EPICS ETCHED IN ECHOES

A STORY SPUN IN SCARLET COMPANION NOVEL

R. DUGAN

Contact:

Renee Dugan

reneeduganwriting.com

renee.s.dugan@gmail.com

PO Box 1265
Martinsville, IN 46151

Book Cover by: The Odd Seed

Map by: Jessica Khoury

ISBN: 978-1-958927-23-6

First Edition: May 2025

DEDICATION

To the One Who wrote the first story, the greatest story of all – Who wrote *my* story. And Who led me back to it when I wandered.

And to all those seeking the strength to tell their tales.
Keep seeking. Keep asking. Keep knocking.
May you find the perfect way to tell it well.

MITHRA-SHA
To Hadrass-Drui
Fablehaven Academy
The Shastah
Belaris
Vallanmyre
Rivrand
The Illusionarium
Erasure
Fallshyre Bay
Galent
DRENNAN PEAKS
Alusia River
Dalfi
The Spine
Casmiss Wood
VENSAIR MOUNTAINS
Leathris
Assida
The Oasis
Kalvikan
Rothmere
To Amere-Del
Port Craythin
Krylan

CHAPTER I
FINDING AND LOSING YOURSELF

N ONE OF THIS WAS happening how I had imagined it.

Not the meticulous packing of my belongings, what few I had; most of them the books that had been my companions ever since I'd made a home here in the Tailbone City of Krylan, the southernmost slice of the country of Mithra-Sha.

Not saying a silent goodbye to the spacious yet cozy room I called home; divested of my usual feline companion, the endless pause as I filled my bag practically pulsed, sunken silence hammering at my eardrums.

Not the gracious but oddly final farewell from the tenant-keeper when I handed him the coin to keep my rooms in my name until I returned, his terse smile dripping polite disbelief like foam from a beer stein.

Least of all had I imagined the question that awaited me when I returned my bartending uniform to Leatrix before the *Ale Alley Pourhouse* opened its doors for the day; the splash of water in the cups rigged to announce the opening door had hardly dribbled into silence when the establishment's stern, ravenly matron fixed her gaze on me across the counter I had spent the last year and a half tending.

"Is this really what you want to be doing, Miss Jashowin?" she asked in greeting. A blunt one that poured disbelief into my center like expert tilts from twin bottles of spirits.

"Of course it is! Why wouldn't it be?" A champagne-bright laugh was my only defense against the unimaginable oddity my life had become in the last fortnight. "Why *wouldn't* someone who's found out her memories are false want to reclaim the real ones?"

Even as I said them, the words did not seem right—nor wholly *real*. But here we were.

Because it turned out the Audra Jashowin she knew—the one I'd thought myself to be until precisely two weeks ago today—was a fabrication of my own mind. A lie written by my own hand, thoroughly etched on my heart; one I'd wholeheartedly believed myself.

A lie I hadn't meant to perpetrate or corroborate...but a lie nonetheless.

A lie only *I* believed any longer. Across the entire land of Mithra-Sha, in places I only knew as vaguely intriguing points on a map strung across the back wall of the *Pourhouse*, the truth of me was held in the minds of everyone who'd known the woman I was before.

The woman I had no memory of.

"Who, indeed?" Leatrix struck out her arms—tanned, weathered, lined with veins and corded with muscle from the decades of labor that kept the *Pourhouse* well-tended and regularly patronized despite the abundance of competition Krylan offered, both in the Mithran quarters and the Ameresh district.

I laid my barmistress uniform across those steady arms, my throat pinching as the threads left my grasp. Like much of what I called my own in this city, I had scrimped and scrapped and saved for it after my immigration to Krylan from the northernmost city of Vallanmyre, the capital of Mithra-Sha, nearly two years ago. Parting with it felt like snipping threads from my own skin.

But according to the tale I'd been told, this was not the first time I had packed my entire life into a satchel and let go of everything that wouldn't fit into its confines in pursuit of something better.

In fact, it was not even the second.

Sliding my hands from beneath the tunic, skirt, and corset, I batted my hair from my brow and begged Luck that the heat flushing my cheeks only marked the mid-spring warmth encroaching on the streets...not an imminent crying fit.

"Well!" The amount of false cheer I managed to infuse into my tone was nothing short of impressive. "Leatrix, I can't thank you enough for the opportunities you offered me. I'm sure you and Nolin will get along just fine."

"Mmm, yes. The dunderhead." Little faith scaffolded her tone at the mention of the barmaster I'd helped find to fulfill my role—a man who, judging from the wide-eyed way he'd greeted me when he'd read my notice on the local board, knew something of the past I no longer recalled. "We'll see if he has as much brain in his skull as brawn on his arms."

Her coarse retort served only to lift my lips in a smile; it had taken many, many months to discover how Leatrix's brusque veneer masked the brilliance of an accomplished businesswoman who knew precisely how to survive the bustle of Krylan. After all, she had addressed me in those same glowing terms before I had earned her trust behind the counter.

I might even miss her on my journey.

"Well, if he doesn't, I'll see you again eventually. Tell him to keep my rag damp and the bartop polished." I patted my hand against it, but that was a mistake; the kernel of reticence I'd buried in hopes of smothering it entirely pulsed with new life at the familiar motion, the same way I bade silent farewell to this place every night at closing.

I dropped my hand swiftly, but Leatrix's eyes—as piercing gray as the silver that threaded her dark hair—fixed on me.

"You know, in all of these injuriously long months you've served as my barmistress, I have never seen you frown or fret," she remarked. "Not until the day the Sha and his entourage graced our threshold."

My stomach shriveled at the memory of that day—one that still sizzled across my vision like a slash of daylight every time I shut my eyes.

A day of poor sleep and forgotten dreams. A day of smiles turned sour. A day of eager eyes masked by tears. A day of gray threads and a teal and teakwood blur.

The day a table of strangers at the *Pourhouse* had acted as if they knew me. As if I should have known *them*. The day Sha Arias Lothar, ruler of the whole country, and his friends—*our* friends—had come to find me, their presence spreading like a spilled drink through the fabric of the only life I knew. And even now, I remembered nothing of them but what I'd learned from bartop gossip about our country's newest leader and those who served alongside him.

Naomi Weathers, a masterful healer, advisor to the Sha; Reiko Aythers, a confident and precise storyteller; Shadress Mahalia Lothar, her keen mind as much a work of art as the ones she made by hand; Wyat Fyerda, Mahalia's bodyguard; Sha Arias Lothar himself, whose father had abdicated shortly after I'd made the pilgrimage south to Krylan from Vallanmyre, the city the Sha's family called home.

And...

Ashen speckles splashed across my vision as Leatrix rounded the bar counter, her smokey shawl offsetting the vivid fuchsia pants that cuffed at her ankles; her grip abraded my hands the same way when she took them, the first time I could ever recall her touching me except to pop me gently over the head in reprimand.

Now she held me fast at the wrists, her hold like iron as she turned me fully to face her. "Audra. You realize you do not *have* to do this?"

Something hot and vicious needled the base of my throat. "You think the Sha and his friends were lying?"

"Luck, no," she scoffed. "They would have no reason to lie, if the only prize was wooing an average barmistress. Which is why it must be true, all of it...what you were, what you *are*, why they sought you out." Her hands slipped from my wrists to tighten around my fingers instead, dancing on the threshold of pain. "Still, you're under no obligation to go along with it. Are you certain you *want* your memories back?"

Hanging a smile on lips that wanted to wobble with weeping was no small feat; but I managed it, clutching her fingers with the same intensity that she held mine. "Of course I do. It hardly seems fair everyone else should remember who I was when I don't have that same privilege." With a last squeeze, I tugged from her hold. "It will just be a quick trip...a sail out to the Isle of Misspoken Stories, a meeting with the overseer of Erasure, and then I'll be back."

It sounded so simple when I said it...not at all like some fantastic voyage from a book.

Leatrix's mouth tweaked at the corners, perhaps hearing the parrotlike cadence as I repeated what I'd been told about the journey—one I'd supposedly braved before. But despite the unspoken notions that filled her eyes like blistering springtime stormclouds, she let me go. "You'd best hope this Nolin is as much an oaf as he appears. I have no intention of holding this position open for you on sentiment, Miss Jashowin. Sentiment—"

"Does not fill seats, I know." Laughing, I backstepped from her, my gaze tumbling to the uniform she'd laid across the counter. The aching stitch in my throat returned. "I...I'm truly grateful that you—"

"Flipping Luck, girl, either get out the door or get this uniform back on!" Leatrix waved me off. "Go find yourself, or lose yourself, or whatever it is young people without their memories do these days. You're far too much of a spectacle for my establishment, anyway."

"If you believe the rumors, I used to be far more of one!" I lobbed back as I retreated over the threshold—then stuck my boots to the top step, breathing deep to chase away the prickle of guilt that pierced my heart.

Poking fun at the woman others claimed I'd once been never struck me right. I couldn't put it to words, but the few times I'd tested it these last two weeks—wielding humor like a shield against all this head-spinning impossibility—it always left a sour taste in my mouth.

Smacking my lips, I swallowed that unpleasant tang away, closing my eyes to settle myself in my own skin before I took the plunge into the unknown.

CHAPTER 2
THE TAILBONE CITY'S SONG

THE CEASELESS CHAOS OF Krylan swarmed my senses at once: the perpetual odor of rifle powder and well-smithed steel from the soldiers who held such a dominant presence in this city...though less of one lately, since our southern neighbors in Amere-Del had loosened their chokehold presence on our shared border.

The rich aroma of countless taverns and public houses, which lined this winding avenue and so many like it in the marketing districts of the Tailbone City. A decadent blend of perfumes and colognes. The cries of hawkers and the laughter of children and the banter of vendors all trying to outsell one another.

The distant music from the Ameresh district, where immigrants in jew el-toned attire sold and shared and lived and loved beneath the minarets they'd erected with their own hands, capped in flags of balanced scales.

The overwhelm of sheer *life* effervesced in this city...the vim and vigor that had promised second and third chances and more from the moment I'd stepped through the turnstile so long ago; since I'd joined the countless folks who had traded lack for luxury in the years since Mithra-Sha had begun to pick itself up from the gutter-heap it had long been banished to.

Banished by—

My eyes popped open, my thumb chafing beneath the strap of my satchel. A cloud scudded across the sun, chased by a breeze that promised the eventuality of rain.

My pulse stuttered out of tune with the Tailbone City's song. I'd become aware of that dissonance for the first time on a night two weeks past—a night spent walking its shadowed streets until sunup, side by side with the Sha's own bodyguard as he poured out a tale of his own. One that had seemed utterly unimaginable at the time.

The story of my life.

Our life.

This sense of discord had seethed beneath my skin ever since; I'd promised to think on that tale, but it was less *thinking* and more *existing* within it that had undone me. Understanding how it shaped the world...how it shaped *me*, and the things about myself I could never fully explain.

There would be no peace in Krylan for me anymore unless I quieted the havoc in my chest...or learned to live with it.

Thank Luck I did not have to guess at how to do that. The method lived in my pocket in the form of a note—a name and a place and a date. The last thing the keeper of my shrouded past had left for me before he'd given me space to think, a parchment scrap he'd slipped into my hand when he'd kissed my knuckles in farewell as the sun rose over our shared, sleepless night.

I had wrestled with the possibilities ever since, all while sneaking glances in every crowd, searching for his face. The face I hadn't been able to banish or ignore or stop flipping *dreaming* about since he'd first cast back his hood in the *Pourhouse*, baring tearstained cheeks and silver-lined eyes...the moment the world had tilted beneath me, shifting everything.

Slipping my hand into my pocket, I clenched my fist around the note.

The date—today.

The place—a few hours' walk from here.

With a last fortifying breath, I took my first step away from the *Pourhouse,* into the future...and back toward my own forgotten past.

The fields that wrapped around Krylan like a scarf also wrapped me in quiet calm.

The breeze rolled warm and briny from the coastal waters ahead, only faintly chilled with the fragrance of the wild alpine slopes that skirted the southern portions of Mithra-Sha. Saline fingers teased chestnut threads from the messy knot I'd tamed my hair into that morning and gave a flirtatious tug at the belt that hugged my skirt to my hips.

As if the world itself towed me along, reeling me down the road toward distant Port Craythin—a hub for sailors and fishmongers. A place I'd never truly cared to visit until now.

Yet with every step, my heart dug in its heels against the siren song of wind and sea. It begged me to retreat to the safety of Krylan's confines, to once again forget I had ever known another life.

A life invented for myself, *by* myself.

Doubt spoiled in the pit of my stomach like poorly pulled ale as I batted aside the piney boughs of the evergreens that fringed the furthest reaches of Krylan, ducking into the shadows that gathered beneath.

This was my last chance to turn back. My last chance to remain the Audra I knew myself to be...a perfectly competent, perfectly capable, perfectly wonderful Audra, despite my family's feelings to the contrary. Despite how few friends I had.

Leatrix believed in me. The customers at the *Pourhouse* were always quick with an extra silver for my efforts. And I had Sheeba, the feline companion I'd found in these very fields. Couldn't that be enough?

I slowed, my bootsteps barely reaching past the rustling the furring of pine needles that blanketed this stretch of the coast—then halted altogether.

"What are you doing, Addie?" I freed the question to the swells of wind churning off the water.

When the breeze came back to me with an answer, it spoke in a different voice—not crashing waves or murmuring pines, but the blunt strike of steel on straw, an echo of my early days in Krylan when I'd found lodgings in a boarding house near the soldiering apartments at the city gates.

The next gust came from behind me, not ahead; it flung my hair into my eyes and chased me forward, twirling me through a gap in the columns of ancient evergreen growth, releasing me at the crescent edge of the coast.

And there, a soldier all but danced.

His performance and props and playstage were the stuff of stories—tavern tales and rumors whispered over half-empty steins. Legends made living. A blade that must have been built from Storycraft...double-edged, crossguard sparkling like smokey glass in the shape of a flame, a winking scarlet jewel encased in its pommel. It whispered like a quill scripting a eulogy, lightweight and effortless in the grip of a man who wore no armor, no shirt at all, striking his foe—a simple grainsack—as it if had personally wronged him.

He snarled and shouted as he hammered it again and again, hitting all its softest parts, and I...I just watched *him*.

The man who was master over the soldiers in Vallanmyre, right hand of Sha Lothar himself.

The man whose note lay crumpled in my limp fist while my eyes fixed on the back of his golden-chestnut hair, the meddlesome breeze revealing gilded threads in every layer chopped short against his scalp, falling rakishly over one side of his head.

Captain Jaik Grissom.

CHAPTER 3
GROUND RULES

THERE WAS A BRUTAL tension and sinuous grace to Captain Grissom that lent credence to every awe-soaked whisper I'd ever head from gossips in the *Pourhouse*: that he was as handy with a sword as a rifle. That he had been a prodigy of sorts, serving first in the army, then the inner ranks of the former Sha, and now alongside Sha Arias. That his incomparable knowledge of the two greatest strengths in Mithra-Sha—Storycrafters and soldiers—had helped build a lasting alliance between the once-antagonistic factions.

That such intimacy with both sword and story made him powerful enough to help lay waste to the Misspoken manifestations of poorly amplified Storycraft plaguing our country.

I had always been grateful he existed, for as long as I could remember. Even when he was only the figment of tales that kept shadows at bay so common folk like me could rest their weary heads at night.

I had never imagined I would actually meet the man. Nor that when I did, he would look at me like the answer to every question he had ever asked himself...like the beating heart at the center of his favorite story.

Nor that, when he spoke to me that first time in the *Pourhouse*—a shattered, pleading command of *"Ayjay. Stop."*—it would feel like I'd broken that heart with my own hands.

The memory weakened my knees. I leaned into the sturdy pine on my left, resting my cheek against the sap-riddled bark as I blinked the heat from my gaze and went on watching him.

Watching as every strike landed true. As the sun limned the lines of his body, highlighting a sheen of sweat that suggested he had been locked in this one-sided duel for hours. As he slashed and cut and cleaved again, his sword positively singing, its vibrations ringing like birdsong down the coast and along the waves. The wind's inhale and exhale kept his shouts and battle-cries like a secret...a muffling force that cast leaves off into the sea with one hand and tore his hair across his brow with the other.

With a deft slash, he brought the blade to rest at the neck of the grain-sack...and halted, head bent, panting. He aimed his gaze off to one side, drawing my attention toward the curve of the treeline to my right.

A feline figure trotted from the undergrowth, a bundle of damp black leaves caught in her jaws. She brought them to Jaik's feet, dropped them, and sat—expectant.

Laughter suited him better than those furious shouts, even hoarse from training. Jaik dropped to one knee, stroking behind the cat's ears...*my* cat, up until two weeks ago. Until I'd learned she'd once been his.

"Who's the best hunter in Krylan?" Jaik laughed as Sheeba stepped elegantly onto his bare shoulders, twining her white-and-brindle body around his head. "Yeah, these soldiers haven't got anything on you."

Purring so violently I could hear it even this far away, Sheeba flopped like a shawl around Jaik's neck. Chuckling, he scratched under her chin.

"Tell me about it. Krylan's mightiest predator. Bet you really miss life out in the cornstalks, huh?" Sheeba raised her chin to invite more scratches, her head bumping against his, and Jaik sighed. "Yeah. Me, too."

Nameless emotion fizzed in the base of my throat; I had spent enough time listening to talk over steins of ale and mugs of mead to know when reflection bordered on regret.

Shoving up from the tree, I padded toward them, clearing my throat as I approached. "Excuse you. You stole my cat."

A shriek pierced from my throat as Jaik whirled, leading with his blade, bringing it to within a half-inch of my neck. Sheeba yowled lowly in protest, claws flashing out, but didn't leap off.

We both froze, staring at one another.

He blinked first, then blinked again, loosening his posture and lowering the blade. "Sorry. Force of habit."

"*Why* is this your habit?" I sputtered.

"You used to..." Trailing off, he reached behind his neck with an awkward cough, delicately extricating Sheeba's claws from his skin before lifting her off and setting her back on the ground. "Ah, nevermind. You have to scare me like that, though? What's wrong with just saying *hello*?"

"Hello, Jaik." The words floated off my tongue, soft as a pour of sweet wine, and both of us stilled again.

My gaze retreated from his…dropping to a scar etched across his chest in a vicious, upraised line. A sight I had seen on countless soldiers before him, all across Krylan…yet bearing witness to its brutal twinings twisted my gut like a mouthful of tainted food.

Forcing a swallow, I tore my focus back to his eyes, opening my palm to Sheeba—who, having promptly strutted out of the apartment door to leap into Jaik's arms two weeks ago, returned to my embrace for the first time since. Her vibrating weight in the cradle of my arms was a comfort I hadn't realized I'd missed, the brush of soft fur on my face dispelling some of the awkwardness that wanted to open its tab in my chest and wrack up an insurmountable debt.

Jaik sheathed his blade and shoved his hair from eyes that were unbearably, achingly gentle, full of a hope more glorious and more difficult to look at than a sunrise striking off every glistening rooftop in Krylan. "Hey. You're *here.*"

"I am." I played with the tufts of fur between Sheeba's toes when she sprawled over the crook of my arm. "I considered your offer, as promised, and…I think it *would* be best. If I went with you to the Isle of Misspoken Stories and met with the Storymaker."

That title sparkled on my tongue like a sip of champagne. I had only the vaguest notions of the One who Storycrafters claimed had uttered the first Wellspoken story—the One who had shaped the world and created a well from which all Storycrafters now unspooled the power to create with their own tales. But even those notions brought about the impression of dark hair and kind eyes and a warmth that brought tears to my eyes. A feeling like a forgotten homecoming. Like I had once stood heart-to-heart with someone, utterly seen, utterly known…and so utterly *loved,* it had taught me to love myself in kind.

"You sure about this?" Jaik backstepped to retrieve his shirt, hanging from a low branch beside a bedroll and tent-pack that had likely been his dwelling the past two weeks. "Like I said, it's not exactly a safe place to go."

"But you *also* said it would be worth it," I reminded him. "And I think you're right. After all, how foolish would it be if I just went on living my life, knowing so much of it isn't real?"

As much a reassurance to him as a reminder to my heart, which still tugged ceaselessly in Krylan's direction. Pleading to return to the safety of the lie.

Jaik watched me for a moment, whiskey-brown eyes overshadowed by the frown that stitched his brows together. "I just…" He broke off, tugging his shirt over his head, then fluffing it over his hips several times without meeting my eyes.

"I don't want you doing this because you feel obligated to. Because of the things I told you."

"Which things?" I arched a brow. "That we've known one another since we were young? That you were *my* bodyguard when I became Master Storycrafter?"

The absurdity of those words launched a pained, scathing laugh into my throat. I had loved books as long as I could remember, but to imagine myself a *storyteller*—and not only a storyteller, but the *best* of them all...

It only made sense *because* it was so fantastical.

"Or do you mean when we traveled all of Mithra-Sha together?" I added, my tone bubbling higher. "Or are you referring to how you were murdered at Tobyrus Lothar's orders, and I rewrote Storycraft itself to save you, and we found each other again, and traveled to this same Isle, and then I rewrote Storycraft *again* to give away my power to every storyteller in the world, and I lost my memories of the past trying to save—"

"You need to stop talking." Jaik smothered my mouth for the briefest moment—just long enough for speckles of salt and citrus on his palm to brush my lips. A hint of his exertion and the taste of whatever fruit he'd had for breakfast that morning.

"Is there anything else I *should* know?" I prodded when he dropped his hand. "Something else that might be making you nervous, Captain Grissom?"

My early impressions of this soldier were of swift wit and an even swifter tongue, a dangerous marriage of traits. One which made the absence of his answer seem far too long, even if it was only a moment or two.

"Nah, think that's about it." Jaik swiped his palm down his trouser leg. "Just...it's strange, you know? Hearing you say all of that like it's just some story to you."

I bit my lips together, swallowing a swell of defensiveness. After all, to me, it *was* merely that—a story told to me by a soldier, like so many others who'd passed through the *Pourhouse*'s doors.

"I'm sorry. I don't mean to make light of it. I know it's more than a story...you lived it." Swiping my tongue over my lower lip, I amended, "*We* lived it. But when it's so *different* from what I know—"

"Saying it like that makes it easier. I get it." Jaik reached over to dig his fingers into the fur between Sheeba's shoulderblades, smiling slightly when she arched into his touch—her favorite place to be scratched. "I mean, Luck knows I wasn't exactly easy to get along with when I was learning all of this again, either, the last time we found each other in Krylan. But maybe you could...not say it like that."

"Fair." I watched the skin shift and slide over his knuckles as he rumpled Sheeba's fur—knuckles scarred and sunstamped from years of soldiering and farming. Years I didn't remember knowing him…and some when I hadn't known him at all. "Could you do me a favor in return?"

"I'll do my best."

"Let's not always talk about what I *don't* remember." Vulnerability stole the brazen undergirding that had allowed me to flippantly deliver the tale of our forgotten past. "It makes this all feel more impossible."

"Ground rules. I like it." Jaik's grin was so bright, I couldn't bear to meet it.

We were quiet for a time, taking turns petting Sheeba. Then, sick of the awkward silence building beneath my skin like an itch, I blurted at last, "Well, if nothing else, this one's affections prove your account is true. She clearly likes you more than she ever liked me."

"Ah, I just had her longer." Jaik took back his hand, stuffing both into his pockets. "But thanks for letting me keep her these last couple weeks. She's been a good distraction."

I could scarcely fathom what emotions this man must be wrestling behind the carefree tilt of his smirk, beneath the depths of those spirited eyes…so I didn't try. Instead, I lifted my satchel flap and deposited Sheeba inside, where she kneaded my spare clothes and settled in at once, chin balanced on the rim of the well-loved leather.

Those garments would be covered in shed fur when I eventually went to wear them. But that familiar nuisance might be some comfort, too.

Jaik blinked at me. "What do you think you're doing?"

"What did *you* think we would do with her?" I scoffed. "She's a cat, Jaik! She can't fend for herself."

His mouth opened, then slammed shut again. He towed a hand back through his hair. "You want to bring her to the Isle of Misspoken Stories? You're serious?"

"I assumed we would leave on her on the airship during the incursion itself."

Jaik barked a laugh, sliding his hand over the back of his neck now. "Yeah, about that. The airship that brought all of us here left for Vallanmyre about a week ago."

I gaped at him. "You stranded yourself here?"

"Airships serve the Sha…I mean, they serve the whole country, but the orders come from Arias. He couldn't exactly leave one tethered in Krylan for my personal business."

Swallowing, I adjusted my satchel, slinging Sheeba's weight across my front. She had gained a fair bit of heft since the first time I'd bundled her inside to escape a cold drizzle, the night she'd followed me home from a restless walk beyond the city walls. "Well, unless you intend to swim..."

"Flipping Luck," Jaik chuckled. "Do I really look that muscular to you?"

"Muscular, no. Mad?"

His chuckle turned to a guffaw, and he swiveled on heel, motioning with a bend of his head. "You haven't seen *mad* yet, tiger. But we're getting there...I've got a ship that can sail us to Erasure."

I surged forward to fall into step with him, pushing back through the trees along the angle of the coast. "A ferry vessel?"

"Eh. You could say that."

"Isn't it too dangerous—?"

"Not for ships who've been helping sort out the Misspoken manifestations in the sea." Jaik swept aside a pine bough for me to duck beneath. "A lot of them are used to it. I heard one might be getting in port here, so I sent a message...either they'd be taking both of us, or they'd just be taking me back out."

To do his duty as a soldier? Or to wrestle with the ripples of the choice I might've made, not to come and meet him today?

I silenced that resonant question with one for him: "But those ships must answer to the Sha as well, don't they?"

"Yeah, you'd still need a special ship for personal business." Jaik tossed me a wink. "Sort of like a pirate ship."

With that—and nothing more—we shoved free of the short span of trees and began the descent into Port Craythin.

CHAPTER 4
THE BAKER AND THE BARMISTRESS

Port Craythin was a deep, many-tiered beehive of hewn stone, its switchback paths and slick, knobby stairs leading down to the falcate of the harbor itself. The crooked teeth of slick wooden wharfs grinned up at us from a mouth slavering with seafoam as Jaik, Sheeba, and I made our way down the rocky trails to the docks; it was nearing nightfall when we reached the harbor, where the silence we'd hardly broken since the pine grove shattered into hawking shouts and whistled shanties and the roar of the sea.

Jaik strode with a confidence that didn't quite owe itself to the title he carried, nor to the soldiering strength of him; he'd clearly been among sailors before, perhaps as a farmhand in Krylan as well as on these missions he sailed for the Sha. He walked with a strut, head high, offering grins and greetings to a handful of fishermen and ferrymen and traders until, at last, we came abreast of the very last of the docks—this one nearly a quarter mile from the rest, so that the ship anchored there showed all the more prominently against the splash of twilit sky.

My stomach wobbled as I studied the veneered prow, the hull rising and falling in repose on the sloshing waters. The sails were trimmed and wrapped in rich plum cloth, and from the railings, globed lights hung, ever-burning...a newer creation of Storycraft that Leatrix had scoffed at for its uselessness. But seeing those undying flames pulse in their settings along the ship's rails, I had to disagree; their ambiance soothed the inflamed stitch that had been thrown in my chest when Jaik and I had fallen quiet during our descent through the port.

Even at a glimpse, there was something *other* about this ship...something homey and beloved in the care that made her shine, in the sound of laughter pouring over the railings, in the fiddle notes that twined up from the deck to greet the first stars peeking over the harbor.

Jaik slowed to match my pace when I lingered, drinking it all in. "How do you feel about sailing?"

"I've…" I caught the words between my teeth, shifting my feet. "I don't *remember* ever doing it."

"Yeah." He inclined a bit toward me. "Well, hey, if you need me to, I can hang a hammock topside. You got seasick before…that seemed like it helped."

"I'd be glad to try. Thank you, Jaik."

His smile brightened every crease and laugh-line carved into his features by the tales I'd heard of him and those he'd lived of which I had no memory. *Yet.* "Anytime, tiger."

We stepped onto the dock, halting at the foot of the gangplank; it, too, was rosined wood, artfully carved. Jaik laid a hand on my shoulder, squeezed once, then called up, "Permission to board!"

He did not speak it like a request.

The fiddling eased. A scoff floated in its muted wake. "Ask nicely, and I just might bloody let you."

Jaik rolled his eyes. "Permission to board, *Captain*?"

A figure claimed the railing, arms folded with casual, lethal grace atop it, his frame tall and broad and so corded with muscle, I might have believed him a soldier himself. He wore springtime attire typical of many sailors who came clambering into the *Pourhouse*: a dark tunic with the sleeves hacked away and the cords half undone. Tattoos blazed like black fire along his arms and across an exposed cut of his chest. And the way he sloped to peer down at us left little doubt he was in command here—not a captain of soldiers like Jaik, but a *ship's* captain, from the roots of his honeyed hair to the soles of his feet planted on the deck, swaying effortlessly with its motion.

Then his bearded mouth pulled down at one corner; he smoothed an inked hand over his mustache and spoke to Jaik without taking his eyes off me: "This her?"

Jaik's hand tightened over my shoulder. "Yeah, this is Audra Jashowin. Ayjay, this is Ryker Kassian, captain of *The Cathan*."

There was something unnerving in the way the Captain regarded me, shoving back to brace his hands on the railing…the fashion in which I assumed most sailors regarded myths of the sea or mirages on the horizon.

Then he swiveled his head to peer at something behind him; and after another indeterminate pause, the Captain jerked his chin. "She can come on up. Your ugly mug, I'm not so sure about, Fishbait."

"Bite my entire ass, Kassian."

"Wouldn't take long enough to make it worth the effort."

Insides churning as if I had taken a plunge into unfamiliar waters—or any waters at all—I started up the gangplank. The height and angle proved unsettling with Sheeba's weight at my front, and I nearly staggered; Jaik freed my shoulder to catch beneath my elbow instead, a necessity that flamed my cheeks with humiliation.

"Fishbait?" I mumbled, desperate for a distraction.

"Look, his quartermaster and I...we didn't exactly get along," Jaik admitted. "So Kassian sort of...tossed me overboard last time."

I swiveled my head as far to the side as I dared. "What did you *do*?"

"Just tread water until someone—"

"To the *quartermaster*, Jaik."

"Ah, nothing that stuck. They've got a pair of good healers on board." Jaik gently pushed me aboard. "Anyway, *that* didn't stick, but the name did. The Ameresh love their nicknames."

Before I could point out how he, a Mithran in blood and bones, had called me by no fewer than two nicknames since our meeting—our *reunion*—mere days ago, we were stepping off onto the deck, greeted by *The Cathan's* crew.

Some were dressed for the work of the sails and seas, cutlasses and daggers, Ameresh pistols, and Mithran rifles strapped to their bodies. Others were dressed down for dancing, barefoot, smiling. Their ages varied as widely as their appearances, men and women mingling with wine glasses and grog growlers in their fists.

All of them looking our way.

I strangled the strap of my satchel, the heat retreating from my cheeks to puddle in my belly so quickly the deck bucked under my feet; it took effort to peel my fist from around the coarse fabric that chafed the side of my neck, to flash three fingers in a weak wave. "Hello. All of you."

Several sailors glanced at one another; no one spoke. Not even Jaik.

And then, pert and stern as a mother reprimanding her children, a voice floated above their heads: "Oh, for Ahim's *sake*, must all of you behave as if you've never seen a woman before? Gyddy, I at least expected better from *you*, Siu is the only thing you look at on this deck if it isn't ill or bleeding!"

A woman brushed forward to the edge of their halted merrymaking, cleaning her hands on a towel slung through her belt. Her rich cobalt dress matched her lacquered nails, the blue opal hoop that pierced her nostril, and the paint that lined her eyelids; her smile plumped her round cheeks and showed a sparkle of teeth, and all at once, *peace* washed over me...as if I'd found a familiar face in a crowd of strangers.

"Lionyra Kassian." She offered a hand dusted with bread flour. "But you'll call me Lio. And you are...?"

"Audra," I said, seizing her hand like the lifeline it was.

"It's a pleasure to meet you, Audra." Lio's eyes dropped to my satchel, then widened when Sheeba poked her head out to take in the deck, amber eyes luminous in the globe lanterns' glare. "And who is *this* perfect little creature?"

"Sheeba." A laugh burst from me when she scrabbled free, plopping onto the deck with tail fluffed. "I suppose she smells fish."

"She must...it's all half of these people will eat, even after more than a year of coaxing on my part." Lio linked her arm through mine, jolting warmth through my whole body. "Speaking of sea creatures, if you've all finished gawking like freshly caught crabs, I'll escort our guests to the hammocks."

"Wait!" A young man's voice cracked from the crow's nest, and down the mainmast he scuttled, freehanding the descent as if he had no fear of plummeting to his death; I didn't take a full breath until he dropped to the deck and sprang up to his gangly height, pointing two fingers at Jaik like the muzzles of Ameresh pistols. "Hey, Captain! You owe me a rematch at dice!"

"Hey, kid!" Jaik aimed the same two fingers back at him. "Never going to happen!"

Laughter burst across the deck, and the fiddle tune struck up again; the sailors parted to let us pass, though many still watched as Lio tugged me through their midst, Jaik on our heels, Sheeba trotting in his shadow.

I fixed my gaze ahead, ignoring the whispers that spiraled like puffs of hearthsmoke on every side. Ignoring one man's voice that nudged a bit louder than the rest. "Hang on, I don't get—"

"Oi," Captain Kassian cut in crossly, "if we slowed down every time you didn't get something, Syd, we'd never leave bloody port. And speaking of leaving port..."

The rest of his words—and the drum of feet hitting the deck as sailors leaped to attention—stayed behind when we descended belowdecks. The muffling quiet enveloped us in the aroma of salt and treated wood, leather and smoke.

Lio loosened her herding hold on my arm. "Don't mind them. Sailors are little known for their tact."

"*Little known.*" Jaik scowled. "Your husband insulted my backside."

"Well, it is a smidge lacking." Lio's eyes sparkled with good humor.

"Some kind of expert, huh?" Jaik grumbled.

"Ship's cook, Captain's wife, purveyor of ports, rear-end expert...I am a woman of innumerable talents," Lio teased, flashing me a wink. "And I'm certain the same can be said about you, Audra."

"You got that right." Now Jaik was grinning in earnest.

Heat scorched my ears. "To hear others tell it, my foremost talents are forgetting things, making this country suffer, and, oh, tending bar on the side."

The humor molded in the air all at once; Lio spun me to face her and Jaik both, pressing her finger to my lips. "Not another word like that, Audra."

"Ayjay, none of what happened is your *fault*." Jaik clapped a hand to the thick beams that bisected the roof of the lower deck, bending forward to catch my gaze over Lio's shoulder. "You just did the best you knew how with the way Luck's coin flipped."

I forced a smile, slipping my arm from Lio's. "I was trying to make a *joke*, you two. I suppose I need lessons from this crew on how to jest like a pirate."

Lio folded her arms low over her waist, studying me from beneath thick, dark brows; after a moment, she said, "Would you like to retire for the evening?"

"Luck, *yes*." The words whooshed out of me, the release of a pent-up breath.

"I've got it." Jaik's murmur soaked into the wooden walls. "I told her I'd string a hammock up topside. She gets seasick."

Lio had scarcely nodded before Jaik brushed past us, bound for somewhere deeper in the vessel. His gaze strafed across mine for a heartbeat—perhaps even less than that—but it was enough to set my stomach swimming.

"Jaik." I reached for his elbow, but he'd already passed me.

Lio snared my fingers instead, squeezing them lightly. "From the tale he shared with us, I suspect you both need time to grow used to things as they are now...not as you knew them. Give him time."

I loosed another struggling breath. "It'll all be moot once we reach Erasure, anyway. How long do you suspect that will be?"

Quiet for a moment. Then, "With how this crew sails, a fortnight at most."

A fortnight until I stood on equal footing with everyone who had once known me.

A fortnight...and then everything would change again.

Swallowing did nothing to touch the dryness in my throat this time. "A fortnight it is."

CHAPTER 5
MAPPING STARS
JAIK

ALMOST TWO YEARS, AND Ayjay still slept the exact same way she had the last night I remembered with her...the night she'd become my wife.

A night she didn't flipping remember.

Two years, and I was as good as a stranger to her.

Sitting on the railing by the helm, I could catch a peek at her hammock on the forecastle—strung up and swaying over the deck. She'd curled up in the dead center of it, one leg stretched out, the other one hiked to her chest, head on her arms.

It was like cutting myself on the edge of Luck's coin whenever I looked at her—because it wasn't only *her* I was seeing.

I could see her right here...and I could see her that night in the Shastah, the only time we'd had each other the way we'd always wanted to. And I could see her in a cabin in the Vensair Mountains, halfway between nowhere and anywhere, sleeping on a cot the same way, shaking while a storm beat the spit out of the walls and not even her Storycrafter cloak could keep her warm.

Then, I'd laid down next to her and wrapped her up in my arms as tight as I could, praying to Luck we'd make it through the night. Now...

Now, she slept half a ship away. Out of reach in more ways than one.

Three different Audras, all living in my head at the same time. And to her, I was nothing more than a story that stepped into the public house and interrupted her life. A stranger who dumped a past a lot worse than the story she'd written for herself at her feet...and asked her to try and remember it anyway.

I could still catch that look on her face every time I blinked—that moment belowdecks when the bitterness had chased out the brightness in her eyes. When she'd talked about the Audra she'd been...the girl whose Storycraft had sent stadiums to their knees, the woman who'd laid out the way to make her people safer, the one who'd ripped apart the world to try and make *my* flipping *death* right again...like she was the villain of the story.

I didn't know what to do with that.

So, while I'd hung up the hammock for her, I'd turned back into the bumbling farmhand who didn't know words from wheelbarrows. But at least I'd remembered to say goodnight before she'd buried herself under the blankets.

A whistle from the wheel cut through the havoc in my head. "Oi. You moon over that lass any harder and you'll sink in the depths come dawn, Fishbait."

I couldn't manage much more than a scoff. "Been there. Done that. Didn't agree with me."

Wood rasped on callouses when Kassian tilted the wheel, correcting our course on some tiny thread I'd have never picked up on. Guess that was why he was the sailor and I was the soldier.

I pulled one foot up onto the railing, leaning back into the rigging. "You talk to the crew about her yet?"

"Aye. No one who sailed with *The Athalion* breathes a word they ever knew her." Kassian was quiet for a moment. "Hardest for Syd. Seems he liked that oddball an awful lot."

"Yeah. Ayjay's easy to like." Which was about all I could push out past the lump in my throat.

When a rogue soldier had spilled blood on this ship deck, Audra had gone half as feral as me. She'd cared about this crew before it had been two crews in one...when it had sailed under the name *Athalion*, when my friend Julas had captained it.

Our friend.

It would've meant something to Audra, before...putting her boots back on these planks. The way it had felt to me when I'd come back to it off the Isle of Misspoken Stories with all my memories splitting my skull, and the second I'd dropped back over the railing, I'd broken down right in the same spot where Julas had died.

Most of that day was still blurry. But I remembered Lio grabbing my arm and just *looking* at me, and right then I'd known that the ship I'd picked to sail me out to Erasure wasn't a coincidence. Wasn't the first time some of them had sailed this far. And I'd found the one person on board who'd known Ayjay better than the rest...who'd looked at me like she was trying not to cry, because somehow, she knew her. She knew me, too.

Back then, we'd thought Audra was back, because *we* had her back. That all we had to do was go find her, and everything would go back to the way it was.

But Ayjay didn't have *us*. She'd looked at Lio like a stranger today, too. Same way she'd looked at Naomi and Reiko and Mahalia and Arias in the *Pourhouse*.

Same way she looked at *me*.

I emptied out the air from the bottom of my lungs, pitching my head sideways into the netting and winding my fingers into the gaps. "Glad they listened. She doesn't need one more person knowing more about her than she knows about herself."

Things stayed quiet for a second. Then a more easygoing voice floated across the helm: "Siu knows me better than I ever will."

I swapped my focus over to one of the ship's healers, Gydeon Nassar; he sat on an overturned crate with the wheel and its captain between us, smoking a pipe. The smile he aimed around it made my skin crawl a little bit...it reminded me of other healers I'd met in my life, like Naomi. People who could see under your skin to the bones beneath...people who knew exactly how to break them.

"You're not exactly a mystery, mate," Kassian snorted.

Gydeon strafed the pipe his way, but kept his eyes on me. "If you lose yourself, is it truly such a bad thing that the pieces are kept in the pockets of the people who know you best?"

"No one's lost the way Ayjay is." Flipping Luck, it hurt just *saying* it. "No one else I know of, anyway."

"Aye? And it sounds like no one knows her the way you do, either," Kassian chimed in. "I'll give you one for free, mate: every sailor worth his salt knows he needs stars and a map to navigate by. That way, if he loses one, he can sail by the other."

"How does that have anything to do with—"

"What he's trying to say is that your wife has lost her map," Gydeon interrupted. "Perhaps she needs you to be her stars."

"Spot on." Ryker snapped his fingers and pointed to Gydeon, then palmed the drifting wheel, staying its course. "Speaking of, she know—?"

"No." I swallowed a surge of sick in my throat. "I mentioned it...sort of. I told her I *had* a wife, but I think with everything else she heard from me that night, she just...forgot that part."

Ryker snorted. "Tell her, you coward."

"Hey." I snapped a glare onto him. "I don't want her to think I'm pushing her into anything she'd not ready for. Being loved by someone you don't remember is a lot flipping different than being *married* to them."

And I *did* still love her. I'd known it the second I'd remembered everything, back in Erasure. When I'd surfaced from our story, sobbing like an ass had kicked me in the crotch, I'd known two things about myself: I was a soldier who used to protect a Storycrafter, not a Sha; and no matter who I was, whatever story anyone told about me, that idiot was in love with Audra Jashowin.

I'd known it the whole voyage on this ship back to Craythin. I'd known when I'd flown an airship to Vallanmyre and found out everyone else remembered, too. I'd known when we'd scoured reports from across the country and finally found out where Audra had landed after she'd fixed the Tearing, given power back to all the stories in Mithra-Sha...and unraveled every last inch of herself to keep me written in the world.

I'd known I was in love with her when I'd stayed outside that public house while the others went in and cried until I couldn't breathe, because seeing her again had knocked the world out from under my feet. And I'd known I was in love with her when I'd stepped through the door and she'd looked at me like she'd never seen me a day in her life.

I still loved her right flipping now, with a gulf a lot bigger than the space between the railing and the forecastle between us.

And if Luck loved *me*, that would be enough to hold the pieces together when she remembered, too.

Kassian was right, even if I wasn't going to tell him that with anything less than another knife to my neck. I'd never know the threads he teased, pulling this ship across the sea...but I knew about other threads. I knew all the threads that tied to Audra's life; the ones she'd told me about and the ones that tangled with mine.

If I could just help her hold onto them without coming apart at the seams, then maybe...

Maybe we could still have a happy ending, after all.

CHAPTER 6
REMATCH

J AIK WAS RIGHT: SLEEPING abovedecks was nearly as comfortable as sleeping in my bed in Krylan. Soothed by the stroke of the springtime breeze that tilted the hammock like a gentle hand, cooled by the whip of water from the whitecap that cut from the prow of the ship, I slept so deeply I didn't even dream. No scarlet threads twined through my drowsing mind; when I woke, heaped under an extra blanket that hadn't been there when I'd fallen asleep, I didn't feel on the verge of weeping.

I roused slowly that first morning aboard *The Cathan,* almost re-freshed—ready to face whatever the days ahead held in store—and my feet touched the sleek forecastle at the same moment Lio bobbed into view at the top of its steps, swaying easily with the ship's movements. Her arms balanced a tray of sticky buns glazed in honey, and my mouth watered when the warm scent of yeast and walnuts tickled my nose.

"Please tell me those are for me," I begged.

Lio arched a brow. "Unless you assume I feed the fish and porpoises as well as I feed this crew, I would say that is a safe assumption, yes."

"I would've guessed it was an offering to the sharks, actually."

"Oh, Audra. That is such nonsense." Lio lowered herself into the hammock beside me, both of us bracing our feet on the deck. "Sharks are tempted by scones, not sticky buns."

"More for me." Grinning, I plucked a bun free, a thick layer of tantalizing glaze slathering my fingers at once. "How did you make these aboard the ship?"

She raised her chin to the ever-burning globes that tinkled like calliope music against the ship's railing. "Those were gifted to me by a Storycrafter who is...a complicated friend. Enough to outfit the galley, and some to string from the railings as well. Now I can heat things without setting fire to the ship."

I popped my finger from my mouth, cleaned of glaze. "That's brilliant."

"Well, I was once considered quite an innovative baker in Krylan."

"You're from *Krylan*?" I hadn't expected to find someone who shared my home, and perhaps my love of it, aboard this ship.

"Where I am *from* is a very long, very complicated story." Lio swirled a bit of the glaze around with her smallest finger. "But I immigrated to Krylan from Amere-Del, yes...the first immigrant to own a bakery outside the Ameresh district." A faint smile twinged across her lips. "*The Secret Ingredient* was my passion for a very long time."

I searched my mind for a speckle of familiarity at the name. "I'm sorry, I don't know that I've ever heard of it."

Sadness glinted in the corners of Lio's eyes, but she swished it away with a flirt of her hand. "No, I imagine not. While we put into port, I visited my old shopfront. It's since become a hatmaker's store."

"Not a bad trade," I offered sheepishly around a mouthful of sticky bun.

"No, but sadly, one cannot eat hats." Lio plucked a bun from the tray and settled the rest in her lap as she unraveled the sticky golden spiral. "Or, at least, they shouldn't."

We shared a laugh, giving the hammock a kick as one to set us swaying gently. On the maindeck, the ship seemed to be changing watch—much of the crew disappearing belowdecks while others ascended, slapping open palms and patting each other on the back as they passed.

"Would you like to meet them?" Lio offered, following my gaze to the fluster of activity below. "Or perhaps you would prefer a quieter morning kept to yourself."

"No, I don't mind meeting everyone." A flurry of activity and unfamiliar faces felt like a day at the *Pourhouse* with its rotating list of clientele—a slice of normalcy in the strangeness my life had become.

We abandoned the hammock, sticky buns in hand, descending from the forecastle to the lower deck. The breeze teased our hair, its zephyrs rushing across the wide-open sea and ushering the ship over the waves with an eager hand; I scouted the deck for a glimpse of the familiar, and Sheeba was the first I found, hovering near the boy who'd challenged Jaik to a game of dice. He sat on a barrel, gutting fish from a sprawl of nets at his feet; she basked on a crate nearby, tufty paws kneading the air, eager for every spare scrap he fed her from his filleting knife.

"That is Camden," Lio grinned, blowing the boy a kiss he pretended to catch and stuff in his pocket, "the youngest and wiliest of us. He apprentices under Annet, our carpenter." A gesture to a woman with bobbed bronze hair treating measures of wood on the far side of the deck. "You could not count the splinters Gydeon and Hasser, our healers, have pulled from that woman's fingers."

Lio whisked me through the rest of the crew like a bar-room dance, a dizzying trade of partners with names and faces I eagerly committed to memory: Jaspyr and Rynshaw and Maryon, Bess and Blaise and Hectyr and Rosemay. A spicy blend of sailors, Ameresh and Mithran and even some from Zandrae-Rath, the land to the east of Amere-Del, and from the isles sprinkled across the sea.

My mind eased gratefully into the vigor of meeting so many new people who knew nothing of me. That gratitude laced my smile wide when I shook hands with Reinera, the quartermaster's assistant, and she invited me to a game of cards if ever I was bored on the voyage.

"I don't see how anyone could be bored *aboard* such a bustling ship," I teased.

Reinera tossed a hand back through her dark hair, rolling her eyes. "You'd be surprised the sort of trouble you can get into with a mix of soldiers and sailors."

"None of that," Lio scolded, checking her hip against Reinera's. "Jaik is behaving himself beautifully...what happened with Wilkes was a misunderstanding."

"Aye? And I suppose that's why Captain's putting him to work as far from Wil as possible?"

I stifled a snort—then jolted when a dark-skinned woman shouldered into our conversation with a curt, "Rei, Syd's looking for you."

"Of course he is," Reinera snorted. "Well, don't forget that card game, Audra."

She swaggered off, and the newcomer thrust out a hand, sharp eyes agleam. "Klement Keen-Eye Drace. Sure you've already met my brother, Kato, our bosun. I'd like to be the first to say I think this voyage is a waste of time."

Lio smacked down the hand she offered me. "You, eager to be the first trading insults? Depths, no!" Teasing laced her word, but also a tinge of warning—as if these two were used to striking at odds, their corners like puzzle pieces that didn't quite fit together.

"Not my point." Klement cinched her arms across her middle. "I mean that there are Misspoken manifestations that need catching and a crew that needs paid, and this isn't a ferryboat."

"Are you *sure* it isn't?" A woman with scarlet hair piled in an intricate, twisted topknot called down to us from the helm—shamelessly eavesdropping on the conversation in such a way that would've likely earned her a blow to the face in the *Pourhouse*. "Think real hard, Klem. Are you *sure* that's not what we are?"

"Just keep steering, Steady Siu," Klement replied crossly.

"I can do lots of things in two and threes!"

"And she must. Because whatever else she's doing, she's always taking my breath away." A bearded, burly, bright-eyed sailor elbowed between Klement and Lio, offering a weathered hand to me; his fingers hung a bit crooked—as if once broken, then mended poorly. "Gydeon Nassar. Siu's my—"

"Wife?" I guessed—and laughed when his grin stretched wider, crinkling the corners of his eyes. "It radiates from you."

"Better that than whatever was radiating from him last night," Siu scoffed, palming the wheel with enviable ease. "I could barely stomach the sick bay with him."

"This you cannot blame on me," Lio warned.

"I know. You're annoyingly unblameable," Klement groused—but her gaze remained fixed on me, undeterred by the crew's banter. "Best make this extra voyage worth our while, Oddball."

I blinked. "Come again?"

Hinges creaked at our backs, and somehow—even before I turned—I knew precisely who had emerged from belowdecks.

Jaik shouldered through the hatch dressed in a plain shirt, tattered trousers, and an oil-stained vest. A shipman's cutlass hung from his waist, replacing the blade with which he'd trained on the clifftop, but his hair flopped roguishly across his left eye again—both eyes cutting straight to me, and the round of his throat bobbing when our gazes locked.

My chest pinched.

Lio swept an arm before both Klement and Gydeon, pivoting them away. "Have either of you seen Bash? I have a question for him about..."

Whatever she would have asked of this Bash, I heard none of it; I stepped to meet Jaik, and he to me, our boots finding the same patch of sunlight to anchor in.

The silence billowed for a moment, heavy and full as the rounded-out sails overhead.

"I'm sorry for being so sour yesterday after we came aboard," I blurted at last. "And I never thanked you for hanging the hammock. Or for the extra blanket last night." I offered him the last sticky bun, the runny glaze gleaming in the sunlight. "Thank you."

"You knew it was me?" A smile eased across his stubbled mouth, and he plucked the bun from my grip.

"Well, yes, Jaik, I did watch you hang it."

"I meant the blanket, *Ayjay*."

"I know, I know." Tucking a flyaway strand of hair behind my ear, I picked a particularly interesting knot in the wooden planks off to the side of our feet to study. "I assumed. It seemed like the sort of thing you would do."

"Hey, well, you're not wrong." He shrugged. "It was nothing. Just got a little cold close to sunrise."

It had; and buried in those warm threads, I'd felt my first shred of true comfort since the arrival of the Sha's entourage had tipped my world on its head like a swift pour of brandy into flames.

"So," I offered brightly, "are you sailing or soldiering right now?"

"Little bit of both." He smirked. "Wilkes—the quartermaster—I owe him a rematch from the last trip."

My gaze hooked on the cutlass lashed to his angular hips. "With real blades?"

He lifted his arm and peered at the sheath himself. "Well, yeah. Have to make sure my joints don't rust out here with all the seawater."

So that he could still defend the Sha properly when we returned. So that he could do his duty—a duty that this voyage kept him from.

A waste of time.

"Want to watch?" Mischief laced Jaik's tone, his grin edging on something wicked that dug me out of my thoughts.

I stared at him, opened my mouth to reply—

But my imagination got the better of me.

Clashing blades. Bellowed cries. Two men at war with one another on the ship's deck, tempting Luck with every stroke of honed, merciless steel.

Jaik Grissom, dueling shirtless, paved in glittering sunlight.

Jaik Grissom, with a sword at his chest.

A blade in his heart.

Bile blistered in the back of my throat; without a word, I swung away from him; I strode blindly to the railing, where I leaned my elbows on the wood and cradled my head in my hands. My stomach tossed and heaved as *The Cathan* rose and plunged over a swell in the sea.

And then, warmth: fingertips balanced carefully on my back. "Audra...wait. What's wrong?" Concern deepened the tenor of Jaik's voice. "You feel sick?"

Sick. That was one word for it.

I couldn't chase the notion of him dueling out of my head.

"I don't know," I whispered, squeezing my eyes shut. "Jaik...don't fight him."

A long, labored pause; then, slowly, Jaik's fingers eased outward until his broad palm warmed through the sea-spray dampness of my shirt. "All right. All right, I hear you. Duel's off."

We hovered there at the railing, the ship rollicking beneath us, and I struggled to snap free of the cords of misery and fear that banded my heart painfully to my ribs.

Two weeks of this...these jumbled emotions, these flashes of feeling that came from nowhere and carved into the pits of me, leaving me breathless, floundering, drunk on despair...

I screwed my eyes even more tightly shut, breathing deeply of the breeze.

We couldn't reach the Isle of Misspoken Stories quickly enough.

CHAPTER 7
THE GRIM OR THE GRIN

To my relief, Jaik kept his word not to duel with Wilkes—and he gave me a wider berth after that first morning aboard the ship, for which I was both absurdly grateful and oddly sad. Captain Kassian put him to work on various tasks, and much of my time was spent with Lio in the galley, which she commanded like a country of its own. We baked and cooked and inventoried stock, all while discussing our time in Krylan…a safer, more pleasant subject than what the notion of Jaik in a duel had stirred up.

I wrestled nightmares where he fought the quartermaster despite my request, and it always ended in tragedy—Jaik impaled through the heart, bleeding out in my hands. Or his decapitated body crumbling onto the deck.

These flashes woke me in a cold sweat night after night. It always took some time for the wind to stroke my tacky hair flat, for my hackles to unbind…for the distant music of Maryon's fiddle from the crow's nest to sing me back to sleep.

The days were better, even when I faced them groggy and at times grouchy; Lio's training in baking gave my restless hands something to do as the miles to Erasure—to my memories—passed in lurches and lulls. And the crew proved as kind as they were rowdy, full of outlandish tales and an effervescence like an uncorked bottle of bubbling wine. A fizz of liveliness that poured through the aching seams of my heart at mealtimes and between bouts of distraction.

That endless, unraveling spool of delight among them made it all the clearer when their bearing changed as one, between a single day and the next. It reminded me of the hush that sometimes stole over a whole tavern, when card games and arguments and conversations fizzled in the same breath…a time Leatrix used to say fickle Luck was flipping its coin, and none of us knew it for certain which side it would land on: the grim, or the grin.

And that was when I knew we were drawing near to the Isle of Misspoken Stories…our own Luck bet on an unseen coin toss.

Faces I had come to know for their cheer hung heavy now as cut apron cords, and mouths given to banter and laughter traded levity for quiet mutterings—a few, even, to prayers. A scudding of sudbucket clouds soaped the wide dish of the sky, erasing the memory of sunlight; and a chill, slick and damp, emanated from the varnished shipdeck. It crawled beneath my skin whenever I was abovedecks, helping with odd-and-end chores, tying simple knots and bucketing fish entrails from the deck with Camden or running food from the galley to the late watches on Lio's orders.

I came to crave the globelight dimness in *The Cathan's* belly. At least there, I could pretend the cold above did not touch me.

"How often have you sailed these waters?" I asked Lio one day while we worked dough together at the counter.

"Many, many times, these last two years." She brushed a flyaway strand of hair from her brow with the back of her wrist. "It is always this way when we draw near the currents around the Isle of Misspoken Stories. But..."

Hesitation, in her voice. In her fingers as they met the dough.

The chill crawled from the planks beneath my stockinged feet, winding its vicious constriction around my calves. "But—?"

"It is not usually so fierce." Lio glanced at the galley doorway. "And not usually so soon."

My back teeth ached, grinding against one another. "What do you think that means?"

"It isn't for me to say." Her dark eyes cut back to me. "What do *you* suppose it means?"

I would never know if it was instinct or guesswork or something far more that nudged the answer from my lips: "Something's changed."

No sooner had the words escaped than a bell clanged, jolting me in place, my hands springing free of the dough I'd been shaping. Lio straightened as well—slower, frowning at the galley's low roof as she dusted flour from her hands. "Merciful Ahim...I *despise* that bell."

She left me with that as swiftly as she left the dough, unlacing her apron while she tore from the galley. Cursing, I whipped my own apron over my head and bolted after her.

Whatever that bell was, it had summoned even the sleeping crew members. Crushed in a torrent of clamoring sailors, Lio and I found each other's hands and held tight, pulling against the currents up the steps to the deck, where we spilled out among a swarm of salt-scented, sweat-tacky bodies.

Shoulders checked against mine with bruising force as *The Cathan's* crew shot for the railings, seeking what had summoned them; the sky was a dizzying blur of black-bellied clouds molding with stormforce, the deck slippery under the first speckles of what promised to become a deluge.

In the drizzly haze, a burly sailor slammed into me so sharply, my stockings lost purchase on the deck. My fingers ripped from Lio's, and I tumbled forward—then shrieked with breathless shock as an arm swooped around my waist, spinning me out of the crush of bodies.

"I've got you, Ayjay—go!" Jaik thrust me toward the steps up to the helm, then whirled back for Lio, catching her under the arm and pulling her after me.

I scrambled up the stairwell on all fours, snatching the next hand that reached down for me—Captain Kassian's, and for the first time, I noticed it was missing a finger. His other hand held a spyglass to his eye; he heaved me up and pushed me around to his far side without looking, then caught Lio's fingers when she mounted the steps. Drawing her near, he slammed the spyglass shut against his thigh and leaned his chest into her back, bracing both hands on the railing on either side of her broad hips. "There's a bloody blockade."

"*What?*" Outrage strangled Lio's voice; she snatched the spyglass from her husband's hand and slipped it open to follow his nod toward the stormy horizon.

"A blockade—against *us?*" I demanded.

Jaik wedged between Captain Kassian and me, jerking his chin grimly at the gauzy veil of rain enshrouding the ship. "You wouldn't think so. But it looks that way."

Tearing my gaze from his furious countenance—angrier than I had seen it yet—I swiveled to face the sea.

I could scarcely discern the waves from the horizon at first, the sky so dim and the water so murky that where they met was a mystery. My stomach swooped at the irreconcilable notion that we were captured in a globe of some sort, an endless wheel turning our lives end over end.

And then, with a flare of light, the world righted itself.

The chain of ships necklaced the sea, a grim, gapped grin of fiery teeth jutting in the lipless, foaming maw of wild waters. Their formation interlocked like the overlay of boards in *The Cathan's* hull, mortared with a wicked arsenal of cleaving prows and speared hulls.

"Bash," Lio hissed, "tell me those are not Old Salt vessels."

I turned to look for this *Bash* she'd now mentioned twice, but it was Captain Kassian who grunted, "Not this bloody far north. Not if they know what's best for keeping their heads."

"Hang on...no." Jaik leaned his weight into his hand pressed to the railing; the other slid to the sheath on his hip. "That's *Arias's* flag they're flying."

Lio shut the spyglass in the span of her palms. "Those reinforcements on their fore and aft are like none I've ever seen."

"And the fire they're flaring isn't a signal *I've* ever seen, either," Captain Kassian growled.

"That's because we've never had to use it before. Arias and I were saving it for..." Jaik slapped a hand on the wood, then spun on the Captain. "Look, just sail me in as close as you can. I need to talk with whoever's in charge."

CHAPTER 8
MESSAGE IN A BOTTLE

From Lio's tales of *The Cathan's* time searching the waters for Misspoken manifestations, I'd gleaned that the command of Mithra-Sha's navy rotated regularly. Sometimes it was a soldier directing the fleet, other times a Storycrafter—power balanced equally between their hands.

Today, command lay with Officer Ravella, a senior soldier with Storycrafted armor soaked tight to skin nearly as dark as the rain-heavy clouds that hung above our ships. She and Jaik met aboard *The Cathan's* deck, their frames paved in flickers of lightning snaking through the belly of the storm. Encircled by the sharp-eyed crew, they shook hands with a sort of terse comradery that made me feel utterly adrift—the only one not a part of this strange world.

"Officer Ravella." Jaik's tone was almost easygoing, but the tension in his shoulders tightened mine in turn. "Appreciate you rowing over. I'm—"

"Not in command here." Ryker shrugged up from the mainmast, stepping to Jaik's side with a scowl that rivaled the thunder. "You want to tell me why we're being blockaded when that bloody island is still a half-day away?"

Ravella shot him an unimpressed look. "That isn't an easy question to answer."

"Try us," Jaik invited lowly, his bulk with crossed arms nearly equal to Ryker's.

Ravella shifted, pitching her weight onto one leg. "Ships have reported an increase in activity in and around the Isle."

"Misspoken manifestation activity?" Jaik clarified.

"Yes, but not the..." Ravella grimaced, drumming her fingers along the crease of her inner elbow.

Ryker's jaw shifted. "The *what*?"

"You can spit it out, whatever you're chewing over. It's not too tough for us," Jaik added.

Ravella's shoulders rippled with a swift, silent intake of breath, then dropped as her exhale steamed the damp air. "Not the sort we're used to facing."

Ryker's eyes narrowed. "Come again?"

"You know how it is, Captain. The manifestations we've faced before, they're...bestial. Beholden to whatever purpose they find in the story that gives them life. But these ones have caught our ships off guard. They sank two crews to the depths before we managed to get the word out."

A muffled curse ripped through the rain; a quick glance over my shoulder showed it came from Syd, the ship's logkeeper, perched on the railing with one arm wound into the shroud fastenings and gutting compassion dampening his eyes. Lanah, the bosun's assistant, linked her hand into his free one, her own damp gaze fixed on Ravella.

Jaik shifted, stroking a hand over his bearded jaw. "The fleet's holding the line now?"

Ravella nodded. "We sent word to Vallanmyre. Storycrafter Nayori is advising...she should be here soon. But orders from the Sha himself are that no one sails in until these strange manifestations are eliminated or contained."

"*No one*?" Jaik echoed sharply.

"I don't recall making the Sha bloody Captain when I signed on to wrangle his beasties for him," Ryker growled.

"If you're one of us, then you're needed *here*," Ravella snapped back.

"I don't remember asking *you*, either—"

"*Ryker*." Lio stepped forward, laying a hand on his arm, her fingers sludged in flour turned sticky by the rain. Fingers that bristled with a sort of staying power I hadn't thought her capable of—but the way they looked at one another was as charged as the heart of the storm we sailed under. It raised the hair on my neck...and lashed my gaze irresistibly to Jaik.

Jaik, who stepped back from Ravella, tearing both hands through his hair, then wrapping them around the nape of his neck. "We can't get through."

No one argued. No answer came at all but the drum of rain on the deck...almost a mocking chorus.

Then Jaik cursed Luck, hands flying back up to shove his hair down again, to streak over his face. "We were so flipping *close*!"

I slipped from my spot with the crew, striding to his side, slipping a hand over his shoulder—a touch he jerked away from.

It burned. I couldn't say why.

"Jaik," I croaked, "Jaik, it's all right—"

"*Jaik*?" Ravella interrupted, her sharp gaze cutting between us. "Captain Jaik Grissom? The Sha's personal guard?"

"Yeah, figured you knew that," Jaik fired back gruffly, dropping his hands from his face.

Ravella's shoulders dropped. "Apologies, Captain Grissom. I haven't had the pleasure of crossing paths with you yet...I didn't know your face."

Heaving a breath, Jaik shook his head. "Not your fault. And it doesn't change anything, I know. You've got your orders."

"It changes nothing for the blockade, no. However..." Ravella stepped nearer, fishing in her pocket. "I have a message for you."

Jaik cursed lowly. "Raz can't give me a couple *weeks*..."

"It's not from the Sha."

Another rain-soaked pause.

"Then who—?"

"Captain, honestly, I couldn't say." Ravella shifted her feet again, casting a glance toward the neighboring ships. "He was a sailor, I suppose, but I've not crossed him in the fleet before, nor seen him since. He's the one who told us how treacherous the waters were turning near the Isle and said we should form up a blockade. If we'd just done it when he suggested, those two ships..."

She broke off, lips pressing thin; then she shook her head.

"He said to give this missive to Jaik Grissom when I saw you. Seemed pretty confident you'd be showing up." She tugged a square of folded parchment from the seams of her armor, damp with seaspray and rain. "After that, he got into his rowboat and headed back toward the other ships."

Jaik snatched the letter, turning his back on the crew while he thumbed the seal. It was like nothing I had ever seen before—a rich ebony wax, the sigil on it outlined in fiery tones. A quill and inkpot.

Jaik's thumb stilled. His breath caught—and held.

Unease drizzled down my spine. "What is it? Who—Jaik—?"

The note trembled in his hand.

"Flipping Luck," he breathed. "He was *here*."

Goosebumps soared up my arms, prickling as high as my jawline. "*Who*?"

Jaik's eyes flashed to mine; flecks of hope sprinkled over the depthless despair from a moment ago, like winks of sunlight sliding through chinks in this never-ceasing cloudbank.

"Come with me, Ayjay. You need to see this."

CHAPTER 9
FLYAWAY SPARKS

MY SHIVERS REFUSED TO abate even when Jaik and I tucked ourselves into a quiet corner in the sick bay, offered generously by Gydeon and Hasser. Perched on one of the empty cots, I shuddered endlessly, watching Jaik kindle the lantern strung from the ceiling with one hand—the other still trapping the note in his fist like it might otherwise flee his grasp.

I mumbled a numb-lipped *thank you* when he tossed a starchy blanket over my sodden shoulders; he sought no warmth for himself, settling on the cot a respectable distance from me, teasing the wax seal with a trembling thumb.

Water dribbled from the soaked strands of my forelock; I scuffed it from the tip of my nose. "Jaik, you're scaring me."

He jumped as if I'd prodded him, shaking his head; water flecked from his hair and spritzed my cheek. "Sorry. I just…" He swallowed audibly, gripping the folded missive between both hands. "Ayjay, this symbol…I've seen it before. In Erasure."

My eyes darted up; his dropped to meet mine.

"It's the Storymaker's mark."

Weightlessness surged in my belly. The breath stole from my lungs. "Are…are you *certain*?"

"Yeah, I've seen it twice now." Another violent tremor sent the paper rattling in his palms. "Flipping Luck…I don't even know what to do with this."

"Because it's from Him?"

He drooped, hands falling in his lap. He stared at the note with something like reverence. Relief. "Because for a second there, I thought we lost our only chance to get your memories back."

The notion twisted strangely in my chest, like one of Lio's braided loaves stretched until the yeasty threads verged on tearing. Swallowing, I scooted closer to Jaik, tying the blanket more tightly around my shoulders. "Well? Why don't you read it?"

Jaik held still a moment longer. Then he cleared his throat. "Why don't, ah...why don't you do it?"

I bent away, searching for his gaze, but it remained transfixed on the note. Avoiding me.

Throat tight, I pinched the parchment and slid it from his hands. He let it go...did not even twitch, palms still upturned, head still bowed, eyes fastened on the wood between his boots.

And just like that, my hands held a note written by the teller of the greatest stories. The One they claimed had spoken the world into being.

I couldn't bear to sit idly with that notion—if I did, I would never keep the courage to read His words. So I thumbed open the seal—carefully separating the wax without cracking it—and unfolded the note.

A puff of something escaped the creases—like dust, but nothing old, nothing moldering about it. Sparkling like flyaway embers from a bonfire, it tickled my nose and glistened in my throat when I inhaled. Like breathing in fractals of pure power.

I shook my head and fought not to sneeze. Nose wrinkled, I studied the perfect, tidy penmanship at the heart of the note—of which there was surprisingly little to speak—then whispered:

Jaik and Audra,

I am afraid the nature of things has necessitated that I leave my place in Erasure for the time being.
If you would still seek me, you will find me—when you seek with all your heart. Begin with landfall in Fallshyre Bay. Be wary of the waves...and of the shadows on their faces.
Whatever you choose, grace and peace are yours.

The note was unsigned but for the sigil of the inkpot and quill stamped below the words; the symbol danced in the low lanternlight, speckles of amber and russet winking secretively against the black when I turned the letter this way and that.

Bone and sinew popped as Jaik's fingers slowly, slowly curled into fists on his knees. "Fallshyre Bay. That's not too far away."

"You truly want to do this?"

Laughter scraped from his chest. "Where else would I want to be?"

Klement's irritation at our first meeting slashed across my memory. *A waste of time.*

Guilt echoed every beat of my heart. "You're the Sha's right hand; his bodyguard. You're needed for more than chasing something like this."

"Chasing the Storymaker Himself out of Erasure, you mean?" Jaik's eyes darted to me. "You heard them...waters are too treacherous to make it to the Isle right now, anyway. Besides, I'm not on the rotation right now—Reiko is. A side trip to Fallshyre Bay's not going to take that long...forget the waves and the shadows. We'll be sailing away from those."

Unease simmered like hot oil in my throat. "If you're *certain*..."

"Are *you*?"

We gazed at one another, him with fists loosely clenched, me with the note strung tightly between mine.

I had agreed to a two-week sail to the Isle of Misspoken Stories. But this...

This was no longer that. I could feel it in my chest, basting my insides with a sort of crystallized conviction—and judging by the embers of thought dancing across his eyes, Jaik could, too.

There would be no simple stroll into Fallshyre Bay to find the Maker of all stories. What awaited us, I could not say...only that it wasn't *that*. It was as if the inhaled waft of this note's contents had dusted my heart with a vague notion of what lay ahead.

"I do still want to find my memories," I murmured. "That hasn't changed. And my board in Krylan is paid for until the year's end."

It wasn't quite an answer; by the narrowing of Jaik's eyes, he'd noticed that, too.

"Fallshyre Bay it is," he said slowly—like a question. Or a test.

I folded the note into quarters and slid it into the pocket of my shirt. "Fallshyre Bay, indeed."

CHAPTER 10
SIMPLE, EASY, FULFILLED

WHETHER OUR CHOICE TO travel to Fallshyre Bay was right or wrong for our sakes, it proved the perfect one to make regardless—I wasn't certain Officer Ravella or the blockade would have survived Ryker's wrath otherwise.

Tension banded my chest like armor that pulled tighter and tighter with every slow mile we sailed away from the string of ships, away from blackened skies and treacherous waters—a tension mirrored in every line of *The Cathan*. There were no more shanties, no more dice games, no more dances. The crew manned their posts warily, eyes forever scouting the horizon, on the lookout for the things Ravella had warned us about.

For the waves and the shadows.

I bundled my hammock belowdecks; it seemed safer than being confronted by the open expanse of the sea whenever I blinked awake from a bad dream.

Day by day, we sailed—and every day, we prepared. Weapons sharpened. Clothing stowed. Two notes burning a hole in my pocket...an invitation to this desperate quest. A call to continue it.

"Do you think I'm a madwoman?"

The vulnerable question fled my lips after days of contemplation, making itself a nest in the warm confines of *The Cathan's* captain quarters. Lio and I had been at work there for some time, sorting through a trunk of clothing hauled abovedecks by Siu. The fine garments it contained would supplement our journey to a breezier Fallshyre Bay. When I'd asked Siu where she'd gotten her hands on such fine threads, she'd cackled like a treed monkey, shook her head, and swaggered out of the cabin.

I didn't need to know stories as well as I once had to know *that* one wasn't meant for my ears.

Fingers buried in rich layers of fur-trimmed leather and stiff-woven fabric vests, Lio hesitated, glancing at me sidelong; the late-day light poured in from the bay window at the aft of the cabin, limning the hoop in her nostril. "I'm afraid you are going to have to be much more specific than that."

I blew errant curls from my brow; I'd asked Noveen, the cooper's assistant, to trim them in anticipation of our journey across the Isle of Misspoken Stories. But in the salty sea air, they'd rebelled, curving into my eyes. "About going to Fallshyre Bay."

"Hmm." Perched on the edge of the cot she and Ryker shared, Lio sorted through several pieces of clothing before she gave me an answer. "Why would I think that madness?"

"Well, chasing the *Storymaker* into port..." I swallowed, resisting the urge to reach for my pocket and play with a square of paper already crooked and curled from the sweat of my fingertips. "It's all a bit...outlandish, isn't it?"

"Yes, it is." Wry humor sketched her tone. "But aren't all stories? Mustn't you be a bit touched in the head to tell them—to *live* them?"

"I just...*Storycrafting*." I rolled the syllables across my tongue. "I don't *remember* having a mind for it. Barkeeping, that was a simple, sensible life. This all feels like...like a balancing act on the edge of Luck's coin."

Spreading a vest across her folded legs, Lio studied me with bright, considerate eyes. "Audra, you seem quite a practical person," she said at length. "And I wonder if perhaps you struggle to see yourself in the role you once played because you struggle to lean into what might be fantastical and foreign."

"It's possible." I toyed with a cowl in my own lap. "Simple feels...safe. When I had simple, I had everything I wanted. And then the Sha's entourage came to our doorstep, and they complicated *everything*—"

"Do you blame Jaik for that?"

Such a quiet question. But it rang in my ears like she'd shouted it.

"What? No!" My fists knotted tightly in the threads. "No, I—how could I? None of them knew I still didn't remember, and...by the time they came, it was too late. There was no turning back."

"If there was, would you?"

Would I?

If I had the chance to rewrite the tale just once more...would mine be a story still of barcounters and bustling streets? Of empty apartments and feline friends?

Would I write Jaik out of it, for the peace of an uncomplicated past and a future untainted by knowing I had once been something else...a far more powerful and, in some ways, a far *worse* woman than I'd always thought myself to be?

"It...would be simpler," I confessed. To Lio. To myself.

She reached for my hand, wrapping my fingers in a grip callused and scarred in strange ways...deep, harsh notches scraped across her palms, burn-marks and small puckerings of flesh that she had not explained to me. That I had not dared to ask about.

"I have had simple," she murmured, "and I have had whatever in Ahim's name all of this is. And I will tell you this, Audra Jashowin...a simple, easy life is not always a fulfilled one. You have to listen for the tune of your heart below the sounds the world makes. You might find the rhythm it beats is a war song or a melody of adventure." Brushing the clothing aside, she scooted nearer to me, tugging me over so our heads leaned together—so that her next words could be quieter, a murmur that soaked into the marrow of my bones. "It might be a sea shanty or a six-string tune. Or, perhaps, Audra, it will sound more like a story."

I nestled my cheek against her shoulder, breathing in the comforting aromas of sugar and cinnamon and powdery flour from her clothing. "I don't know why that terrifies me."

Her lips pecked the top of my head. "Because, to hear others tell it, the story of your life has been tragic as often as it has been truly happy. But tell me if you could ever go back to Krylan and think your life simple again, if you did not pursue this quest to its end."

Slowly, I pushed myself up from her, wiping the lids of my dry, burning eyes. "No, I don't think I could. It's like those adventure books I read to Sheeba...the ones that kept me up all night. Sometimes you have to know how the story ends before you can sleep. You have to turn the last page and close the book, or you'll spend all night tossing and turning anyway."

"That's my girl." Lio smoothed a hand down my hair. "Audra, it's all right to be frightened. But it's also good to know what it *is* that frightens you."

Groaning, I pitched forward, burying my head in my hands. "Flipping Luck, I wish we could bring *you* with us. Speaking with you about all of this is easier than speaking about it with Jaik."

"I've grown ridiculously fond of you, you know." My heart leaped at Lio's words—and that freed my laugher all the swifter when she added, "And I have also faced *my* story, and written it how I like. And that is with my feet on this deck, thank you very much." A deep breath, a discomfited frown as she fit her hand over her middle. "Even if it isn't treating me kindly just now."

Concern lifted my head fully from my hands. "Are you all right?"

"A bout of seasickness, that's all—it comes for even seasoned sailors now and again, and I am less seasoned than most." Lio fluttered her fingers my way. "Nothing good conversation and distraction won't solve."

"Fair enough." Still, I peered closely at her as she reclined on her palms among the nest of clothes. "Do you suppose you'll return to the blockade?"

Lio arched a brow. "Have you been acquainted with my Bash? Perhaps we might have, before...but now that he's been told to do it, he would rather sail to the depths themselves."

"That does sound like him." I huffed a laugh—then gave over to the spurring of curiosity that rankled in my chest, turning to face her in full. "Why do you call him that...Bash?"

Lio paused a moment, a certain distance overtaking her gaze—gentling it with memories I suspected I would never be privy to. For a time, only muted scuttling and creaking along the hull broke the well of silence.

"Bash was the piece of Ryker I fell in love with first," she murmured. "The man he once was...the one even *he* believed to be lost at sea." With a swift shake of her head, she stirred from the memories, looking to me once more. "Sometimes, love does not happen all at once. It comes to us step by step, piece by piece...like a dance. With Bash, it was his smile first. He was pure sunlight to me. So when the darkness in him shoulders forward, I seek the sunshine. It reminds me that even at his worst, he is still the man I fell in love with. Every piece of him."

"You make it sound so easy," I sighed. "And so *romantic*."

"Merciful Ahim, it wasn't always," Lio laughed. "We've even held knives at one another's throats. But I made a choice...I chose him. And I keep choosing him, even when it's difficult."

Wood rasped and scraped, needling against the sudden discomfort that chafed in my heart.

Could it be as simple as choosing? Was I meant to choose Jaik, in all of this? Was that why I was here?

Did he *expect* me to? Was that why he seemed so nonchalant about abandoning his duties for a time?

I opened my mouth to give voice to those thoughts—and all of a sudden Lio slashed a hand against my chest, her eyes fixed on the wall at the stern of the ship, beside the window. A frown pinched her thick brows.

At first, I feared she might *season* my lap with the manifestation of her seasickness. Then...

Another creak. Another scuttle. Another soft, subtle, sawing echo.

I met Lio's narrowed gaze, my own eyes wide.

Three beats of shifting boards. A soft *plink* as a shard of wood shot inward, bouncing off the floor.

Outside the window, something shifted—a blackened stain rearing back and slamming into the glass.

Lio and I shot to our feet, and she cursed, jerking me back as wooden boards buckled and bowed and glass splintered under the next slam. The next. The next.

By the time we stumbled backward to the door, something knobby and coal-dark had *shoved* itself through the hole in the wood, widening the gap.

Lio fumbled blindly behind her, found the doorknob, and ripped it open. We tore from the cabin as one, spilling onto the deck, Lio's cries wrecking whatever peace prevailed with the blockade long lost on the horizon: "*We're being boarded!*"

And then Ryker's bellow, booming like the thunder to her lightning: "You heard her! Raiders, on your posts!"

My gaze leaped wildly around the deck, finding Jaik on the other side of it, his hand on his fire-guarded blade, his focus on the helm—not seeing what I saw.

Not seeing the shadow unfurling at his back, clambering over the railing whisper-silent, drawing a mangled, lethal-tipped dagger from the tatters at its flank.

"*Jaik!*" I screamed.

The dagger skewered downward.

Jaik tilted and whipped sideways, the weapon grazing just shy of his collarbone. Pivoting sinuously on heel, he parried the strike—then swore at the top of his lungs, ripping his blade free and staggering back toward us. "*Whoa!*"

Innumerable shadows joined the first, cresting above and tumbling over the ship's railing, staining *The Cathan's* deck like spilled spirits. They looked like sailors themselves, but—*wrong*. Skeletal, dressed in shreds of sinew and severed muscle, pitiless fire burning in the pits where their eyes should have been.

Lio gripped my shoulder, wheeling me back the way we'd come—toward the Captain's cabin, its door swinging ominously on creaky hinges...and to the figures shambling through it.

"What *are* those things?" Syd's shout shook as he closed in on Lio's other side; together we backed toward the mainmast.

My spine bumped against something warm, living, solid, and breath hitched in my lungs when Jaik's voice floated over my shoulder. "If I felt much like taking a coin flip right now, I'd say some Captain tried to manifest themselves a Misspoken crew."

My heart abandoned my chest, splashing into the pit of my stomach instead.

"Bloody *wonderful*." Ryker's voice floated down from the helm; judging by the tension that girdled it, these Misspoken manifestations were present above as well. "If this *ferry mission* gets me killed, I'm taking you with me, Fishbait."

"Good flipping Luck," Jaik muttered under his breath.

And then, like a tether cut free...all at once, the Misspoken sailors attacked.

CHAPTER II
SCARLET ON GOLD

I HAD NEVER FACED battle before that I could recall. And I never, ever wanted to again.

Not with these screams, curses, and cries. Not with the head-piercing echo of steel on steel, the cracking echo of rifleshot and firing pistols, the slap of blood on wood, the crunch of bone.

Not with the loss that stormed *The Cathan's* deck.

The Misspoken sailors did not crumble easily; they felt none of the pain that girdled the screams of the crew who fell victim to their serrated blades. Skeletal frames cleaved across *The Cathan's* face like weapons themselves, and in moments of the first attack, the deck dissolved into a single heaving mess of bodies, some living, some a horrific imitation.

I cowered against the mainmast with Lio at my side, hands gripping the sleek wood backward to steady myself.

There was nowhere to turn. Nowhere to run. All around me, chaos; within me, chaos. I had no weapons; there was a knife in my satchel, stashed belowdecks, but would it even do any good against these grinning, grisly abominations?

Pleas to Luck wadded uselessly in my throat. I couldn't unstick my feet to find shelter; I couldn't tear my gaze away from the carnage, the bedlam as skeletons and sailors dueled across the deck.

I couldn't *breathe*.

Like she had a drop of hidden Storycrafter skill herself, Ravella's tale of warning had come to life before our eyes: the force that had sunk two ships before the blockade locked into place.

A threat that had once been *mine* to oppose as Master Storycrafter.

How had I ever survived?

How could I ever go *back*?

A frightened shout tore me from those thoughts. Through the heave and twist of battle, I caught sight of Camden.

Nearly a dozen Misspoken nightmares had cornered him between the railing and the steps to the helm. Sheeba was wrapped around his shoulders, claws dug in, hissing, spitting, swiping at any skeletons that dodged close.

And there were plenty of them. Far too many.

"*Cam.*" Lio's furious gaze rivaled the Misspoken sailors' firebright glares.

"Lio, no," I hissed—then cried, "*Wait*!"

But it was too late; Lio snatched her skirts in one fist and hefted one of the sacks of goods pitched against the railing near the mainmast in the other—then she *flew*.

These last few weeks aboard *The Cathan* had not painted a picture of Lionyra Kassian as someone with a prowess for battle. My mind had sculpted her in softness, in peace, in power of a different sort.

And yet, when she tore into the fray, she became something more than a baker, more than a ship's cook. She stepped into the chaos like a dance, with floating steps and a ferocity even Misspoken manifestations ought to have feared. Whirling between the skeletons, she hefted the sack in two hands and struck them at the joints, bashing bones out of place, skewing knees and ankles and hips with perfect, precise aim that sent the creatures clattering across the deck away from Camden.

As if she knew exactly where to strike to incapacitate, and expended no excess energy. And despite my terror, watching her battle her way to the boy's side with a determination that likened her more to this crew than anything I had seen about her yet...

Something in me ached. Something in me *yearned*.

Lio struck and slammed and shoved her way through the throng to Camden and Sheeba, and for a moment they dueled with their backs together, the boy with his dagger and the baker with her sack, knocking skeletons flying; when the ranks thinned for a moment, Lio whirled and gripped Camden by the collar, gesturing wildly to the crow's nest. With a deft nod, he sprang toward the mainmast. Sheeba hunkered around his neck with eyes so full of fright, the black of her pupils eclipsed the rest.

"Come with me!" Camden bellowed as he skidded to my side; then he jammed his dagger between his teeth and vaulted up the handholds in the mast, Sheeba swaying on his shoulders.

I spun to follow, hefting myself up the first two notches before a terrible sound dropped me back to the deck, spinning me on heel.

Lio had not followed us.

She couldn't. Because a Misspoken sailor had backed her against the railing and driven its blade through her shoulder.

Panic burst in my head, the strangest silver-blue-and-gold starburst spraying across my eyes, a muffled, tinny ringing filling my ears.

Its echo sounded strangely like fireworks.

And the next thing I knew, I was screaming—screaming until fear took the form of rage, my voice dropping from a piercing shriek to a guttural *roar* that ravaged my throat. And I hurtled across the deck toward the wicked, wasted manifestation of a sailor as it tore its mangled blade free of Lio's flesh and raised it to strike again.

Lifeblood spilling across a shipdeck.

Blood painting my world.

Scarlet on gold. Crimson on umber.

"Get away from her!" My cry belted out like thunder, and I took a running leap, smashing into the skeletal seaman's side, hurling us both away from Lio. Its blade skipped and skimmed across her other shoulder, narrowly missing her throat.

We slammed to the deck, living flesh tangled with the living dead, those serrated ribs catching my wrists and holding them fast like shackles. I shrieked, kicking, writhing to free myself as its skull revolved *backward* on the column of its spine.

The burning ember sockets of the sailor's eyes held me captive, a scalding inferno that truly burned as it latched onto me, and for a moment, it seemed as if those flames pulsed more brightly—as if something tempestuous and *knowing* kindled in the depths of its skeleton stare.

It couldn't be—

Recognition?

Before I could blink that thought away, the skeleton revolved the entire column of its spine, hands wrapping its crooked cutlass, twisting it backward—then it cleaved down toward my neck.

"Ayjay!"

"Lionyra!"

Twin shots exploded in tandem from the helm and forecastle, and the sailor's skull shattered like glass, pelting my face with shards of bone; its body jerked left with one impact, then right with the other.

Running footsteps. The wail of a blade leaving its sheath. Then bone gave way with a horrific *crunch*, and I toppled backward, wrists weeping blood, chest heaving, terror sharpening every breath to a blade that knifed from my battered throat.

At the next blow, the skeletal figure shattered like spilled brandy and badly thrown dice across the deck; then the Captain slid on his knees across the wood, tumbling down at Lio's side.

"Lio," I gasped her name as I crawled to them.

Ryker had already cast aside the cutlass that had knocked the sailor's bones tumbling; he filled his hands with Lio instead, heaving her up from the deck, cursing when she cried out in pain and catching her hand when it leapt for her own shoulder.

"Not yet, not until I get a look at it—'ay, Cam's safe." His voice roughened even as his grip gentled, and he settled Lio against the railing. "You did good, Seasplitter."

Lio's eyes, wet and rived with anguish, flicked up to him; a smile traced her mouth. Then her gaze strayed to me, and that smile wobbled. "Oh, look at you...you look like a half-drowned alleycat."

Heart lodged in my throat, I grabbed her unhurt hand and wound our fingers together.

New shadows rose around us—these ones steadier. Fuller. The crew forming a bladed and pistoled crescent around their Captain and cook—and me—and struck out at the amassing army of Misspoken sailors while Ryker tugged off the rich maroon kerchief that bound Lio's hair and deftly wound it around her shoulder. Though his touch was featherlight, swift and soft in ways I had not seen before, still Lio's mouth cracked downward at the corners; she doubled up, her forehead slamming into the crook of Ryker's neck, a moan sliding through her lips and losing itself where the pulse throbbed visibly against his flesh.

The wound itself had not been dealt anywhere I might have assumed to be deadly; not in the heart, not in the neck, not in the belly. But the blood...

It surged and heaved like the waves we sailed on. Too much of it. *So* much of it.

Ryker did not speak. But the wild dart of his gaze about the deck as he cinched the kerchief tighter said enough—what I assumed was a fruitless search for this ship's healers, neither of whom I saw in the grouping around us, nor in the crush of battle beyond.

My stomach dropped. "Is she going to be all right?"

"As if I'd bloody let her go." Ryker's tone was shadow and storm, the depths he swore by quaking at the threat in his tone.

And something...*something* in me unfurled to meet the fury in his eyes when they leapt to me.

The intensity that wreathed his words—I *knew* it. My bones knew it, my blood, my heart. A whispered echo wound down every corridor of my being, curling my muscles in sharp twists, clamping my hand more tightly around Lio's as she panted and heaved.

The tension did not abate when Ryker knotted the makeshift bandage and swooped Lio upright, half-sprawled in his lap; we held her between us, sheltered from the havoc of combat at our backs.

"I know it hurts, sweetheart, I know...'ay." Ryker palmed damp strands of dark hair over Lio's ear, clutching the back of her head against him. "Steady. Steady."

I've got this. I've got you, I can fix this, just keep your eyes open, all right? Keep looking at me...

A hollow hum throbbed in my ears, pain blistering in my middle like salt in an open wound—a strange, strangling *need* to tear my eyes away, to search the deck for a different face amidst the chaos. Whiskey-dark eyes and a roguish smile.

But I couldn't. Not when Lio stirred, pushing back from Ryker to find his gaze, her own misty—but still fierce.

"I am—I will be *perfectly* all right," she panted, her head dipping a bit with every breath, her hand covering his over her shoulder. "But this crew will not. Not without you."

"If you think I'm going to—"

"I *know* you are going to keep fighting, because *The Cathan* will join those other crews in the depths if you don't!" Lio's voice was nearly lost under a fresh clatter of blades, a brutal volley of rifleshot.

Had I truly been someone who tangled in messes like these before? Of her own volition?

Was some part of me that woman still?

"I'm all *right*," Lio croaked, straining to shove backward from Ryker's grip. "This is nothing Gyddy can't manage. This ship needs its Captain...you must go. *Go*, Blackhand! You know what you're facing."

His eyes flashed to me, lips peeled back, breath seething between his gritted teeth.

"I've got her," I assured him—half honesty, half fear of what would happen if I didn't.

Ryker swore so colorfully, my ears heated; then he tore off his black captain's coat and cast it around Lio's shoulders like armor. He planted a fierce kiss on her brow, stabbed his blade into the deck, and jerked his head at me. "Move your arse, Oddball!"

I slid in to take his place, wrapping my arms around Lio's chest; together we tugged her to her feet, and she swayed into me. Ryker withdrew his arms a fraction at a time, as if he feared she might crumble again...and he would trust no one else to catch her if she did.

"You two get belowdecks, lock yourselves in the sick bay, and don't stick your heads out until Siu or I come for you," he barked. "Clear?"

"Aye, Captain," I panted.

Ryker shoved a hand through my hair, mussing the sea-sopped locks; then he snared Lio's chin, pressing his forehead to hers for a heartbeat.

The last I saw of him was the blur of a bloodstained black shirt and sandy hair spearing into the heart of the Misspoken crew, his holler of "*Come on, you ugly bastards!*" half-muffled under the pop of firing pistols.

Lio and I stumbled for the hatch belowdecks like a staggering, one-sided spider. Ducking volleys of rifleshot, swiping blades, and skeletons, we pitched down beside the hatch, and with one hand I ripped it wide, shoving Lio down onto the first step. I swung my legs around to follow her—

A many-headed shadow reared at my right, six fire-eyes burning, gap-toothed maws agape, and the nearest of three converging skeletons whipped its dagger toward my face so swiftly I didn't even have time to scream—or to comprehend why, with an entire deck of sailors to engage with, they sought *us*.

Only a faint squeak of shock escaped me when those bony fingers exploded into powder, the blade barely grazing my cheekbone, whipping my head toward the railing.

The railing where Jaik racked the riflebolt, took aim, and fired again—bursting the first skeleton's skull into dust. Then bringing down the second and third in two volleys swifter than heartbeats.

Gratitude and disbelief stole the rest of my voice. For a heartbeat, we stared at one another.

Jaik dipped his chin; then he spun to fire on another skeleton, and I slithered belowdecks, banging the hatch closed at my back and jamming the bolt home.

Ryker would just have to break it.

Lio had already reached the base of the steps and the crew's quarters beyond; she'd pulled a blanket from one of the hammocks, wadding it against her blood-soaked shoulder. The other she leaned to the doorframe, binding Ryker's coat tightly around her curves.

"What fun," she wheezed.

Panting and shaking, I wedged my shoulder beneath her armpit and helped her down the hall to the sickbay.

We found it deserted—Gydeon and Hasser must've been abovedecks after all, just lost in the fray. But my mind burned with the vaguest impressions of what to do…a memory living in the muscles of my hands, notions that floated with the scents of cotton and freesia.

Lowering Lio onto the same cot where Jaik and I had read the Storymaker's missive, I lit the lantern and hunted for gauze and bandages and tinctures. Quietly, Lio directed me to this and that…powders and salves she had seen Gydeon use. Then, while I sat before her, she told me how to use them, with all the confidence of a bartender mixing a brew, or a baker with a recipe…or a storyteller crafting tales.

"I don't know how you can be so calm." My voice shook. "I would be screaming my entire head off if I were hurt like this."

"This is not the first wound I've ever taken, Audra." A wretched, rueful tiredness laced every word, a perfect marriage to the slump of Lio's shoulders and the half-mast of her lids. Her fingers flexed in the folds of Ryker's coat, and when I sprinkled stinging powder on her wound, she turned her face away, burying her nose in the folds of the collar and inhaling deeply. It was several strained moments before she loosed that breath and added, "I wish that I could even call this the worst. It isn't."

"Would…would you tell me about the others?" I tipped a generous pour of antiseptic onto a cloth.

Lio's eyes squeezed shut. Slowly, she nodded.

And there in the throbbing stillness of the sickbay, with the distant, thunderous echoes of battle raging above our heads underscored by the soft and silent tears rolling down her cheeks and soaking into the collar of the Captain's coat…Lionyra Kassian told me a story.

Of a girl stolen away. Of a woman raised in hate. Of beatings and bloodshed and grief and sisterhood. Of wounds both seen and unseen. Of escape, and capture again. Of high seas and mountain fortresses, port towns and prisons.

She whispered to me of a man in a cloak, first gray, then blue, who'd saved them all—and my wide eyes leaped from packing herbs against her shoulder, finding her exhausted gaze fixed on me as she slumped back against the wall.

"You didn't know it then," Lio whispered, "and nor did I, but...when you unbound the power from within yourself, when you gave it all away to the world and its Storycrafters, you saved this crew. You saved *my* life, at the precise moment when I needed you most."

Thickness clotted my throat; I focused again on her shoulder, smoothing down the gauze, then wrapping bandages slowly and meticulously around her shoulder and bicep. "At least some good came of what I did with all that power."

"*Some* good?" Lio's other arm lifted, her fingers taking my chin, forcing my head up until our gazes locked again. "Audra Jashowin, every person in this crew I love—my *family*—owes you their lives. Your selfless act made all of this possible." Her hand faltered into her lap, but now her fierce stare pinned me in place. "Why do you suppose I was able to convince Ryker to sail you and Jaik to Erasure? He knows as well as I that neither of us would be drawing breath now if not for your sacrifice."

Heat seared my throat. "I didn't know—"

"I'm aware." A fatigued smile teased the corners of her lips. "And that makes it all the more precious. You see yourself as the woman who tore stories from the world? That is not the part of your story I remember. *I* remember the moment you restored them, regardless of what it cost you. I remember when hope was lost, and you gave it back. To my *friend*...a man who wept with joy for it." She leaned her head against the wall again, freeing me at last from the tidal force of her gaze. "You look into your past and you see red. I look into it, and I see blue."

Sniffing back the scorch in my nose and eyes, I returned to tending her shoulder. But it was nearly impossible now through the haze of tears clouding my vision.

The night Jaik had told me of our past, I had glimpsed an Audra Jashowin who'd worn a cloak of scarlet and unbound the endings from stories. The one responsible for years of lack and suffering in Mithra-Sha. The one responsible for her own lost and forgotten memories.

This Audra who Lio spoke of—a stranger to her at the time, a myth and legend now—I didn't know her, either. A life-saver. A giver of endings, not a taker of them. It was a piece of the story Jaik had told me, but it had seemed a slim sliver of it, curled and crumbled at the corners like a scrap burned in a mighty fire—the flames of what I'd done wrong. The poor choices I'd made.

It was different to hear Lio tell it. To know that in the moment I'd rewritten the world again, I'd unwittingly saved the life of a woman I would one day call *friend*.

It made the Audra I'd been feel less separate from the one I was now...the one who'd thrown herself at a Misspoken manifestation to save Lio's life.

And all at once, I was laughing...a hysterical, jumbled chuckle that pulled Lio's focus back to me. I leaned away from her, burying my face in my own bloodstained hands, and laughed until I wept.

"Flipping *Luck*," I gasped into the gaps between my fingers. "Oh, *Luck*, what *happened* today?"

Lio's breathy chuckles joined mine, pain-riddled but still pleasant somehow. "Depths if I can even put it to words. It's always an adventure with you, isn't it?"

"I honestly don't know." I palmed my cheeks, pressing upward until the rounds of them nearly obscured my vision. "How flipping *terrible* is that? Oh, I have to get those memories back. I can't be as useless as I was today."

"None of that! I won't have you calling the woman who saved my life *useless*."

"I did do that, didn't I?"

The sound of wrenching metal—followed by tread of uneven footsteps—echoed unmistakably beyond the sickbay door, putting to death our humor in half a heartbeat. Both of us straightened, or tried to; Lio hitched halfway through, bracing her bandaged shoulder with one hand, and I swiveled toward the door.

Staggering, slow boots brushed to a halt.

In the silence, we held our breath.

The doorknob twisted—caught. Then began to rattle.

This time, I didn't hesitate; I swiped a sturdy refuse bucket from its hook on the wall and stalked to the door, bracing myself before it. There I spun one swift, reassuring glance at Lio; she offered a deft nod in reply.

Bearing down the deepest breath I could, I waited for the knob to rattle again—then I seized it, spun it, yanked the door in, clutched the bucket in both hands again, and *swung* with all my might.

A yelp. A curse profaning Luck. Then a hand swooped around my makeshift weapon and snared my wrists, jerking me out into the hallway.

"What *is* it with you and buckets?" Jaik hollered against my ear.

Lio lost her breath in an audible rush. The bucket clattered from my hands—and I lunged, wrapping both arms around Jaik's neck before I could even think. Before I could wonder why the only place I wanted to hide was with my face in the crook of his shoulder.

He stumbled backward at my weight, struck the wall, fisted his hand gently in my hair...and crushed me against him as fiercely as I pressed him to me.

"Audra, hey, hey..." Jaik kissed the top of my head. Somewhere past us, I heard another set of storming bootsteps, another living body skirting us swiftly enough to cast a breeze through my hair. "You're all right, tiger."

"Are *you*?" I croaked.

A shaky laugh erupted from his chest. "You're not going to believe this, but I'm better than all right, right now."

And at last, that tight, coiled fervor in my muscles abated. My laughter shook as well, tears searing the backs of my eyes, sobs strangling the only two words I could choke free: "You *idiot*..."

"Hold that thought." His fingers unbound from my hair, crawling down my shoulders, hitching me nearer to him by the small of my back. "Hey. I want you to do something for me. Tell me five things you see right now."

CHAPTER 12
HALFWAY TO DYING
JAIK

DAYS AFTER THOSE MISSPOKEN sailors boarded *The Cathan*, I still couldn't really feel everything that hurt. Dagger nicks, sword slashes, a cracked rib where one of them had gotten hold of a rifle and clobbered me in the side...it was all muffled in the back of my head.

But the places where Ayjay had pressed in, held on to me when I'd gone to get her and Lio out of sickbay...I remembered *that*. Like muscle-memory—same as firing a rifle or swinging a sword. Like my body had a craving for every place she'd fit herself in when she'd knocked me back into the hall with her arms around my neck.

Flipping Luck. I was aiming to be pretty useless before long; sooner we found the Storymaker, the better.

We rolled into port a little worse for the wear a week after the attack—holes gouged in our flanks, a dozen sailors laid up who'd need an infirmary stay, Lio among them—but, thank Luck, no casualties. Perks of sailing with pirates...they scrapped even harder than soldiers. If I could've just talked Kassian into training the whole fleet, we'd probably lose less of them wiping out Misspoken manifestations.

Different problem for a different day.

I knew we were in Fallshyre Bay the second I woke that morning—the difference in the speed, the tension on the ship. Even as Arias's bodyguard, I'd spent my share of time with the fleet dealing with Misspoken manifestations the last two years. My body knew the change in tides...not as well as a seasoned sailor, but enough that even groggy, I could tell we'd arrived.

Groaning low in my throat, I rolled over in my hammock—and came face-to-face with Ayjay.

She'd been sleeping belowdecks ever since the blockade, which...fair. And it made sense she'd landed in a hammock close to the steps, same as me, because she'd had slim pickings by the time she bunked with the rest of us.

Still. I let myself think maybe the fact she'd gone for the hammock next to mine meant *something*.

This close, with just a little stale ship air between us, she looked the most like the Ayjay I'd known more than half my life. The ease in her face, the way she mashed her pillow against her cheek, the little bit of drool gathering in the corner of her mouth.

I swung my feet to the floor, gripped the edges of the hammock...just watched her for a minute.

Then, tempting Luck, I hooked a strand of her curly bangs from her brow with my smallest finger, shifting them away from her lashes.

"Morning, beautiful," I mouthed.

Letting myself pretend for a second that things were the way I wanted them. The way we'd been fighting for—for more years than you could count with one flick of Luck's coin spinning in the air.

She stirred a little, burrowing her nose in her blanket, huddling deeper in the hammock.

I beat a coward's retreat before she could catch me in the act.

Thank Luck I didn't have to go abovedecks right away—didn't have to see Fallshyre Bay yet. I let it stay something that lived in my head, floating harmlessly on the nearby horizon, while I made my way through the ship's narrow halls to the quartermaster's workroom.

Now, this part of the ship, I loved. The smell of oil, polish, and cold steel welcomed me in like a friend the second I swung the door open. Which made up for the wary look the quartermaster shot me when I whistled a greeting from the doorway.

Also fair. I *had* gone after him with a sword that one time....and bowed out of the duel he proposed to make up for it. And I hadn't been able to make myself tell him why—mostly because I didn't want to remember Ayjay looking the way she had on the deck when I'd told her about the whole thing.

But I'd given him the only peace offering I could manage without breaking my word to her: my sword laid out on the worktable in front of him, where he pitched himself with folded arms, examining the tooling on the leather sheath.

"You manage it?" I asked, stepping across the table from him.

"Aye, she's buffed and polished." Wilkes tilted his head. "You weren't wrong—the make is like nothing I've ever seen or worked with. And I've seen plenty, Grissom. Blades of all kinds, from all sorts of lands...Zandraen diamond daggers, Navarian venom-blades, even Kaynite silverswords. *All* sorts, pouring through thieving hands in Korsa. But this is something else."

"Probably because no one actually smithed it." I shrugged when his eyes popped to mine. "It's a long story."

"I gather, given how you begged *me*, of all people, to buff it for you." With a grunt, he tossed me the sheathed sword; I slid it out a few inches, letting my breath out in matched increments until I was sure—

Yeah. He'd done a better-than-decent job. The few nicks and scrapes I'd found after the battle against those skeletons were as good as new. Didn't even tarnish the steel. Which was a relief, because Misspoken manifestations were the only things I'd ever found that could dent this sword...and I wasn't eager to lose it to a scrape with them.

"Looks great." I slammed the sword back into its sheath and tossed him as much of a smile as I could muster up. "Listen, I'm sorry about all the...you know. Last time. Going off on you the way I did. You didn't deserve that."

His brow shot up.

"All right, well, last I knew you, you did. But—"

"If I held a grudge against every person who ever raised a blade against me in defense of what was theirs, I wouldn't have the strength to climb out of my hammock every day," Wilkes snorted, spreading his hands on the edge of his weapons table. "The *last you knew of me*, I was sent on orders from the Del's Own Blade to capture the woman you loved. You didn't do half as much to me as I would do to anyone who tested the same with Reinera."

I whistled. "You've got it bad, friend."

"There is something that tells me you have it worse. I'm not the one who sent one of the Del's best blades on the run with sheer feral loyalty. And I'm not the one sailing on a mad adventure to reclaim her lost memories."

"What can I say? She was worth it then. She's worth it now."

Hinges creaked, and the door glided open; I stifled a curse when the lanternlight in the hall framed Kassian, arms folded, pitching himself through the doorway.

First time I'd seen him since he'd barged into the sick bay after me the night of the attack, scooped a half-conscious Lio up off the cot, and carried her to their cabin. Looked to me like he hadn't slept since then—shadows painted on under his eyes, wrists a littler leaner, face a littler gaunter.

Yeah. I got that.

"Everything good in here, mates?" His voice scraped more like gravel, too. "Or do I need to start knocking heads together?"

"Just getting what's mine." I bared the blade.

"If you make it a point to defend my honor like this all the time, you'll make your wife jealous," Wilkes scoffed.

"Mate, you haven't got any honor. Just the best smithing hands a pirate can buy."

"And does she know you flirt with me as well?"

Kassian scoffed, but he didn't give his quartermaster a look; he stared me down instead, the same way he had our first night out of Krylan.

Tell her, you coward.

I was stepping off this ship with a lot more than I'd come onto it with...but still without Ayjay's memories. Hard to know what to say or how to feel, when the wrong parts of me were poured full.

"Give us the room, Wil," the Captain finally said.

Not a request, and the quartermaster didn't treat it like one. He threw me a nod and strode out, clapping his hand on Kassian's shoulder on the way past; the Captain cuffed him on the wrist in turn, but he kept looking my way.

When Wilkes was gone, Kassian stepped inside. Toed the door tighter behind him on his way across the room to me.

He stopped just shy of arm's reach; I still bothered taking stock of whether he could swing at me from that distance.

"You talk to her yet?"

I scoffed. "Why are you so obsessed with Ayjay knowing she's my—?"

"I meant about those skeletons, mate. How they all went to the hatch and tried getting after her once she was belowdecks."

All the hair on my neck stood up. "Didn't mention it, no."

Because, honest to Luck, I didn't want to think it through. Seeing that one abomination turn itself inside-out trying to chop off her head was bad enough. Then there were the three who'd chased after her and Lio before they'd made it belowdecks.

But that hadn't been the end of it. After Ayjay and Lio had gotten clear, bolted the hatch...we'd managed to end the battle fast because the skeletons had poured all their focus into ripping through that bolted door.

And they'd almost done it. The lock was a mangled mess by the time we shattered that last bag of bones, and I'd overheard Kato and Lanah muttering about how there was no fixing it. They'd need to craft a whole new one.

Thing was, those manifestations had had a deck of sailors carving them in pieces...a whole crew to fight. Why'd they been so focused on the flipping *hatch*?

The way Kassian was staring me down, he knew the answer. He knew I knew it.

And he knew I didn't want to say it.

"Could've been the kid they were after," I muttered. "He was the one they had pinned down when our girls got in the fray."

Kassian's knuckles jumped like maybe he was figuring out he was in decking distance, too. "Don't bring Cam into this, I'll handle him. Point is, that skeleton turned on *your* lass. Second Oddball stopped shaking in her boots and took a stand, the tide turned. We all saw it."

"You think that's part of what Ravella meant—about the manifestations acting different?" The second the question left my lips, another thought jammed into my head—something I liked even less. "Wait. Raz knew we were coming...there's been chatter for weeks around the fleet that I'd be coming back through. You don't think—?"

"The beasties sunk those two ships looking for *her*?" Ryker put his head on a slant. "Now, that'd be a thing, wouldn't it? Who knew, and how'd the manifestations hear it—except for the bloke that sent that missive to you."

"It's not the Storymaker." If I was sure of anything in this flipping world, at least I knew *that*. "No, this is...something else. But He would know what's happening, and why."

"Might." Ryker smoothed a hand around his mouth, then hooked his fingers around his chin and stared me down. "If this is what we're up against, I wouldn't even know what to call it, mate. Except a whole heap of trouble on your horizon."

I bit down on the groan that wanted to unwrap from my chest. I could handle this—I'd handle anything that was trying to keep Audra away from me. Just had to do what I always did...tighten my grip on my steel and straighten out my spine. "Thank Luck I've got this, then...only weapon no Misspoken manifestation's ever been able to survive."

Kassian put out his hand; I passed the sword. I wasn't about to start singing his praises from the top of every tower in Luck's two-toned cathedrals, but I'd sailed with *The Cathan* and its crew enough times to know where I needed to worry about its captain and where the waters were safer.

Kassian tossed the grip lightly in his hand, rotating and weighing it; then he palmed off the sheath, lifting the blade to study it in the lanternlight. Arms folded, I pitched myself back against the edge of the quartermaster's table. Watching him.

His eyes traveled up the length of the blade and back down again. Then they flicked my way. "She give this to you?"

I swallowed back the heat that tried to claw up my throat. "Yeah. When I made bodyguard, officially...after my proving period."

One of the longest, hardest years of my flipping *life*. I hadn't expected much to change between us after it was over...until Ayjay had handed me a paper-wrapped present, grinning like a cat that caught a canary, and ordered me to open it before she lost her mind.

"It's a Storycrafted sword," I added, watching Kassian brush his thumb over the edge of the blade. "Pretty much unbreakable. Misspoken manifestations are the only things tough enough to give it a dent."

"Makes sense. Story against story, or some blasted thing." Another nod, then Kassian slid the sword back into its sheath and offered it out to me; but when I grabbed it, he held on, trapping my gaze with his. "You remember what I said to you, last time you were on my ship?"

"*You make problems with my quartermaster, I'll chuck you into the drink for fishbait?*"

"Before that."

"*I've seen a less pretentious face on the ass-end of an anglerfish?*"

His eyes skimmed thoughtfully up to one side, calculating. "*After* that."

Irritation tugged my hand against the sword, trying to slide it from his grip. "Seriously, Kassian, you run your ramble-hole so much, I don't—"

"*The way you talk about that lass, it's like you were born ready to die for her and you're already halfway doing it.*"

I stiffened, staring him down; he stared me right back.

"Mate, I know you need her," he rumbled. "But there's folk out there who need *you*. Best make sure you don't lose yourself on the way to finding her."

Scoffing, I gave the sword another tug. Didn't budge. "Right. Like you wouldn't do it for Lio?"

"Difference is, I'm a pirate. No one but the crew to miss me when I'm gone." He dragged at the sheath, and I was just off my balance enough the move dragged me a step closer to him, too. "I'm not the Sha's bloody bodyguard. And I'm not the one fronting the game that keeps this crew paid. So, if you *don't* mind, I'd like to see you make it back in one piece."

"That's the plan." Because Luck knew what'd happen if I didn't, and Ayjay got her memories back.

Kassian's gaze drilled down on me like a knife sneaking closer to my jugular; then he let go and pushed the sword at me, rocking me back on my heels. "I mean it. You'd best get her right, and fast, Fishbait. Things are getting worse...those Misspoken beasties are just the start of it." A scowl twisted his mouth. "And if they're plundering ships looking for a fight with a certain someone...seems like we could all use a few more stories on our side."

CHAPTER 13
CHASING ADVENTURE
JAIK

SOMEONE MUST'VE RUNG A bell I'd missed belowdecks, because by the time I followed Kassian up out of the hatch, most of the crew was milling topside. A few of them—Osred, Annet, Syd, and Lanah—were staring off the bow of the ship with a look like they were staring down a phantom on the face of the sea.

And I couldn't blame them; I probably looked like I'd taken the same punch to the gut as Reinera, one arm wrapped around the mainmast and her temple tilted against it, when I stepped up beside her and laid eyes on the city pushing up through the shawl of fog skirting the bay.

Fallshyre proper wasn't really much to look at. A mix of wood and wattle-and-daub houses and shops, wide eaves, sloped roofs, fountains and cobblestones. A lighthouse with mirrors beaming fire our way, cutting through the early-morning mist.

But for some of us...it was more than that.

I gave Reinera's shoulder a squeeze—gave the tension in my hands somewhere to go. The rest of me chased the same memories as her: a freezing portside town. A snow fight. A different captain and a crew that was half the same.

"What would Julas have thought of all of this, do you suppose?" Reinera eyed the city like the answer to that question lurked down its narrow sidestreets.

Its secret little back alleys.

"Luck if I know," I said hoarsely. "But he probably would've complained less about the trip."

"And charged you more for it." Reinera checked her hip against mine. "I'm sorry you don't have what you're looking for yet, Jaiky."

"We'll get there. I'm just glad we didn't lose anyone to those skeletons."

I didn't have to say it—I knew she heard it, the look she shot me.

As ready as I was for Ayjay to remember everything—to have my *wife* back—I wasn't ready to have the blood of any more friends on my hands for it.

Without another word, Reinera beat a retreat to the helm where Siu manned the wheel. Heart wedged halfway up my throat, I watched Fallshyre swell up ahead of us, taking shape through the mist. Like a memory come to life.

This could be over tonight. Everything could be right by the time I woke up in the morning.

I knew that was a fact. So why wouldn't my heart get right with it?

Fingers grazed my back, jerking me out of my own head, and I glanced down. Audra slipped up to my side, offering me my satchel; hers was already strapped across her front.

"Good morning," she offered with it—and a little smile that dug in right over the scar on my chest that still twinged sometimes on cold days.

"Morning, yourself." I took the satchel and ducked into the strap, fitting it over my head. "Hey, we made it."

"Almost." Her eyes sparkled with sleepy humor. "Who knows what could happen before we make landfall?"

"Who dumped you out on the side of the bed that felt like tempting Luck?"

"Maybe this is what *excitement* feels like, Jaik. You should try it sometime."

My throat was doing its best to tie itself in a knot. "You don't want to see me excited, tiger. I get clumsy."

"Luck forbid the country's best soldier might trip and break something."

"Only thing he's breaking is my heart, sailing us on pointless voyages like this," Kassian announced his return with that jab—he'd found who he was looking for while I'd been rooted at the mainmast.

Lio's good hand was tucked into the Captain's. Her other arm was still in a sling—from what Ayjay had told me, the stab through the shoulder hurt her a lot less than the fact that she couldn't knead dough right now. So she'd had Ayjay doing it for her...something she'd loved learning.

She was going to miss this ship. This crew. She didn't have to say it; it was written in every line of her body, the way she stepped to meet Lio and wrapped an arm around her waist, leaning their heads together.

I cut a look at Kassian, watching his wife and mine hold onto each other like they never wanted to let go, and right then, it hit me...that maybe he was in this for more than the coin. Ayjay mattered to different people in different ways. Whether you loved her yourself, or loved someone who did.

"Oi." Another figure broke in on us—moody, scowling, shoving between Ayjay and Lio, keeping his eyes fixed off the side of the ship. Camden, with Sheeba lounging in his arms, purring so loud I could hear it even with Kassian and Lio between us. "So...I guess you'll be wanting her back, huh?"

I swapped a look with Audra; she was already staring me down, turning my grief back on me like a knife to the heart.

"Actually," she whispered, "I think it's best if Sheeba stays here."

"Wait...you sure?" Cam's voice pitched higher as he swiveled to face her; he was already hugging our cat against him like he was afraid we'd rip her back out of his hands.

"Sailing her to the Illusionarium and back was one thing." I rubbed the nape of my neck, trying to ease the heat that kept climbing the longer Ayjay held my stare. "And Fallshyre Bay's another, but..."

I trailed off. Didn't want to be the one to say it, with the way Audra's mouth pinched and her eyes narrowed.

I wasn't going to risk chasing her off with a lot of guesswork.

"You think the Storymaker's already hiking his britches off somewhere else?" Kassian wasn't the same kind of worried. That figured.

Ayjay tore her gaze off of mine, and I let my eyes shut for two seconds, debating whether it was worth leaving the Captain with a bloody mouth to remember me by.

"We'll find out when we make landfall," Ayjay said. "But Jaik is right. It's not fair to drag Sheeba ashore when it's clear she's happy on—"

"*Thank you*!" Cam's voice cracked, and when I popped my eyes open, he was half-strangling Sheeba against his chest, his smile wider than a horizon at sunrise. And judging by the sway of her tail, she didn't mind it a bit. "I promise, I'll take better care of her than anyone *ever* has."

"We're betting on that, Cam." Ayjay turned to scratch between Sheeba's shoulderblades, and I wished I missed the way tears started building on her eyelashes.

"Remember—she likes her whitefish soaked in milk," I muttered, easing up at her side to smooth Sheeba's ears between my thumb and forefinger. "And in the winter, just let her get under the blankets with you. You'll both be happier that way."

"Right. Got it. Absolutely." The kid was half-blinding me with that grin. "Don't worry, I won't let her forget you...I'll tell her stories about you two all the time. And you can come see her whenever!"

Flipping Luck. I hoped that ended up being true.

My hand bumped into Ayjay's, and we pulled back at the same time. Her eyes tripped my way, then speared off to the side when Lio stepped nearer, adjusting her silk-scarf sling. "I'm going to miss you, Audra. You've been a wonderful friend."

I didn't know how she'd kept that up all this time. Pretended like she'd never met Ayjay before...acted like having her back this way wasn't the best and hardest thing she'd ever faced.

But maybe that was the right way to do things; because the way Audra scrambled to hug her, crushing her close, careful of her shoulder...it was like they *had* been friends for a lot longer.

Maybe I should've led like that, too.

"I'm so grateful for you," Audra said, peeling herself away from Lio to glance at Kassian. "For all of you. Thank you for sailing us to the Illusionarium...for risking your ship for us. I'm sorry it was for nothing."

"Far from *nothing*," Lio scolded. "It was a gift to meet you. And to see Jaik again."

"Debatable," Kassian muttered—then jerked back, dodging the elbow Lio aimed at his ribs.

Should've aimed lower, in my opinion.

"Besides," Lio added, a mischievous twinkle in those dark eyes, "something tells me your adventure is far from over. It's time you went and chased it."

Audra's shoulders tipped back and her chin tightened. I knew that look—it called to the soldier in me like a command. Had me straightening *my* spine and raising my head just like hers.

"Let the chasing begin," she muttered; and with one last squeeze and kiss to the brow for Lio, one last scratch for Sheeba, she turned and strode toward the gangplank.

Kassian jerked his chin after her, his stare hollering at me to remember what he'd said when we'd rolled into port. And as much as I would've enjoyed snubbing him just for fun...I had to nod. Because I was going to hold onto that for a long time, like it or not.

Especially if trouble kept shaping up for us the way it'd started to out on the sea.

I swooped down to kiss the top of Sheeba's head, letting that croaky purr soak into my ears one last time. Then I threw on my satchel, saluted the crew with two fingers, and slid down the gangplank after Audra.

CHAPTER 14
BACK IN THE BAY
JAIK

Fallshyre Bay clobbered me like a left hook to the side of the head.

Everything. All of it.

The smells hit first—fish and resin and leather and sweat slapping me across the face the second my boots hit the dock. Then the cleaner, spicier smell of pine underneath, riding on the wind's back down off the hulking shoulders of the mountains that edged the city.

Then it was the sounds...shouts, orders, hawking, violin strings, the slapping surf on the dock feet spearing into the water, clanging tools, the wind whistling through the trees and between the foothills.

Brine and bile soaked my tongue. I couldn't unstick my boots from the damp planks, not even when Audra strode off down the wharf on a mission from the Storymaker himself.

She didn't get it. Any of it.

This was just another town to her. Something we had to go through to get where we were going. A notch on a map hanging in a public house.

For me...it was a whole lot flipping more than that.

It was *The Song Beneath the Sea*. It was a boarding house and a bed that was always still warm when I sacked out in it, wrung dry from a long day of labor. It was a winter storm in spring, it was a dance and a snowball fight.

It was a back alley I went to in my head so many times, I was almost ready to lay eyes on it again. Maybe.

If I could just get my feet to *move*.

Audra made it all the way to the gutting stations and fishmonger stalls before she noticed I wasn't behind her; then she spun around, thumb hooked in her satchel strap, whirling so fast her bangs bounced into her eyes and her hair slapped her cheek.

I couldn't help wondering what it'd be like to shift the hair off her face. To push her up against another alley wall and have a first kiss for the third time in our insane lives.

"Jaik!" she called back. "What are you waiting for?"

For you.

The two words dropped through me like flipped coins doing their best to land on the miser's side.

I hauled in air, forcing it down through my lungs so I could finally tear my boots off the planks and follow her. One step at a time, straight into the past.

"Just taking in the view." Not a bad job keeping my tone light—the Ayjay I knew would've picked up on it. But this time she just rolled her eyes and shifted her weight from foot to foot until I fell into step with her. "So, where to first?"

"Shouldn't you tell *me*? You're the one who remembers being here before."

Luck, didn't I.

I stared up at the end of the wharfs where treated planks graded up into cobblestone—the road we'd walked down hand-in-hand, years ago, my shirt on her back and her kiss branded on my mouth. Thinking we had it all figured out, bad as it was—that Ayjay was some kind of murderer. That that was the worst thing we'd be facing together.

Idiots.

We couldn't have been walking back up that way any more different—any more strangers, at least on one side of things.

I cleared the clot out of my throat. "Yeah, so...there's some decent taverns here. Maybe start there."

"You think the Maker of all stories is sitting in a *tavern*?"

"No, I'm thinking gossips are, and if He's anything out here like He was back on Erasure...He's going to start a lot of talk wherever He is."

Audra hooked up her lower lip and blew her bangs out of her eyes. "Fair. What if we split our time? I'll take the taverns, you take the public houses? Gossips tend to congregate there as well."

"You got it." I wasn't about to send her off to the public houses, any-way...she was too likely to wander into the one she'd worked at while we'd stayed here last time, cobbling together coin for our passage out to the Illu-sionarium. And the last thing she probably wanted right now was someone else in a new place treating her like a familiar face.

"Jaik? Hello?" Audra snapped her fingers right under my nose, puffing it full of the yeasty smell of the bread she'd been kneading for Lio the last few days. "What do you think?"

"About what?"

Her lips twitched, that perfect balance between amused and annoyed I used to rile out of her on purpose. "I asked where you thought we should meet after we're through."

I didn't let myself think about it for more than a second...otherwise I'd second-guess myself. "There's a pretty good tavern in the middle of town...*The Song Beneath the Sea*. Hear their swordfish soup is pretty good. Want to give it a shot?"

Her nose crinkled. "Honestly, I could do without fish for a while."

Flipping Luck, I wanted to kiss the tip of that nose.

"Maybe just...meet at the fountain at the center of town, then," I croaked out. "Can't miss it."

"Deal." She flashed me a smile sizzling with excitement. "Good luck."

"Same to you."

Right. We were going to need a whole lot more luck than either of us ever had, if this was going to go our way.

CHAPTER 15
SOMETHING SPECIAL
JAIK

I T WAS HARDER THAN I'd thought it would be, staying focused and keeping my eyes off the side alley they wanted to jump to every time I left another public house. Or a coffee shop. Or a shop in general.

There was enough gossip to keep a nosy person fed for days in Fallshyre. Who was tumbling who, who'd made a bad business deal about what, which ships were coming and going and what their cargo might be, how the weather was, whether the new Sha was better or worse than the old one.

I probably heard more about Arias than anything or anyone else the whole day—maybe because, after a couple of years as his bodyguard, I was used to hunting for his name from every mouth in a room. Gauging threats in the way people said it...whether they were just curious, or happy with him, or angry. Or angry enough to *do* something about it.

My head was pounding like a forge hammer on steel by the time I left the last public house and stepped out into the late twilight, my feet meeting lanternlight splashed across the cobblestones at the heart of the town. The flames were strong, the lighters still moving around the square, setting them off—and on the edge of the bubbling fountain, Audra sat cross-legged, pulling apart a pastry.

I just stopped for a minute. Measured my breathing. Cobbled my composure together. Then I swaggered over, dropping down on the lip of the fountain beside her. "Either that's a celebration pastry, or you had as much luck as I did."

"Fair guess." She offered me a hunk of flaky dough; I took it, even though my appetite had just decided to drown itself in the basin behind us.

"Nothing, huh?"

"Not a whisper," Audra sighed. "At least, not of anything worth pursuing. And you?"

"Lot of opinionated folks who see and hear a lot...which I guess you'd expect from a port town." I shrugged. "But, yeah, about the same. Nothing that sounds like..."

Like, what? What was I expecting, exactly? Dark towers with gardens inside them? Books with all our names and stories written on the pages? The Storymaker hadn't fit my expectations either time I'd gotten inside Erasure...so why was I bothering to *expect* anything here at all?

"Do we have enough coin for rooms at a boarding house?" Audra asked. "We could try again tomorrow...the morning crowd may have heard something different."

"Yeah. Maybe." I clapped my hands on my thighs and pushed up, turning to offer her my hand—

And froze.

Not because I'd seen dark hair, plain clothes, kind eyes—the things about the Storymaker that stuck.

Not *Him*.

Audra blinked at me—then swiveled to follow my gaze. "What do you see? Jaik?"

"*Jaik?*"

The crack in that adolescent voice—it'd changed since I'd last heard it. But I still knew it.

"*Audra!*"

She jumped at that shrill shriek—and that kicked a laugh from me that built up on itself when a pair of kids came *flying* out of a shop door across the square. A dark-haired, dark-eyed brother and sister, skidding across the cobblestones and crashing into me at the same time, tackling me down to the ground.

"Ow!" Even though I meant it, pain firing through a few of the places I'd taken hits in the fight against the skeletons, worst in my ribs, I couldn't stop laughing, either. "Hey—Zeik! Lainey! It's great to see you guys."

The kids who'd teased out one of Audra's most powerful stories the last time we'd visited Fallshyre Bay still hung onto me even when I pushed myself up; Zeik pulled back first, tumbling on his seat, grinning at me. "What are you *doing* here?"

"It's...it's a long story." I ruffled his hair and cut a look at Ayjay, still perched on the basin's edge, watching us with a bemused smile.

"Well, and we know how you love stories!" Lainey flashed a dazzling grin Audra's way. "You look beautiful with your hair that way."

Audra's smile widened—and softened. "Thank you, Lainey."

My heart jumped for a second before I remembered...right. I'd said their names.

They didn't seem to catch that she didn't know them. Didn't remember building snowpeople and ice forts with them, dancing with them, having a snow war with them. Didn't remember making all that happen for them, for...

The breath whooshed out of me. I glanced at Zeik, trying to find the right words to ask...not wanting to hear the answer even if I got them right.

But, Luck...I had to try.

"Hey, listen," I rasped. "Is...?"

"Ziek! Lainey!" A cranky shout cut through the conversation. "You never *wait* for me anymore! And Mama says I'm not supposed to be the one who carries all the bags!"

Zeik smirked, and called over his shoulder without taking his eyes off of me, "Yeah, well, should have thought about that before you started looking like the kid who *does*."

Another laugh jumped out of my chest, and I slapped a hand over my mouth—then dragged it down to let my grin loose when another little boy hobbled into view down the street. One leg a little shorter than the other, one eye fixed, staring, but...

Flipping Luck. *Alive.*

Laith stopped, bags of food dangling from both hands. He cocked his head, looking me up and down. "Wait. I feel like I know you. Do I know you?"

"Beats me, Laith Winterhart," I grinned.

He dropped the bags, eyes blowing wide. "Flipping *Luck*!"

"Don't swear on Luck," Lainey scolded. "Mama says it's rude for little boys."

"I'm not *little* anymore!"

That was right—he almost came up to my shoulder now. This kid who'd been so sick the last time we'd seen him, his brother and sister hadn't expected him to see another winter.

If Ayjay had remembered—if she'd known what this meant—

I shook off that thought, pushing myself up with a hand on Zeik's shoulder. Then I pulled him and his sister up by their collars. "Let's get you kids home...it's after dark. And on the way, *your* turn to tell *me* a story. I want to hear about anyone new in town who's been spreading stories like Audra's."

Audra slipped from the basin and hurried to Laith, taking half the bags from him without a word; Lainey watched them for a second, then tucked herself under my arm, whispering, "What's wrong with Audra? She didn't even hug us."

"Not that we were asking her to, or anything," Zeik scoffed, rubbing under his nose.

"Audra...she got hurt." Best I could do—something these kids would understand better than most. "She doesn't remember much, and what she does, it's...different from what we remember."

Zeik's sharp eyes narrowed. "Different *how*?"

"She knows she was a Storycrafter, but she doesn't remember being one."

This time, Zeik cursed Luck—and Lainey didn't correct him. Her hand clapped over her mouth and she stared up at me with glistening eyes. "But...doesn't she remember *you*?"

Grimacing, I mussed her hair. "I wish."

"But that's awful! You were so in love—"

"Ew, Lain! *Gross*," Zeik groaned.

"Hey, who told you that?" I squeezed her tighter under my arm.

"I saw you *kissing*." Lainey beamed up at me, then pointed off to the side of the square. "Right over there! It was so romantic."

That did it.

I couldn't help it—I looked.

Down that alley I'd been avoiding all day...dark without the light strands from *Spirited Sunrise* filling it up. Dark with memories I couldn't share with the person who mattered most.

Dark...but I could imagine it brighter. Feel the curves of Ayjay's body against my chest and hips, the twist of our fingers pressed against the alley bricks. The way her lips danced on mine. Branded on me...just like when she'd jumped into my arms in that ship hall and buried her face in my neck.

"Yeah," I rasped, thumbing the corner of my eye. "Yeah, Lainey. It was something special."

CHAPTER 16
THE DOVE AND THE DREAMER

Zeik, Lainey, and Laith led us to the very outskirts of Fallshyre proper, to a two-leveled home aglow with candlelight. The rounded transom window above the door grinned golden in the gathering dusk, welcoming us down the last narrow span of twisting avenue to the stoop of the wattle-and-daub abode.

The children raced one another up the three steep steps, the oldest boy—Zeik—bursting in hollering for his mother, his sister Lainey crying on his heels, "You'll never *believe* who we found!" and smaller Laith griping, "Wait for me, *I* want to tell her!"

Jaik snagged my elbow gently, towing me back toward him when we reached the base of the steps. "You want to know, or figure it out for yourself?"

The question gave me pause, my hands hidden in the pockets of the form-fitting jacket I'd scavenged from Siu's things, my eyes on the door left open on its hinges.

Now that I had left Krylan, it was possible I could encounter anyone, any-where, who had known me before. Mithra-Sha was a land of potentially intimate strangers. Some, like these, it was clear Jaik knew; but he had told me of my years traveling the Spine alone, my feet guided by the storymade glass road that traversed through the heart of the country, connecting it from Head to Tailbone.

He couldn't always defend me. He shouldn't always have to be a bulwark between my mind and what it didn't recall.

"Stories used to be my life, didn't they?" I loosed a long, steadying breath. "So I suppose I should try my hand at learning to tell them from what I see around me."

Jaik's fingers gave a deft, reassuring squeeze. "If you get lost somewhere in those pages, you just let me know. I'll come in there after you."

Then he let go, brushing ahead of me to take the steps first—to take the brunt of the familiarity that was all but promised with the shadows leaping long down the inner hall, coming back this way.

Gratitude lobbed thickly in my throat; I padded quickly up the steps after him.

The three children and their mother met us in the doorway, and I knew her at once. Not a memory—a familiarity. In the dark circles stamped below her eyes, the sunkenness of her cheeks and the creases around her mouth and brows that suggested these things were perpetual, and inward. Not an affliction that could be cured by deep sleep or good food, nor drowned in the bottom of a tankard...though I'd lost count of the number who'd tried, crossing the threshold of the *Pourhouse* with those same stamps and sinkings, and leaving with them even deeper.

This was a woman who had come to the very ends of herself countless times...and clawed for *more* strength beyond that, and more faith, and more hope.

And that hope ignited in her eyes, shattering through the fatigue like the spread of milk poured into rich, dark coffee when her gaze found mine.

"Oh, Miss Jashowin," she breathed—and stepped past Jaik to wrap me in her arms.

And I let her; I leaned into her, even. Because the way she spoke my name made me wish like never before that I *did* remember her.

Something wonderful had happened here—something I had been part of.

If only I could recall what it *was*.

When the flurry of embraces lay behind us, the children's mother gave us her name at last—Avriet. Her husband, Sloan, was kept late at the fishmonger's, but she refused to hold back dinner on his account. And she refused to let us graciously decline her offer of a meal once we beheld the modest furnishings and the scarcity of the cupboard.

"We may not have much," Avriet nodded to her children to unpack the food sacks with which they'd burdened their youngest brother in the market square, "but I have all of my children around my table at night, whether it's bursting with food or not. And that, I owe to you, Miss Jashowin—so I won't take no for an answer."

That casual explanation lanced through my chest like a skeletal seaman's sword. I gripped the back of one of the hand-carved seats around the table when my knees turned to water. "If you're *certain*..."

"I have rarely been more certain in my life." Avriet winked—a gesture that erased years and tension lines from around her eyes.

And all at once, I couldn't say *no* at all.

The dining room and kitchen shared space, a cozy warmth emanating from the iron cooking surfaces, the wooden countertops, and through the bay windows behind them that spanned a breathtaking view of the distant Drennan Peaks. It was no ship's galley, but it harbored a different sort of intimacy...a flare of nostalgic heat that made me ache for my childhood home in a way I hadn't since long before I'd immigrated south to Krylan from Vallanmyre.

I joined Avriet at the stove, adding spices to the soup simmering in a pot there, chatting about recipes Leatrix had shared with me while Jaik helped the children set the table. A laugh bubbled in my chest when he lifted Laith under his arms to retrieve cups and bowls from the highest shelves though he must have been nearly ten years old and more than half my height.

Luck, I wish I remembered them.

We gathered around the table for a meal of fish stew and warm, fresh bread; and while we ate, Avriet added, "You'll have to forgive me my forwardness, calling you by name when you came in. That must have come as a surprise, since we weren't properly introduced during your last visit."

I shot a glance at Jaik, who'd taken Lainey's chair while she wedged herself in with Laith, throwing elbows to reach their bowls. He paused with another spoonful halfway to his mouth, his inscrutable gaze fixed on me.

"It's among the least surprising things I've encountered lately." I revolved my gaze back to Avriet. "There's nothing to forgive."

She nodded, a fresh and different sort of tension bracketing her mouth when she spooned through her soup. "It wasn't long after the pair of you left Fallshyre that a soldier and his entourage came through, asking questions about you...calling you by name. No one in this town has ever forgotten that day, or that man."

"I didn't like him." Lainey shuddered.

"No one did." Jaik's voice was a bass thrum that rattled through my chest—that set my heart scrambling, desperate to know what he knew. Desperate to *remember*. But every blink of my eyes only ignited an embered dash of red hair, red blood, searing red across my vision like rage. Like *hate*.

I shifted, pain pinching in my shoulder and ribs. "Did he cause trouble for you?"

"Not as much as he would've liked, I think." Avriet shot a look at Zeik, and he flashed her a mirthless grin that left me wondering if he'd taunted the soldier, perhaps—taunted him on *our* behalf. "That wasn't even the strangest thing."

"Not too long after that, we sort of…forgot to think about you." Lainey quartered her bread and then picked those pieces into ones even smaller. "For a long time."

"And then, just a few months ago, Sloan brought you both up at dinner." Avriet shook her head, a wonderous smile touching her mouth. "And now here you are, dining at our table. I can hardly believe it."

"Something we have in common," I murmured into my next slurp of spicy soup.

"So, what else happened after we left?" Jaik demanded, his eyes cutting to Laith.

Avriet followed his gaze—and that shine overtook her eyes like the starlight floating in through the windows.

"Well, after a certain unprecedented snowfall that spring, a healer came through again. A man who'd wanted to help us, but he wasn't certain he could if the weather didn't turn." Excitement eased the exhaustion from her face like spillage sopped up by a bar rag—every stain wiped clean. "That freeze helped grow some herb…I'm not certain what it's called, I couldn't say the name of it even when he explained a thousand times. But the tinctures and tonics he made from that precious little plant…they ate away the disease in Laith's body. He's been healthier as long as he stays on his medicines."

"And I take them *all* the time," Laith added proudly. "It doesn't even make me gag anymore!"

"You *gag*," Zeik shot back.

"I do not!"

"Flipping Luck." Jaik fell back in his chair, smoothing a hand over his mouth, his eyes leaping back to me—damp. *Tearful.*

Disbelief dripped down my spine; I sat back as well, setting aside my spoon, my stomach squirming too much to swallow another bite.

"We hope to travel to Vallanmyre, someday," Avriet added fondly, watching her boys bicker and Lainey elbow Laith, trying to eat around their squabble. "I've heard stories of the Sha's advisor, that Healer Weathers…they say she's the best student Harrow Hall's ever graduated. I'd like her to see Laith, to advise on his regiment going forward."

I met Jaik's gaze swiftly; he blinked, the sheen clearing from his eyes, his expression morphing back to that guarded impersonality.

Knowing the question that seared my tongue; leaving the choice to me.

I watched Laith, stealing bites of his brother's bread—and Zeik letting him, with a moody eyeroll belied by the quirk of his mouth.

I did not need to remember this family to know they had faced—and evaded—a devastating tragedy. Nor did I need to remember Naomi Weathers to know that the stories of her—of *us*, of nearly a lifetime of friendship—were true.

"I'm familiar with Healer Weathers." Avriet flung her head high at my words, and all three children fixed me with wide-eyed stares. "If you like, I could send a missive. I'm sure she would be happy to come to Fallshyre Bay and meet Laith."

"Oh, Luck." Avriet tucked a hand around her collarbones. "We'd never want to impress—and the..."

A furtive look at the children, then at us—heavy with unspoken things.

"Sha's personal bodyguard, here." Jaik folded his arms behind his head, stretching his long legs under the table. "You took us in, fed us, and covered our backsides when a rogue soldier went on the hunt for us a few years back. I'd say a consultation with one of his advisors is the *least* the Sha can fork over. What do you say, tiger?"

"It's coppers and scraps," I assured Avriet, and her smile widened in a way I'd never seen on *any* patron's face in the *Pourhouse*—a joy and relief no drink could ever bring.

"Then...yes. Yes, we'd be *delighted* to meet with her! Thank you—thank you both so much."

"We'll make it happen," Jaik assured her.

Shaking her head, she rose, fetching both of our bowls and plates, her expression nearly dazed with disbelief.

"He was right," she laughed under her breath. "Everything *is* changing."

I blinked, cutting a glance Jaik's way; but before either of us could speak, Laith slid from his chair and snagged Jaik's arm. "Come wrestle with us!"

"What, now? Right after dinner? You're out of your mind!" Jaik laughed, letting the boy haul him to his feet.

"You're just scared we're going to *beat you*," Zeik taunted.

"No, I'm *scared* I'm going to heave your Ma's soup all over the rug." But Jaik bundled a boy under each arm and charged through the doorway across from where we'd entered—into the warm glow of the fireplace painting the slim sliver of the walls visible beyond.

Lainey rose as well, her eyes bright. "Mama, I'm going to write down questions for Healer Weathers! It will be like I'm her apprentice...this is so exciting!" Clapping both hands to her cheeks, she bolted for the opposite doorway—back down the hall to the foyer, and up the stairs with clamorous footfalls that shook the whole house.

"You certainly have your hands full," I laughed, gathering the rest of the plates and bowls and carrying them in the balance of my arms to the iron washbasin.

"Morning, noon, and night," Avriet chuckled quietly. "But I'd have it no other way. There's something about living life after you've caught a glimpse of how it could change...it makes everything easier to bear. Even my hardest days now are nothing compared to the hardship we faced before you did what you did."

"I'm just glad to have helped." Even if I had no memory of what it was, precisely, I had done...it had helped this precious, kind-hearted family. And for that, I *was* grateful beyond words.

Avriet and I washed dishes and stored soup together, talking of everything and nothing—weather and town gossip and Sloan's work and the things she did to earn coin on the side while schooling and caring for her children. All the while, another question sizzled on the tip of my tongue...but I held it at bay, waiting for Jaik, whose wrestling match with the boys echoed loudly from the next room over.

"I'm sorry for Sloan to miss this," Avriet sighed. "He works so hard."

"You both do." I touched her arm. "And it shows in the lives of your children. And in your kindness. Thank you."

"Taking the pair of you in is the least we could do after what you've given us." Avriet covered my hand against her arm, giving it a shaky squeeze. "And you *will* stay the night, and as many nights as you're here...I won't see you shell over a single coin for board as long as you're in Fallshyre, do you hear me?"

"Yes, ma'am," I laughed.

Another of those lighthearted winks, and Avriet released my hand, slapping her dishrag over her shoulder and surveying the kitchen. "You're no slouch yourself when it comes to cleaning, Miss Jashowin."

"I know my way around tending bar...and cleaning up after unruly patrons." I tipped my head at the sitting room doorway, and Avriet snorted.

"I'd nearly forgotten that's where the children met you...serving in the public house." She strung the rag from a hook beside the sink. "Isn't it strange, the power that lurks in the plainest places?"

Before I could answer, Avriet whistled. The wrestling ground to a halt, and a muffled voice floated from the sitting room: "Yes, Mama?"

"Time for baths and bed."

A collective of groans—Jaik's among them—had me bursting into laughter. Avriet rolled her eyes and strode for the hallway to the foyer, calling as she went, "You'll see them in the morning, they're not about to float off like ashes!"

I went the other way from her, stepping into the sitting room doorway to find the space beyond as warm and inviting as I'd pictured it. The wide hearth crackled with flames, heating every nook and cranny of one wall full of books, the other lined with windows, the third housing a writing desk. Lainey sat on one of the couches, scribbling furiously in a notebook, while Jaik and the boys tussled in front of the fireplace.

Grinning, I leaned my head against the doorframe, watching them wrestle like small soldiers. Though Jaik pulled his blows and gentled his arms, it was clear he'd been doing this for so much of his life. And it was clear from his grin, from the easygoing glint in his eyes, that he cared for these people. That they truly meant something to him.

They had meant something to me, as well.

Jaik rolled to one elbow, catching my stare—and smiling in a way that lit up his eyes from the inside out. That revealed flecks of gold amidst the brown, just like his hair.

My heart did a swift, swooping turn in my chest.

Perhaps I'd just been too distracted to notice before, but...he truly had a captivating smile.

Another whistle floated from the stairs. "Zeik! Lainey! Laith! *Now*, my loves!"

Lainey growled, snapping her journal shut. "But I didn't get to wrestle *Jaik*!"

"Laggers are losers," Zeik taunted—then yelped when Jaik mushed his face into the rug.

"Bold words for the kid eating the floor," he teased...then let Zeik up and cuffed the back of his head. "Rematch, tomorrow. *Before* breakfast."

"*Fine,*" Lainey sighed...then squealed with rage when Zeik pushed himself to his feet and bolted down the hall.

"Race you!" he bellowed over his shoulder. "Last one upstairs has to take a cold bath!"

"No fair!" Lainey tore after him, leaving just Laith with Jaik and me.

The boy was slower to rise than his brother, but there was an odd determination to the way he hobbled over to the hearth, lifting something down from the center of it; my heart thundered and tripped when he came to me in the doorway and grabbed my hand with his smaller, thinner one.

He had a musician's fingers, built to shape wild and whimsical things. To tell stories in their own way.

"Here. You should have this." He flashed me a shy smile, all front teeth, and dropped something into my hand. "Winter already came back. I think you need to bring back what's missing for you, too...a lot more than I do."

"Laith!" His mother called from down the hall. "Upstairs! Now!"

"Coming, Mama." His smile widening to a full-fledged grin, he turned and hobble-ran down the hall...leaving me leaning in the doorway, staring down at the small, sculpted glass dove in my hand.

CHAPTER 17
HOLD MY HAND

PULSING QUIET OVERTOOK THE house after the children disappeared upstairs; I settled myself on the sofa Lainey had abandoned, shifting her journal to the arm and snagging a crocheted blanket off the back of the hand-carved wooden frame. Its fibers smelled of woodsmoke and herbs, a comforting aroma that puffed around my head when I cocooned myself in its folds.

It was cozy. Comfortable. *Homey*, in a way *The Cathan*—for all the intrigue of its crew—could not match. It made me ache for Sheeba's weight in my lap, for a book in my hands. For solitude and stillness both inside and out.

I craved a life like this. I hoped to fickle, flighty Luck it waited somewhere beyond the end of this journey.

Jaik slipped back in from the kitchen, drying off his hands...pausing and taking in the sight of me bundled in the blanket before the hearth. His mouth twitched, but all he said was, "You all right?"

"Would you believe I'm missing Sheeba?" A laugh shook itself free. "I know it sounds foolish, but she was such a comfort. Especially at night."

"I get it. I used to sleep with her on top of my chest...right over this." He tapped a knuckle against his heart, where a lateral scar showed the place a knife had slid beneath his skin...ending his life. Setting in motion every step that had led us to the mess we were in now. "It helped me sleep, most nights."

I stared at the thinnest seam of that scar peeping through the undone buttons at the top of his shirt.

It's only a story. Not something I remembered living. Witnessing. Enduring.

His death. His *loss*. The casual way he spoke of it...

Sourness budded on my tongue. I tore my gaze away.

Jaik slouched into one of the shabby armchairs across the fire from me, propping a foot up on the arm and wrapping his hands around his knee. "So. You heard what Avriet said, right?"

My nerves tingled; I twisted on the sofa to face him. "About things changing?"

He nodded, brows creasing, a divot striking low between them. "Someone telling her they would."

"You don't think—?"

"I'm pretty sure I *know*, tiger." Hope sparkled in the dark relief of his gaze. "We just need to find out for sure."

Those words sprinkled the air like ashes and embers, making it impossible to relax for nearly another full hour—until Avriet's steps thudded down the stairs and along the hall toward us. Jaik and I both swiveled to meet her arrival, his tension mirroring mine; but neither of us spoke while she undid her apron straps and cast it onto the desk, then freed her hair from its messy knot and tousled her fingers through the inky waves—the same texture as Lainey's.

"Flipping Luck, getting them to sleep when they're excited is like wrestling a pack of wolves." She darted a wry smile my way. "And for the last few years they've demanded two stories every night. I can't imagine why."

I offered an unsteady smile in turn, my pulse clamoring in my wrists and behind my knees.

"So, Avriet," Jaik swooped in, his tone casual and his stiff posture anything but, "about why we're here."

"You mean that you didn't come only for the scintillating company of my wild, wonderful children?"

"I mean...they're the best part of it," Jaik lobbed back easily. "But that's not it, no."

"Would you happen to know anything about a man visiting Fallshyre Bay," I added carefully, "someone who came to town for the first time recently, within the last month or so?"

"You'd remember Him if you met Him," Jaik's tone softened slightly, "or saw Him. Dark hair, dark eyes, brown skin, wears brown robes...really friendly. Wise as all Luck. The kind of person you'd just want to sit and have a drink with and tell Him your whole life story."

He broke off, the unspoken thread of that thought dangling like severed twine between us.

Or let Him tell you yours.

Avriet frowned, tucking one hip against the wall, arms folded beneath her bosom. "Now that you mention Him...as a matter of fact, yes."

Jaik gripped the back of the chair in one hand and lurched upright; I slid my bunched legs off the sofa, swiveling to face her. "You *would*?"

She hesitated a moment. "Laith met someone like that at the market…He was a traveling healer, I believe. Selling tinctures and such. He and Laith had the longest conversation…Laith hasn't stopped talking about Him for days. Well, until he had *you* two to talk about." A mild shake of her head. "His remedies were half the cost of the usual healer's, so we were able to purchase twice as much for Laith. He was such a kind man, and…so oddly familiar."

Something tweaked deep in my chest. A smile plucked the corners of Jaik's mouth. "Yeah, I believe that."

Avriet held up a finger and vanished into the kitchen again for a moment, leaving us trading curious glances; when she returned, it was with a small scroll pinched between her fingers and a puckered line forming at the meeting of her brows.

"It just so happens He gave us this receipt with the tinctures we bought. He said not to open it and not to throw it away…that I would know who it was for when the time was right. I thought perhaps He meant for Laith, but…now that you ask, I have the oddest feeling it was really for you."

Jaik lurched off the armchair and joined me at the sofa, sliding in at my side just as Avriet passed over the scroll. I sat myself tall, and Jaik stretched out an arm on the chiseled wood behind me, leaning over my shoulder so that we could read together:

Audra and Jaik,

I have been called away to Belaris on crucial matters. The past beckons.
Seek me there.

I met Jaik's eyes, my stomach churning with dread.

Belaris. I knew it only from maps and tales rasped out by the most seasoned sailors who'd ever stumbled into the *Pourhouse*, desperate to drown the strain of a long voyage in ale. That mountain town in the northeastern foothills of the Drennan Peaks had a reputation for ruggedness, for being a melting pot of rough-hewn characters as unpredictable as the slopes they'd carved the town from.

Jaik's eyes narrowed, too—but not with the unease that turned my limbs to lead.

"Belaris." He caught the corner of the missive between his thumb and forefinger and chafed it gently. "Flipping Luck. I know that place."

Judging by the pitch of his tone, the way the words scraped from him…it was not pleasant knowledge.

Doubt writhed in my chest; I did my best to smother it, to fix a smile in place for Jaik's sake—and for the sake of my wobbling courage. "Well, we have that, at least. *Knowing it* should make the journey easier, shouldn't it?"

Jaik's gaze crawled up from the letter to meet mine; there was something depthless, fractured in his stare. Something that made my heart cringe and cower behind my ribs.

"There's no need to decide on a journey like that tonight," Avriet broke in gently—a matronly balm to the unseen wound bleeding in the space between us. "I'll fetch blankets and pillows, if you don't mind sleeping in the room."

"Not a problem," Jaik mumbled. "We've had worse."

That was painfully true. Sofas and floors were leagues better than sleeping under bridges in Vallanmyre and Krylan—both of which I'd done for some time before I'd stitched my life together again.

A life that was doing its best to unravel at the seams, every stitch picked by the razored edge of Luck's coin.

"Well," Avriet said when neither of us offered more, "I'll just find those linens."

She excused herself with quick, deliberate steps; still, neither of us spoke until the landing creaked above our heads.

"Belaris, Jaik?" I prompted softly.

His jaw feathered with tension. "You sure you want to know? It was back when you were Master Storycrafter."

My heart leaped and then plummeted so swiftly, lightheadedness stole through me.

Did I want to know? Could I bear to?

Could I afford *not* to, when the Storymaker's steps spritzed light over a place that introduced such darkness in Jaik's eyes?

I laid a hand on his knee and squeezed gently. "Tell me. Please."

Jaik drew in a strangled, shuddering breath, his shoulders caving in a bit when he released it. "It was the first place I really almost lost you."

Pain chased itself from my shoulder to my hip and back again in a zip of heat. "Oh."

"We were on a mission out there, from the Sha...busting illegal Storycraft rings. People using and abusing Storycrafters for sport." Fury puckered the corner of his mouth, his stare fixed and unfocused on the missive held between our hands. "My guard slipped after some stupid argument we had, and...they got past me. Got to you."

Anguish wetted his tone; a fresh glimmer of pain echoed along my stomach from hip to hip, like the portend of fierce nausea.

"You came to my room in the middle of the night, you were bleeding out...I barely got it together enough to save you." A slow, unsteady shake of his head. "That was the last time I let myself fail as your bodyguard."

I wasn't certain what to say to any of that—to a memory that birthed such agony in his tone. To a pain I'd been dealt in kind, but no longer shared.

Was I meant to *miss* memories like that? Of nearly bleeding to death, gutted and gasping, terrified, with no one in the world to turn to but Jaik Grissom?

Jaik—who *had* saved me. Barely, perhaps...but barely was better than what *I'd* managed, apparently, when the Sha had *him* attacked and murdered.

"Thank you," I said—for lack of anything better to say. "For saving my life back then."

He blinked, and his gaze cleared a bit. He dropped his hand from the missive only to smooth down his knee. "Belaris isn't an easy place for me to go back to, Ayjay. In here," he knuckled his temple, "or out there. I don't know—"

He broke off at Avriet's return, and we rose swiftly to meet her. Our next several minutes were blessedly consumed with making sleeping arrangements by the fire, building blanket nests and pillow mounds while Avriet explained quietly when Sloan would return, and a note she'd left for him on the door warning him not to disturb us.

When our spaces were settled, we all milled a bit, gazing into the flames; then Avriet said, with a touch of false cheer, "Well, that's everything, I suppose. The pair of you look as if you have plenty to discuss...I'll leave you to it."

I caught her hand as she turned away, squeezing with all my might. "*Thank you*. For your kindness."

A hint of a tear glimmered in the corner of her eye when she clasped my hand in both of hers. "Thank *you*. For everything you've done for my family."

With a quick smile for Jaik, she was gone—away with her own swell of emotions that matched the heave and rollick of mine, as if we crossed the waves aboard *The Cathan* again.

I wished I had Lio to talk with…someone to whom memories were stories, not heavy things full of their own weight and depth.

But it was only Jaik and me, dressing down for the night, bundling ourselves in blankets, laying side-by-side before the fire with a respectable bit of distance between us.

For a time, only popping embers and crackling flames punctured the silence. I chafed the blanket in my fingertips, the soft sensation of fabric sliding against my calluses soothing me like stroking Sheeba's head.

"This family is so generous," I murmured at last. "We should—"

"Already slipped a couple silvers in Avriet's coat pocket. Should help take the edge off."

A smile scrubbed across my mouth, and I leaned my head to one side, studying his profile in the firelight. "You're a good man, Jaik Grissom."

"Learned from the best," he fired back easily—as if we'd had this conversation a thousand times.

But the ease evaporated as the moments wore on…as I took in the cozy walls, the wide windows capturing the breathtaking scenery of the moonlit night over the mountaintops, and the truth that we were *here*, in a stranger's home, being treated nearly like family.

"Jaik," I whispered toward the low-beamed ceiling, "what happened here?"

He understood the question, simple as it was—just like I'd hoped he would.

"That storm Avriet talked about…the one that helped the herb grow, the one Laith needed?" He must have been waiting for my nod; when I gave it, he added huskily, "That was *you*, tiger. You did that. You made it happen."

Shock hefted me up on my elbows, my hair tickling between my. "I did?"

"Storycraft." Jaik edged out a nod of his own, head still cradled on his folded arms. "One of the only times we agreed it was worth it, to flash your power in public. You gave Laith a winter to remember, because we weren't sure he'd get another one."

But he did. The notion sparked between us.

He'd gotten *many* more winters. Because of me. Because of my Storycraft.

Heat drizzled all along my arms and legs, smoldered in my core, stormed my eyes. I stretched back out, draping one arm over my face, but it was not enough to hold the tears from escaping. In moments, the crook of my elbow was dewy with them.

That precious boy…his glass dove tucked in my satchel…

He was alive because of my Storycraft. Because the power I'd used to tear apart so much of the world...I'd used it to stitch together this family.

"Ayjay?" Jaik's voice rasped nearer—higher. Like he was leaning above me. "Hey. Tiger? Are you crying?"

"It's a good cry," I mumbled.

He was quiet, for a long moment. Then he murmured, "Want me to hold your hand?"

I did.

He laid down next to me, nearer than before, our shoulders brushing; and he reached across himself to grip the hand that dangled next to my cheek, my arm still covering my eyes.

Jaik Grissom held my hand while I wept...for this family that had danced on the bitter edge of unspeakable loss. That had been saved by a power that could take away so much...but that gave, too.

My power.

You did that. You made it happen.

"We're going to Belaris," I choked out, my voice wet and wavering and breathy.

Jaik's thumb stroked over my knuckles. "Yeah. We sure are."

CHAPTER 18
ENDLESS SURPRISES

AN UNSPEAKABLE TENSION TWINED the air between Jaik and me after our first night in Fallshyre Bay.

It was a strange, shared strain...the urge to leave the port, to be on our way north through the mountains to Belaris. But there was a longing to remain, as well. To play and rest with this family who had taken us in as their own.

We stretched out the days a bit—gathering supplies for the cooler mountain climes, securing mounts to travel north. It was a relief that Jaik purchased extra weapons, fresh ammunition, even if I despised the shadows that stalked his gaze while he did it. As if he was expecting—*preparing*—for another attack like the last in Belaris.

I filled my days baking bread the way Lio had taught me, showing Lainey how it was done, purchasing food I knew would keep and snares to catch our meals after that ran out. Outfitting us in my own way, though my fingers itched with a sense of uselessness...a restless disquiet that plagued my footsteps to the markets and shops and back again.

By the time we were ready to leave—after several days, and several more coins hidden around the house for Avriet to find—I was nearly leaping out of my skin. All of my disappointment in the Storymaker's ongoing absence had evaporated by now.

I simply wanted to be on our way.

Still, farewells were difficult...among the hardest I could remember and, judging by Jaik's equal reluctance, among the most difficult of those I didn't.

He embraced each of the children in turn...even Zeik, who fussed and groaned beforehand and then fisted his hands in Jaik's long, fleece-lined coat and clung to him for longer than either of his siblings had.

"You three, stay out of trouble." Jaik mussed Zeik's hair and mashed the boy into his shoulder. "Be good to your parents. And each other."

"We will. *Promise.*" Lainey wiped her nose on her wrist.

"And you're still going to talk to Healer Weathers, right?" Laith demanded of me.

"As soon as we finish our business in Belaris," I vowed, squeezing him sideways under my arm. "I'll send her back with your glass dove, so you know for certain it's her."

"Good thinking." He hugged me back with a crushing amount of force given his spindly shape. "I hope you find what you're looking for."

Heat budded in my eyes. "So do I, Laith."

Avriet held me the longest, while Jaik broke away to shake tired, yawning Sloan's hand. Her embrace reminded me achingly of Lio's—a warmth seasoned with spice and the richness of honest, untempered affection.

"We are so thankful for *both* of you," Avriet murmured against my ear. "If you're ever in Fallshyre Bay again, please, don't hesitate—"

"We'll come straight to your door before we even set foot in a tavern or public house," I laughed, squeezing her to me.

I didn't need the memories Jaik had of this family to cherish the ones we'd made this time. From wrestling and reading to the walks we'd taken during the warm nights to watch the lighthouse and spot the phosphorescent algae lighting up the distant beaches across the bay...

It was the sort of living that had held urgency in abeyance. That made leaving so *difficult*, even knowing what lay ahead.

But before my heart was truly ready, the last flurry of embraces came to an end. And with satchels full of provisions and hearts full of the love of a family I doubted either of us would ever forget, Jaik and I wound toward the outskirts of Fallshyre Bay and its communal stables.

Our mounts awaited us at the fringe of the stableyard, already tacked and tethered, watched over by a wide-eyed stablehand who I suspected had some interest in soldiering. That would have certainly accounted for the slack-jawed awe with which he beheld Jaik while we greeted our horses: a buckskin mare and a black gelding.

"Kyren." Jaik clapped a hand on the mare's shoulder. "Kova." He scratched the gelding's haunch.

"Pleasure to meet you." I held my open palm beneath Kyren's muzzle, a corner of my heart melting and stretching like taffy when her whiskers brushed my skin.

A last wink of coins swapped fingers between Jaik and the stablehand, like fickle Luck grinning our way; then Jaik slipped back to join me, one hand brushing my shoulder lightly. "You all right?"

"Why wouldn't I be?" Flippant words that spoke nothing of the ache that stabbed low in my gut when I glanced back over my shoulder toward Fallshyre proper.

When Jaik said nothing, I accepted the silence for what it was—something to be broken and changed.

Sliding a foot into the stirrup, I hopped and heaved, throwing my free leg over Kyren's back and shifting to center myself in the saddle. I smiled down at Jaik—then faltered a bit when he stared up at me, mouth agape.

"What?" Defensiveness hefted my tone high. "Leatrix lives in the farmlands around Krylan. One thing led to another, I lost a bet, and—"

"She taught you to ride." Jaik shook his head, his tone rolling with disbelieving humor. He gripped the saddlehorn and swung into Kova's saddle—a smooth slide of powerful muscle that sparked an ember of heat low in my belly.

I'd practiced enough with Leatrix's ancient nag to be comfortable in the saddle, but Jaik made it look natural. And somehow very, very provocative.

"Never stop surprising me, Ayjay." He gathered the reins and turned Kova with a click of his tongue.

"Oh, I don't intend to," I shot back, grinning—and with a spurring shout, I urged Kyren ahead of him, from the stableyard, toward the stony northern foothills...toward our next adventure.

CHAPTER 19
DANCES AND DAGGERS

The wilderness welcomed us with open arms, consuming us that first day away from Fallshyre Bay. We sank into the temperate embrace of craggy foothills swathed in pine, our brows and cheeks kissed by the breeze. It took some time to find my rhythm with Kyren's gait, but once I settled into it, the world widened around me; my ears caught the distant rumble of waterfalls tumbling down clefts and crevices, my eyes straying across hind trails and clots of stone that cast shadows across our path.

My lungs couldn't draw in enough of this clean, wild breeze, so different from the congestion of spices and oils and bodies stacked atop one another in Vallanmyre. In Krylan.

To hear Jaik tell it, these wide-open spaces had once been such a part of my life...buried under a tale *I'd* written about a mundane and unhappy time in Vallanmyre, until I'd made my way to the Tailbone City.

I prodded a bit at that notion, at that *past* as we rode that first day mostly in silence, drinking in our surroundings. And I found it...lacking.

There was a muffled, muzzy quality to my memories of the middle portion of my life. To *all* of it, really...a shadowed, jaded overcast I had always attributed to some sort of wishfulness for a better life. A happier one.

But it wasn't only that. The world beyond the bustle of Krylan was so *brilliant*, so beautiful, so vibrant and alive in such a different way. Every corner and curve seemed gilded in the sunshine, every scent and sight and sound sharper. Clearer. Cleaner.

I loved Krylan. I had loved my life there...a life self-made. Yet, compared to these open spaces, even the Tailbone City had been dim. *Everything* had been dimmer until the Sha's inner circle—until *Jaik*—had come through the door.

Had my world been muffled with mourning, all this time? Had I spent years grieving for friends and family, for faces, for *memories* I had forgotten...and had some part of me stopped its tears, raised its head, gasped in a breath when it had seen Jaik Grissom living? Had it reached out to the old friends around that table in the *Pourhouse* even when they'd seemed strangers to me?

So much had been missing. Not only true memories, but the truth of a world I'd allowed myself to forget.

Made myself forget.

I couldn't sop the silly smile off my face all day while we rode. Bar songs hummed in my throat and my fingers danced at the base of Kyren's mane, rearranging the thick ebony locks. And Jaik was silent as we went, except to occasionally add a whistle to my tune.

I didn't think his smile slipped even once, either.

It was only as evening encroached, dipping our surroundings in sly, slithering shadows, that a small knot of anxiety tied itself in my gut. But like a fresh bar rag, it soaked in my thoughts and expanded, leaving little room for appetite by the time Jaik signaled to make camp for the night.

We halted in a meadow sloped between the foothills, dotted with wildflowers; Jaik set to work at once, tethering and untacking Kova with a smooth proficiency that harkened to his time as a farmhand. My hands much less skilled for that particular task, I loosened Kyren's tack for him and then set about clearing space for a cookfire.

Silent, tandem work guided us as the sun lost itself through the gaps in the trees, swallowed by the sliver of the sea visible through chinks in the westward foliage. I was glad to see it—glad to have the landmarking, to know the waves would be at our left hand much of the way to Belaris.

But watching the blackened span of water choke down the sun while I struck kindling alight and swabbed tallow on the small iron pot I'd purchased in Fallshyre Bay, my throat tightened. My mind crowded with memories of what shadows could hide...shadows just like the ones crawling with spindly-limbed grace across the meadow behind me.

I nearly leaped out of my skin when a *crunch* like snapping bone split the air; half-whirling on my heels, I found Jaik's eyes where he crouched several yards away, hacking low limbs off a pine with a hand-hatchet.

Brows raised, he mouthed, *Sorry.*

Biting my lips together, I spun back away from him.

So much could go wrong on a journey like this—so much already had gone wrong, between the blockade, and the Misspoken sailors, and the Storymaker being called away to Belaris. And that newest missive hung heavier than the others stashed in my pocket.

Somehow, I doubted that matters crucial enough to demand the *Storymaker's* attention—the One whose first story had shaped the whole world—were happy ones.

We heated dried meat and a few tuberous vegetables in a broth in the small cookpot over the fire, the rich, sappy smoke hanging in a cozy haze over our heads. But I couldn't relax; I sipped and chewed listlessly, my wandering mind turning the shadows to enemies. Turning the way ahead treacherous in my mind.

Jaik polished off his portion and set aside his spoon, leaning forward in the firelight with his arms bent around his loosely-cocked knees. "All right, Ayjay, what's eating at you? And don't tell me it's *nothing*, you about clobbered the cookpot over when I sneezed a few minutes ago—"

"Jaik...I want you to teach me to protect myself," I blurted out, tearing my gaze from the shadow-soaked meadow to his wide-eyed face.

A rogue laugh burst from him.

"Why is that *funny*?" I groaned, tossing my spoon back in the pot.

"No, sorry, I just..." He knuckled his mouth but failed to wipe away his grin. "It's been a while. You serious?"

"Yes, I'm serious." Pulling the pot from the fire, I spoke down toward it. "I never want to feel as helpless as I did when those skeletons struck *The Cathan*. I want to be capable, even without Storycraft...ready for Belaris and beyond." Bearing in a deep breath, I flicked my eyes up to his. "And who better to teach me than the head of the Sha's personal guard...the best soldier in the Mithran army?"

All the humor dashed from Jaik's gaze at once; palming the leaflitter and pine needles at the edge of our small campsite, he vaulted to his feet. "All right, so, let's do it. Let's start. Right now."

"Right *now*?" Disbelief—and a bit of fear—scathed along my spine.

"Well, yeah, Ayjay...who knows what's out there?" He jerked his chin at the meadow around us, then met my dry look with a grin that faltered swiftly; he dragged a hand back through his hair. "You're right. Belaris is as black as the bad side of Luck's coin on the best days. Better make sure you're ready for it."

My pulse thundered in the base of my throat. I hadn't expected him to take my offer without a bit of protest over something like wasted ammunition—a bit of banter and back-and-forth. Now that he agreed so willingly, all the tension I'd built for an argument fizzled into anxious nerves.

Shakily, I climbed to my feet, brushing pine needles off my trousers. "All right. What do I do?"

"Well, first...you need to loosen up." Jaik rounded the small fire, palms held out. "Mind if I—?"

"No, please. You can touch me wherever you need."

He hesitated a moment too long—then, mercifully, let that slide by. Which unfortunately did not spare my *smoldering* cheeks when he took my shoulders and backed me deeper into the meadow, where hardy mountain grass closed around my ankles and the light dimmed somewhat.

"Here we go...easy." His voice a deep, throaty rumble, Jaik massaged my shoulders, down past my elbows, to my wrists. He seized them gently. "Does anything about swordplay, knifeplay, feel familiar to you?"

I held his gaze, a sigh rolling up from the depths of me. "It should, shouldn't it?"

"Don't look at me like that," he laughed. "You weren't a swordmaster. I just had you trained good enough with a dagger that you could get yourself out of a tight spot if someone gagged you."

Dizziness spun through my head at the notion that such danger had been *commonplace* in my life...common enough that Jaik spoke of it casually, as if it was a possibility any given afternoon. A crisis solved between breakfast and dinner; not the sort of terrifying notion that had chased me practically running through Krylan's streets at times, hoping to Luck that the beady-eyed gazes I'd caught lurking down dark alleyways, watching me pass, had only been my flighty imagination.

Not the reason I had my own dagger stashed in my satchel, one of the first items I'd bought once I'd made a home in the Tailbone City.

"I don't know how you do this," I muttered, half to myself.

Jaik studied me for a long moment. "You know how to dance?"

Relief picked at the knot in my belly. "Waltzes, two-steps, jigs..." I broke off, swiping a bit of bitterness from my lips with a jab of my tongue. "But that's no surprise to you, either, is it?"

"Hey. I didn't ask if you'd been taught, I asked if you *knew*." He crouched, sliding a dagger from his boot, then straightened and held it out to me in the flat of his palm. "How do you remember learning them?"

"I don't," I admitted, stepping near enough to pluck the dagger from his hand.

Its heft surprised me—not how *much* it weighed, but how familiar that weight felt. As if I'd carried it many times before.

"I've just known as long as I can remember," I went on quietly, keeping my gaze on the blade; when I tilted it just right, it caught a glint of moonlight peering through the trees over my shoulder. "I used to join in the dances at the *Pourhouse*...it was one of the best ways to earn a few extra coins on a slow night."

Jaik nodded. "All right. You hold that...just keep it in your hand, don't point it at me." He tilted his head this way and that, rolling a kink from his neck; then he said, "Waltz."

I wrenched my gaze from the blade to his face. "What?"

"Come on. Show me how you waltz."

"Jaik—"

"*Ayjay*." Laughter bubbled beneath his tone, and he sloped his head, hair falling rakishly into one eye. "You want me to teach you? Or not?"

"Swordplay! Not a dance!"

"Hey, well, everything's a dance." Still that light, errant tone as he stepped nearer, taking my hands—guiding the one with the blade to rest on his shoulder. I flipped it swiftly, keeping the pommel aimed at his neck.

His grip curved around my waist, bringing me a step nearer. His other hand met mine, fingers twined in the space between us.

And then we waltzed.

Embarrassment studded my skin with goosebumps as we followed steps with no music, no melody to carry us—only the sway of grass stroked by the wind's fingers. The rustle of the treetops. The shifting stamps and snorts of our mounts. The two of us stepping and spinning and turning beneath the rising moon, our breaths matching rhythm, my eyes a few aching inches from the scar peering over the folds of Jaik's shirt.

"How is this teaching me swordplay?" I whispered.

"*Just* wait." Jaik drew out the first word into a handful of syllables, leading me into another turn through the meadow.

And right then, I had the ridiculous urge to give in. To forget blades and defenses. To lay my head over his chest and let the beat of his heart be the music that drowned out everything else.

The tension unspooled from my muscles. I swayed toward him.

"There we go," Jaik laughed softly—then spun me back to the start of the waltz square, murmuring under his breath, "Block. Parry. Strike. Parry. Block, parry, strike, parry..."

One word for every step. Backward, sidestep, forward, sidestep. A pattern that repeated with every beat and turn of the dance.

The hair on my arms rose. I shot backward to the end of his grip, meeting his sparkling smile with a grin of my own.

"You're getting it," he said—not a question. "Block, parry, strike, parry—"

"Jaik Grissom, you're a *genius.*"

His laughter was louder this time, but still muted, somehow...reined into the space between our bodies. "It's not a perfect pattern, obviously. Not all enemies make for good dance partners." Another turn through the calf-high grass, whisking us toward an untrodden pocket of the meadow. "But once you get the steps down, you can change up the dance."

Emboldened by the notion, with the next turn I did just that; twining my fingers more tightly with his, I spun out from his grip on my hip, and he twirled me as if he'd expected it—a pirouette through a pocket of grass that leaped alight beneath my steps.

A plume of iridescent insects puffed up from the earth, skirting my body in a sparkling shimmer like embers cast from a collapsing campfire. Delighted laughter surged in my throat—then burst free when Jaik whirled me back to him by the hand, lifting me effortlessly with a swoop of his broad arms around my thighs.

We whirled in a galaxy of worldbound stars, the insects scattering and lofting around us, no sound to be heard but our laughter winding together with every pivot through the meadow. I cast myself back in Jaik's grip and flung my arms wide, drinking in the moon, the spangled sky, the emptiness and *rightness* of it all.

Alone, but not lonely—not when we were together. Truly free...as if this place was meant for us, and we were made for it. For moments like these.

Tears scorched my eyes, blurring the world when Jaik lost his footing all at once; we crashed into the grass together, splayed on our backs, dizzy and breathless and still laughing.

"Anyone who fights *that* way with me," I gasped, splaying a hand over my fluttering stomach, "I'll have no choice but to marry him."

Jaik coughed low in his throat, rolling to an elbow. "Next time, I'll keep it serious. I swear on Luck's flipping coin."

I hiked myself up on both elbows as well. "And what if that's a vow I'd rather you not keep?"

He blinked. I bit down on my brash tongue.

Silent, we stared at one another.

"Do you want to keep going?" Jaik's question was the softest thing he'd spoken in this evening of soft things...and yet it boomed through me like thunder.

All at once, like the insects dimming back into sleepy dimness in the meadow far beyond us, my streak of courage winked out. "I think that was enough for the night."

Jaik said nothing; but he took my hand when I rose and offered it, and he dropped it hastily once his boots brushed the ground.

Quietly, we made our way back through the trodden grass to the meadow's edge and our low-burning fire. The mountain wind whisked through my clothes, burrowing under my collar, and I shivered; the brush of it felt familiar, like a twin to the breeze that had chased me to Jaik's side on the edge of Krylan.

The moment we reached the thin corona of remaining firelight, Jaik crouched beside his satchel and delved into the depths, speaking without glancing my way. "Here, I've got...you probably don't want it, but..."

My heart stilled as he bundled an ash-gray cloak from the satchel and offered it out to me.

There was no familiarity to it—none at all—and yet my heart *knew* it. My mind placed it like a book slotted into a shelf, a story aware of its own telling and eager to repeat itself.

It was the gray cloak Jaik had worn into the *Pourhouse* the day we'd met—reunited.

But it was more than that.

It was a gray cloak found in a sealed room in the Shastah—a mystery whose gossip had traveled through tavern doors on new tongues for years afterward. It was a Storycrafter's raiment discovered with a journal in the pocket—a detail known only to the Sha's bodyguard. And now, to me.

It was...

It was *mine*.

Colorless. Sooty. Forsaken by time and change and choice.

"I know," Jaik said huskily, as if he could hear every thought trapped behind my trembling lips. "But it doesn't have to be anything...just a cloak to keep you warm out here."

Not a cloak that had once been Master Storycrafter scarlet.

Not a cloak that had ever meant a thing.

A protest danced on the backs of my teeth—that I had other clothing. Things I'd purchased in Fallshyre Bay, things I'd brought from Krylan, things given to me by Sui. A jacket and my traveling blanket would be enough. I didn't need this mantel of a forgotten past draped over me, weighing down my body.

But though my tongue itched to decline, my fingers was already stretching, my feet already moving. Closing the distance between us. Tugging the cloak until Jaik released it, freeing those colorless threads to spill in murky folds through my hands.

A knot forged iron-thick in my throat when I held the cloak strung in the span of my trembling fingers. "This...this will do wonderfully. Th-thank you, Jaik."

He didn't remark on the tremble that seized my voice. He only nodded and turned to lay out his own bedroll and sleep things while I turned away from him.

Bunching the cloak in my fists, I brought it to my face and breathed it in.

Jaik's scent—sandalwood and weapon polish and a hint of the rich balsam soap he used—saturated its creases. A testament to how close it had been kept, how reverently it had been carried all this time. All these years, he'd kept it...even when he hadn't known who I was. That I'd ever existed at all.

I hardly knew how to hold all of that devotion. How to fit my hands around the shape of it...to carry it. To make it make *sense*. To make sense of a world where, even forgotten, I'd been held.

So I didn't try. I stepped around the fire, laid out my things—and cast the cloak over my feet when I laid down, drawing it up over my shoulders.

It fit like an embrace. Like a homecoming.

And when the breeze stirred over our campsite this time, teasing and taunting with its errant touch, it almost seemed to carry a whisper on its swells.

Welcome back, Audra.

CHAPTER 20
NO TIME AT ALL

THAT FIRST NIGHT IN the meadow beyond Fallshyre Bay forged the imprint of a repeating pattern for Jaik and me, shaping our days and nights.

By the lengthening spring daylight, we picked our way higher in the foothills—deeper into the northernmost stretch of the Drennans. Alpine trees and craggy heights became as familiar as the city streets that lay behind us...and etched a place just as permanent in my heart.

Around every bend in the horizon, another mountain peak revealed itself, often still capped in snow at the heights. Waterfalls and roaring rapids played us a tune better than any tavern song while we rode, and we took turns naming birds by their cries and animals by the flirt of their shadows disappearing into the next pocket of evergreens framing the hind trails and occasional peddler paths we traveled.

In the last dozy glow of dusk each night, we practiced the steps of a waltz. First, with the weight of a dagger in my fist; then with sticks in hand, which we knocked lightly together in another repeating pattern—the block, the parry, the strike, the second parry. Over and over, until my muscles knew precisely what to expect; until evening stole the last of the light and we had no choice but to retreat to the fireside again.

After that first night away from the Bay, Jaik was never anything but confident and cordial in our dances. True to his repute in every regard, he was a soldier putting a barmistress through her paces...never touching me longer than was necessary, never pulling me closer than the waltz and the weapons demanded.

I cursed fickle Luck for the parts of me that wished we could return to that first meadow, that first dance, in more than merely my dreams.

If I asked him to, Jaik would go there with me again. And beyond it. And that was the war that chafed at my edges, sanding down my boldness and resolve as the days turned to one week, and the first bled into the second; *I* was all that stood in the way of exploring forbidden, fascinating places with this wonderful and willing companion who was both stranger and friend.

And I was an insurmountable foe. My own doubts, my own anxieties...they were enemies Jaik couldn't teach me to block or strike. Particularly not when they wanted things that only made sense in the scarlet void between waking and sleeping...in fits and starts like echoes ringing in my head.

Those things kept me awake for countless nights. They prodded gaps in my joy, dimming my wonder at the Mithran landscape as it passed in soaring steeples of stone and lush valleys of wildflower blooms.

They married somehow perfectly with the gloominess of a rainsoaked morning that found us deep in our second week. The peaks on every side of this latest valley we traversed were half-shrouded in clouds, even the lower passes visible across broad chasms wrapped in thick, sweeping shawls of showers. I shivered and hunched in my cloak, and Jaik in his thick leather coat, the wool-lined collar flipped up to mask his cheeks.

What am I doing here? The silent question raged in my mind in tune with clopping hooves on slick rock, a progression so maddeningly slow I nearly screamed. *Why are we* doing *this, when we could be anywhere and doing* anything *else?*

The rest of Mithra-Sha was enjoying warmth and sunshine, unburdened with forgotten pasts and colorless cloaks and secret shame that had to be made right. And here we were, Luck's least-favorite children, freezing and sodden, half-stuck to our saddles, and—

Jaik's low whistle sliced through the drumming of the rainfall, bringing my head whipping up. "There it is."

The storm, the bleakness of this stony divot, and the grimness of his tone all shaped the sight I expected when I nudged Kyren abreast of Kova—so that, at first glance, Belaris felt more like a memory than Fallshyre Bay ever had.

It loomed at the valley's end, abutting the next clefted peak like a hissing cat backed against a wall. A broad, curved entry gate guarded deep layers of rock croppings, edifices all forged of the same weathered stone. It was as if the entire city had been chiseled from one mountain—even the spires of a cathedral for two-faced Luck, with its one side cast in deeper shadows than the other, and a soaring jut of outstretched stone at the city heights.

"How inviting." I sank my chin deeper into my cloak.

"Yeah, whatever's the *opposite* of inviting, that's this place." Jaik snugged the reins a bit, halting Kova when he threatened a sharp sidestep. "This is one of the oldest cities in Mithra-Sha...and the proudest. They don't get many strangers here, and the ones they do usually are trying to sell something they don't want."

"At least we have that in our favor. The Storymaker's arrival should have turned a few heads."

"Good point." Jaik's breath puffed in cool clots on the damp air. "Just...stay close to me, all right?"

He clicked his tongue and nudged Kova in a slow plod toward that crescent wall and the broad, deep arch hewn into it. Head tilted back, I watched the city stretch higher the nearer we rode, the mountain at its back and the tallest of all its structures thrusting up into the cloudbank. Whatever that uppermost building was, it was the most ornately carved, even from a distance—high and sharp and bell-towered, by the look of it. And if my eyes didn't deceive me through the tattered veil of rain, there was a span of a stone bridge funneling from that tower's edge into a gaping maw in the mountain itself.

Awe strangled me at the sheer craftsmanship of it all...and for the first time, I wished I had more than paltry words to describe the sight before me. My tongue dazzled with something like a faded taste from childhood...a sugary powder of a flavor, a tangy odor that if fully captured, would twist like a key and unlock some forgotten portion of my heart.

But it only tantalized; it wouldn't turn true. And with every pulse of my heart and every jarring step closer we clopped, hooves clanging on rock, my irritation fanned and feathered out.

I was chilly. I was saddlesore in my haunches and hips and back, and stick-sore everywhere else. I was *exhausted*. And all of this for memories of places like this that had nearly taken my life. A whole past full of death and near-death.

Today, it didn't feel worth it. Today, I yearned for the comforting embrace of blissful ignorance. But there was none to be found as Kyren and Kova picked their way to the gate—and from the shadowed interior of the arch, a pair of men slid into the open. Leather and fur strapped their broad chests and thick limbs, and their belts hung low with serrated blades bearing cruel, hooked ends.

Jaik reined Kova ahead of me, the gelding's broad haunches forcing my mare to a halt. "Stand down. We're not here to cause trouble."

"Funny way of introducing yourself," the man on the left sneered up at us, undeterred by the height our horses granted; the flash of his pale teeth was a stark contrast to the umber of his skin. "Almost makes a man think you *are* here to raise a ruckus."

"I didn't say we weren't here for a ruckus. Just not the kind that'd cause trouble." Jaik snugged the reins again when Kova shifted. "Friend of ours said to meet him here in Belaris. We just want to find him and be on our way."

The man on the right cocked his head, spilling a tumble of golden-red hair over one shoulder. "Odd place to choose a meeting. Not often on anyone's route."

"It's on ours."

The man glanced at his companion, who regarded us shrewdly—unblinking.

"You've got three days," he growled at length. "If you can't find your friend by then, well...Luck's flipped against you. Either way, you're finished."

"Seems fair," Jaik said—before I could protest that just three days of searching, in a city of this magnitude, was utterly absurd.

Gritting my teeth, I glared at his back, nudging Kyren after him toward the archway. The men parted as if to let us pass without further contestation; but when Jaik rode abreast of him, the redhead flashed out a hand, snaring Kova's cheekstrap and halting him in place.

The gelding sidestepped and whinnied shrilly; cursing, Jaik brought him back under control, twisting toward the guard. "Hey, you want to watch how you're handling my horse?"

"I know you, stranger?" The man's question was tight, terse—and as pointed as the tip of the blade he rested against Kova's rounded barrel, right beside Jaik's ankle.

My breath caught. My own fingers floated toward the side of my saddle—I'd wedged my dagger there after our second night of practicing, just in case I ever had need of it.

Luck, don't let me need it now.

Jaik raised a brow. Unlike when he offered *me* that look, there was a mocking edge to it...and something dangerous seething beneath. "Trust me, friend...if I'd been to Belaris before, you'd know about it."

After a long moment of silent staring, the man scoffed, leaning his blade out of the way and freeing Kova with a bash of knuckles to the bridle. But his eyes tracked after Jaik as he trotted on through the depths of the arch...a look that raised the hair on my arms.

I was almost glad when they watched me go instead. Because a sense, deep and festering like spoiled hops in my belly, warned that if they knew the chaos Jaik had been involved in during our last visit, we wouldn't have three days here.

We might not have any time at all.

CHAPTER 21
ALL ABOUT BREAKING PROMISES
JAIK

T HE STONES OF THIS city were mortared with Ayjay's blood.

No one else could see that. Anyone who heard me say it would call me crazy...even her. Even if she'd remembered our last visit here.

But I could feel it. It was soaking into my bones, too, every step through the streets.

We dismounted on the other side of the gate; if those guards decided to take a second look my way, I didn't want to be a horse's height above everyone else. Not that there were very many people around...not in this quarter. Mostly beggars in rags, their wide, wet eyes watching us pass, widening a little more when I thumbed a few coppers into their cups.

I knew how bad they had it here. They'd been some of our best informants when we'd come here to bust up the rigged Storycrafter matches; Ayjay and I had heard firsthand how hard it was to eke out a living in Belaris if you weren't dealing under the table. And with how little foot travel they saw from outside the mountains, generosity was hard to come by.

That hard of a life hadn't made the dealings here any less disgusting. But it did explain how people could claw themselves into a space where they saw drugging and capturing and abusing Storycrafters for coin as a Luck-loved alternative to poverty.

That poverty had spread its fingers a little farther than our last visit; it ripped awnings from shops, molded wood over booths and sidestreets, picked out chunks of stone from the walls and dropped them into the street like a bored soldier pulling pebbles off the edge of a path during patrol. People pushing handcarts shot us looks balancing on a knife's edge somewhere between suspicion and interest when they saw the horses we were leading, the cloaks we were wearing.

I met every stare and didn't blink until they looked away.

When the road finally curved up from the base of the city—and widened enough for Audra and me to walk side-by-side—it was like my lungs had space to stretch, too. Taking in a deep breath, I let my focus slide up the high stone walls that bulked the street in from either side; guards were on watch up above, like they always were, half-hidden by the stone teeth that capped the flat tops of every roof and building.

Lucking lot of good they'd done last time, when someone had shoved a knife into Audra's gut on a walk from the tavern to the boarding house we were staying in.

I flexed the tension out of my hand, curled my fingers in slow—then glanced at Audra when she took in a deep breath herself. Ready to say something.

"So. Three days." Every word cut short, like she was chewing on glass—trying not to snap. "That isn't much time."

"About the best we can do without throwing clout." And I wasn't about to try that again...not when it had led to her stalked and stabbed the last time we'd been here.

She scoffed under her breath—definitely biting *something* back—but she didn't argue, just said, "Well, I suppose we could start the same way we did in Fallshyre Bay. Taverns?"

My stomach clenched and heaved up, every muscle went tight...I wanted to punch one of those stone walls soaring over our heads just to let out the strain.

This was a bad idea. And the Storymaker...I hadn't doubted Him much since the first time we went to Erasure, but I wasn't good enough not to wonder if He was punishing us for something. Making us come back *here*, of all places.

"Jaik?" Audra buffed my backside with the edge of her boot, knocking me forward a step. "Taverns, or no?"

Luck, no.

"Yeah, probably," I grated out. "But we stick together."

A harsh laugh burst from her. "Believe me, I had *no* intention otherwise."

Which was about the biggest difference between her and the Audra I'd come here with the last time. The *only* time, I'd sworn to myself.

But I was all about breaking promises lately.

So that was what we did, just like in Fallshyre. Dipping in and out of taverns, taking turns ordering—my food in one, Audra's in the next. Her drink, my drink. Sipping on chipped wooden travel cups full of spicy cider and nibbling on roasted turkey legs, we skirted the edges of a few markets, keeping warm even in the shadows of those tower-high stone walls.

"What do you suppose is on the other side of that bridge into the mountain?" Audra asked after a few hours, jerking her chin up at the glimpse of spired stone we could catch from the laundering corner of Belaris.

So far, even down here where all folks did was talk, we hadn't picked up much gossip about anyone fitting the Storymaker's looks or the way He carried himself. It was just a lot of talk about new faces in taverns and how this rain was making everyone's lives more miserable than the sobbing half of Luck's two-sided face. So I settled for the change of subject, at least for now.

"Escape tunnels." Pinning my cup between both hands, I jerked an elbow up at the scrape of a tower over our heads. "I mean, they wind through the mountains for *miles*. That tower...used to belong to someone who challenged the Lothar family's right to rule, way back when. And they knew the Sha wasn't going to take that lightly, so they made themselves a way out. A few of the tunnels collapsed over the centuries, but for the most part they're still pretty well excavated."

She blinked. "That's fascinating."

"Sure is."

"Do I want to know how you learned that?"

"Someone dared me to go explore them last time I was here."

Her eyes flicked to the tower, then back to me. "*I* did, you mean."

"I'm not saying it was you, and I'm not saying it wasn't...I'm just saying some sassy Storycrafter baited me to go as deep as I could, then stole my coins and took off for the tavern while I was gone."

She snorted into her cider cup. "That doesn't sound at all like me."

Neither of us had much to say for a while after that; the next thing that came into my head wedged its way in when the shadows from the walls started spreading out, turning thicker, souping the air with a feeling like these weren't streets we wanted to be in after dark.

Like I didn't already know that.

"Think we should call it quits for the night." I slowed down a little so I could keep myself right between Audra and the latest marketplace we'd wandered into. Gossip must've stopped flying here hours ago; folks were packing up the last of their wares—most of them wool-lined leather, boots with the kind of grooves that could help you balance on slick mountain rocks, and the kinds of hand-carved arrows and bows most mountaineers picked over rifles. Less of a crack-and-echo, so less likely to kick off an avalanche.

Still, there were more than a few eyes darting our way, and not like they were searching us out as prospective customers. More like they wondered how much the rifle and sword strapped to my back and the satchels we carried might be worth.

"Agreed." Audra slipped her hand into the crook of my elbow, firing a shock all the way through my arm. "Let's try the taverns one more time. It's sunset—the clientele will be changing. And evening patrons often tell different stories than daytime ones."

I had to give her that; she knew taverns.

She picked one I'd never been in before, the kind that wore *rustic* like a badge of honor: game trophies mounted on the walls and strung in the low-roofed rafters, hide pelts hugging the floor, serving counter probably offering nothing but what the people hunted themselves. It sure smelled like it—smokey, gamey, sweaty.

Audra slipped her hand from my elbow down to spin her fingers between mine; then she hauled me between the zigzag tables to the counter and let me go so she could fold her arms on the edge and bend over to shout at the barkeeper above the noise: "Two bowls of venison stew, two mugs of ale, please!"

"That'll cost ya a few silvers, lass," the grizzled graybeard grunted.

Audra arched a brow. "For venison and ale?"

He shrugged. "Hunters brought the deer in fresh today. Been all day skinning it. Have to make up for the lost time."

"Mmm...no." Audra slanted her head. "Because every cook worth his salt knows venison is best aged by *several* days, and judging by how easily these gap-toothed patrons are chewing through it, it's more than a few days aged." She flashed him a smile that somehow managed to balance on that blade's edge between sweet and tense. "I'm happy to pay good coin for good food. What I'm *not* willing to do is be swindled by someone who thinks I know nothing about how tavern food is made."

The barkeep met her smile for scowl, and I shifted my feet, reining in the bone-deep need to put a hand on my sword.

"Know something about taverns, do ya, lass?"

"I've served in several. So I know precisely what the food is worth."

They stared one another down for a few more seconds; then the old man grunted, "One silver for the pair of ya. Same as I'd charge anyone here...you can ask around."

"No need." Audra softened up, delving into her pocket for coin I hadn't even seen her lift from my satchel.

Some things never change.

The barkeep's brows shot up when she dropped a silver and two coppers by his gnarled hand.

"As I said, I'm happy to pay good coin for good food," Audra added quietly. "And it truly smells delicious."

Grunting, the barkeep shuffled the coin off. "Find a table. Food'll be out in a minute."

I kept a hand by the small of Audra's back while we turned, scouting for seats. "Not bad, tiger."

"Leatrix taught me everything she knew about haggling." Audra shrugged modestly. "It turns out, wherever you go, people are just people."

"Unless one of 'em's the Storymaker," I muttered, giving the room a once over and hoping against hope I'd catch a glimpse of dark hair and soft eyes in between the hard edges of all the day laborers and hunters taking up the place.

No look from Luck; but we did spot a table and shove our way to it, sliding in under a pop of banter a few tables down. I folded my arms on the notched tabletop and leaned toward her. "So. New plan for tomorrow?"

She matched my posture, drumming her fingers under her elbows. "There must be some city overseer for a place this large. Perhaps we could ask them for insight."

"Maybe." I tilted a hand. "Problem is, they usually ask for more in favors than they can give back. I'm wondering if we should head to the beggar's corridor first."

Audra frowned. "Why?"

"Because if we're going to end up paying *something*, I'd rather we pay it to people who actually need it. And, besides...we worked with the poorer people here last time. Some of them might remember my face...might be willing to do it again."

Her lips tipped up at the corners. "Well. Good for us."

"It was your idea." I shot her a wink. "Anyway, I'm thinking with the Storymaker...He seems like the type to be helping the destitutes more than He's drinking in taverns."

"So our paths may cross down that corridor regardless." That tilt of a smile turned to a full-fledged grin. "Jaik, that's brilliant."

"I have my moments."

A barmaster wedged himself into the conversation right then, banging down bowls of venison and tankards of ale and then whisking off without so much as a *Enjoy your food.*

Fitting for Belaris.

"Terrible service," Audra muttered, stabbing her spoon into the broth and sipping it; her brows shot up, and her mouth wrinkled down at the corners. "But, decent food."

We tucked in for a few minutes, spooning through hearty broth and chunks of the tenderest venison I'd ever had. I kept my eyes on the tables around us, trying not to watch Ayjay too close...she'd always had a problem with people staring her down while she ate.

"You know," she said suddenly, jerking my attention back to her; wiping ale foam from her top lip, she glanced out the gritty tavern windows, "even if the beggars don't know anything about the Storymaker's whereabouts, they're *from* Belaris. They're likely to overhear things that won't be spoken in our presence. We could always pay them a bit extra to serve as our eyes and ears in parts of this city that wouldn't let us in."

"Good thinking." I couldn't wipe the smile off my face. "You're catching on quick."

"You make all of this seem so easy." She shrugged. "So it feels easier when I'm with you."

Luck was tying its mask strings around my throat and squeezing with every-thing it had. I cleared out the tightness, but then it felt like the air was hanging empty between us. Just waiting for me to fill it with *something*.

"Ayjay." Her eyes darted up to me, and my throat dried out all the way; I cleared it, tried again. "Listen, you—"

When the tavern door slammed open, my first thought was, *soldiers*.

Second was, *Flipping Luck, why'd I have to be right about that?*

Because it was the same ones who'd slowed us down at the gate, and they shouldered inside like they were on a mission.

I dropped my spoon and shoved back, halfway on my feet before one of them stuck his fingers in his mouth and whistled—so loud the whole room clammed up at once.

"Everyone needs to return to their lodgings. Immediately."

Grumbles fanned through the tavern; my eyes snapped to Ayjay. She'd start-ed to relax when they didn't make a beeline for us, but now her shoulders snapped back and her gaze bolted to mine.

"What *for*?" someone demanded. "Night's just kicking off!"

The whistler shifted his feet, hand on his sword pommel. "Curfew just went into effect."

"Curfew in this city is a *myth*," the grizzled old barkeeper snapped. "What's got you lads shaking in your pinchy new boots?"

"Watchtowers spotted something out on the trail...something they didn't like."

My knees went out like someone kicked them, dumping me into my seat. I couldn't pull in a breath deeper than halfway through my aching lungs.

Luck—come on—no...

"*Something* isn't good enough to lose business over," the barkeeper argued. "Spit it out. What's out there?"

The soldier stared him down—and answered the last thing I wanted to hear.

"We don't know what it is."

CHAPTER 22
WATCHMAN IN THE NIGHT

IT WASN'T JUST OUR tavern.

Jaik and I shoved through packed streets to the nearest public house, his hand on the small of my back. He was a world-wrecking sort of silent, the kind that soured my stomach and made the remnants of the tavern food crumble to ash on my tastebuds. Terrified nausea churned in my gut by the time we reached the public house and slipped inside.

We linger in the confines the lower foyer just long enough for Jaik to secure us board, my back pressed to his and watching the room fill up with the spillage from the nearby taverns, likely trappers and townspeople who couldn't afford a homestead of their own. They all bustled with talk swept up in their coattails like dirt from the streets...whispers of *something* spotted lurking in the lower passes, and approaching the city.

Something that moved like no natural creature. Something that either the gossip or the guards on the watchtowers reported as a corporeal shadow, flickering in and out of existence...far away one moment, closer the next.

That was all the talk I caught before Jaik ushered me upstairs to our room—where he barred the door and slid his sword from its sheath. The hair on my arms stood at attention to its shrieking call, like a creature of the deep belting out a battle cry.

"Jaik, what *is* this?" I hissed.

"Hopefully nothing." He barely turned his face my way. Just enough that I caught the bristling tension of his clenched jaw, the flex of his stubbled cheek. "You should lie down. Try to rest. We may need to leave first thing tomorrow."

That was unfairly sensible, given the circumstances. And I obliged—not because I was tired in the least, but because I needed to think.

Because the way he'd reacted didn't feel like the *sensible* thing. Not for a soldier in a city of people. And perhaps I could have blamed it on our history of Belaris, but it didn't feel like that, either.

It felt like Jaik labored under a different urgency than mine.

That he knew something I didn't.

Hounded by that thought, I barely slept all night. And I knew Jaik didn't sleep at all; because every time I turned over, kicked the sheets and blankets, fought and failed to find a wink of slumber...there he was.

Sword braced across his knees. Back to the wall.

Watching the door for *something* to come barreling through.

CHAPTER 23
SUSPICIOUS, SINISTER CITIES

OUR SECOND DAY IN Belaris dawned as bleak as the first—still sodden, still shadowed, still hopeless in almost every regard. And that hopelessness, that bleakness, had found its way deep under my skin when Jaik finally stood and said without looking back at me, "Nature calls. Don't leave this flipping room, and if anything comes through that door, you put this sword through its chest."

He tossed the blade to me, then hurried out just a hair slower than a sprint.

Oh, that was a coward's way out.

I tossed up my hair in a hasty knot, stashed the sword under the crusty blankets, and clamored down the steep stairwell after him, sword in fist, ducking beneath the last stretch of wooden overhang at the base and pausing with my hand against it, searching the faces in the full common room.

It seemed no one had dared risk going outdoors since last night's unexpected curfew, and I couldn't blame them...but this was far too public a place to hold a conversation like the one burning the back of my tongue, particularly in a city as distrusting as Belaris.

Well. The other option wasn't conventional, or by any means ideal...but it would certainly deter any listening ears.

Gathering my breath and my courage in the same sweep, I gave chase after Jaik, winding through the parlor. When he ducked into the communal washroom, I caught the door he kicked in his wake, slipped in behind him, and shut it with a sharp *click*.

Soundless, sure-footed and even surer-handed, Jaik pulled his dagger and spun, slamming his palm to the stained wood beside my head; in the narrow space, that sharp pivot and single forward lurch was all it took to put the blade to my throat.

My harsh swallow and the hitch in my breath lifted my skin to meet the dagger's edge; Jaik froze for a heartbeat, then ripped the knife back, turning the blade against his arm. But his other hand still braced the door beside my head.

"*Ayjay*? What in flipping *Luck* are you—? I told you to stay put! This isn't a room for two!"

I bit back the sassy retort that it *could* be, depending on one's intentions; instead, I sank further against the door, widening the space between us. "We need to talk."

"In the flipping *washroom*?"

"Focus, Jaik!" I snapped my fingers, and he straightened, sliding his hand from the doorpost at last, stabbing the dagger away in its sheath on his belt; then he turned from me, tapping the faucet on, skinning from his shirt.

Heat budded in my cheeks. "What...what are you doing?"

"Washing up." He bent to brace his forearms on the stained porcelain rim. "It's a *washroom*, Ayjay."

In his mind, I supposed it served as fair enough payback for following him in the first place—and startling the wits out of him, though he'd startled me just as much.

Guarding my fluttering stomach with folded arms, I averted my gaze to the grimy window across the room. "Whatever is out there, Jaik, whatever's frightened a city like *this*...what do you know about it?"

"Who says I know anything more than what we heard?" Jaik splashed water on his stubbled cheeks, speaking down into the basin. "You think shadows on the path and mountain folk not knowing what's out there isn't enough to get a man's hackles up?"

"Don't play coy with me. You're terrible at it."

"You didn't used to think so." He pushed back again, slapping handfuls of water on his forearms and scrubbing vigorously; my eyes tugged of their own accord to his bare back, faintly scarred and suntanned, and to the gooseflesh that puckered it in perfect pebbles.

"Jaik." His name emerged breathier than I'd intended. "Just *tell* me."

A long pause, filled with the gurgle of water struggling through the public house pipes. Jaik sopped a hand through his hair; he wetted the hem of his cast-off shirt and scrubbed his chest, his back still to me.

At long last, he turned, nudging the tap off with his hip and folding his arms as he dropped his weight back against the sink. My gaze traced the scar over his chest—over his heart—and I swallowed a surge of sourness, forcing my eyes up to meet his instead.

"After you and Lio got out of the scrape on *The Cathan*—" I had to bite back a retort that that was putting *lightly* what we'd faced on those decks, "—you probably noticed how fast I came after you."

"I know, and I'm grateful you—"

"Ayjay, we mopped up those skeletons in a few minutes. Because all they were focused on was tearing through that hatch and getting to *you*."

The hearing numbed in my ears; I stared at Jaik, and he stared back, fury dancing across the sheen of his brown eyes, turning them the shining amber of a bartop veneer.

"You..." I could barely give breath to the word. "You can't *know* that."

"I know what I saw. Kassian saw it too. It was real, Ayjay. Those skeletons wanted *you*, they were trying to go after you—I don't know why, but they were. And I think that's what Ravella meant when she said they were acting different, the way they sank those ships. Not just picking a fight, but..."

I drew my arms tighter across my chest, holding the warmth into my middle. It did little for the chill that found a way to twist around my spine and lace tighter than apron strings. "You think those Misspoken manifestations were looking for *me*. That they...they killed all of those sailors trying to find me on *those* vessels."

Jaik's eyes flicked up to me then, the grooves around his mouth softening slightly. "I know it doesn't exactly make sense—"

"No. It doesn't." The cold perforating my chest turned my words brittle like cracking ice. "Because everyone says—and *you've* said—they're nothing but mindless creations made from broken, amplified Storycraft. They have no reason—*no reason*—to be *hunting* for *anyone*. And especially not for *me*!"

"You're right, I get that. You don't owe the world anything more than you already gave up for it."

Now fury burned hot in the back of my throat. "Well, it seems everyone and now, apparently, every flipping *thing* in this country gets to have an opinion about my life and my past and what I *deserve*...except for me. And I can't say I appreciate being *hunted* for things I don't remember doing, by *manifestations of Storycraft* that are supposed to be senseless *beasts*, who know absolutely *nothing* about me...who could have crawled into the *Pourhouse* and taken this out on me before I had any *chance* to defend myself or the people I cared about!"

"Yeah, I—"

"No, I'm not finished!" I cut across Jaik, all of the rage that had been pounding in my temples since we'd arrived in Belaris bursting free all at once like an uncorked bottle of shaken wine. "Do you have any idea what this is like, Jaik?

Every layer of the past I peel back, it's like finding rot under a barcounter! All of these horrible things soaked under the surface of *someone else's* life, but do you know who has to deal with the consequences? *Me!*"

He said nothing this time, his jaw firming, his lips pressing tightly together. But I didn't stop. I couldn't bear to.

"It's like I'm being punished for someone else's mistakes." I tore my hands back through my hair. "Flipping Luck! You think I'm being hunted, Jaik, and for what? For choices made by an Audra who was entirely different from me! And *I* have to pay the price for them. I have to live with everyone looking at me like I'm her, *treating* me like I'm her, and now, apparently, *punishing me* like I'm her, too!"

Jaik tipped toward me, hands braced back on the edge of the sink. "Listen, we've faced things like this before. Storycrafters, Misspoken manifestations, soldiers...Galan flipping Fiordona." His teeth cut in a vicious line for a moment before he added, "You've never let *any* of it stop you from doing what you know you have to. Don't start now, all right? The Audra I know would—"

"I'm not *her*, Jaik!"

My shout clapped like thunder in the small washroom. Jaik all but flinched, drawing back from me.

"Do you even look at me and see *me*, or am I just the ghost of another Audra to you?" I snapped. "Because you talk to me sometimes like I'm half a person you're just waiting to put back together...but I'm *not*. Maybe my memories aren't true, maybe they're different from what everyone else knows...but memories or none, I *know* who I am, and I know I'm real. I'm *enough*, just like this. I don't have to be like *the Audra you knew* to face this."

In the throbbing silence, Jaik rocked back against the sink, loosing a shallow breath. "You're right. You're right, I...I just keep breaking promises, huh?" A swift, deprecating smile. "I told you back in Krylan I wouldn't always talk about how things used to be, but..." Trailing off, he shook his head, knuckles leaping as he gripped the edge of the sink. "But, nothing. I'm sorry, Audra. Forgive me?"

Sipping in short breaths of my own, I edged out a nod. "Yes. I forgive you. All I want if for you to look at me and see *me*, because I'm the Audra who has to survive it. Not the person you're used to having all these adventures with."

He nodded.

"Good. because I'm *not* the Audra you knew," I repeated softly—just to hear myself say it again. "And I need you to understand why it infuriates me *so much* when you treat me that way...because I don't think like her, I don't act like her,

I wouldn't make the choices she made, but I'm still the one being punished for them. And I didn't ask for this."

Jaik studied me for a long moment, the round of his throat bobbing several times. Then he rasped, "You wouldn't make the choices she made. Like bringing me back?"

Speechless, struck silent, I stared at him. He stared right back, a tinge of redness crowding his lower lids—exhaustion? Grief? Despair?

I hated to be the cause of any of it. And I despised that it didn't change the truth of my next words: "I don't know how to answer that, Jaik."

A humorless tilt at the corners of his lips. "You know, when people say that, it's like they think it lets everyone off easy. Like it's not an answer itself."

I raked my teeth along the inside of my lower lip. "*Jaik.*"

"No. I hear you." He flashed one palm my way. "You're not her. So let's drop the subject and talk about what we're dealing with here."

You're not her. Why did my own words sound so *wrong* when they came from *his* mouth?

But now was not the time to argue.

I tucked my hands behind myself, pressing my haunches against the door. "That thing the soldiers spotted in the pass. You think it's another Misspoken manifestation."

Jaik toweled off his arms and chest vigorously—as if he was trying to rake away the subject of our latest conversation. "Yeah, I do. The fact no one seems to know what they're dealing with makes me think it's probably here because of us."

"Or we're here because of *it.*"

He paused, eyes widening, gaze fixed on mine.

"You think that's why the Storymaker came here," he mused at length. "He *wanted* us to follow Him—to deal with this thing."

"He wanted us to learn about the danger." Nodding, I bit the loose skin at the side of my thumbnail. "So we could stop it?"

"Or stay ahead of it. No sign of Him in the city…no whispers in the taverns. I figure He can move without being seen if He wants, so…"

"Perhaps His *crucial matters* were these Misspoken manifestations…warning us about them."

"Right." Snapping the flecks of loose water from his shirt, Jaik towed it on over his head. Maneuvering around in the narrow space in such an artful, precise way that no inch of his body brushed mine, he reclined against the sink again. "How do you want to dance this?"

I dropped my head against the door, spine flush to the wood. "It's not safe here in Belaris...and it may not be safe for anyone who knows me, or anyone who associated with me." The words dried my mouth—the sheer absurdity of them. How impossible such a notion would have seemed before I'd met Jaik Grissom and learned of my past. "I think someone else needs to manage the Misspoken manifestations here, while we search for the Storymaker."

"Arias," Jaik said without hesitation. "We can drop two birds with one shot. Go to Vallanmyre, put Raz and Reiko on alert, and warn your family, too. We don't know who's crafting the stories these things are coming from...we don't know if they'd try to hurt the people you care about for leverage."

The words struck like a tankard swung at the side of my head, gonging violently through my skull and piercing pain behind my eyes and cheekbones; my family, from whom I was estranged by own my hand...their professions harmless and unassuming, their paths taking them nowhere near danger's door. The thought of them suffering for my sake choked me speechless.

Had I somehow suspected, years ago, that this might happen? Was that why I had written myself a narrative that chased us apart from one another? I couldn't begin to fathom the prospect of seeing them for the first time in so many years only to tell them they were threatened by the mere fact of our shared blood.

"Hey." Jaik closed in on me in the confined room, raising one hand at level with my face, but not quite touching me. "Ayjay, I know that look. Listen, it'll be all right. We'll warn them—"

"What if they don't want to see me?"

The words shrank as they emerged from my lips; it was far from the greatest worry I should've had, and yet it was the first vulnerability to escape me, staring up into Jaik's eyes.

He hesitated a moment longer; then his hand settled on the side of my neck, his thumb brushing the line of my jaw.

I did not pull away.

"Trust me," he murmured huskily, "if they miss you even half as much as I did, then seeing you is the only thing they want right now."

My throat stoppered like a corked bottle; I struggled to swallow the lump even as Jaik started to draw away, ripping his gaze to the door over my shoulder.

"First things first, we need to get out of this city. You grab the packs, I'll settle up our tab. We'll head straight to the stables...we can be in Vallanmyre in three days, tops."

He started to pull away; seized by a stroke of reckless compulsion, I clapped my hand over his, holding his fingers flush to the side of my neck. "Jaik, wait."

His eyes widened a fraction; his chest, inches from mine, stilled.

"Just because I don't know how to answer your question doesn't mean I've made up my mind," I whispered. "The reason I don't *know* how to answer is because the answer I want to give makes no sense for a woman who just met you a few months ago."

He stared at me for a moment, then dropped his gaze to my hand cupping his around the side of my neck. A flicker of a smile traced his lips—true enough this time to till the soil of his deep brown eyes.

"Think I can live with that."

A last graze of his thumb beneath mine, unleashing a torrent of gooseflesh down my sides that boiled into simmering heat in my core; then he slid his hand around the back of my neck and tugged me up from the door, and for a wild, heartstopping, toe-curling instant, I thought—I thought he might—

His other hand snaked around me, and he swung the door open. Freeing my nape and brushing past, he murmured in my ear, "Don't wait in here too long, tiger. That'll give the other patrons something to think about."

I aimed my elbow into his ribs, but he bent away from the blow, striding through the open room toward the service counter.

For a moment, I paused, breathed...collected myself. Calmed my racing heart and quieted a swell of disappointment I had *no* purpose feeling right now.

And then I spun on heel and jogged across the parlor, to the sloped stairwell and up to our room. At least afterward, I could blame my thundering pulse on exertion...and on eagerness to be free of this city of suspicion and sinister Storycraft in the mountain passes.

I shouldered open the door, stepped into the narrow quarters where neither of us had gotten our coin's worth of sleep—and tripped to a halt.

I had one moment to register that the space was not empty. To pinpoint the aberration just over the threshold.

Something that should not have been. That stabbed a knife of terror straight through my faltering heart.

It was like a thing viewed through falling water...a winding, lissome column of shadow vaguely impressing the shape of a person. Shuddering and insubstantial, it pulsed with an inner fire that reminded me sickeningly of the skeletons aboard *The Cathan*—a burning ember essence revealed by twists of shadow as it thrummed larger and smaller with every breath.

Was it breathing? I couldn't be certain; but I *felt* the stare smoldering under the shadowed hood of its cloaked frame, the edges of that black shroud falling like a pall from bone-thin shoulders to the floor. The hem snapped out and pulled back in spidery talons, ushering it in a glide across the floor.

It drank me in the same way I stared at it—horror and revulsion staining the air between us. Something like *hate* fuming the room's stale atmosphere. And not from me.

We don't know what it is.

But now *I* did, for certain. I knew that Jaik was right.

This was a Misspoken manifestation.

And it did not beset the public house with the cruel mindlessness I'd always heard in tales of these creations hissed over tankards in *The Pourhouse*.

No—it *erupted* with incandescent rage, flinging itself straight at me.

CHAPTER 24
DOOM AND DOWNFALL

The creature's piercing, otherworldly shriek blended into my scream as I dove for the bed, fumbling for Jaik's sword and hefting it to strike; but the creature blurred out of focus in a blink, then rematerialized so close I gagged on the rotten-flesh reek of it. Its gnarled fist, far more corporeal than the rest of it, struck my wrist.

My hold unlocked from the blade's grip the same instant the creature smacked me across the throat. All the air choked from my lungs, and I slammed against the wall, head cracking backward. Darkness mopped up my vision, only a pinprick shining through when my shoulder clipped the edge of the cot on my way down to folding in a heap on the floor.

The creature swayed in rollicking shadow, weaving toward me; survival outshone shock, and I dug my fingers into the moldering wooden floorboards, clawing out from its reach. Wheezing, head and throat throbbing, I gathered my breath for one shout—the only one I had a prayer to Luck would help me.

"*Jaik!*"

A twine of living darkness crunched my nose, the violent blow slamming my head back into the floor; before I could reach for the sword again, the creature fastened spider-talon fingers around my throat and swung me up from the floor.

Dimly, through the pain shrieking in my temples and the narrowing of my throat, I was aware of my hair strands caught in the splintered rafters. That this *thing* unfolded over nine feet in height, that reddish glow in its middle expanding, feeding life into every inch of it.

Making it all-consuming. Making it fill up the whole room, everything I could see.

Pain blistered through my head. Blood gushed down my throat, and I gagged, stroking weakly with one hand at the arm that held me; but it was all slippery shadow. Impossible. Unreal.

My doom and downfall made both tangible and untouchable.

The creature's mouth gaped, a new world of crimson flame revealed by its yawning maw. Its inhale pierced my thundering head like a scream in reverse, sucking in the whole world. As if it would devour me in a single swallow.

But even that ear-rending snarl could not altogether muffle the thunder of bootsteps up stairs. Down the hall. The *crack* of a door sailing open and rebounding, the muffled *thud* as it met an outstretched hand, shoving wide again.

"*Audra?*" Jaik's voice—cracking halfway through my name. "Ayjay! *Hey*—whoa, ugly!"

Rifleshot pounded through the room; it stole what remained of my hearing.

The shadow smothered my world.

CHAPTER 25
FALLING IN REVERSE

WAS THIS **WHAT IT** felt like to fall in reverse?

The world tore past me, muffled and inky. But flickers lit up the dark, bright and bleeding like ribbons of flesh peeled away from the bone.

Those flashes, blinding bursts in the night, they were...familiar.

Kindred.

Cursed.

Fear raked its clawed fingertips down my spine.

Fury devoured a hole in my chest in scarlet fire.

Disbelief clapped irons around my wrists and ankles, speeding my fall through the all-consuming nothingness.

Grief tore my throat like a neverending scream.

Hatred lit up my heart like a rifleshot.

I was falling, falling, enslaved to it all—

Crashing into something soft. Muffling. Something that wrapped around my shoulders and knees—and then the freefall turned to a tilt, as if I was flying parallel to the world. Jouncing and hurtling through it.

Faraway...shrieks. Screams. Violence and animosity incarnate, awakening the pain in my spine, my chest, my throat, my heart, my hands and feet.

But those sounds were fading.

Somehow...somehow, I was faster.

Was it really me? Or was it this smothering softness, smelling of leather and hard soap, that somehow outpaced all of the devastation that wracked the world behind us?

I didn't know how long it was until the falling ceased. Until everything became so disorientingly still, like taking the first step off a ship deck again; until pressure shoved against the base of my spine, and coldness bladed against my shoulders and back. Until hands gathered my face.

"Ayjay—Ayjay, hey! I know you're with me. Show me those eyes!"

The darkness was worse than nothingness, it was the worst of *every-thing*—so why was I clinging to it? Why was I so frightened to heed those summons?

Weak, bloodsoaked whimpers traveled no farther than the wool-fletched leather gloves thumbing the edges of my lips. The cold rekindled every pain in my head, my throat, my temple and shoulder.

"Luck, *no*." That wretched, rasping, *gasping* plea dug through the darkness and burrowed straight into my chest, quieting the pulsating fury there like a kiss stole breath. "No, come on, Ayjay...please, *please*—this can't be happening. *This can't be happening again*!"

Again—

Vines of scarlet and gild entwined behind my shuttered eyelids.

Jaik—Jaik?! Arias, put him down—tell me what happened! What happened *to him? Jaik—open your eyes! Jaik? Jaik—please, don't leave me, don't leave me, don't leave me*—

It has to be this way—do you understand that?

You're a murderer, you're a murderer, *I despise you, I hope you rot, I will never, ever serve you again*—

I know you don't want that. Not really.

I. Want. Him. BACK.

A breath whooped into the bottoms of my lungs, raking my eyes open to blinding skies, to frigid mountain cold. To the warmth of a pair of gloved hands still cradling my jaw, thumbs pressed to the corners of my mouth. To silver-streaked eyes and a mouth hanging agape with panting breaths.

To Jaik Grissom, bowed before me on his knees in a narrow alleyway, forehead nearly touching mine as he crouched between my sprawled legs. As he held my face and searched it, ensuring himself I was with him.

Was...was I doing the same?

"Ayjay—" His voice broke; his hands dropped, just to tear at something—the hem of his shirt—and to lift it to my aching face, his eyes focused on the wounds that impossible creature had dealt me; but the pits of them were blown wide like a man in shock. "I shouldn't have sent you upstairs alone, I just dropped my guard for one second—just like last time, and I didn't think...Luck, I'm so *sorry*—"

The words tore from him like the separating of the cloth that dabbed my throbbing nose; they danced on the verge of hyperventilating.

He needed help as much as I did; who knew where the memories were dragging him, the things he had seen in this city the last time we'd come?

But what could I do? What was it he had done for *me*, after the attack aboard *The Cathan*?

"Jaik, wait—wait." My voice scraped out, barely louder than a rough whisper as I caught at his wrists; but he brushed me off, still dabbing my cheek. "Tell me...tell me five things you see."

"There's blood all over your face."

"All right, that's one—"

"It's the *only one* that matters right now!"

His next dab landed a bit roughly, and I cursed, catching his hand with all my not-impressive strength this time. "Stop, Jaik, you're hurting me!"

He froze, staring at me, his chest heaving.

Slowly, I guided his fingers back to my face, teaching him by touch how I *wanted* to be touched; and his movements matched mine, his other hand returning with the tenderness I craved...carefully cleaning away the blood, mindful of the wounds he couldn't see throbbing beneath my skin.

"Tell—" Again, my voice scraped raw from my throat after just a few moments of silence. My hand found the hinge of his elbow and squeezed, anchoring me in this place; refusing to tumble back through whatever freefalling darkness that *thing* had thrown me into. "Tell me you *killed* it."

Somewhere far away, glass shattered. An inhuman shriek—followed by several *decidedly* human curses—lofted onto the wind.

Through gritted teeth, Jaik retorted, "Seems like I didn't. So, it's one of those manifestations that's impervious to rifles. Not my favorite kind."

Hands sliding under my arms, he shot to his feet, hauling me with him. The world tilted and dipped, and I swayed in his hold, but I blinked away the darkness clinging to my eyelashes.

I wouldn't go back to that place with its shadows branded on my skin. I couldn't afford to.

"We need to *move*," Jaik growled. "Can you?"

"Help me."

Jaik dropped one arm around my waist, pulled mine across his shoulders and steadied me with a hold around my wrist.

And then we hobbled, nowhere near quickly enough, out into the winding avenues of Belaris.

CHAPTER 26
MY TRUST IS YOURS

THESE CITY STREETS WERE mortared with my blood.

It plopped from my nose and chin, no time to stanch the flow as Jaik half-hauled me through the streets—and behind us stone sundered and wood crunched while a Misspoken manifestation of shadow made flesh *hunted* us, shattering every obstacle in its way.

Horror dripped the same metallic tang as the blood dribbling down the back of my throat, swarming my stomach with nausea like spoiled milk. I wanted to fold down and close my eyes, to catch my breath and sob. But we kept moving, elbowing through fleeing crowds, running where we could, slogging ahead where the foot traffic thickened—until, finally, Jaik spun me out of the mash of moving bodies and down a narrow alley.

Splashing through puddles of Luck-knew-what, we crossed the shadowed sidestreets and bobbed back out into the current of marketers flowing through the arterial street of Belaris, a pocket familiar from last night's venture through the city.

I tugged against Jaik's grip around my waist. "Left!"

He didn't hesitate in heeding me; we hobbled into the next plaza, our destination gleaming like a beacon ahead, its ratty doors flung wide. Familiar notes of honey and hops and homecooked food—and delectable venison—reached for us like an embrace. I yanked Jaik across the roughcut stone span to the door of the same tavern where we'd eaten the night before.

We staggered past the daylight patrons, a far sparser gathering; and then we collided with the counter, where the same grizzled barkeeper met us with raised brows, a frown line etched between them. "Someone really worked over your face, lass."

"Someone is still trying to," I panted, fresh blood freckling my tongue.

He stared at me for a long moment—time we didn't have to spare—his jaw working like he was chewing over a fatty piece of his own venison.

"All that blood on your face," he murmured, "I see you now. You looked just like that, last time you paid us a visit. Didn't recognize you, with the lighter hair and the gray cloak." His narrowed gaze leaped to Jaik. "I remember *both* of you."

Jaik angled a bit, tucking me back and jutting his shoulder between me and the barkeeper. "Don't make this something it doesn't have to be, friend."

"Wouldn't think of it," he scoffed. "We've seen what happens when we turn against your kind in this city...and you know we swore an oath a long time ago that we wouldn't allow that sort of nonsense inside our streets ever again." He dipped a sharp nod. "We've spent years making up for what most of us turned a blind eye to back then."

"Then you'll help us?" I demanded—no time for warmth or formality, when that creature was wrecking its way through Belaris as we spoke.

The old man cracked his knuckles. "Every man and woman worth their steel in this city knows you don't lay a finger on a Storycrafter. And they know what happens if that oath's broken. So you tell me who worked you over, and we'll deal with it our own fashion."

"That's not going to work," Jaik cut across the disbelief—and a rush of heady *gratitude*—that looped itself around the next stumble of my racing heart. "This isn't something we've faced before."

"Try me, son."

He clearly meant it; but no one, not even in this city, was prepared to face what danger roamed on our heels.

I wasn't even certain *we* could face it.

"That thing the soldiers warned us about last night...it's hunting us." The words blurted over my split lip, thick with gathered blood. "We don't know why, but it is. We need the fastest way out of this city. Just tell us where to go, and we're *gone*."

The barkeeper studied us a moment longer, his eyes widening by a fraction. Debating, perhaps, just how much old oaths were worth.

Then, gruffly, he jerked his head. "Git back here."

We staggered around the counter, and the barkeeper jammed his heel into the floor just beneath it; a hatch sprang up on ready hinges, revealing a laddered black tunnel below.

"Rum running tunnels," he explained without a glint of shame. "Gets you to the depository by the stables. From there, up to you to make it out."

Gratitude tightened my already-painful throat like that creature's fist wrapped around it again.

Something had changed these people. Touched their lives. Turned them against their own ways, at least as it pertained to hunting and harming Storycrafters.

And I had a feeling I knew precisely what—and *who*—that was.

My gaze strayed to Jaik...pressed against my side, chest heaving in silent breaths.

Whatever these people had done to me, he'd made them fear for it. Had made them allies in our future need.

"Thank you," I croaked.

"No need for it. Doing us a favor...trouble follows your kind in. Faster we get you out, the better."

Jaik cinched his hold tighter around my waist. "Looks like our three days are already up."

We plunged down the ladder into the tunnel.

We moved swifter belowground, without crowds to contend with or fear shackling our strides. I could almost limp on my own by the time we reached the tunnel's end—a broad uphill slope in the earthy terrain. Something I could only assume was meant for handcarts full of rum barrels.

At the crest of the slope, we pushed out into a dark storeroom—but it wasn't silent. Voices clamored through the seams of the walls, coaxing up the hair on my neck as Jaik helped me up the incline and shoved the door shut behind us.

Furious bellows volleyed outside the depository walls as we crept for the door in the single-room edifice; it sounded like they were between us and the stables.

"...how absurd all of this sounds?" A strident voice demanded as we reached the door and pressed ourselves on either side of it; I leaned into the blessedly-chilly wood, numbing a bit of the pain in my temple while we listened. "Those Storycrafted abominations are just as worthless as what made 'em—they don't have brains in their skulls! They don't behave like that."

"I know what we saw this morning!" A woman snapped back—then hocked and audibly spat a wad of wet phlegm like a seal on an oath. Jaik and I traded glances, noses wrinkled, as she barreled on: "You remember those Storycrafters came through during the drought and tried to sell us on how they could craft us those plowbulls? Well, that's what we saw out there...flipping cattle twice the size of a real one, black as pitch and fire in their eyes, goring trees out at the roots. They were carving a path this way!"

"Goring trees, they could plow down stone walls just as well," someone added fervently.

My stomach plunged into the depths of me; I stared at Jaik, wide-eyed. He paled in turn, pressing his knuckles into the wood.

"Not our first clash with this Misspoken rabble," the first man retorted. "Let's have ourselves a look."

"Jaik," I hissed. "They'll be *slaughtered.*"

"Not necessarily," he breathed back, tilting his temple to the wall. "Rifles and blades sometimes can bring them down."

"But if *not*—"

"They need Storycraft. I know." As boots mustered and tromped away from the depository, Jaik lurched back up straight. "Which means we need to get it to them. *Fast.*"

We ducked out into the chilly morning, eerily still after the chaos in the heart of Belaris; but how long until that wraithlike creature found us? Until those Misspoken bulls breached the city walls?

"We can't risk being tangled in a fight against Misspoken manifestations," I panted as we crossed the depository and the vacant street to the communal stables where we'd boarded our mounts the day before.

"You got that right." Jaik's gaze floated back to the town proper. "Which is why we're taking a different way."

"The tunnels," I breathed.

With a grim nod, Jaik launched a few steps ahead to the stable doors. "And if Luck decides to love us for once, maybe we'll pull the attention off Belaris...and still stay enough steps ahead that those flipping things don't catch up."

Everything else was a blur: tacking. Mounting. Wheeling at a breakneck gallop through the streets, ignoring the people we crashed past, the crates and baskets we sent tumbling and rolling. It would be far worse for the residents of Belaris than a few dislodged items if it came to a fight against that wraith in their streets—because that would be a fight Jaik would make certain was as fierce and bloody as it had to be to keep us both safe.

So we laid low on our horses' necks, and we flew—even when shouts bolted up behind us. Even when a horrific shriek took shape on the wind. Even when the sloped streets quaked and shuddered, and power pierced the air like the humidity before a summer storm…we flew.

All I let myself see, all I let my heart know, was the cobblestone streets rising ahead of us, and Jaik's bellow: "Don't look back, Ayjay—*don't look back!*"

All of Belaris shuddered to its roots as we vaulted the winding staircase fixed to the stone tower's exterior; I buried my face in Kyren's mane and trusted her to follow Kova, my whole body coiled tight to the saddle and refusing to witness the height that manifested tangibly around us. In thin air, in cloud-dampness, in falcon screeches and wrung-out cries from far, far below…the world was too much.

I couldn't bear it. I could barely breathe until my mare's uphill lurch evened out. Until Jaik whooped with defiant joy, and then I peeled my head up at last—and lost all my breath in a rush.

The world was wide open before us—distant, fang-mawed mountains, swooping valleys, a vibrant blue sky. Clouds *below* us. City depths full of shadows, full of shouts, full of movement flowing like water through the streets as we galloped past burbling stone fountains, hand-hewn benches, and potted trees, skidding over the open expanse where a waterfall gushed from the mountain face and tumbled down at the backside of Belaris, branching into twin rivers flowing down the valley.

My nerves buzzed with the wish for words to describe this city that would stay with me long after we were gone…even with so much terrible that had happened in just a single day.

These people were strong, hardy, shaped by rock and rain, by toil and triumph. And by the mark Jaik and I had left on our last visit here, bidding them by a memory inscribed on the soul of Belaris itself to be better. To battle their cruel urges. To be known for the strength of their own hands, not the power stolen by the imprisoned labor of Storycrafters. And to see us out today, when they remembered us, when we needed it most…and to stand against the Misspoken manifestations with their own might.

"You changed this place, Jaik." my panted words echoed strangely off stone walls as we plunged into the first of the mountain tunnels—and Jaik reined Kova in from a gallop to a trot.

"Maybe." His voice, too, was muted by the darkness. "But you had to bleed to make it happen."

"I was going to bleed anyway." That much felt inevitable, with the mealy, metallic taste still saturating my throat. "Not everyone could have turned that suffering into something good. But you did."

"Ah, I didn't do it for them." A pause carried us several feet through the blackness—far enough that the light dimmed at our backs, and my gaze adjusted to seek veins of mineral ore that ran in silver spangles along the roof. "I'm sorry I let that thing get close."

"That wasn't your fault. And...even as terrified as I was, back in that room, I knew you would come for me."

After a a long moment, his shaky laugh rattled against the stone walls. "You know, this city was the first place you ever told me you trusted me. After...after you were hurt, when you finally woke up, you said that was why you came to me. Out of everyone. Not a healer, not a city guard...you came to *me*, even though we had a lot of bad blood between us back then. You trusted me to put you back together. To make you safe again."

I knew that, as clearly as if I *did* remember it—because I would make that same choice again. Now. Today. And any day after.

I couldn't recall the last time I'd had someone I could turn to my loneliness, to share a private joy, to confide and quiet my fears; nevermind someone I could call on if there was danger, if there was trouble. If I was harmed in some way.

I'd lacked for any of that in Krylan. But now, no matter where the road took us from here, even if I returned to the Tailbone City and he to Vallanmyre and we held nothing between us but the memories of the journey we had made to this place, to this moment...

I had Jaik Grissom. Someone I wouldn't hesitate to reach for in my time of need. And I knew, without a shadow of any doubt, he would reach back.

"Things were different after that." Jaik's quiet voice jerked me back to the moment—to the fierce, fluttering feeling that consumed my chest. "Promised myself, no matter what, I'd never do anything to lose your trust."

"For whatever it's worth, Captain Grissom...it's still yours."

His breath caught audibly, and with such a sharp pain I was glad I couldn't see his face.

We said nothing more as the mountains swallowed us whole.

CHAPTER 27
INTO THE LIGHT

Darkness cloaked our world for days, broken only by seams of shining mineral ore in the walls, cavern glow-worms unfurling from long spans of the ceiling, and the occasional beam of light slicing through weak chinks in the stone walls. In some ways, it was too much like what I'd seen when that Misspoken manifestation held me captive—before Jaik had shot me free of its hands. It took the first two days of travel before I could sleep without jolting awake, terrified I would see heart-heat pulsing in the darkness as that thing came alive from the strands of shadow soaking the tunnel.

My only comfort for a time came from those rare peeks of light that fell across us like hopeful, warming hands...and painted a sluice of water flowing through the heart of the mountain paths, which Jaik kept perpetually on our right. The tunnel seemed to be carved along its winding and wending way, and Jaik struck a course by it like a sailor navigating from the stars.

"Water has to come out somewhere," he said, "and wherever it does, so do we."

That assumption sustained me as the days of gloom slowly elapsed—even as three turned to four, and fear pinched low in my gut that we still hadn't reached the capital.

But, then again, we were traveling a significantly different path than most took between Belaris and Vallanmyre; it made sense that it would take longer to wind through these mountain passes than to traverse the roads used by peddlers and travelers beyond. And Jaik seemed to share none of my concerns with the passing time; he rode loose and easily in the saddle, his attention scouring the stone walls and turning us down branches in the tunnels following the whisper of moving water that sometimes I could scarcely hear.

All of those were sensible comforts...and they still weren't enough to quiet my racing thoughts our fourth day in the tunnels, and into the fifth. I couldn't tell a story to save my life anymore; but my imagination still possessed a finely-honed edge for conjuring up the worst scenarios.

"Jaik?" Nervousness fletched my tone, needling it along the narrow stone walls that hugged against our horses' flanks midway through the fifth day; we were climbing in absolute darkness, and my summoning Jaik was only half concern for asking a question; the other half simply couldn't stand the unshattered gloom.

"Right here, tiger." His tone was still easygoing, floating back through the dark.

I swallowed. "You're *certain* you know where you're going."

"About as sure as I was last time you asked."

I blew out a breath, tickling my brow with the stirring of my hair. "I don't mean to pester, I just—"

"Don't like the dark for long. I know." The tenderness of his voice suggested he had *always* known that about me...another gossamer thread tying my present and my forgotten past.

Before I could ask him to tell me some tale of that lost beforetime—to take my mind away from this place—all at once the tunnel widened, with a whoosh of freer air that tumbled straight down into my lungs. Kyren's steps lightened, as if she relished the feeling of space without stone stroking her sides and shoulders. I bent my face to her mane, then jerked away sharply when I realized the bristly hairs had more than texture now. They had *definition*—distant sparkles of light on the paler strands woven into the dark.

My gaze shot past her bobbing head to find Jaik's profile in glittering silhouette—and far beyond *him*, a gleam of gold bouncing off a curve in the cavern wall.

Sunlight.

A whoop of relief cracked from my mouth, and Kova danced sideways until Jaik brought him back under control. His chuckle joined mine, and together we nudged the horses at a trot toward the glow—toward the budding echo of falling water. It took shape and gained clarity as we rode, so that before we even rounded that sunlit bend, I knew what awaited us.

The cave mouth jutted through a tumbling curtain of water, an endless, roaring sheet that surged from what I could only assume were the foothills that framed northern Vallanmyre. The resting place of the Shastah.

Steel snickered in its sheath as Jaik drew his blade; leaning against the arch of Kova's neck, he thrust the blade into the shimmering sheet of water, parting it like a veil to allow a glimpse of the city of my birth.

Vallanmyre was precisely how I remembered—the surest of all my memories, in fact. Laced with glass bridges, capped with domes and flat roofs, its thin streets dewed in shadows which fell from Fablehaven Academy and the lofty heights of Harrow Hall nearby, the academies of Storycrafter and healing. My gaze riveted on them until Jaik withdrew his sword, plunging the impression of the city back behind the shimmering wall of water once more.

"Well, how about that?" For the first time in days, Jaik laughed; and though the tension of our time in Belaris still bracketed his eyes, relief tilted the corners of his smile. "Right where we wanted to be."

"It would seem the Sha's detractors didn't just hew tunnels for their own escape," I mused. "They carved themselves a way to the capital itself...a way that would be almost impossible to follow unless you already knew it was there."

"Now, *that's* a story."

My wounded cheeks and mouth itched and throbbed, bringing to mind all too clearly that creature made of stories and shadows, too.

I snugged the reins and nudged Kyren forward. "We should report to the Sha."

CHAPTER 28

FAMILIAR FACES, STRANGE PLACES

I COULD NEVER IMAGINE a life where I had walked into the gilded halls of the Shastah with anything but the awe and wonder that rendered me speechless when we approached it now.

Any courage I possessed was found in Jaik's hand wrapped around mine after we stabled the horses and hurried through the morning markets, through the spice-rich air, all the way across the prismatic glass bridges until finally we reached a door accessible only to soldiers—a guarded door Jaik strolled toward with a breezy confidence I didn't share.

Not just because my palms were sweating at the thought of the people—the forgotten friends—who waited inside. But because of the sheer breadth of the glittering, gilded Shastah, and the formality of the guards who saluted Jaik and parted out of the way to the door grooved into the hilltop where the Sha's home perched. And because of how they peeked at me as we hurried past, hand-in-hand.

And then we were brushing the doors wide, and stepping into the vaulted halls I'd once called *home*—as casually as I said the same about Krylan.

Beautiful, *simple* Krylan. Nothing at all like the sights before me now.

The long, sweeping corridors; the high, arched windows. The few tapestries and nicknacks gleaming in nooks, welcoming us with sun-limned grins. The primly-dressed servants bowing their heads in respect, in recognition of Jaik—a few trailing me with wide-eyed looks.

Soldiers barked greetings and *welcome backs* to Jaik—then faltered a bit when they caught sight of me, the same as the ones who'd guarded the outer doors. The tips of my ears heated; I was almost compelled to squeeze behind Jaik's broad shoulders, something I hadn't wanted to do with *anyone* since I'd hidden from schoolground bullies behind my brother's back as a girl.

At least...that was what *I* remembered.

"Can't a Captain command his men not to stare?" I grumbled as we hurried through the halls.

"Nah, they're just checking out the bruises all over your face."

"Jaik...walk me back through that sentence and tell me which words *exactly* were supposed to be comforting."

"Just saying it how it is, tiger." His fingers flexed gently around mine. "Soldiers admire scars."

How nice.

But I forgot all about bruises and stares when we mounted a gilded, pearl-banistered flight of steps and twisted around a corridor, striding toward a pair of sleek, soaring wooden doors set at the end. So artfully carved they appeared almost liquid to the touch, they should have been nothing but inviting in their majesty.

So why did my feet drag as we crossed the hall? Why did a weight drop through my middle, like my heart and lungs had cut free from their strings?

I ground to a halt. Jaik swung around to face me like he'd expected this—and the grooves hewn around his eyes and mouth suggested the same.

"Jaik." I raked my hand up my opposite arm, bunching my sleeve. "I don't want to go through that door."

"I get it," he murmured, taking a step back toward me. "But it's not what it feels like, Ayjay. Just trust me, all right? I'm walking through it with you this time."

This time. But what had happened last time that my body kept score of?

Luck, I didn't think I *wanted* to know. All I was certain of was that I would never walk into that room unless Jaik was holding my hand.

So I laced my fingers between his again; and together, we entered the Shastah's Convening Chamber.

It was opulent in the extreme—more golden finery, a glass-smooth floor, drapes drawn wide to let the sun splash in. Those breaking golden rays danced over the Sha's seat, and the one beside it that would one day be occupied by his Shadre.

But no one occupied either one today. Instead, there were five people gathered at a table set for six—a round council setting in the center of the chamber.

And around it perched the same five people in the same exact chairs they'd taken up around a similar table at *The Pourhouse*, months ago. The day my life had turned upside-down like an emptied shot glass drunk dry.

Sha Arias Lothar was the first to raise his head from his hands—his spine cracking the seatback as he took us in, recognition lighting up the bearded counters of his face, hiding the dimple of his smile. "Well, flipping Luck—would you look who it is. Sensed we were meeting without you, Jaik?"

"I figured the sudden urge to punch you in the face came from *somewhere*," Jaik drawled, tugging my limp arm and resistant feet toward the table. "Should I be worried about my job?"

"We tried to fill the position, but no one else was stupid enough to take it," Storycrafter Reiko Nayori tossed back airily, draping one arm behind her seat and dipping her head to me.

I couldn't bring myself to return the gesture...nor could I only see this room as it was now, and the table where they sat. My ears clamored with the tales from *The Pourhouse* of this same chamber, vacant except for a gray cloak and a forgotten journal found nearly two years ago behind its locked doors—no evidence at all how they had gotten there. A mystery drunkards loved to pretend they could solve after a hard day's labor in the Tailbone City.

No one ever had uncovered the truth. Because, after all, that had been *my* cloak and journal—the same ones tucked in the satchel that bumped against my hip.

Naomi Weathers scooted her seat back a bit, half-rising to greet us; her dusty brown hair was scrunched over one shoulder, tamed beneath a green-stitched handkerchief that matched perfectly with her emerald healer's cloak. It offset the sheen in her eyes, somewhat...a hope I was about to be the death of.

"Addie?" she said, so cautiously it struck an ache through my heart. "Addie, your *face*..."

"That's what I've been saying for years." Reiko's grunt lacked any true venom; her livid eyes charted my healing wounds just as the soldiers' had at the Shastah door.

"It's nothing," I mumbled.

Naomi studied me for a moment longer; then she fell back in her seat, frowning. "She still doesn't remember us."

Reiko tossed up her hands; the Sha's sister, Mahalia, dropped her gaze to the tabletop, her already petite-frame shrinking further as she tugged her fingers through her dense curls. At her side, a dark-haired soldier—Wyat Jaymes, Jaik had told me after I'd failed to recognize him at *The Pourhouse*—touched her shoulder and shot me a halfhearted smile.

"Long story." Jaik pulled out the last chair at the table, and I sank into it—too saddlesore and weary to argue. "I can tell this one, if you want."

"Please." Leaning my elbows on the table, I bunched my other sleeve and rubbed gooseflesh from my arms.

"I'm dying to hear it." Reiko flicked a narrowed glance between us. "Because something tells me it has to do with the blockade and these Misspoken manifestations everyone's talking about."

Dread, it turned out, felt precisely like claws of shadow wrapping around my throat. "*Everyone?*"

"We took word from *The Cathan* by carrier fowl," the Sha explained, "and from airship by the soldiering forts among the Drennan Peaks."

"Something's got the Misspoken manifestations stirred up," Reiko agreed. "Not just the ones out in the waters, but the ones we haven't rounded up yet inside Mithran borders."

Jaik and I swapped glances as he leaned his folded arms on the back of my chair.

"I take it you two know something." Naomi's attention strafed between us.

"Probably more than we want to," Jaik grunted.

"And still less than we'd like," I admitted.

"Luck help us," Reiko groaned. "She doesn't have her memories back and they're *still* finishing each other's sentences."

"By all means, inform us." Arias rolled his hand. "Because Reiko has been to visit the blockade and come back again, and despite their reports we still can hardly make grim-or-grin-sides of what's happening out there. Manifestations sacking two ships is one thing...but the report from *The Cathan?*"

Jaik's gust of breath ruffled the back of my head. "Yeah. We think, both times...those Manifestations were after Audra."

The chill that doused the table might as well have thrown shutters over the sunlight. Yet Jaik's proclamation blunted before it could pierce my heart...perhaps because, just after *I'd* learned his suspicion, that wraithlike creature had all but confirmed it.

Naomi bent her fingertips on the table's edge. "I'm...I'm sorry. *After—*?"

"Misspoken manifestations don't *go after* people," Reiko protested. "Not specific ones. They're not fully formed enough for thought and reason. At *best*, they retain a single-minded sense of purpose to complete a task...to destroy, to consume anything in their path. But not to *go after* a particular someone."

"I'm telling you what we saw," Jaik argued. "We went to Belaris—"

Naomi's eyes bulged. "Are you out of your flipping mind?"

"Let me finish, all right?" Jaik's fists creaked over the back of my chair. "We went there looking for the Storymaker after He left us a missive...the townspeople saw something watching the city from out in the mountain passes. Some kind of wraith, it turns out. Next morning, it got the jump on Ayjay."

Every eye at the table snapped to me...charting the bruises and scrapes on my face. The raised welts on my throat.

And that was besides the nightmares of freefalling that still woke me in cold sweat, different points of my body aching. My chest, my throat, my wrists and ankles—

"Watching...like it was plotting how to reach her?" Reiko's tone rounded with skepticism.

"I wish it didn't seem like it, but...yeah." Stubble and skin rasped as Jaik rubbed a hand along his jaw. "Like it was waiting for me to drop my guard."

"And it didn't act alone," I added, before he could fall full-tilt into the shame that undercut his tone. "The townsfolk spotted more Misspoken manifestations that same day...plowbulls sundering the forest, on their way toward the city."

Wyat's eyes blew wide. "Two attacks at once?"

"Or just one," Jaik said. "From two sides."

Arias leaned back in his chair, folding his brawny arms low against his hips and fixing Jaik with a look of arch-browed disbelief. "You believe the thing—the so-called *wraith* that attacked Audra—set the plowbulls against the city?"

"I think it stirred them up," Jaik said. "It can't be a coincidence, not with the way we've seen Misspoken manifestations act in the past."

Another silence swirled through the room, sopping everyone's faces with a similar slurry of dread and shock.

They didn't want to believe it any more than I had, when Jaik had confessed his suspicions in Belaris. But we were beyond being able to outright deny anything...all of us, in our own ways, had seen too much.

"Do you know who crafted it?" Naomi ventured at last.

Jaik and I traded heavy glances, touched with despair over a subject we had grazed against—and failed to make shape of—when we'd crossed the mountain tunnels.

"No idea," Jaik admitted. "Someone powerful. Maybe someone with enough of a grudge to make a manifestation that can focus on just one person."

"A grudge...because of the Tearing?" Mahalia's voice was barely louder than a whisper. "Retribution for what Storycrafters lost back then?"

"Maybe." The very notion made my chest ache with fear—with *fury* about just one more thing the Audra I'd *been* had put into motion, that I was suffering for. "Maybe they remembered me and decided to do something about it."

Reiko's eyes narrowed slightly. "Well, then we'll do something about *them*. But first, how did you escape that thing in Belaris?"

"Outran it," Jaik admitted. "Which isn't going to last for long. So we can't stay long, either."

"But we needed to give you the word," I added. "And Belaris needs aid. It's already been too many days since the manifestations were spotted in the forest." Who knew what had happened to the town after we'd fled? Had the Misspoken Manifestations taken their leave once they'd lost their quarry—or stayed to wreak havoc in our absence?

"I can leave with a contingent by airship tomorrow." Reiko twisted in her seat to address Arias. "And alert the coalition that the manifestations are acting irregular."

"I'll get word to the soldiers if you handle the Storycrafters," Wyat offered—then shot a guilty glance at Jaik. "I...I'm assuming you're going with Audra, right?"

Jaik favored him with a snort. "Sharp kid."

Something uncomfortable bubbled in my gut—the thought that if life had gone differently, in a story I no longer knew, perhaps it would have been Jaik and I leading such endeavors. Seated around this table together with friends.

"But not tonight," Mahalia protested, jolting me out of that thought with a stab of confusion; when I blinked at her, she amended, "You can't leave *tonight*. You need to rest after your journey from Belaris... and Naomi should see to Audra's wounds. And I simply won't let you leave without dinner."

I swiveled to glance up at Jaik; he drummed his fingers on the seatback, then cocked two in what equated to a shrug.

Up to you. All risks considered—what we stood to gain and lose.

An endless possibility of danger. But also a promise of soft beds and good food and, *Luck*—of being surrounded with people we could trust.

And a kind delay to other reunions in this city I didn't want to think about just yet.

I eased out a slow breath. "Dinner would be *wonderful*."

CHAPTER 29
MEASURING UP

I N SINGULAR ACCORD, NONE of us broached the subject of Belaris, or Misspoken Manifestations, or my still-missing memories that night. No one mentioned how Reiko and Wyat arrived later to dinner than the rest, carrying the air of difficult work soon to be done.

Instead we gathered in Arias's rooms, sprawled on cushions around a table sat low on the floor, and enjoyed my favorite meal: braised beef, sourdough bread, and cheese. The perfect tavern food.

Arias regaled us with accounts of city life in Vallanmyre, of silly spats and market feuds he'd been solving for weeks. Naomi told with a healer's clipped efficiency of the work she was doing in Dalfi—which remained her home, despite her place in Arias's council.

"Is it worth traveling so far between cities every time you're needed here?" I asked as we polished off the meal—and greeted the servants who brought mugs of cocoa for the whole table.

"Anything is worth it, if it means being where you belong." Naomi waved an airy hand, sipped her cocoa, then pulled a face. "Not enough maple syrup."

"Is there ever enough for you?" Mahalia teased, folding her hands around her mug and settling back against the edge of the sofa that cornered the table.

"She must offset the heavy cream in it somehow." Arias winked, and Naomi rolled her eyes.

"I can drink cocoa however I like, you absolute degenerates."

"Yeah, yeah." Jaik mimed a yawn, popping marshmallows in his mouth. "It's like an art form with you."

Mahalia pressed a hand to her chest. "Ah, *art!*"

"I've heard you dabble?" I glanced at the smudges of charcoal on her left hand—which appeared just the same as the ones she'd sported in *The Pourhouse* the day we'd met.

Or...met again, I supposed.

"More than dabble. She drowns," Wyat snorted—then dodged a back-handed swipe from the Shadress, sloshing a bit of cocoa on his pants. "Ah, my *uniform*."

"It'll wash out," Jaik assured him, eyes dancing with wicked delight as he glanced between the pair.

"Actually," Mahalia inclined toward me like a woman about to share all the secrets of the known world, "Reiko and I are designing a storybook for children! I'm creating the art pieces. She's writing the story."

"That sounds lovely." And it did...a sharp reminder of the kinds of books I'd enjoyed during my simple nights in Krylan with Sheeba, before forgotten lives and shadowed wraiths had stalked my footsteps. "What sort of power does a tale like that hold?"

"Absolutely flipping none." Reiko's broad grin was mostly teeth. "But you wouldn't *believe* how excited my nieces and nephews are to read it."

"Hmmm." I blew steam from my cocoa mug. Truly, I hadn't thought of it like that before. Most of Storycraft and the telling of tales that I knew enshrined the power in them...not the purpose beyond it.

"Maybe the best thing to come out of those years of lack was a lesson." Sinking back on her cushion, Reiko shrugged her folded arms. "It's all right for a story *not* to be some perfect, poignant thing. For it to just exist to *exist*, to be worthy because of its own merit, even if it isn't the sort that changes lives."

"Exactly!" Mahalia grinned, lacquered nails dancing on the sides of her own mug. "This country got so caught up with believing stories and the people who tell them are only as good as the most powerful thing they can do."

"But not anymore." Swirling his cocoa to the sides of his mug, Arias tossed me a grin. "Now that the fear lies behind us, this country's begun to see that not every tale told must be tremendous and overwhelming and life-changing."

"That's made things easier for Storycrafters," Reiko added. "Less weight on all our shoulders to perform, to *measure up*." The cocked brow she angled my way suggested the measure they'd been trying to reach had something to do with me.

And yet...the lifting of that burden had something to do with me, too.

"It's taken *me* a while to accept that," she admitted after a beat, sinking a bit deeper in her seat. "I was used to Storycraft as a competition...always trying to tell the next tale that swept everyone off their feet."

"But now we're creating something that's just small and silly and sweet. That *matters* to these children, even if it won't lay new roads or shake the foundations of our country." Mahalia flashed her friend a beaming grin. "And I think that's making all the difference in the world."

I slipped a glance at Jaik; he watched the volley of conversation quietly, but the brightness in his eyes, the way his gaze fixed on me, unleashed a torrent of butterflies low in my belly.

You taught them that, tiger, he mouthed.

Luck. It seemed I had. Something else good that had come from the so-called Tearing. Something only time had revealed.

Stories, allowed to be stories...and storytellers, simply allowed to tell them.

I wasn't the same Audra who'd struggled beneath the burden of her craft, of the demands heaped on her shoulders in these very halls, but...

Somehow, unbelievably, I had the sense I'd done her proud.

CHAPTER 30
THE LOOK OF RUNNING

Naomi and I were the first to leave dinner, with a lift of her healer's satchel from the floor behind her and swoop of her head to gesture me after her. "Shall we see to your face?"

The offer freed the breath trapped tight in my breastbone. I was almost too eager to abandon the warmth and banter that filled the Sha's parlor, my nerves jangling after hours of keeping up with conversation that lost me in bits and pieces bereft of memories the rest of them shared.

"You looked as if you could use an escape," Naomi remarked as we stepped out into the hall, shutting the door on an arm-wrestling match between Jaik and Reiko. "And a tincture or two."

I rubbed my goosefleshed arms as we strode down the hall. "It's wonderful to be here, somewhere safe, particularly after Belaris. I just…"

"It's overwhelming. I understand completely." Naomi's hand floated over my shoulder, pivoting me the way we should go. "Living alone in Dalfi, and then coming here, it…it's infinitely different. Infinitely more difficult after you've left the bustle of the Shastah behind."

I blinked. "Is that why you haven't moved back here since joining the Sha's inner circle?"

Lips pinching off to one side, Naomi shook her head. "Not entirely."

She offered no more than that. I knew better than to pry.

I expected Naomi to lead me to what must be her rooms in the Shastah; instead, we went to what a space that was undeniably Jaik's. Our satchels, carried off by servants before dinner, hung from the back of one of the seats near the dusky hearth, along with his rifle and my dagger sheath.

I supposed there was no point in carrying all his weapons now, knowing the rifle had done nothing to destroy the Misspoken manifestation in the public house.

A shudder wrapped around my limbs as Naomi shut the door and strode to the hearth; she stoked up the fire, then settled on a ottoman before it and gestured me over. "I thought you might feel more comfortable doing this here. Jaik's rooms are some of the most secure in the Shastah."

"I can see that." Iron shafts crisscrossed the windows in a tasteful diamond pattern, and every piece of décor on the walls looked as if it could be transformed into a weapon of some sort. "It's hard to believe sometimes that he lived here. *Lives* here."

"That's just whenever he stops moving." Naomi shifted away a bit when I sat; then she raised her fingertips to my temple. "May I?"

"I think you must."

A smile tweaked her mouth; then she set to work examining my wounds, probing the bumps on my forehead and temple, the lacerations on my face, the raised wheals around my throat. Her hands were shockingly gentle—they almost rendered me embarrassed by how clumsily I'd treated Lio's shoulder aboard *The Cathan*.

"Be honest," I murmured, staring into the flames while she dabbed a stinging tincture against my hairline. "How many times have we done this?"

Naomi blew a breath through pursed lips. "More times than I care to count. *But*," she tugged a tacky adhesive bandage from her satchel and tapped it lightly over a cut at the corner of my eye, "I knew that was the risk when we became friends. And I still wouldn't trade it for the world."

Wincing, I let my eyes fall shut—playing off the sear of heat across my eyes as if it belonged to the tenderness in my skin. Not across the face of my heart. "You, and Jaik...all the friends I've met on this journey so far, really..." Lio's face danced again across my mind; I swallowed thickly. "I've never known people like you."

"You've never *known* that you've known." Naomi prodded my chin, rounding my head her way so that she could lather more tincture onto my cheekbone—with the same efficient grace that most people applied cosmetics. "But we know *you*."

The woman I had been. But would they hold the same affinity for the Audra they *didn't* know—the barmistress whose only real friend was her feline companion?

Sucking breath through my teeth as Naomi grazed a tender spot on my cheekbone, I forced a sheepish smile. "I'm afraid I'm not as exciting a person as you remember."

"I don't know...sailing with reformed pirates, tangling up with Misspoken manifestations, chasing the Maker of the Wellspoken World...that all sounds *exactly* like the Addie I've always known." A shadow grazed her eyes, and she dropped her hand as she added, softly, "*Almost* always known."

I swiveled to face her fully when she sank back on the plush sofa behind the ottoman. She didn't have to voice those thoughts lurking behind her eyes; though it was little more than a tale told to me, I knew precisely what she meant.

"Was it...easier, for you?" I ventured carefully. "Forgetting me after the first Tearing?"

Stuffing her hands in the pockets of the long cardigan that fell to the backs of her knees, Naomi answered with the frank honesty of a seasoned healer: "Absolutely, yes. In some ways. But there was also a hole in my life that I never stopped trying to fill...with other friends, with busywork, sometimes with crying fits I couldn't explain." She flashed a lopsided smile. "Addie, even if you lose people—or give them up—you can't ever be rid of them completely. You'll always have that ache, and you'll always try to soothe it somehow."

Like storybooks read in solitude. Like looking at a tavern door sometimes, kicked with a feeling like you were *waiting* for someone particular to walk through the door.

"Do you want to tell me some?" I asked. "About what we were like as friends?"

A shocked laugh crinkled the corners of her eyes, nearly squinting them shut with the width of her smile. "Me, tell *you* a story? Next you'll want to stitch up *my* wounds."

"Well, I would if you needed me to."

"Oh, I *know*." Falling deep into the sofa cushions, Naomi spread her arms on the seatback and tilted her head until her hair spilled loose over the winged wooden back. She was quiet for a long moment; then she spoke up toward the rafters: "We were just girls when we met. I was attending Harrow Hall. You had just come to Fablehaven Academy..."

And for the next hour, I followed Naomi down a path Jaik could never have shown me, despite all he knew about my past; the places trod by two little girls growing up into women together. One with a mother and one without; one with a passion for stories and one with a fervor for healing. Girls who traded nights at each other's homes and scribbled homework together beneath fiery autumn trees. Women who ranked potential suitors and told stories of the wildest outcomes of their adventures, together and apart.

"But then you left, didn't you?" I asked at a lull in the tale—somewhere between one of my many missions with Jaik and the next. "You moved away to Dalfi. Why?"

Naomi's lips parted, then pursed sharply. She was quiet for a few heartbeats; then she said, barely more loudly, "Everything was growing complicated in Vallanmyre. I needed a fresh start."

"Mmm, I can understand that. It sounds as if we all wanted something similar by the time the world fell apart."

Naomi winced. "Well. I had an easier time getting mine than you did. But I sort of always knew about you and Jaik. I never said anything, because of the implications for you both, but...I hoped for the best."

And we, apparently, had gotten the worst. *Jaik* had suffered the worst, in these very halls.

I shuffled my fingers together, then flexed them, cracking my knuckles. "What about you? Is there someone *I* should know about?"

"Oh, Luck, no." Naomi's eyes flicked aside. "Though there have been *plenty* of offers...handsy soldiers and lovestruck strangers, and the occasional friend who wishes he could be something more." Her attention hung a moment longer on the door, in the pause that followed...then landed back on me. "But something always frightens them off...whether it's my reputation, or my interest in poison studies, or my *four older brothers*." Wrinkling her nose, she shrugged. "One reason or another, I haven't met my match yet."

"If there's a man out there who can match Healer Weathers for ambition and talent, I will *certainly* have to meet him."

"You and me both." Naomi drummed her fingers on the arm of the sofa, then pushed to her feet. "I really should go, Addie. It's a long walk back to my father's house from here, and it's already late."

I supposed it was, but, Luck, I wouldn't have minded staying up telling stories with her all night...just like we had as girls.

But she was already reaching for her satchel; and it was now or never, my only chance to keep a promise I'd made in her name.

"Actually," I pushed up from the ottoman, stiff from so much sitting, "before you go, there's one last thing..."

"With you, Addie, it's never the last," Naomi smirked. "Let's hear it."

Retrieving my satchel, I pulled out the glass dove from its most padded pocket and offered it to her—a parting that tore off a piece of my heart. "There's a little boy in Fallshyre Bay who was sickly, but he's on a regimen that's helped with it…I may have told his mother you'd be willing to see him. When you have time."

Naomi's smile softened as she accepted the dove from me. "If it matters to you to ask, then it matters to me to visit. Of course I'll look in on him. What's his name?"

"Laith."

"Hmm." Her eyes twinkled a bit as she put her head on a slant, studying me. "I think I've heard that one before."

Scoffing, I fell back on the ottoman and chucked a pillow at her; she caught it and hugged it to her chest, balancing her chin on its beaded edge before she tossed it down on the sofa behind her.

"Do you know where you'll go next?" she added.

I shifted on the ottoman, letting its plush warmth half-swallow my haunches. "Not really. Away from whatever that thing was in Belaris…but we didn't exactly have our course set besides visiting Vallanmyre."

Which was unnerving. Not only because the Storymaker might disappear without a trace, rendering all we searched for fruitless…but also because the longer we were in this city without a reason to go, the greater the risk of the wraith finding us here.

"Well, wherever you go, it's bound to be dangerous if that state of your face is anything to go by." Naomi delved back into her own satchel—this time pulling out, not a remedy, but an entire book of them.

I didn't have to be a healer to know as much. The edges stained with salves and the binding hand-stitched, by the look of it, the book's deckled pages and thick leather cover tooled with mushrooms and ivy screamed of an herbaceous existence.

"I want you to take this." Her tone firmer even than her skilled hands, Naomi pressed the tome into my upturned palms. "Don't even think of arguing, I have four copies of the same book. But what you and Jaik are facing…I don't like it. I don't like the implications or the risk of it. The only way I'll be able to stand watching you two walk out of this city and back into danger is knowing you're armed with some piece of knowledge in case *this*—" she gestured to my bandaged face, "—happens again."

"I wasn't going to protest." I hugged the book against my chest, insides warmed with the smell of old pages and ink wafting from its corners. "Thank you. I already feel better just having this in my hands."

"That's always been you with books." Naomi's breath snagged after the words; mine did, too.

Then she turned away from me, busying herself gathering the tools of her trade; melancholy bit at the edges of my heart as I watched how deftly she cleaned and packed things away, marveling that a quill and parchment must've once felt so familiar and natural in my hands. The way bar rags and tankards had come to be.

"I wish I knew me the way you do," I blurted out—an honesty I hadn't even felt rising up in me until it was set free.

And I almost wished I could take it back.

Naomi tugged her satchel closed; then she swiveled her head, peering up at me sideways. "You still can. If you want to."

"Do I not seem like I want to?"

"You seem scared." She swung her satchel over her head and adjusted it on her hip. "Which is perfectly understandable, given what we discussed before dinner tonight. All I'm saying is...keep the course, Addie."

"I'm trying. It's just..."

"I know," Naomi said simply—and with a smile that was anything besides. "I know running when I see it."

Balancing a hand on my shoulder, she pressed a swift kiss to my cheek. Then she was gone, striding for the door, swinging it wide—nearly colliding with Jaik in the frame.

Relief tore the breath from my chest at the sight of him...knowing I wouldn't have to spend a moment alone in this room the way I had the one in Belaris.

He and Naomi exchanged a brief, quiet conversation; then he slung an arm around her shoulders, hauling her tight against him. Her answering hug was equally fierce; he kissed the top of her head, and she ducked under his arm, out into the hall—with a parting kiss of her own blown my way.

Jaik stepped inside, shutting the door and leaning back against it. "Hey."

"Hey, yourself." I gathered my legs onto the ottoman, scuffing my thumb along the frayed hem of my trousers. "Who won the arm-wrestling tournament?"

"Ah, Raz. He's really been committed to those muscles ever since he made Sha."

"I suppose that makes the country feel safer...having a Sha who can fight for himself."

He dragged his bottom lip through his teeth like he was fighting a smile. "Yeah, it's needed that for a while." Hands stuffed in his pockets, he sauntered toward me. "Mind if I—?"

"No, please...it's your room."

"Eh. There's that." He dropped onto the ottoman, stretched out and propped up on an elbow. "So. How you feeling? About coming here, about whatever's next?"

I rubbed my forehead—then jerked my hand back when I crumpled the edge of Naomi's bandage. "Better, knowing the people in Belaris will receive help from the Sha. But still not settled about the rest of it."

"Yeah?" It wasn't an agreement; the lilt of his tone was an open invitation to discuss how I truly felt.

"I know you're right...that we have to warn my family. But i don't know if I'm brave enough to face them."

"I hear that." He drummed his fingers on the ottoman. "Look, you don't have to tell them yourself. I can handle it, if you want me to."

The notion was as much a relief as it was a coward's choice.

"No, it should be me. If I've brought the danger to them, I should be there when they hear about it. It's just..." The words soaked my tongue in tangy truth, more readily spoken since Naomi had voiced them first—a truth that I hadn't felt ready to admit until now: "I'm scared, Jaik,"

"Hey. I know, tiger." Pushing himself up on one hand, he raised the other—hesitated—then swiftly tucked a lock of hair behind my ear, setting a trail of pleasant warmth alight along my temple. "But you're not walking into this alone. I'll walk into it with you, and we'll walk back out together."

Everything in the world had become so unpredictable—especially since Belaris. But I had this, at least: the certainty that, no matter *what* came, Jaik was at my back. And at my side.

For once, I chose not to overthink it; not to chase the *maybes* and *what ifs* down their variegated paths. If I did, I would never stay in this city long enough for closure.

"All right," I murmured instead. "Tomorrow, then. Let's go and see my family."

CHAPTER 31
COMING HOME

THE WAY TO MY parents' house was familiar from every corner of Vallanmyre.

I had grown up in the home my mother had inherited from her father, and him from his, its roots sunk into the crust of the country's capital nearly back to its founding. It was the house where I'd chased my siblings after days wiled away in the market, fingers and cheeks tacky with the residue of sugared cinnamon bread we could never make last until we raced one another up the front steps. It was the house where, according to Jaik, I'd told my first tale—unleashing a snowstorm inside the same walls where I'd been rocked to sleep in my mother's arms, sung across raging fevers by my father, teased and tormented and talked through childhood heartbreaks by my sister Marli, shown how to pinch and bite and beat up boys who pulled my braid by my brother Raff.

Some of it I remembered. Some of it Jaik had told me. And it was still nearly impossible to unweave what I thought I knew from the memories I'd forgotten when I stood at the base of that familiar stoop, my heart and head at war.

In my mind, they despised me. They'd abandoned me. I'd abandoned *them*, leaving for Krylan without so much as a farewell. In my heart, there was a different truth told to me: that they'd forgotten me. Then searched for me. Then lost me again. And, if Jaik was to be believed, they'd never stopped loving me at all.

Still, I couldn't make my feet unstick from the streets of Vallanmyre, to chase the mirages of my pigtailed younger self and my cocky-grinned brother and my sassy, nurturing sister up the steps to the door.

Someone had painted it scarlet. But in my memory, it was still deep, dark oak.

A door slammed in my face. A memory that was not real.

Or was it?

"Hey." The gentlest brush of a hand to the small of my back as Jaik stepped to my side.

"What if they're angry with me?" The words brushed over my lips, quiet and quavering. "For bringing trouble to them...for everything that happened when I was Master Storycrafter?"

"Does it change anything?" Jaik's hand dropped away. "Angry or not, they're still your family."

His words dripped through me like warm mead, filling my core with courage.

He was right; this was not about me, it was about them. And I could take a few blows of disdain, even of disappointment or rage, if it meant telling them what I had faced...what might endanger them because of me.

Bearing down a deep breath, I wiped my sweating palms on my trouser legs and hastened up those familiar steps, my toes dodging the weaker stone just to the left of middle on the top one; then I was on the stoop, and knocking.

Then fidgeting. And waiting.

No answer.

I glanced hastily at Jaik; he rolled his hand toward me, goading me on.

Biting my lips together, I knocked again—longer and louder.

"Coming, coming—hold your coin!"

My breath snared to a halt at the sound of my mother's deep, husky tone, always balanced on the verge of teasing; and the air didn't return to me, stealing my voice when the latch unhinged and the door swung wide.

And there she was. Everything I remembered. Everything I'd yearned for and resented in my years in Krylan...a bitterness birthed in false memories.

The same dark hair I'd tried to style mine after as a girl. The same sharp, bottle-green eyes that could cut through any lie my brother and sister and I told, no matter how well-concocted. The mouth that had formed my name over and over while she swayed me to sleep—a first memory, an impression not even time or twists of Storycraft had stolen.

But there was thick silver warring for dominance against the deep umber of her hair now. Those eyes were masked a bit behind half-moon glasses. And that mouth dangled open, caught on a breath, too, her hand bracing the door.

I laid mine to it as well, half-fearing she would shut it.

"Addie." A breath rushed over her lips. "*Addie*?"

I managed a hiccupping, open-mouthed swallow. "Mama—"

She pulled the door a bit wider—and confusion cut the noose of fear and relief from around my throat.

A little boy perched on her hip, baby-round face drooping with sleepiness, eyes red-rimmed. In his chubby fist he clutched a threadbare ragdoll rabbit—an old toy of Raff's, one my mother had stitched a dozen times when Marli and I ripped off its ears and legs in tug-of-war matches with our brother.

"Who...?" The word was a strangled puff of breath; I barely choked past it, "Who is *this*?"

"Oh! Oh, Addie, this is Henri." Her eyes darted to the thick weave of his dark hair settled against her shoulder. "He's...he's Marli's."

Marli.

My wetnurse sister, who the healers of her adolescence had said might never have children of her own...who had been drawn to the orphanages and infirmaries and public nurseries for a place to spend her love of children when her body might never endure carrying her own.

She had a *son*.

I had a nephew.

Choking on heat, half-blinded by tears, I reached out a hand. "Oh, hello, Henri. It's so good to meet you."

"Nana," he mumbled, turning his face into my mother's neck.

"Don't be frightened, Henri," Mama crooned, jostling him a bit on her hip. "This is your Auntie Addie. She's my baby, just like you're Mama's baby."

A sob erupted from my chest, and at that sound, the door crashed back on its fastenings. My mother surged out onto the stoop, catching me against her before my knees gave way; I broke down in her embrace, weeping against her opposite shoulder, clutching her and Henri to me. And she gripped me as tightly as she held him—by my back first, and then my neck, and then by a fistful of my hair.

"Addie-cake." My childhood nickname shattered in the tumble of her tearful voice. "My Addie, you're home. You're *home*."

I no longer knew where that was. I hadn't in so long.

But here, in my mother's arms, it felt like the start of finding out.

CHAPTER 32
NO PART OF IT

MY REUNION WITH MY family was a dizzying blur of tearful embraces, disbelieving demands, and so much warmth I felt as if I would burst with it.

When my mother first released me, it was only to beckon Jaik up from the streets to receive his own crushing squeeze—her sharp *"Where have you been?"* answered only by his sheepish, "Sorry about that, Mama Jay."

Then it was down the familiar front hall to the broad, cozy kitchen, where Marli's question of "Who was at the door?" transformed to a shriek cursing fickle Luck when she turned from mixing a bowl of cookie dough at the counter and met my tearstained eyes.

Another flurry of hugs. Tears. Questions. Sitting on the stool at the center island—the same stools where we'd measured our heights as children, hoping to Luck we'd be the first to brush our bare toes on the ebony-and-ivory tiles beneath—I heard learned of Jordin, my brother's partner in the lumbering trade, now Marli's husband and Henri's father.

Mischievous and grinning, Marli reminded me about Sera, the florist who'd inherited the shop at the end of the street from her own father, over whom Raff had been mooning for decades—and who, at long last, he'd worked up the courage to court. Mama told me of my father's flourishing architect business, and how she herself had retired from logbooks and accounting with the city officials when Marli had given birth nearly a year ago.

Perched on the stool next to Jaik's, I took my third warm cookie from the plate and sampled it with a tongue that turned everything to the taste of cinders.

So much had changed in my absence. And I had spent too long resenting my family, believing they didn't love me, that they were ashamed of me; I had fled from them to the Tailbone City to begin a new tale of my own, and now…now they had written entirely new chapters of their lives, in which I played such a broken, uncertain role. Their stories had taken on new twists, with spouses and children and grandchildren who wouldn't know me from a stranger on the street; who, according to Jaik, might never have even been told about me at all, from these lips they loved who hadn't remembered I existed until only a few months ago.

And I couldn't blame them for it. *I* had left. I had chosen Krylan over them. I had written memories that turned me away from them. And even knowing their disgust and dislike of me were falsified—a protection of sorts put in place with the desperate swish of my hand as I'd rewritten the Tearing—there was still a prickle beneath my skin when the silence swelled. A vague wondering if the awkward pause had its roots in something foul and even furious.

It was Marli—classically—who ruptured that quiet like a lanced boil, forever the one who preferred a moment's despicable discomfort over ongoing pain. "So, Addie...where *were* you?"

"Krylan," I admitted, setting my half-eaten cookie on the counter and rubbing my face with both hands. "Working as a barmistress."

Marli snorted, then waved a hand when I picked my head up to glare at her. "Sorry. Go on."

"That's it," I grumbled. "I was working at a tavern in the Tailbone City until Jaik found me."

"Shortly after we all remembered *again*, I gather." My mother's voice was quiet from where she sat in the doorway to the dining room, laying out a scattering of kitchen utensils for Henri to play with.

"Got it in one." Jaik aimed a cookie at her, clicked his tongue, then bit into the warm dough with a groan of delight that teased my core. "Sorry I didn't stop by to see all of you first."

"It's been a chaotic handful of years." Mama waved off his apology. "We didn't even remember *you*, Jaik, and that is saying something indeed."

"Hey!"

A smile tugged at my mouth, but swiftly faltered. "I'm so sorry...for everything this family endured on my account."

"Oh, don't be like that," Marli scolded. "If nothing else, it taught us that life is a lot flipping duller without you in it."

"Even with all of these new faces to love," Mama added, "it always felt as if something was missing around the table on family supper nights. Your father mentioned it every single week."

Hope pricked the edges of my weary heart. "He did?"

"Just you wait." My mother winked. "He's going to be thrilled to see you. We're so glad you're home."

That word again, trembling through me like a hot summer wind.

Home...it was here, but it wasn't. With all of these changes. With unfamiliar names and faces.

I felt more welcomed in my family's arms than I had in longer than I could remember. But I had also never felt more like a stranger.

Mama wasn't wrong—my father's delight at my presence was almost as smothering as the hug that lifted me off my stool. And it made up almost entirely for the much cooler shock that emanated from my brother Raff when he strolled in a half-hour later, followed by a burly man who looked so like Henri he could only be his father.

"You're back?" Raff demanded the moment he spotted me at the counter, helping Marli plate up baked grouse and potatoes for dinner.

"Hello to you, too, ass-head."

"*Audra*!" My mother whipped my arm with a dishcloth. "Flipping Luck...all of those years at Fablehaven Academy and you *still* can't think of a better insult for your brother."

"Sorry, Mama." But I wasn't—and I didn't think I'd ever meant the insult more than when Raff rolled his eyes, foregoing even a sideways embrace for me to give one to my mother and one to Marli instead.

"I'm going to walk Sera over," he said—then added my way, "Try not to disappear for a few years again while I'm gone?"

"Keep talking, and I'll be tempted to."

Raff scoffed, then jerked his chin in a nod across the room. "Grizz."

"Raff," Jaik shot back from where he bounced Henri on his knees, sitting with his back to the wall. *Ass-head*, he mouthed my way when Raff hurried out of the room.

"So, who's this?" the burly man asked, dropping a kiss on Marli's head. "And who's the stranger bouncing our son?"

"Not a stranger, I've known Jaik Grissom since he was a scrawny bean-pole playing soldier," Marli teased. "And this...this is my sister." Her eyes slid sideways to me, depths pulsing with quiet wonder. "Addie, this is my husband."

That much was obvious even without the tale she'd told me; the way he beamed at her with one arm wound around her waist was no different at all from how Gydeon had looked at Siu.

Jordin shook my hand, his smile faltering not a single stitch. "Jordin Haversen. Pleasure...Marli's mentioned you recently. She said you were out traveling the world?"

"Something like that."

My mother swooped in just then to take over plating the food, and my father tugged me aside to tuck me under his arm. Though he chatted relentlessly about his business and its burgeoning growth these last few years, an odd tension curdled the air—unspoken questions and untold tales leaving me far from hungry by the time Raff returned with Sera Jameson in tow. After a brief, polite introduction to a girl I'd only known through my brother's adolescent swooning, we all settled in to eat...and the silence took hold.

Jaik's boot grazed mine under the table while we all served ourselves; I wondered briefly if I had the courage to grasp his hand, to soak up a bit of his soldiering strength for myself.

In the end, I didn't. But I wished I had, when—after only a few bites—Raff said, "All right, so, I'm assuming no one had the guts to ask while I was gone." He jabbed a fork stuffed with grouse my way. "What in flipping Luck *happened* with you?"

Of course the question came from Raff.

I set aside my own fork, giving up on my wilted appetite. And then I told them everything—the things I remembered and what Jaik had told me about the truth of my past. He lent his voice effortlessly where I needed him to, filling in the holes in the narrative, parrying the questions that left me lost for words with no answers dredged from the depths of my misremembered history.

We passed the whole meal that way, and afterward, there was a new sort of silence—not even the scrape of cutlery or chewing mouths to break the terrible pause. I almost wished Henri, asleep in a dozy drape on my father's shoulder, would wake and fuss.

Anything to shatter this endless, aching quiet.

I thanked fickle Luck for Jordin Haversen when he twisted in his seat and pinned Marli with a wide-eyed look. "Beautiful, when you said your family was *complicated*—"

"Oh, shut your ramble-hole." My sister swatted him on the chest.

"He's right, it's a lot to take in." Raff spanned an arm across Sera's seatback. "Forgetting, remembering, forgetting *again*...I mean, don't get me wrong, Addie, we looked everywhere for you the first time, but—"

"There is no *but* to that, Raffael Jashowin," my mother scolded.

"I've never heard of *any* Storycrafter with that sort of power." Sera's summer-sweet voice twisted with uncertainty, and she tugged her fingertips anxiously through the tufted end of her charcoal-dark braid.

"No one does anymore," I assured her quietly, puddling a bit of the gray cloak in my lap; I'd worn it for security, for the sense of steadiness it brought whenever I wrapped it around me, but...in that moment, when all their eyes fell on it, I almost wished I'd left it tucked in my satchel. "Your memories are safe."

Marli frowned. "Safe from *you*, you mean?"

I raised my eyes to hers, then let them drop again—and tugged my fingers from the folds of my cloak.

"I'm far less concerned about what happened to us," my father rumbled, one hand braced gently on Henri's back, "and more about what was done to *you*. To both of you."

"Tell me about it." Jaik scrubbed his knuckles over his chest.

"I can't believe our Sha would..." Mama broke off, pursing her lips together, appraising us carefully. "Actually, no. I *can* understand. I remember how stressful those last several years in his service were for you both. How you would come to visit just weeping with exhaustion, Addie...you said you no longer had a voice. That you were only a weapon for him."

"He never deserved your help, anyway," Raff grunted.

My stomach pitched uneasily; these things they spoke of with such certainty...they were shadows glimpsed through a veil for me, like a city lying beyond a curtain of falling water.

Intangible. Beyond my grasp.

"But, people dying and being written back to life," Sera fretted, "and all of our *memories* being played with..."

"Honey, that's never going to happen again." Raff tugged gently on her earlobe. "Right? You heard Addie. That power's gone."

Jaik shifted, arms folded, chair creaking beneath him.

"And now you're looking for the *Storymaker*?" Jordin laid a hand back through his thick, wavy air—the precise shade and texture of his son's. "As in, the One who wrote the *world* into being?"

I blinked. "You know Storycrafter lore?"

He shrugged. "My father was a violet-cloak. I've dabbled."

Jaik nodded. "Nice."

"Yes, we're searching for the Storymaker." I tucked my cloak in bunches and loops over my fingers again. "To see if there's any hope of restoring my memories."

"What about your *Storycraft*?" Marli demanded.

An odd, simmering resentment scalded my throat. "Well, *that*, I gave away so that every *other* Storycrafter in all of Mithra-Sha could possess their power again. So I don't *know*, Marli."

She held my gaze. I held hers.

"I'm sorry, Addie." Her words struck like a blow to the gut. "I know Raff and I weren't particularly...supportive of your stories. But it was such a part of you, such a thing that brought you joy, and...I'm sorry it was exploited by someone you should have been able to trust. And sorry you had to give it away to right someone else's wrongs."

"Yeah," Raff muttered. "It shouldn't have gone that way."

I needed no memories of the past to be certain this apology had been a long time in the making; nor that it was the only one I would ever receive from siblings just as wily and stubborn and proud as I was.

"Thank you," I managed. "That means everything to me."

Marli flashed a lopsided smile. Raff cleared his throat, tapping his fingers on the back of Sera's seat.

For a while, there was silence again. My mother broke it this time: "So, the Storymaker...you suspect He's here? In Vallanmyre?"

"Not...not precisely," I hedged.

"We're here for a different reason," Jaik added.

"Surely not because you missed us *so much*," Marli teased, rising and gathering the dishes.

I glanced at Jaik; he held my gaze for no more than a moment, but the tilt of his brows as he read my eyes mirrored all the strife of the last week.

And here, at the threshold of it all...

I couldn't do it.

I couldn't be the one to say it, after all...to shatter this fragile sense of peace. To see the wonder and acceptance in my family's eyes go cold. For them to regard me as a different sort of threat—not to their memories this time, but to their very lives.

Biting my lips to stanch their trembling, I could do nothing but blink at Jaik. Swiftly, he nodded. *I've got this.*

And just like that, I could breathe again—as Jaik scraped his chair back and rose, and said, "Hey, Raff, Jordin, Papa Jay, can I borrow you for just a second?"

Selfishly, perhaps, I was glad he wasn't telling them all at the table. I wanted my mother's serene smile and Marli's roguish good humor for just a little while longer.

I helped Marli sweep up the dishes while my father passed a still-sleeping Henri to my mother's arms, and the men all retreated to my parents' study; my sister washed and I dried the platters while Sera put away the leftovers, and we talked of nothing and everything. Sera's business, Marli's whirlwind courtship and marriage to Jordin, my time in Krylan—tending bar, sharing life with Sheeba, learning more of my trade from Leatrix.

"I never would've imagined that sort of life for you," my mother remarked, bouncing and swaying Henri around the isle counter to keep him asleep, "but it's clear it brought you happiness. I'm glad for that, Addie."

I halted in the motion of swirling the drying cloth over the last plate, teeth grinding the inside of my lower lip.

I *had* been happy. Or at the very least, content. And all of that I'd traded for a bruised and lacerated face, for nightmares, for danger and uncertainty and sorrow and little else to show for it yet.

Setting aside the dish, I slipped past my mother to the dining room, scrubbing down the table—a familiar motion that belonged to a simpler time. A simpler life...even if it had been a lie. I missed the utterly unassuming nature of it. The sheer predictability. The warmth and weight of Sheeba's purring bulk on my feet at night, the textured pages of well-known books to read, the absolute certainty of what the next day would bring, and the next, and the next.

Luck help me...I no longer knew what each *moment* would bring. And I had brought this on myself.

With the table cleaned to my mother's standards, I padded back toward the kitchen...then halted.

There was something so *normal* about the scene unfolding between those familiar walls: Sera and Marli laughing as they stacked and put away the plates. My mother giving her back a much-needed rest on one of the stools, Henri snuggled and soothed against her again, his face buried in the hinge of her shoulder.

This was the pace of their lives now. *Their* familiar and predictable.

And I was not part of it.

Before I could unstick my feet from the doorway—before I could find a way to fit myself back into their midst—Raff, Jordin, and my father stepped in from the hallway, grave-faced. My mother glanced questioningly at my father; he shook his head. But Raff went straight to Sera and caught her in a crushing embrace. Marli watched them, narrow-eyed; when Jordin approached her, she laid a staying hand on his chest, shaking her head. "Tell me what's wrong."

A lump lodged in my throat; shame and regret blackened my core like dousing shadows.

Biting down tears, I backed from the doorway, hurried through the dining room's second arch into the hall...and slipped quietly out the front door.

CHAPTER 33
A STORY UNTOLD

I N THE BELLY OF the evening, rocked to sleep in the arms of commerce's waning labor and only certain districts awakening through freckled patches of lanternlight, Vallanmyre could have been anywhere. Most closely, it resembled Krylan, though lacking the bustling nightlife of the Ameresh district Lio had once called home.

Tonight, I missed her so fiercely the longing accounted for at least a small score of the tears dripping down my cheeks.

Lio had never once looked at me the way my family had tonight. She'd sidestepped seamlessly to make space for me, a new friend with no qualms about the woman who'd twice torn the world. There had been no fear in her, in the crew, at what I'd done. They hadn't regarded me the way Sera and even Raff had...like some fiendish, Misspoken manifestation that could only be trusted to raise havoc again.

Arms folded, hugging my elbows to myself and cinching my ashen cloak to my ribs, I quickened my pace.

Familiar streets. Memories real and false. An infliction *I* had inflicted on myself—and on Mithra-Sha. And now I was the only one who believed these streets had ever been my bed, the only one living beneath the burdensome memories that beat against my skull, telling me they were *true, true, true*—that I had lived beneath *that* bridge, bathed myself in *that* river, begged on *that* corner when my latest prospects ran dry.

The loss of my power, I understood. I fully fathomed what I had given up for the Storycrafters of this country. But tonight, it was the continued loss of my memories that plagued me...a loss no one else shared.

And why? Why hadn't they returned, the way even my family's had?

I'd taken their absence for granted until now...a problem to be solved when we found the Storymaker. But now the notion haunted me, pursued me through Vallanmyre's winding streets...

What if my lack of real memories was punishment for the fear I'd wreaked on innocent women like Sera? For the unhealed wound I'd dealt to strangers and friends alike in this country? Did I have any right to pursue this path, to try to change things for myself *again*?

Luck's coin had flipped against me twice. What would happen after a third toss?

Distant thunder rumbled from the west, it echoes vibrating in the soles of my shoes. Before I'd reached the next block over, gentle spatters of rain freckled my cloaked arms and dampened my hair. Cursing Luck, I flipped up my hood and lengthened my stride—but the deluge caught me in the next market. Through the misty veil of rain, I squinted at the signs framing the square: tailors, tinkers, leatherworkers, an apothecary, and a bookbinder—the only one with the shop windows still aglow.

How oddly fitting.

Gritting my teeth, I hurried across the square and tested the door, half-hoping it would prove itself locked; but the glass-paned wood slid wide without so much as a creak, and I slipped into the bookbinder's shop, chased by the next, closer crackle of thunder.

The interior chafed at my senses like a dream nearly grasped but not quite held; a softness, a welcoming warmth to the high, dark shelves and the neatly-bound pages they held, waiting to be bound. The rich scent of tooled leather, the tang of ink both new and ancient, even the rich amber hue of the light...all of it soaked my senses and chased out a bit of the rain's chill.

The shop itself felt feather-edged, a tome waiting to be tested and taken in.

Carefully, I wove between the shelves, mindful that my damp cloak brushed against nothing; in the recessed aftbof the shop, I located the service counter, which made room for a small till, a nameplate...and everywhere else, books. A towering stack of them completed, a heap of them not yet done, and behind it all an elderly man perched on a stool, deftly stitching bound pages to a leather cover.

Halting, I cleared my throat. "Hello, I'm sorry to intrude, just—"

"You were caught in a storm," he said without looking up, "and this was the only refuge you could find."

Warning zinged along my nerves. My arms tightened over my middle. "How did you know that?"

He raised kind eyes to me, dark and lively beneath the snow-white brows that shadowed them and the beard that framed his gently-smiling mouth. "You are dripping, my dear."

I pulled my limbs in sharply, shy of ruining any of the papers that reached for me with testing fingers over the shelf edges and counter. "Could I just stay here until the storm lessens?"

"You may stay as long as you like."

He returned to his work; I shifted my weight, reticent to make the same return to my dour thoughts. Crying in the streets was one thing; crying in front of kindly strangers was entirely another.

"Are you..." I peeked at the nameplate on the counter, "Gareth?"

"I am not." He winked. "Simply watching the shop and catching up on a bit of his work while he's out courting his lady. And you are—?"

I opened my mouth, then clapped it shut again.

I wish I knew. But who would answer such a simple question with dramatics?

"Audra." Best not to give him my full name; who knew if someone bound in books might also be bound to resent the person who'd once taken their endings away?

"Audra. That is a beautiful name." Another warm smile, this one loosening a stitch of tension between my shoulderblades. "May I inquire as to what you're doing out at such an hour, and in such a storm, Audra?"

"Would you like the truth?"

"You know, I appreciate that you would ask." He set aside the book, perching his fingers loosely-clasped on the counter's edge. "Many who inquire do so out of politeness. But, yes, I truly would like the truth, if you feel like giving it."

I fingered the edge of my cloak, swallowing back another lump of tears threatening to erupt from my throat and dash across my eyes. "I think I'm running from something."

A frown tugged at his brows. "Are you in danger, my dear?"

"No—well, yes. I mean, I was. But not here in Vallanmyre, I don't think, at least not yet." I pressed my lips together, fighting the tremble that darted across them. "The truth is...I think *I'm* the danger."

To my relief, he didn't seem to take the words as a threat; he slid his elbows onto the counter and propped his mouth against his fingers. "Would you care to elaborate?"

I supposed it should have felt strange to speak of any of this to a man I'd just met; but wasn't that what had made Lio such a safe harbor? It was my family and the people who knew me before who'd looked my way with so much mixed emotion. Even Jaik.

Oh, Jaik. He was likely out searching for me in this storm, but I wasn't certain I could bear to face him. Not when these raging doubts made me wish I could cheat my way aboard an airship and return to Krylan tonight.

"I just…" I wandered nearer to the counter, to the lanternlight…the warmth this stranger emanated, like shelter from storms both inside and out. "I'm just afraid I'm making all the wrong choices. That I made them before, and I'll make them again."

"Hmm. Yes, I can see why that would trouble you. No one enjoys the feeling of making mistakes."

A wretched little laugh punched from my throat. "No one makes mistakes quite like me."

"Truly? No one else in all the world?"

"No one *I've* ever heard of." I folded my arms on the counter's edge and rested my chin atop them. "And maybe that's the trouble. If no one else has ever made these choices or walked this path, how can I know whether the decisions I'm making are the right ones?"

"Well, there is wisdom in experience…and wisdom in counsel," the elderly bookbinder offered. "Perhaps your purpose is not to walk a path, but to forge one. And to forge it with the aid of those around you."

The words found some purchase in the slippery surface of my aching heart—but to keep it, they dug in like claws. "I just wish I wasn't always the one carving routes no one else has ever walked. Living stories no one else ever tells."

"I imagine that must be difficult, indeed. But what if the road was given to you to walk because you *are* capable of walking where no one has? Of telling a story no one else has told?"

The talons in my heart gave it a gentle tug—pleading to embrace the notion that I was not overwhelmed, but equipped.

I buried my face in my arms. "I would like to think so, but it's hard to imagine I'm capable of that after all the trouble I've caused. That I'm…"

Worthy.

Fingers tapped the wood near my head. "I have lived a very long time, Audra, as I'm sure these grizzled whiskers attest." He gave me a moment to free a giggle before he added, "In all that time, I have never known a person who did not cause trouble. Can you believe it? Not even one."

I opened my mouth to protest—he didn't know *me*, the trouble *I* caused, and he might throw me out of the shop if he heard—

"I have also never known a single person who was not loved by someone, somewhere. A cruel son with a mother who still kissed his portrait before bed each night. A wicked daughter whose father searched to the ends of the country for her. An unfaithful man whose children forgave him. A murderous woman whose lover believed she hung the moon and stars." A slow shake of his head. "I believe in forgiveness. I believe in repentance. I believe in homecomings after the worst times. But these things are certainly not easy. The question, I think, is not whether you are able to go where you're going...it's whether you are willing to face what lies beyond arriving there."

Conviction and blows to the face, it turned out, landed *precisely* the same way. They knocked the breath out in the same sharp sweep. They rendered the same terrible pain.

Arriving. It meant facing the truth of my past.

Going. It meant owning and embracing a portion of the fear in Sera's eyes. The disdain in Raff's scowl. The threat of abominations made with power like mine.

It would mean every story Jaik had told me became *more* than a story. I would have to live it. Carry it. Accept it.

My part in it. Not something that merely happened to another Audra. Not *her* choices, not *her* mistakes, not the things done to *her*—but *my* choices and mistakes. The things *I* had suffered that infuriated my family, that made Jaik so distant at times. These things kept at some cozy distance by the murkiness of forgotten memories today could become the griefs and guilts so heavy I might not be able to crawl from my bed tomorrow.

Was that a homecoming I could bear?

I had thought so, after Fallshyre Bay, after the joy we'd found in Laith and his family. But now, having survived Belaris, having seen the trouble this life brought to my family's door...

There was not only joy. There was pain...enough to put the few people I *did* remember in danger.

"Is it wrong if I wish I had never been given this path to walk?" I whispered, raising my blurry gaze to the bookbinder.

"Not at all, dear girl." A hint of dampness sparkled in his eyes as well—or perhaps that was a trick of the tears in mine. "A purpose is a heavy thing to carry. But it is worth asking yourself, I think, whether you would truly be happier without the path...or simply if it would be *easier*."

"Does the difference matter?"

"I believe it does. Because if something is worthwhile to you, you *will* find a way to fight for it...ease or not. And it's good to know which is which before you decide to step off the path in a fit of weariness." He patted my arm gently. "Do that, and you may find life is a different sort of difficult."

Like Krylan. The thought bolted through me at the brush of his touch—memories of an engulfing loneliness. Of a painfully predictable existence. Of believing myself cast out and forgotten by the same family who'd embraced me with all their might tonight.

The family I'd fled from—into the night, into a storm, without so much as a farewell. Just like I'd left last time, stepping off the path.

Gripping the counter's edge, I shoved back from it. "Flipping Luck...I have to go."

"Ah! Before you do..." The bookbinder turned and rifled through the towering stack at his side, sliding one book from the many; it was laced with a leather cord, tightly tied. The tarnished charm of a crossed quill and sword dangled from the meeting of the strings. "You should take this. It sounds as if you could use a good adventure to escape into when yours becomes overwhelming."

"Oh." My breath caught at the beauty of the leather cover laced with swirls and curlicues, etched with echoing patterns of curves and twists like smoke and embers. I couldn't help running my fingers over it, feeling the depths of those artfully-hewn divots.

But when would I have time for adventure tales, with everything we faced? Did I even want to escape into the realms of fiction, when reality was so terrifying of late?

I jerked back my hand. "No. I mean, no, thank you, I'm so grateful for the offer, but...I don't need any more books. My...the Sha's advisor just gave me one on healing, and it's all I have space for in my things."

The practical. Not the poetic and picturesque. Not until our quest was finished.

"I understand your concern...not all books are for all times. Besides, if ever you're ready for such a tale, I'm certain you'll find a copy again." Once more, the old man flashed the cover my way; then he tucked the book under his arm. "I have business in the back, but stay as long as you like, Audra. That storm seems a frightful one."

He hardly knew.

"Thank you," I said quickly as he turned away. "For speaking with me about this. And for your advice. For whatever it's worth, I think you're right about me."

"Well, if I am," he cast a last smile over his shoulder, "then I suspect you will be just fine."

He retreated into the shelved recesses of the shop—and barely had he gone before the door brushed open, ushering in the rumble of thunder, the drum of falling rain, and a familiar voice cracking with concern: "Ayjay? Hey, you in here?"

All the breath tumbled from me in a rush. "I'm here, Jaik."

He darted between the bookcases just as I turned to face him, his hair tousled, every inch of him dripping. "Thank *Luck*.. What happened back at the house? Someone say something to you?"

"It's...no, it's not them, Jaik," I confessed. "It's me."

He frowned. "What do you mean?"

I brushed a spot on the counter clear, then gripped the edge and hopped up on it, putting my eyes at level with his.

"I'm scared," I admitted, and the contours of his body tensed. "I'm scared of that Misspoken manifestation and what it did to me. I'm frightened for my family, and I...Jaik, I'm terrified of what happens when I remember all of this. What I did, what was done to me, all of it."

"Ayjay, there's nothing wrong with being afraid." Jaik eased his palms onto the counter's edge on either side of my thighs, sloping toward me; fresh tears sparkled across my vision as the scent of rain and leather leached from his clothes. "Flipping Luck, I'm scared out of my mind half the time. But you—"

"I'm afraid of remembering you, too."

His hands flexed on the wood, as if they might drop away. As if he couldn't bring himself to let them.

"If I remember *everything*, then I have to remember *you*." The words stumbled on my tongue. "I have to remember losing you...again, and again, and *again*, and now that I'm starting to...now that I feel like I..."

Flipping Luck, why wouldn't the words come?

"Jaik...from what you've told me, it seems like all we do is find each other and lose each other again. I have lost you *so much*," I choked. "I don't think I want to remember what it feels like to lose you all over again."

Jaik gazed at me for a long moment, the sharpness of his jaw and the roundness of his cheekbones and the gold tracing in his eyes all highlighted in lanternlight.

And the single tear that slipped from his lashes, sliding down his cheek.

"I get that it's hard." There was scarcely any volume to his husky voice. "I get that you shouldn't have to do it. No one should have to do what you're doing. But, Audra, listen...I need you to fight for me. I need you not to give up on this."

On us.

But...would I be happier if I did?

Tonight, no answer came swiftly. Not to my mind. Not to my lips.

So instead I seized Jaik by the collar of his shirt and pulled him near; I wrapped my arms around his neck, rested my cheek on his hair. His broad hands splayed across my back, and he tugged me to him until he was crushed in the gap of my legs, his face resting over my beating heart.

We huddled there, wrapped up in each other, for Luck only knew how long; while the storm raged, and the bookbinder lurked somewhere in the shadows, allowing us the space we needed to weather the tempest together. While tears and rain melded until it was impossible to say which was which.

Until, beneath the heat of Jaik's relentless grip, I could breathe again, and unbind myself from him, leaning back to rest my hands on the broad spread of his shoulders. Our damp gazes met—and held.

"I'm still trying," I whispered. "I just need you to know why it's so hard for me. Why I'm so afraid."

"I hear you." He hooked a damp strand of hair from my cheek, tucking it behind my ear. "And I want *you* to know I'm not letting anything happen to you. I've got this...I've got you, tiger."

Somehow, it meant far more than bodyguarding or escorting on this search. It was all I was, my flaws and fears and feelings held in his hands. It was my heart, every piece I thumbed over a shard at a time, safe in his grip.

It was the only sure and steadfast thing along this path.

And it was the strength I needed to slide from the counter. To take his hand. "I'm sure I frightened my family, running away like that. I should go back and apologize."

"You sure? We can leave right now if you want."

Wouldn't that be simpler? The easier path?

I shook my head. "No. I need to be with them...to start making new memories that are true. And to show them they don't need to be afraid of me. That I'm not letting anything happen to *them*, either."

Jaik's hand flexed around mine. "Proud of you, Ayjay."

By the time we slipped out the door into the storm, the lanterns were dimming in the shop; and when I paused at the mouth of the street to glance over my shoulder, it was so utterly dark, it might as well have never been open at all.

But the hand tucked in mine spoke otherwise. And the stirring of conviction in my chest said infinitely more.

This path was not an easy one. Or a sane one. Or a safe one.

But it was the one *I* had been given to walk. So I would keep walking, through the doubt, and the fear, and the pain.

Because if I didn't...no one else would.

CHAPTER 34
SHOW YOURSELF

NONE OF MY FAMILY said anything condemning or cruel when we returned. There were soft, warm blankets to ease our chill, and my mother's arms around both of us for a long, long time.

Then we gathered in the sitting parlor, and my father was the first to speak—with that deep, unsparing rumble of his. "I'm going to have a word with your brother and sister, Jaik. They're good Storycrafters. I'd like to have them keep an eye on the house, maybe walk Marli and Sera to and from places for a bit."

"Watch out, Raff," Jaik said airily, draping an arm along the sofa behind me. "Lyam's going to steal your girl."

"As *if*," Sera sniffed, swiping her thumb along her lower lashes. "Raff's already warned me you Grissoms are nothing but trouble."

"Nothing but," I agreed, digging my elbow into Jaik's thigh. Sera shot me a shy smile.

"Trouble or none," Father insisted, "Lyam and Adele are practically family, too. Addie helped them with their schooling...they'll be more than eager to help keep an eye on things until the matter of these Misspoken manifestations gets sorted."

"And I'll have a word with the Sha," my mother added—as if just anyone had Arias Lothar's personal ear. "If things become dangerous in any way, I'm sure we can shelter inside the Shastah."

Unease squirmed in my chest. "I'm hoping to Luck it won't come to that."

"The point is, if it *does*, we'll be ready," Marli assured me, leaning from the armchair where she perched to squeeze my hand. "And none of this is your fault, Addie."

"Well," Raff began.

"No, Raffael, you swine," Marli snapped, "it is *not her fault*. No one deserves this...to be stalked and hunted by *creatures*. That's just cruel."

"Yeah, well, Raff does cruel pretty well," Jaik fired back with a pointed look at my brother.

"No fighting," my mother said sternly, and both men looked to opposite sides of the parlor. "We all knew danger was inherent when Addie became a Storycrafter. We also know it's inherent in chopping down trees."

"And in architecture," my father added gruffly. "Every profession has its risks and rewards. The question is up to the person whether the passion is worth the price."

I found myself mulling that notion even as my family dispersed—Jordin and Marli to take Henri home, Raff to escort Sera back to her apartment before he returned to his. Soon it was only Jaik and I still in the sitting parlor—him seated on the sofa while I wandered to the blanket basket, choosing my favorite knitted throw to replace the damp blankets my parents had taken into the kitchen to launder.

I couldn't remember where I'd gotten this one, but somehow its soft multicolored hues made me think of peddler fairs and a man with a laugh like Naomi's.

"Jaik?" I began, hands still tangled in the blanket. "What my father said, about passion—with us, did it feel—?"

I pivoted on heel as I spoke—and broke off midword.

For the first time since we'd come back in from the cold, my gaze snagged on the mantel...and something caught my eye.

My breath hitched. "Mama? Did someone come to visit while we were gone?"

"No, no one," she called back from down the hall. "Who would be out and about in this storm, Addie?"

Who, indeed—but perhaps One who commanded them?

I glanced at Jaik. He blinked at me.

As one, we lunged for the hearth—slamming into each other and scrabbling like cats over a beached fish, swiping and grabbing for the letter wedged between my father's handmade Ameresh clock and my mother's Hadrassi crystal-crusted egg collection.

"*Oof!*" I caught Jaik's elbow to the side, shoving me back; he cocked the letter skyward between two fingers, holding it above my head.

"Ah-*ha!*" he chortled—then doubled up with an undignified gag as I launched myself into him, tackling him back against the sofa and sending us both to the floor.

"Audra? Jaik? There had better *not* be anything happening there that you wouldn't want these old eyes to witness!"

"Just—Jaik—*losing*!" I crawled up his chest and snatched the letter from his hand, then spun to sit over his ribs, peeling at the edges.

"Just Ayjay being a *sneak thief*!" Grabbing my hips, Jaik dumped me off and dove for the letter when it fluttered from my hand; cursing, I rolled over on top of him, crushing my back over his and flattening his chest to the floor as I reclaimed the prize.

Pinned under my weight, he groaned into the rug and didn't fight back again. Smirking and panting, I nestled my head back into the muscular dip between his shoulderblades and read aloud:

Audra and Jaik,

I fear my duties in Belaris kept us apart from one another. But it was good you came to Vallanmyre.
I must journey on to Rivrand, in the Vensair Mountains. I await you there.

"Rivrand..." Jaik moaned into the carpet.

Pinning my elbows on either side of his ribs, I propped myself up a bit and twisted to look down at the back of his head. "Do you know it?"

"Not really. Heard of it, but I can't think of where or why."

Likely not somewhere we had visited before, then.

Were we ready to go now?

Sinking down with my back to his again, I dragged one foot absent-mindedly up the inside of his leg. "It's no safer out there than it was when we left Belaris. We still don't know where that wraith is now...or who created it, and where *they* are."

"Yeah. But it's not any *more* dangerous that we know of. And we made it all the way from Fallshyre to Belaris not knowing what we were up against."

"Fair point."

"Ayjay?"

"Mmmhmm?"

"Kind of can't breathe."

"Oh! Right, sorry." I rolled off of him, tucking my knees underneath me; Jaik flipped onto his back, cocking one arm behind his head—casual as if he'd just sprawled out to warm his bones by the fire. He watched me with guarded curiosity that made my stomach prickle.

"So. Are we going?"

I dragged my fingertips down the letter, watching for glints of gold in the ink—marveling at the fact that the Maker of the Wellspoken World had somehow been inside my parents' home. And wishing with all my might that I could have just found Him *here*.

Why not wait for us? Why not show Yourself?

"Of course we're going," I sighed. "Now I have even more questions that need answers."

CHAPTER 35
DAY BY DAY, DANCE BY DANCE

I T WAS BOTH GRIEF and relief to say our farewells to Vallanmyre; to share one more flurry of parting embraces with my family and with our friends in the Shastah. To accept gifts of food from my parents, gruff advice from my siblings, supplies from Arias and Naomi, Reiko and Mahalia.

With our satchels and saddlebags heavier by far than when we'd fled Belaris in so much haste, we made our way with leisurely determination to the east—toward the foothills of the Vensair Mountains that curbed the border with neighboring Hadrass-Drui.

And that was where the relief settled in; to no longer have to be a bit of two Audras, the one who'd forgotten and the one they all remembered. To cut the tethers of a performance better left to the acting troupes I'd so enjoyed in Krylan, and simply be myself...with Jaik. Where every day, pretense felt lesser.

Every day, I was learning to be my whole self around him; and every day, he took that in stride, whatever it meant at the time.

Easy days. Difficult ones. Days of waltzing with daggers in our fists and days of lying on our backs around the campfire, scratching Kova and Kyren beneath their whiskery chins while we searched the stars for constellations and patterns.

Now and again, Jaik asked me how I felt. If today was a day of chasing, or a day of running away.

It eased, in time...the debilitating fatigue when my heart and mind swept from one extreme to the other, and the shame that I could be so fickle. The humiliation at the notion that I was failing, somehow, by wanting both to flee and to pursue, and wanting them so achingly much whenever one took precedence over the other.

Jaik took every swing of my mood in stride; we were two ships sailing in tandem, crossing an endless ocean toward a shadowed horizon. But where my smaller craft strafed one way or the other as it went, Jaik's vessel held to its bearing and cleaved the waves toward true north. It was as if the stars themselves guided him—an unfaltering map across these tumultuous seas. And I was moored to him, my lines wound to his stern, so that even when I strayed, my horizon was secure.

And on that horizon...Rivrand.

We made our way toward it day by day, dance by dance, with renewed hope—hearts bolstered by full saddlebags and full bellies. Lush summer forests in the lowlands bowed aside to make way for the hardier evergreens and alpines that had become so familiar during our crossing in the Drennans. We traversed meadows and streams and rivers, scouted a path marked by the steam curling from village chimneys and town-center bonfires.

Sometimes, when I assured him I was ready to hear it, Jaik told me of when these things had been our life together; he spoke of a duty-bound past traveling from one place to the next, by airship or by horseback, to meet the needs that arose across Mithra-Sha.

I could hardly fathom when such needs had been my responsibility. But I was prepared to meet the needs of each *today* that greeted me, head full of birdsong and billowing scarlet dreams already slipping from my grasp.

We rode. We raced. We bantered and argued. We climbed and climbed toward Rivrand.

After nearly two weeks of eastward bearing, we angled our course south. The mountain peaks closed around us.

Another fortnight passed, this one dotted with storms—but aberrant of any wraithlike shadows, for which I was grateful. Whether something kept it at bay or it simply struggled to find us in the vast wilderness, I didn't dare dwell on the notion too long. Whenever I did, fear and fury sparked in my fingertips...sensations I could only outrun by putting my heels to Kyren's sides and riding with all of my might from one patch of sunlight to the next.

Who knew where that creature would strike next? Had it attacked Vallanmyre in our absence? Or had it perhaps sensed the Storymaker's presence there, when He had brought us the latest missive weighing heavy in my pocket...and moved ahead, lurking along our path to Rivrand?

And who in flipping *Luck* had created this creature? And *why*?

I was ready to put all of that cruel mystery behind us as the days wore on. Desperate to have my answers, and my memories, so that we could conquer the dark. So that I could shed the prickles of rage that occasionally woke me at night, smarting like a stomachache.

So onward we pushed, with all our might...closing in on Rivrand.

But it was not Rivrand we found first, after all those weeks of riding.

It was a mountain refuge we rode across, all of a sudden one day…deserting the depths of the trees, trotting Kova and Kyren along the edge of the stream we'd been following for the last handful of days into a broad swath of meadow, and catching a glimpse of a lovely but modestly-sized log cabin at the far end. Smoke curled from its stout chimney, and its porch faced our way. A swinging bench stuffed with pillows swayed from hinges beneath the eaves by the touch of the breeze.

Jaik reined Kova in, shielding his eyes against the midmorning light. "Huh. Looks like an outpost, but…a lot more lived in. And not by soldiers." He cocked his head. "Unless they're soldiers with a real love for beaded pillows and crocheted blankets."

"Aren't *you*?" I nudged his knee with mine, then clicked my tongue, urging Kyren forward.

We had nearly crossed the meadow when the cabin door swung wide, with an almost musical cry of creaking hinges. But it was no soldier who emerged, nor someone I might have considered a first watch for trouble from the north. It was an elderly woman, her hair snow-white but her frame strong beneath a dark, flowing dress stirred by the breeze that skirled the hem around her ankles. Her bright green eyes, even from a distance, shone with a keen mindfulness—and when they speared our way, I drew Kyren sharply to a halt, dragging her chin nearly to her chest.

Something thrummed in my mind. In my body. An awareness, a wakefulness that, even muffled, still demanded my fully attention.

"Ayjay?" Jaik's tone dipped with concern.

"I…I know her."

"Maker's tales!" The woman's exclamation bolted shock straight to my bones. "Audra Jashowin? I should have known, with the reports of manifestations haunting these hills of late, I'd catch you wandering the mountains straight to my door!"

I shot Jaik a swift look; the one he returned me was equally mystified.

It was the first time we'd met someone he didn't remember, either.

Unease stroked along my bones; I didn't dare relax even as I nudged Kyren closer, and the woman descended the porch steps toward us, her dress fanning like an inkstain on the mountain breeze that poured around the cabin's corners. We met just beyond the base of the stairs, and she perched her hands on her hips, studying us both. "Well? Have words failed you after *all* this time?"

"Do we know you?" A bit of metal crept into Jaik's voice; Kova's tack jangled like warning bells as he trotted up to my side.

The woman paid him no mind; her gaze, sharp as a quill's nib, pierced into me. "Surely you haven't forgotten me, Miss Addie. That would be insulting indeed."

Embarrassment colored my cheeks. I ground my lower lip between my teeth, and with a swift glance, Jaik edged Kova ahead of me. "Actually, thing is...Audra's sort of forgotten all of us." His tone was brittle with final warning. "So you'll have to give us your name."

The woman cocked a regal brow—the only sign she might be fazed by such news. I suspected it was the only sign she would ever give. "Ovalia Andriss. Former Headmistress of Fablehaven Academy."

Jaik's eyes blew wide. "Flipping—that's right! *That's* why I knew Rivrand, Ayjay...you told me the Headmistress was retiring up here after your Master Storycrafter trials."

"Then you must be Jaik Grissom. Flattered and charmed to meet the infamous bodyguard who betrayed our best girl." Ovalia's eyes did not drift from me. "And you, Audra Jashowin, the most intriguing student I ever had the challenge of discipling...I am sure there is *quite* a tale behind that vacant look and the colorlessness of your cloak." A sharp, almost daring twist to her lips had me sitting taller in my saddle...a call to craft that my mind did not remember, but my body held the script of it down to the core. "And I am dying for you to tell me a story."

CHAPTER 36
COMMUNING WITH THE CRAFTER

O VALIA WELCOMED US INTO her home with a familiarity that clashed against my awkward sensation of meeting a perfect stranger; she whipped about the small kitchen, directing Jaik to toss our satchels and saddlebags in separate rooms, one of which I suspected must be hers. Me, she put to work gathering a meal of bread and cheese and carved turkey.

When we settled in at the table, Jaik and I tore into the food with as much manners as we could muster—which was arguably little. It was wonderful to have foods like these again, after weeks of foraging and eating meat cooked over an open flame.

"It seems you've come quite a way," Ovalia remarked, quartering her own portions neatly and eating in small, swift bites as she watched us; the habits reminded me a bit of a hawk. "To what do I owe the *stunning* surprise of seeing the pair of you?"

Jaik froze with a hunk of bread halfway to his mouth, eyes flicking my way.

I swallowed my bite of cheese and turkey; it scraped going down. "Would you ever believe the Storymaker led us here?"

Ovalia offered a slow blink. "The Storymaker Himself. By dreams?"

"No, by actual letters." Jaik reached into his pocket, and I into mine, finding my share of the letters we carried—from *The Cathan*, from Fallshyre Bay. Together I laid them with the one Jaik had carried from Vallanmyre, pushed to the center of the table.

Ovalia slid them closer, poring over them while we hastily consumed the rest of our portions...sharing a sense conveyed by a mere glance that the opportunity for eating was about to be sacrificed for explanation.

"Fascinating," Ovalia breathed, following the articulate curls of the lettering with a fingertip. "This is stunning. I've heard myths and legends of such communing with the Crafter of the first Wellspoken Story, but no one expects to see such things in their lifetime."

"Well, I've gone in twice." Jaik draped an arm around the back of my seat. "And Ayjay's going for her second, too."

"Is there anything you might have heard to suggest He's here in Rivrand, like His note says?" I finished my own plate and stacked it with Jaik's.

Ovalia shook her head. "Nothing which might have prepared me for all of this. And one would think that I, of all people, would know if the Maker Himself had shown His face nearby." A slight divot grooved between her brows. "But it would be less a surprise to see Him now, of all times, with recent happenings."

Dread soured the meal in my belly. "You mean the Misspoken manifestations."

A sharp narrowing of those hawkish eyes. "Indeed, I do."

Jaik folded his arms on the tabletop and dropped his head to rest on them; the strength of his shoulders sagged away. "*Great.*"

"Don't be that way," Ovalia chided. "No such threat has reached us yet. Rivrand proper lies two miles further to the south, so I invite you to give it a good scouring...just know that I do suspect if some fantastic stranger had found His way there—the *Storymaker*, of all things—I would certainly have been told."

Which meant He likely wasn't here. *Again.* "Oh, of flipping *course.*"

"Hey. Don't worry, I've got this." Jaik squeezed my shoulder and shoved to his feet. "You two, catch up. As much as you can," he amended for my sake. "I'll scout around the village, see what I can pick up."

I had never been gladder to leave him to it; though discomfort had dogged my heels around my family, around my friends in the Shastah, here with Ovalia it was dimmer, somewhat. There was a presence about her like the mentor in every child's adventure tale I'd read during the long, lonely nights in Krylan...a sense once did not need to know her to *be* known by her. Whether it was a first meeting or something as utterly unbelievable as my circumstances.

The moment Jaik was gone, Ovalia turned to me, the stern line of her mouth softening. "Chilled tea? On the porch?" The words lilted like a question, but she was already sweeping back toward the modest kitchen to retrieve the tray.

A smile tugged at my lips, and I trailed after her, muttering under my breath, "Somehow, I suspect *that* bit of my story has already been written for me."

CHAPTER 37
TO LIVE WITHOUT STORIES

OVALIA'S WRAPAROUND FRONT PORCH offered a truly breathtaking view of the meadow and the mountains crafted artfully by the first Wellspoken Story—or so Ovalia reminded me when we took seats on opposite ends of her porch swing; and though I had been immersed in such sights, and the sounds and scents of the Vensair range, for weeks now...I still could hardly sip my raspberry tea past the emotion that clogged my throat.

Such beautiful corners of Mithra-Sha were open to me now, the turned pages of a never-read tome. But unlike the books I'd tired of back in my apartment with Sheeba, somehow I felt as if I'd never grow bored of these views.

"So," Ovalia's thoughtful voice cracked several minutes of silence after she'd badgered the truncated version of our tale—and *my* story—from me. "This is quite a journey you've been on, Miss Addie."

"That is certainly one word for it," I muttered into my next sip of tea.

"I can't say I'm grieving I passed the Headmaster mantle to Thiago before all this nonsense." Ovalia flicked a bit of condensation from her weathered fingers. "I had my fill of ridiculous Storycraft the year you graduated."

Heat pulsed in the tips of my ears. "I hope not on my account."

"You wrote quite a bit of my resignation letter, yes." Teasing flavored her words. "But there was also the mess with the soldiers-in-training becoming more brazen, more rebellious against Storycraft...and there were other Storycrafters in your year and surrounding that made me feel as if I'd met my match for the first time in all my years at Fablehaven." A slow wag of her head. "Yours was a generation unto itself. Some of the brightest minds, the most exceptional imaginations I've ever had the pleasure of helping cultivate. But...many Storycrafters from origins I had not experienced, with fires in their bellies that were difficult to tame."

"People with a double-portion." The whisper floated from my lips, at one with the stirring of wind through the distant pines.

"Yes, something like that."

Another bout of silence...hers lost in the past, mine in my imagination of things I had lived.

"Could you..." The words stuck a bit on my tongue; I had to swallow them and hunt for a different approach before I could force the words past the knot wedged in my throat. "Is there any Storycrafter you trained, who you could think of, that could have crafted a Misspoken manifestation like the one we're facing now?"

Ovalia hummed low in her throat, eyes narrowed across her sweeping lawn—as if she expected the wraith she'd heard rumors and my account of to come slithering from between the pines at any moment.

Luck help us both if it *did*.

"If what you say is indeed true," she said, "then only two come to mind. One who left these lands long ago, bound for Amere-Del. The other..."

Eagerness—something almost like *hope*—shoved me to the edge of the rocking seat. "Yes?"

Brows arched, she swiveled her focus back my way. "The other went on to become Master Storycrafter."

Grimacing, I fell against the hewn backrest. "Well, that's far from helpful."

"You only asked me who I *know* of with such power, Miss Addie. You've forgotten that some Storycrafters are imbued with power beyond Mithran borders...and there are others within them who never visit Fablehaven Academy. I'm afraid I can only tell you what I've encountered, not all that exists in the world."

Hope sputtered out like a snuffed candle. It appeared the Storymaker hadn't pointed us this way for Ovalia's help in identifying the Storycrafter powerful enough to have shaped the wraith.

"Well...can you tell me about yourself, then?" I ventured when my disappointment threatened to sour into despair. "What has life been like here in Rivrand?"

"Exceptionally ordinary." Ovalia chuckled. "Which is precisely what I require after the ruckus of Vallanmyre. It's certainly a different pace of life...and I've come to crave it. I've taken up painting and crochet...and haven't touched Storycraft since my first day in this home. I've found other pursuits more rewarding since."

"I can see why. You have a lovely home to keep here."

But it was more than that; the easygoing fondness in her tone made it clear that Rivrand was her Krylan. It was a heart-home, the way the Tailbone City had felt for me. And right now, sipping tea on the porch and watching the breeze tease the treetops and stir the meadow grass...

Today, such a pace seemed far better than the next pursuit looming on our horizon if Jaik found nothing in the village. If all we had to carry from this place was another heartsick defeat and a wraith on our heels.

"What has it been like?" I hedged. "Living without Storycraft, I mean."

Ovalia's gaze slid sideways to me; I ignored the look in favor of scrubbing condensation from the sides of my cup.

"Restful," she said at length. "Quite restful, in fact. I very much needed the time apart from it, those first few years...and then the urge to dabble simply went away." A quiet snort. "And then, of course, those years when I couldn't finish a story...no one could. And by the end of all that, even when my cloak regained its color, well. The desire has not returned. I don't suspect it ever will."

Something uneasy wriggled in my belly. "Why is that, do you suppose?"

Ovalia lifted one shoulder in a shrug. "All your life is an awfully long time to tell stories, Miss Addie. Students in Fablehaven learn what it is to tell, and tell, and tell...often when they wish to be doing anything else. Some even bow out of the Academy under such duress, and they should. Because there are times that life will demand a Storycrafter craft a story when they feel they have nothing at all to give. And one must learn if they can press onward, or surrender in those times."

"Everyone deserves an opportunity to rest," I protested. "They *need* that."

"Yes, they do. But when you choose Storycraft, you choose the risk that the times you need rest and the times you *can* rest will not be one and the same."

The question is up to the person whether the passion is worth the price.

Frowning, I washed my mouth with a longer swallow of tea.

"Anyway," Ovalia went on, "now is *my* time of rest, and I haven't felt any tremendous urge to tell stories ever since. Rivrand has rarely been in need of them...it's a hardy place, and its people have only infrequently been touched by Storycraft at all. The few times I've considered using my talents to solve a problem here, they've figured it out for themselves before I could finish the debate with my own head and heart."

A sharp laugh cut free from my throat. "It seems you chose the perfect place to settle, then."

"Oh, I was very deliberate in my choice, you can trust that."

And I did. Even without my memories, I had a good sense that Ovalia—who reminded me in many ways of Leatrix—was not a woman who did anything by half-measure. Not least of all deciding where she would live out her peaceful retirement.

And yet, here we were, in such an unassuming corner of Mithra-Sha, a small village tucked away in the mountains...and our paths had crossed. The student and the headmistress, coming together for the first time in over a decade.

There was no coincidence to it...no more than there had been in meeting Laith's family, or being drawn to Belaris.

Whether or not Jaik found Him, and whether Ovalia could tell us anything of who might've crafted the Misspoken abomination that hunted us, the Storymaker had guided us to this place for a reason. And that reason, I suspected, was the very woman sitting across the bench from me, sipping her tea, studying her beautiful home.

Perhaps it was even the question branding my tongue, which I'd wondered from the moment she'd welcomed us inside.

I stared down into my glass, wrestling the subject for a bit longer...seeking the right way to broach it. Then, at last, I gave up getting the words perfectly right; I was no longer that Audra, after all.

"Given the life you've lived since your retirement," I blurted, "do you suppose you can enjoy the rest of your days without Storycraft?"

Ovalia was already shaking her head before I'd finished speaking—not in negation, but a teacher's subtle scolding. "You're asking the wrong question, Miss Addie." She paused, then, her gaze searched the mountain-studded horizon. "Or, well...it's the right question, but spoken the wrong way."

I cocked my head. "I beg your pardon?"

"I see the lessons in inflection did not linger with you." Smirking, she sipped her tea. "The question isn't whether you *can* find fulfillment and happiness in a life without Storycraft. Because, of course you can. Plenty of people do...people who have told tales all their lives, and those who never have." Her gaze arced back to me. "The question is whether *you* can find fulfillment and happiness without it. *You*...Audra Jashowin."

The hair on my nape prickled. "Well, I've lived this long, haven't I?"

"Indeed." No lessons of inflection were needed to register the polite disbelief in her tone. "You've lived...but have you been happy?"

I shifted, the weatherworn seat creaking beneath me. "I *have* to make peace with all of this. Even if I have my memories back, that won't restore my Storycraft. It seems foolish to build so much joy around something that can be lost like this...torn away from me like this."

"True. Storycrafting is as fickle as flipping Luck, even with power in the endings again. It can come and go on its own whim, like calling a snooty cat. One day it may bring you joy, and the next, suffering." Ovalia chuckled. "But so can love. So can the labor of your hands, not your lips. So can friendship and parenthood and healing and any sort of craft you might put your mind to." She inclined, elbows on her knees, hands folded around her cup as she pierced me with that severe stare. "You are going to lose things. Have them torn away. But is the joy worth the pain, Miss Addie? It seems a frightfully empty life, to have nothing because someday you will lose something."

Somehow, it didn't feel as if we only discussed Storycraft anymore.

My heart thudded out of rhythm, and I swiped my tongue over my lips. "I don't know when the losing becomes too much. And when it does...am I going to lash out like I did before?" Setting my cup aside, I rubbed gooseflesh from my arms. "The world won't survive being torn again like it was. And I don't think people will stand for that, either."

"Hm." Ovalia's monotone hum welcomed more words—so I gave them.

"What if that's why we haven't found the Storymaker? What if He's furious with me for what I've done?" The fear bubbled hot and sticky on the back of my tongue. "Perhaps He doesn't *want* me to find Him."

Hearing myself speak the words pressed an ancient, ugly bruise on my heart; it stirred up a sense of being unwanted. Unlovable. Almost...

Forgettable. And expendable.

"It seems to me," Ovalia mused when I kept my silence, "that someone who has seen the terrible things a power can do is more likely to wield it gently. And that someone who has witnessed the good and the ill she has already done, as if through another's eyes, would be better equipped to write a more noble journey for herself in the aftermath."

A faint ember of hope pulsed beyond the pain in my chest; swallowing, I reached for my cup again. "I hope so. I truly do."

Because, if I couldn't...

Then did I want my memories back at all?

CHAPTER 38
LOVE LOST

I WOKE THE NEXT morning in a foul mood again. Talk of loss and anger and broken hope stuck through me like bar knives, not to mention the fruitless pursuit of a potential culprit for all of our suffering from the one person who knew Storycraft better than most. If Ovalia didn't know who might've crafted the wraith, no one else would—no one but the person who'd done it, who carried so much hidden resentment and hatred of me that they wrecked lives across Mithra-Sha to reach me.

An inescapable fate, if I didn't know its source. And beneath the tattered shawl of rainclouds far across the meadow, my outlook was equally dour.

I was exhausted—from restless sleep, from the trek, from all our travels since Krylan. And here we were, in another strange place, with strange people...and according to Jaik, the Storymaker's fingerprints were all over Rivrand, in tales told and miracles of healing and help before we'd arrived, but there was no sign of Him.

He'd abandoned us. Again.

Wounded pride made comfortable space for doubt to simmer, like a sauce overthickening. My appetite spoiled; when Jaik asked me to come with him to peruse the town for more sights and signs of the Storymaker, it was an odd blend of pettiness and fatigue that had me refusing. Adamantly.

"What even is the *point*?" I snapped, ripping clothing from my satchel to wash and hurling them into separate piles on my bed; I didn't dare glance at Jaik, though his presence filled up the doorway of the small room like every other shadow of a forgotten past crowding at my heels. "I'd just go with you, and we'd walk ourselves weary in that village, and for what? Just to be given another letter, so we can travel to *another* place, so I can have myself tied in *more* knots? No, thank you...I can wallow just as well *here*."

"Look, I know it's hard," Jaik said as I yanked my satchel shut and tossed it into the upper corner of the bed. "But the Storymaker knows what He's doing, Ayjay."

"Does He? Does He *know* He's driving me mad? Does He know how much all of this is breaking my heart and making me want to tear out my hair?" I spun on him, hands perched on my hips. "Because if He does, Jaik, then I'm not even certain I want to meet Him! I might be tempted to take a swing at His head, with the way I'm feeling today."

A strange sorrow pulled through Jaik's eyes. "Don't do that."

"What? Swing at Him, or say I might?" I flung up my hands. "If He's as wise as you say, I'm certain He already knows I want to! Or He would, if He would stay in one place long enough for us to catch up to Him! But, no, He would rather drag my heart through absolute *filth*, force me to confront everything I was and am and can *never* be again, as if that will somehow make me a better person!"

"You want to talk about getting your heart dragged?" Jaik lurched up from the doorway, shouldering into the small room. "You think this is easy for *me*, tiger? Being out there, looking under every rock, getting my hopes up and then getting them crushed? But I'm still trying—I need you to keep trying, too!"

"Why? Because misery loves its bedfellows?"

"Luck, no! Because I need us to be sure we tried *everything* before we talk about giving up." He slammed a hand backward through his hair. "*I* have to know I tried everything."

"But you might be better off if you didn't!" I dipped a hand to indicate the length of him. "Look at yourself, Jaik...you're run as ragged as me. Why don't we just stop this nonsense and admit that the Storymaker fled Erasure, and keeps fleeing, because He doesn't *want* to be found? At least, not by the likes of us."

Guilt drizzled my tongue like hot honey in the wake of those words—there was not a single flavor of truth in them. But my wounded heart found some cruel pleasure in saying the worst possible thing.

Jaik's jaw squared like a fighting stance. "I don't believe that. I can't. After everything, He's not doing that to *me*. I know He's not just leaving me in the middle of all of this, not when He *knows* what I've got at stake."

"Well, Luck loves you, then, but it still hates me...because I can't be sure He cares about *me* at all!"

"So don't look for Him for yourself. Look because *I* need you to...*I* need us to keep looking for Him, Ayjay."

"Why?" I demanded. "Why are you behaving like you're the one who's suffered so much, the one He's going to change everything for? *I* lost my memories, *I* lost my power, *I* lost the new life I built in Krylan—"

"And I lost my *wife!*"

The thunderous clap of that retort stole all the hearing from my ears. All the breath from my lungs. It stopped the very beat of my heart.

For one moment—two—I was weightless. Untethered from the world.

Then my senses crashed back in a roaring tide, a thundering pulse, a harsh swish of blood, all pushing my breath from me in a choked gasp: "*What?*"

Humorless laughter ruptured through Jaik's gritted teeth, and he palmed both hands back through his hair this time, tying his fingers together at the back of his head. "Flipping Luck...yeah. There it is, Ayjay. I figured you forgot that part after our talk in the tavern in Krylan—"

A book of adventure tales. A soldier's curiosity. That same agonized flicker in the depths of his eyes.

My wife used to love stories like that.

Oh, *Luck*—

I *had* forgotten; when he'd made that offhanded remark, perched on the stool across the counter in the *Pourhouse,* he'd been no one but a legend. Nothing to me. And then, with the truth of our past revealed in a nightlong walk through the winding city streets, to the glittering edge of the Ameresh district and back again, all the way to my door...I'd let that part slip through the seams.

Because *Captain Grissom* could have had any wife, any family, and it would never have mattered to me. He was only a figment of a story from the capital, a gossip scrap come to life, sitting on a barstool. But *this* Jaik—the Jaik I'd sailed with, fought beside, danced with in a meadow, taken to my family, slept beside under the stars—this Jaik I shared a past with, and a present...

I hadn't held onto that small slip of truth about *him*.

About *us*.

My knees buckled. I staggered backward, gripping the bedframe and bowing down to my seat on its edge. "I—we—we were—?"

"I mean, was it completely official? Probably not." A scathing chuckle scratched deep in his chest. "It was sort of thrown together at the last minute, like most of our plans. But we both *meant* it, and you..." He shook his head. Shook free a thread of silver lining his lashes, a bead of dampness scouring down his stubbled cheek and dripping off his jaw. "You went into that Convening Chamber with my ring on your finger."

Shock bolted through me.

The flipping ring.

Luck help me. There *had* been a ring clutched in my fist when I'd woken under a bridge in Vallanmyre, ready to change my life, to rewrite my story...because my head had already been built of new memories. *False* ones.

A family heirloom, I'd thought. A piece I'd sold to begin my new life in Krylan.

Jaik's ring. My *wedding* ring.

A sob rolled up from my throat; I slapped a hand over my mouth, bowing into my bent legs, tears budding in the corners of my eyes. "Oh, no. Oh, *Jaik...*"

"Hey—listen, don't..." He stepped nearer to me, then hitched to a halt. "Ayjay, don't—"

"Why didn't you *tell* me?" The words cracked over a second sob. "When you told me the rest of the story? How could you think I didn't want to *know* I was *married*?"

His throat jerked harshly; he padded to the bed and gripped the opposite corner, lowering himself slowly at my side. "Because it's like you said...you're not her. You were a different woman when you made those vows, and...it didn't feel right. Holding you to them, when you don't remember making them." His gaze slid to me, then darted away again. "And I didn't want you to think I was using it against you."

"To *guilt* me?"

"To force you. Before you were ready. If you ever were."

My breath and my tears stopped all at once, and I could only stare at him, gaping through the gaps in my fingers.

This man...this cocksure, silly, impossible soldier...

He was in love with me. Of that I'd had little doubt since the night he'd told me of our past, though I had rarely allowed myself to dwell on it.

But I hadn't realized the depth, the breadth of that love. The flame he was carrying, a fire stoked close to his heart, sheltered in secrecy and hidden behind scarce touches and fleeting looks that must have meant the world to him...and more.

He loved me enough to let that love be entirely my choice. To hold onto it for himself...but never to allow the flame he bore to burn me.

Even in Krylan, the few times I'd looked twice at strangers in the *Pourhouse* handsome and kind enough to catch my attention, I'd never dared to daydream of a love that powerful.

Under any different circumstances, it would have been so simple to fall into it. To be swept away by it. If there had been no history, no forgotten past.

But then...perhaps that was what we both needed. A sweeping away. A free-fall.

So I shifted nearer, until my leg pressed to the length of his. Until the fire in his chest lit the edges of my world. Until the warmth pulled me in, nearer and nearer; until I could swoop an arm around his back and tug him to rest his head on my shoulder.

"Jaik, with how things have gone, I think we both know...I may never have my memories back." He shuddered a bit in my grip, a resigned rise and fall to the line of his shoulders that rocked through my whole body. "But maybe that's what's wrong with us."

"I don't follow," he said huskily.

"Well, we've both been looking so fiercely for the past...perhaps we're losing sight of what matters. What's right in front of us." I leaned my cheek against his hair. "Jaik, I'm *here*. And you're here. That alone may not be enough to mend what was torn, but isn't it enough to begin writing a new story?"

A slow, careful breath rose up through him, lifting his back in a measured swell; then it slipped free, and his hand slid onto my knee, tightening gently.

"You're right. I've been spending so much time focused on getting your memories back, I haven't been thinking about making new ones with you." He sat up from me, leaning back just enough to swivel and thread a strand of hair behind my ear, and to hold my gaze so fiercely, my stomach danced with butterflies. "So, let's try this: for right now, I'm Jaik Grissom, you're Audra Jashowin...and as far as anyone knows, we met in a tavern in Krylan where you were tending bar, and that's as much of a story as we've got. Now...you want to get out of here and go do something worth remembering for the rest of our lives?"

A grin tore across my face. "I'd *love* to."

CHAPTER 39
JUST STAY

JAIK

I F I'D BEEN A Storycrafter, I probably could've come up with a hundred ways our second day in Rivrand would've gone. And I still wouldn't have come up with this one.

We didn't head to the village at all, just swiped some more bread and cheese from Ovalia's kitchen; then we were heading out toward the mountains, talking about all the bread Audra had made with Lio on *The Cathan* and all these dishes she'd learned to cook at the *Pourhouse*.

She told me more about that place on our hike through the trees than she'd mentioned all the months we'd been riding out this way. What she'd loved about it; what drove her crazy about it. The things she missed and the parts she was glad she didn't have to think about anymore.

While we climbed a steep, stony pass, I told her about being the head of the Sha's retinue and all the soldiers in Vallanmyre...what that was like. How sometimes it was the easiest thing in the world and sometimes the job was so heavy it felt like it was burying me alive. And how when I was there, I couldn't stop thinking about something happening to Arias...but when I was out here, traveling with her, everything was easier.

"Why do you suppose that is?" she mused.

I shrugged, stopping to hold a pine bough out of her way. "Best guess? I got used to being one half of something—sword and story. And while you were gone, there was no one watching my back. So it made it harder to watch his."

She didn't say anything, but I caught her tongue poking out from the corner of her mouth the way it always did when she was really thinking about something.

We ended our hike where the path leveled out: at the top of a waterfall roaring down about twenty feet to a hot spring. Steam curled off the surface like it wanted to wrap around our ankles and pull us down.

"Perfect," Audra grinned. Then she started shucking off her shoes.

"Whoa, whoa—what are you thinking?" I ripped my satchel off and dumped it off to the side.

"I'm thinking that I love to swim, and I haven't done hardly any of it this year." Hastily, she swirled her hair into a knot and bound it with a strip of leather from around her wrist. "So I'm going to make some memories. Are you coming, Jaik?"

And with a mischievous smile, she took a running start and jumped off the edge.

So that was how we did it: made memories with dives and plunges. Went under the waterfall and climbed around for a while, catching rainbows in the palms of our hands. Eating warm bread on the rocky shore and talking about everything. Nothing. The stuff that mattered and the stuff that didn't. Sparring with sticks, until the dance pulled us too close. Until we forgot to pretend we were at each other's throats.

Until it got to the edge of something more and we'd both pull back. Go back to talking, back to something safer.

Or at least, a different kind of dangerous.

"What was it like, being married to me?" Audra asked with her head on my shoulder. We laid ourselves back against the rocks beside the waterfall, angled to watch the sunset, and I ran my fingers through her damp hair, finding my way through all the tangles by touch. Wishing the rest of this was so easy to navigate.

"Best night of my life," I said—and meant it.

"That's all you can say?" she teased, snuggling in closer.

"Hey, what do you want? I was scared out of my mind for most of it." That barely described what my head and heart had been going through when we'd said our vows, knowing she'd rewrite the Tearing—and maybe write me out of the narrative again—the next day. "But it was the night I got to love you the way I always wanted to...not hiding it, not worrying about getting caught, not feeling like loving me was putting your life in danger or the other way around."

She was quiet for a second; then she said the thing we'd both known, deep down, for a long time: "We deserved better."

"You got that right." I rested my cheek on her hair.

We stayed quiet for a while, until the sun slipped out of view; then Audra went to grab her dry clothes, and I sat there soaking up the steam and imagining what it'd be like if this was all we had to do with the rest of our lives. Hot spring swims, hikes, talking about the past and dreaming about the future.

It would probably be nice. Easy.

We'd get bored out of our skulls.

As much as Ayjay and I were made for loving each other...we were made for more than that. For fighting for things and protecting what was ours. For telling stories and living them.

I knew it. And I couldn't help hoping she still felt it, too. Even on hard days like today, when the Storymaker seemed like He was on the other side of the world.

Audra padded back after a while, dropping the satchel beside my hip and folding herself down behind me. Her knees curved in under my armpits. Her arms looped around my chest, and her cheek landed on my shoulder.

"You're so warm," she grumbled. "It's unfair."

"Yeah." My breath puffed out, halfway to a laugh. "Add it to the list, tiger."

She didn't move. Neither did I. Not for a long, long time.

Not until her weight slumped hard on my back. Not until her arms slipped...would've plopped in my lap if I hadn't caught her wrists, holding her arms around me.

Her sleeping breaths whispered on my neck when her head tilted sideways at a funny angle. And just like that, she was asleep...using me for a pillow. Like we'd done this a hundred times.

And we had. Just a hundred times she didn't remember.

But she'd remember this one. And so would I. A day we stopped being a soldier and a former Storycrafter on the hunt for lost memories. A day we were just *us*, and, Luck...that was enough.

I couldn't lose sight of that again. Couldn't lose sight of *her* when I was looking so hard for the Storymaker. I had to find a way to hold onto both...keep us moving without dragging her with her heels dug in. Without leaving her behind.

It was a wild balancing act. But after today, I wasn't about to let it go.

I wasn't letting go of her.

It was the dead of night when I finally carried Ayjay back to Ovalia's cabin—and that was just because I had to, or my hind end was going to freeze to the rock.

Carrying her kicked up a lot of memories...some I was better off without. The way she fit in my arms was just like always—like the times I'd hauled her exhausted out of danger after fights, sword and Storycraft against whatever this country threw at us. Same way she'd fit when I'd carried her to healers in Belaris after I'd stopped the bleeding, and to safety down near the border with Amere-Del after the Del's people had tried to drag her off to his castle—head on my shoulder, breath on my throat, arms around my neck. She'd wrapped them there tonight, too, half-asleep the second I stood us up from the rock.

I wasn't sure how I was going to set her down and walk away, but I needed to start figuring it out; because, before I was even ready, we were coming up the steps to the cabin, and then I was ducking us inside.

I tossed a nod Ovalia's way—curled up under a blanket by the fireplace and shooting me a *look* over those half-moon spectacles of hers. Then I shouldered into Ayjay's room; careful not to move her head any way that would knock her awake, I settled her against the pillow and eased down at her feet. Pulled them into my lap, unlaced her boots, took those off. Tossed them onto her satchel so they wouldn't make any noise. Then I just sat there, rubbing her toes, staring at her sleeping face.

If we could have a hundred nights like tonight, maybe we just needed to start over.

I mean...flipping Luck, she *knew* now. The secret I'd been keeping. And she'd still gone with me today.

That had to count for something. Just wished I knew exactly how much and what for.

But I wasn't ready to give up yet. Not on the Storymaker. If anything, today was proof He was plotting something. Because I wasn't missing how every step down this road brought Ayjay a little closer to her courage, her sass, her strength...everything she was made of. And a little closer to *me*.

Whatever was waiting at the end of it...He had to have something wild up His sleeve. We just had to get there. And get through days like today, when taking that next step made us both feel like we were about to crack in half.

Blowing out a silent sigh, I slid out from under Ayjay's feet and tugged the blanket up over her shoulder; I was about to let go and let myself out when fingers I'd know anywhere wandered up, snagging mine on the edge of the quilt.

"Jaik, stay." Her voice was blurry with sleep—digging itself straight into my middle.

It was a second before I even realized what she'd said. What she *meant*. Then it was a few more before I could catch my breath again.

"Are you sure?" I croaked.

A fluttery, fatigued little smile; then she scooted back, making room for me at the edge of the bed. "Just stay."

Don't argue. Don't ask. Just stay.

Luck, she didn't have to say it twice.

I toed off my boots and slipped under the blanket, rolling over with my back to her. Giving her some space, some privacy.

Her hand found the hinge of my shoulder; she tugged me toward her, and when I let her guide me onto my back, she snuggled into my side. Settled her cheek on my shoulder. Rested her hand over my heart—over the scar itching under my shirt.

I grabbed that hand, played with her fingers—and choked down the biggest lump that'd ever lived in my throat. "Ayjay…"

"Shut your ramble-hole and go to sleep." She nuzzled closer, her voice already fading out against by the last word even before a yawn cut it off.

Smiling knocked something warm and wet loose, slipping down my cheek. "You got it, tiger."

CHAPTER 40
AIM AND LET GO

WAKING IN JAIK'S ARMS should have been one of the greatest new memories I had made yet. It should have been all warmth, and coziness, and even a touch of shyness, with my head over his heart and his heat surrounding me. After the day we'd had before—knowing he was my husband, the first thought that greeted me on the cusp of awake and asleep—perhaps it should have even led to something more.

Unfortunately, I had no time to savor it. None at all.

Because what woke us was not a slow stirring, not a gentle stretch of muscles, not a soft, *Hey there, tiger*.

It was a slamming door that had us jolting apart, bolting up with our hands pressed into the mattress, fingers knocking awkwardly together in the chilly gap between us. It was wide eyes and pounding hearts and a stumbling curse flying off Jaik's lips as we stared, disheveled and half-dreaming, at Ovalia's stern form filling up the doorway.

Her gaze raked over us, then snapped to my face; and I knew at once that the severity of that look could not have anything to do with the position in which she'd found us.

"Trouble in the village," she said.

Another curse against fickle Luck; then Jaik flung off the covers, jamming his feet into his discarded boots and throwing mine my way. "What are we looking at, here? And, flipping Luck, don't say it's—"

"Misspoken manifestations."

The breath rushed from me all at once; my boot dropped to the floor with a dull *clump*. Jaik, too, froze, his hand halfway to his sword. "Tell me that's a joke."

"Captain Grissom, no Storycrafter jokes about such things," Ovalia snapped. "These are beasts that only myth can conjure...I hardly know how to describe them, and you know words do not forsake me. They were howling and shrieking in the hills shortly after your return last night, it's a wonder the pair of you slept through such a ruckus. I'd hoped they would pass us by from a distance, as they've been doing, but a runner's just arrived from the village, terrified out of her boots. She claims they've come down as if something's driven them straight for the village."

Driven them—

My eyes snapped to Jaik's face; he held still for only a moment longer. Then he slapped on his sword belt, starting for the door. "Well, something's about to drive them *back*."

"Jaik." I slid on my other boot, frenetic energy cooling into something that noosed my wrists and ankles, turning every movement sluggish.

Disbelief. Shock that our wildest suspicions seemed about to be proven true, after all.

Fear, thumping in the mostly-healed wounds scattered across my face.

Horror, that it might happen again.

Jaik spun on me, paler than I had ever seen him—or ever *remembered* seeing him. "I'm not letting that thing get close again, tiger."

"To which *thing* are you referring?" Ovalia demanded. "Or are you supposing the wraith, too, is here?"

Jaik palmed the side of his neck. "I don't think Luck loves us enough that it would be anywhere else."

There was something chilling in that my first glimpse of Rivrand proper was a graveyard sort of quiet. The livid tension thrumming the air had me wrapping my fingers more tightly than ever around my dagger, slinking in Jaik's shadow to the outskirts.

Jaik didn't bother with the rifle this time—we both knew it was useless against the Misspoken wraith. Instead he palmed his fire-handled sword, gaze strafing around the village.

"Where *is* everyone?" The bass scrape of his voice ignited something deep in my core—a kindred awareness of just how eerie the silence was.

"I don't know," Ovalia replied, tone equally brittle. We had left the runner who'd brought the news—a girl of barely twelve—at Ovalia's cabin.

Safer, we hoped, than what should have awaited us here.

Except that *here*, on this cool, overcast, foggy morning, there was...nothing. Nothing but the thickness on the air.

No screams. No howls. The village slumbered in repose; when I twisted around, easing in backstep with my shoulders pressed to Jaik's, all I saw were vacant chiminies and communal firepits, a few lonely strands of gossamer spiderweb that drifted from eaves and overhangs.

Though it seemed a bit early for seasonal decorations.

I caught a strand between my fingers as the damp wind teased it past me. "*Sinister Sundown* preparations?"

Ovalia seized my wrist in a bony-fingered grasp like a vise; even her rich brown skin sapped of hue. "*No.*"

And then, the first scream.

A scream I *knew*—that piercing, otherworldly wail that had deafened me in our room in Belaris. That had proceeded a horror like none I'd ever known.

And somehow, down to the marrow of my bones, I *knew* it...knew what it was as if I had uttered the shout from my own lips.

"It's a battle cry!" Tearing from Ovalia's grip, I whirled to stand beside Jaik—to behold what that scream unleashed against us.

Spiders.

They emerged from over and behind every home, every forge, every shop—fanged, bloodstained beasts, some still carrying the bodies of Rivrand's people bound up in silk threads from their bulbous, cratered, rotting abdomens. Eight eyes to a head, multiplied and multiplied and *multiplied*, hundreds of pitted, ember-like fires gleaming in their horrific faces.

Carnivorous spiders, more and more of them scrambling over the village rooftops, ripping up the thatching and wooden boards with their taloned legs like serrated daggers, skittering our way. Every one was at least half the size of the buildings they rambled over—and some were not entirely spiders at all.

Beast heads and clawed arms and *human torsos* wove out from their bulging thoraxes, white-eyed faces still with eight dripping sockets, their overlong jaws slack with soundless screaming. Even those dripped blood from their chins and teeth, hissing and snarling as they advanced.

My bowels threatened to empty.

"Back, back, back!" Jaik elbowed me behind him as he sheathed his sword and swung his rifle from his shoulder. Ovalia retreated as well, weapon in hand, a battle cry of her own tearing from her chest and booming through the stricken village:

"Let me tell you a story!"

And all at once, the stillness broke in a cacophony of chaos—bellowed words, power like a lightning strike raising the hair on my arms; thunderous rifleshot, the blur of Jaik's hands as he loaded, racked, and fired, over and over, bringing down abomination after abomination with deft shots to their humanoid or bestial heads.

But with every one that fell to a shot, more spilled into the gaps, forcing us to retreat, and retreat again—until my back struck the side of a house and I rebounded, slamming into the broad planes of Jaik's back. He stumbled a half-step, then righted himself, loading, racking, aiming—and cursing as a disjointed human arm cleaved in from the left, smashing the rifle muzzle and ripping the weapon from his hands.

I lunged, grabbing for the stock as it whipped past me; the heft of it crunched a bruising blow across my palm, and then it was gone, tumbling into the muddy streets.

Jaik swore and spun on Ovalia and me, his eyes cutting to her first. "You think you can circle around, try to draw out and bring down that wraith?"

"No Misspoken manifestation can survive Storycraft," she seethed. "And it certainly will not survive *mine.*"

"Good. Go!" She was gone in a wrench of her currant-red cloak, before I could even beg her to be careful; then Jaik seized my shoulders, pushing me back beneath the eaves. "Stay here!"

Terror ripped along my spine. "Jaik—"

"You stay *here!*" He whipped his sword back from its sheath and spun it deftly in one hand as he whirled to meet the converging manifestations.

Dozens of them. Screaming, shrieking, chittering, howling horrors spoken to life by a forgotten craft.

Bile sweated in my mouth. A violent retch jammed in the base of my throat.

"*Come on!*" Jaik bellowed—and lunged to meet them with a reckless courage I would never possess. That let him run from me when all I wished was that he would stay.

So *I* stayed, and he went to war. Against these beasts forged of some story I dared not imagine, that had made them vessels of venom and viciousness against which no man could be a match.

But Jaik fought and felled them in a hailstorm of ichor and cracking carapaces, in a mess of animal howls and human screams. He battled brutally against creatures beyond mortal reckoning, an unstoppable force unto himself.

The Captain I'd heard so many tales of in the *Pourhouse...this* was the man they'd spoken of. The one who'd knit swordplay and Storycraft together, to erase abominations like these from our country's narrative forever.

He was a soldier—among the best Mithra-Sha had ever seen. He was the Sha's bodyguard, head of the army in Vallanmyre.

He was *Jaik. My* Jaik, cocksure, silly, sweet, and savage in his own right. And I did not need a lifetime's worth of memories to know that against this many Misspoken manifestations, he could only stand his ground so long.

I did not have the Storycraft Ovalia possessed...I had only a dagger and a dance.

And I had Jaik. And he *needed* me.

Hitching back my terrified breaths, I gripped the dagger in both hands. I centered my posture, squared my shoulders, leaned into the might of my muscles—just like Jaik had taught me.

And I danced.

A feint to the left-hand side, dodging a spidery leg that slipped past Jaik's waning guard and speared toward me; a lunge forward, bringing the dagger up and back in a cleaving arc that struck *something*—

Gelatinous ooze sprayed my arm. The spider clicked and cried out, rearing as it stumbled backward, gashed through the chest by the Luck-loved sweep of my knife.

I dared not hesitate; I flung myself at the gap between its eight razor-tipped legs, twisting and whirling out into the narrow span where Jaik did battle against far, far too many Misspoken manifestations.

They were everywhere, clawing and bobbing up along the homes and winding toward us on silksteel threads, or scuttling by the pull of their human-hands, upside-down in the advance.

I gave myself no time to think, to hear, to feel. I jabbed and dragged, jabbed and dragged, only dimly aware of the relief that these ravenous horrors were not skilled in swordplay. I'd have been no match for them then; my only advantage lay in the months Jaik and I had danced these steps, and the feral instinct that set me apart from these beasts I battled.

Jab and drag. Jab and drag. Every step bringing me closer to Jaik, until we were feet apart. One chittering, jolting revulsion left between us.

Screaming my fury, my exhaustion, my fear, I plunged my dagger into its abdomen with all my might—then screamed again, a pitch so high it tore my throat as the creature wheeled on stumbling legs, cracking its jointed hinges against my side. I stumbled, the muddy village streets slick with blood, and tumbled to one knee.

A bellow split the air—Jaik, shouting my name like the sundering of the world at its very seams.

Coarse, scraping weight crashed over me, the spider's blade-tipped feet jabbing into the soil on either side of my head. It loomed above me, pincers dripping venom, pasty gray flesh of its humanoid torso oozing tarry blood as it plunged its hands toward my throat.

Silver shimmered. The flat of a blade twisted between us, the vibration of fang on metal jarring through my whole frame, stuttering the rhythm of my heart.

Jaik spun up off a knee beside us, shrieking blade on bone, jerking the spider's human head his way. Steel plunged through flesh, hammering the beast between its eyes, and as it reared and squealed and thrashed in the throes of death, I plunged my hands into the dirt and shoved myself backward, scrambling to evade its flailing limbs.

"You all right?" Jaik shouted—then broke off with a blistering howl of pain as a bulging body swung in from the left and collided with him, flinging him away from me.

"*Jaik!*" I grabbed wildly for him, but my fingertips raked to bleeding against needle-sharp abdomen hairs instead as the spider whipped past and landed with a horrific squelch, smothering Jaik under its weight.

Cursing, I staggered to my feet; the spider pinned Jaik in the cage of its legs, and though steel flashed, no killing blow sent the creature reeling.

It held him pinned; and my hands were empty, my dagger gone—

The rifle.

It still lay in the mud, kicked aside at the base of the town's well.

Staggering upright, I hurtled toward it, dodging swipes from more slavering arachnids.

A wild *boom* shook the earth. T the south, a curtain of shadow spiraled high as smoke, blotting out the sun for an instant; the spiders recoiled in the loft of shadows, but I didn't allow myself to hesitate.

Sliding on my knees, I snatched up the rifle and slammed my back to the well. Twisting on my haunches, I dared to peer over it.

Who knew *what* Ovalia had crafted with her story on her way around to the wraith; but now they dueled in sparks of liquid lightning and formless void, every slam of their power against each other knocking my heart out of rhythm.

We had to help her. But first—

I lunged to my feet, rifle stock jammed into dip of my shoulder, racking the shot into place just as I'd watched Jaik do—but I had no clear shot on the spider that held him trapped.

So I stepped backward instead—up onto the rim of the well.

A strange, liquid familiarity coated my bones, guiding the heft and swivel of my arms. For a moment it was as if hands slid beneath my elbows, gripped my hips, strengthened my stance and swiveled my muscles.

It's easy. You just aim—

Breath dropped down, down, to the base of my lungs...and held there.

And squeeze?

My sights found the spider's rearing, thrashing head that dodged the slim silver strafe of Jaik's sword.

And let go.

A trigger click. A puff of air.

The rifle erupted, jamming backward into my shoulder, nearly flinging me off the well—but in the same instant, the spider's head burst in a bloodied shower. It slumped forward, burying Jaik beneath its weight; his pained bellow burst louder than the rifleshot. It deafened me. It deadened the world in the silence that followed.

A tinny ringing fizzed in my ears; hurling the rifle stock into the mud, I lunged down from the well and tore across the village proper, slamming my shoulder full force into the spider's contorted carapace. It bowled over, legs crooking inward in a ghastly spasm, fangs jutting skyward like a defiant flag waved.

Beneath it, Jaik slumped, one hand over his middle, chest heaving for breaths. His other arm, outcast, still held his sword.

"*Jaik?*" I fell against him, hauling at his hand. "Jaik, let me see—!"

"M'fine," he slurred. "Just knocked the wind out of—"

Agony exploded through my ankle, snapping up as high as my hip—and then I was gone, ripped away from Jaik, his fingers snagging and slipping through mine between one breath and the next.

The world skimmed, skidded by, my chest barely brushing the ground as I flew backward through the village, my ankle roped by something that seared like *fire*—

And then, darkness.

Darkness absolute and incarnate.

I was falling again.

CHAPTER 41
HOW THIS ONE ENDS

*W*HAT DO YOU THINK *you know of sacrifice? Your service is not sacrifice—it is for the greater good.*

We've given enough—

We have to do this.

I plummeted forever through the shadows.

I have to mend the Tearing. I have to make this right.

Close your eyes, Jaik. Let me tell you a story.

I knew nothing of sky from earth, head from feet—right from wrong.

All I ever do is lose you.

Lose myself.

Forgotten. Cast out. Expendable.

We have no daughter named Audra Jashowin.

Stone slammed my knees. My head jerked up.

The world was still vast, endless shadow, but I no longer fell through it. I knelt on it, crumbled before it.

Before the wraith.

It glided toward me on reaching and retracting vines of utter darkness, tendrils of smoke that reeked of decay and despair. Its textured, slouched frame guttered as it glided toward me, and the fiery heart still pulsed visibly between its emaciated ribs.

I jerked backward, and pain erupted through my shoulders as smoldering shadow manacles bound my wrists, jerking me down into a slump again before the creature.

"You did this!" I cursed it, wrenching against its hold. "You brought those creatures here, attacked this village, *all* of those towns—*why?*"

Its arms rose, hands smoothing back along the vague definition of its cheekbones, its temples, down its shoulders. In the sunken pits of its skeletal countenance, twin pools of fire ignited—eyes cleaving straight to mine.

And when they did, it was as if it launched a blade through my chest.

Fear etched itself on each of my bones.

Fury inked the edges of my every exhale.

Disbelief twisted my tongue to a hopeless knot.

Grief wrote itself on the face of my heart.

Hatred consumed me.

"What *are* you?" I seethed, pressing my knuckles into the cracked shadow-stone beneath me.

A withered arm extended, sleeve falling back to bare a pocked, webbed, rotting arm of pure dark flesh, like spoiled ink; a grisly hand, every finger sharp as one of those spider's talons, cupped my chin, clawed tips pricking blood from my jaw.

Let me tell you a story—

A cacophony of disjointed impressions flashed across my eyes like searing sunlight.

A tavern dripping in flowers. A broken window. A rifle aimed at my face. A lamppost glazed in deep violet tones. A wild white horse. A snowy forest—a towering skeleton and slavering hounds lit with the same inner fire as the wraith—as the skeletons aboard *The Cathan*—

Unbearable pressure built in my head, tumbled down my throat, poured out of my mouth. A scream, endless, eviscerating, as the impressions scrawled themselves on my mind faster than I could even begin to understand them.

Snowfall. Starlight. Lamplight. Gold coins, cities awash in color, ocean waves, a hundred, a *thousand* scarlet threads tying the world together—

Help me, Jaik—help me—please!

Memory—voice—which was it? Had my scream found words?

Wood varnished in blood. Dozens of eyes—familiar, somehow—watching me with regret and grief and anguish.

Piercing, consuming cold. A world of gold. Blood. Tears. Regret on top of regret on top of—

Breath on my middle. Hands on my back.

This is how we fix it.

I'm dying to hear how this one—

Shadows *exploded*.

Daggered shards of darkness tore past, whipping me off my knees, slamming me flat on my back; for an instant, the wraith loomed above me, its talons sunk into my jaw, its fiery eyes and burning inferno of a mouth both agape. Piercing me through to the heart...pinning me as surely as if it had run me through.

Another wave struck it—a wave of pure, iridescent light, and it burst into a thousand smoky filaments.

The pain in my jaw vanished; lurching up onto my elbows, I rolled over in the sopping mud of Rivrand's streets and choked back bile as I watched it go.

Disseminated. But not destroyed. Its tendrils unspooled in a ravel of ink to the outskirts of Rivrand proper—where they met another wave of light, and darted into the encroaching forest.

The light did not dissipate; it crystallized, a shimmering barrier of rippling opalescent brilliance that veined and spidered overhead, forging a fragile web of blinding daylight.

And nothing hurt worse than the assault of that pearlescent glow pouring across my face, sizzling like flame held to flesh. I buried my face in my forearm, nausea cracking against the side of my skull over and over, blood sliding wet and oily against my jawline.

A hand on the back of my head. Then another, prying my chin up from the bend of my elbow. "I know it hurts, Ayjay, but you've got to look at me—I need to see you, all right?"

For that voice—and only that voice—I braved the agony of the searing light after such deep shadow. With several harsh blinks, I managed to squint in the glowing aura—and when I cranked my head to the side, at first I saw only blood.

Deep red, blood-red, pouring between my fingers—

"You're hurt," I whispered, fumbling my hand free from beneath my body to touch the weeping gash on Jaik's middle. "Liar."

"I'm not the one who was screaming for help." His voice shook as he caught my hand, guiding it down from his torso. "Flipping Luck, Ayjay, I'm so sorry."

"Get her on her feet, Captain Grissom." That voice—sure and strident—had I ever heard it so undercut with exhaustion?

I pried myself to my knees, every muscle aching, my throat a sore mess...but I wanted to face her on my own strength as she approached us.

Ovalia strode through the wreckage at the outskirts of Rivrand, one hand still extended where she had directed the power of her Storycraft to go. Behind her, a vivid currant hem trailed on a wind of her own making...not quite the scarlet of the Master Storycrafter's legendary cloak, but the closest I'd ever seen.

This woman whose light had sent the shadows running. Whose story had shaped a barrier, a bastion around her home. Who walked with her head erect though her chest heaved, whose hands were in fists though they trembled to the shoulders.

She had done this. Saved us. Her *Storycraft* had done that.

Insatiable hunger panged in the base of my throat; I had the absurd urge to touch her cloak, to run its hem through my fingers.

To see if a bit of that color would leech into my aching, swollen hands.

I tucked those away between my knees, fighting that urge when she paused beside us. "Are you all right?" I mumbled instead.

The Headmistress huffed, folding her arms over her narrow chest. "I will be after a good rest. I am entirely too old for the sort of adventure tales that power demands, Luck smile on me."

"But you did it." Jaik rested a hand on my back, rubbing slow circles as if he needed the contact to ensure himself I was still there. "You turned that thing into *tatters*."

Ovalia's eyes met mine—a quiet confirmation that felt oddly kindred. A questing glance to confirm I had seen—and ascertained—what she had as well.

"It wasn't destroyed," I croaked. "Just...dissolved. For now."

"I'm afraid it will return." Ovalia waved a vague hand skyward. "Hence this barrier. Light seems to repel such a shadow-crafted being, however—"

"You can't keep it up forever."

Ovalia slowly shook her head. "A thing Storycrafted of a tangible element—stone, wood, glass, even—such a thing can endure beyond the tale teller's might. But light is a tricky thing, just as shadow is. Not entirely corporeal."

Jaik fell back from his heels to his haunches. He stared unseeing at the distant forest where the creature had vanished. "So, you're telling me that *Misspoken manifestation* is—?"

"Impervious to Storycraft." Ovalia's tone deadened, robbed of all strength at once, touched by a horrified sort of wonder I never wanted to hear again. "Two tales I told to trap and end it...neither was its undoing. I served as Headmistress in Fablehaven more than half my life, Captain Grissom, and I will tell you this...in no lore book or ancient tome I ever read has such a thing been recorded."

Hopeless dread burned like crackling kindling behind my eyes.

There was no doubt anymore—that wraith held sway with its Misspoken kin. It could influence them, somehow...guide and direct them to hunt its same prey. And that meant wherever we went now, whatever manifestations had not yet been brought down by the coalition of soldiers and Storycrafters...

They could be weaponized against us by a creature even Storycraft was useless to kill.

And I had no doubt it *would* try again. The creature's hatred and fury still cloaked my skin like embers and char. Grief and despair sank down into my lungs in a fine sifting of ash, threatening to finish what the creature's fingers had begun around my throat back in Belaris. My breaths staggered and stacked atop one another like erratic quill loops, tightening with every cursive curl.

"The villagers?" Jaik's question only dimly touched my ears.

"Some fallen, no doubt." Ovalia's answer was equally and oddly distant. "The blood—but see the webbing over certain doors? Perhaps they trapped—to consume later—"

"Ayjay? Ay—whoa!"

Jaik's shout was the last thing I heard before I fell into darkness of a different sort—the blissful black nothing of unconsciousness.

CHAPTER 42
FAILING BY FLEEING

JAIK

I T WAS HALF AN hour before Ayjay came to—and a lot longer before she stopped shaking.

Even after I helped her to Ovalia's cabin, checked the punctures on her face, then helped her get a hot bath going and took watch at the door. Even after Ovalia came back and told us she'd gotten the villagers out who were still alive, and the barrier was still holding up…Ayjay just kept shivering.

I knew a little what she was thinking; I could see it in her eyes, in the way she was hugging her knees to her chest and resting her chin on them while she stared out the washroom window. So I sprawled out with my back to the door, rifle across my lap, and used some of the needle and thread Naomi had sent me off with to fix the gash on my side—just to keep my hands busy.

It wasn't even that deep. But it had slowed me down—enough that I hadn't grabbed Ayjay before that *thing* had dragged her off and did Luck-knew-*what* to her underneath that blanket of shadow.

Not even a blanket. More a barrier, a lot like Ovalia's. Something as strong as Storycraft. Something had kept me *out* even when I'd been shooting and swinging at it, too wild to even *think*, hearing her screaming for help through it.

She hadn't told me yet, either. What it was doing to her. It had to be more than cuts on her face, because she'd gone tearing through Belaris with me after a lot worse.

But now she was just sitting there. Staring out the window.

For lucking *hours*.

I snipped off the thread, gave my side another douse in disinfectant—Luck, I could've sworn Noni picked the stingiest stuff just to make me miserable—then ripped my focus to the bathtub when I heard a mutter.

Ayjay was frowning at the barrier poking above the treetops, her lips framing words I could barely pick out.

Dying to see how this one—

Something twisted up in my stomach. "What are you mumbling over there?"

She jolted, water sloshing, and shook her head. "Nothing. Will you hand me a towel?"

I grabbed one off the hook behind the door, swirled it around my fist, and lobbed it her way; then I closed my eyes to give her some privacy while she toweled off.

Finally, footsteps padded across the floor. She sank down beside me, arm-to-arm, and I could feel she'd finally stopped shaking.

"What do we do now?" she whispered.

I let my eyes open, but kept looking at the low-beam ceiling. "The way I figure, if the Storymaker was here, He would have done something to stop what happened today. So we're either too early or too late to catch Him...and either way, we can't stay."

"Unless He *is* here, somewhere nearby, and He wanted to see what we would do about the wraith."

"Yeah. Maybe." I couldn't forget He'd waited me out in Erasure to see if I'd scale the tower on my own before He'd given me a hand. "But I don't know if that's a risk we can take. Ovalia scared that thing off, and she's holding it at bay with the barrier, but—"

"We saw what it took from her to forge it. If the wraith returns with *more* of those abominations, it might be more than Ovalia can manage." Ayjay hugged her arms around herself, leaning back against the door beside me. "But what if He *is* here, Jaik? What if we're *this* close?"

"Then we just have to hope He gets why we're going." I shrugged. "That He'll find us again."

She turned her cheek to the door, peering at me with earnest, exhausted eyes. "And if this is a test, and we're failing it by fleeing?"

"Ayjay, listen..." I pulled my legs up and shifted on my seat to face her. "We're not doing anyone any favors by staying. We're just going to make more trouble for this village, and that's not right, either. They went through enough today."

"Then what now? We don't have a note follow this time."

At least I'd already thought out this part while she was soaking, so I could offer her more than bad news. "I know somewhere we can go—somewhere a lot more fortified than this. Better for facing the kind of clout these manifestations are swinging. I'd feel a better about bringing trouble with us there than just about anywhere."

She pulled in a deep breath, then rushed it out, blowing a bead of water from the tip of her nose. She didn't say anything.

My gut twisted up in a knot. "Unless you're not wanting to keep going."

Her head jerked up. "What?"

"I mean, Ayjay, look at what just happened. You know, back in Vallanmyre, our friends were right...all of this started when we went after the Storymaker. Maybe if we stop looking, the attacks stop, too."

Audra rubbed her arms. "You truly think one is happening because of the other?"

"It didn't start until you left Krylan with me."

A line cut between her brows. "Tell me you aren't blaming yourself."

Luck, she knew me too well, even like this. "All I'm saying is...you keep getting hurt. You keep being *hunted*. I would get it, if you wanted to lay off the chase."

And maybe I'd sleep easier at night, too. But I wasn't going to have her making any kind of choice because of me, because of how *I* felt. Not when I was the one who'd dragged her into this in the first place.

She swiped her knuckles against the clotted punctures on her jaw like they were just inkspots she could wipe off. "What was the point of any of this—what we and others have suffered—if I just walk away now?"

"I don't know about you, but to me, a choice isn't really a choice unless you know what it is you're choosing," I shot back. "So, you came with me...you saw what's out here, what's waiting outside of Krylan. You *know* what you're saying no to. This way, you've got no regrets, no second-guessing. You know what you got yourself into and what you got out of, and that's...that's how you make a clean break."

Her eyes jumped up to mine. "A clean break from what, precisely? From you?"

"Luck, I hope not." I slipped a hand around the back of her neck, rubbing my thumb on the dip at the base of her skull. "Ayjay, you were *everything* with Storycraft...and you're everything you were back then without it, too. This isn't about making you back into a whole person. You can be that, with or without your stories. Your memories. It's about whether you can be *happy* without them. And...safe. Because I don't want you dying for this."

"I'm afraid that wraith won't stop even if *I* stop looking for my memories." The words were barely louder than whispering, and Ayjay craned her head back into my touch. "When it had me today, Jaik, and back in Belaris—"

She broke off. Swallowed so hard, it made her collarbones jump and her shoulders arch.

"I don't want to hear it if you don't want to tell me." Biggest lie I'd ever given her.

She shook her head, stayed quiet for a minute; then she murmured, "I don't know what it's usually like, with Misspoken manifestations. But every time this one touches me, I can *feel*...so many things. So much rage, so much *revulsion*, so much terror and sorrow, it's as if those things are trying to corrupt me. After Belaris, I was able to ignore it, for the most part."

Oh, Luck. I didn't like the way that sounded.

"So...what about this time?" I nudged when she didn't say anything.

Biting on her bottom lip, Ayjay smoothed her hands over the towel draped on her cocked knees. "I've been sitting in here for hours trying to fit my hands around those feelings. Trying to push them down. But it's still there, Jaik...it feels like drowning."

"Hey." I slipped an arm around her shoulders, and she leaned against me, head so heavy on my shoulder it was like she'd dropped unconscious again. Only this time, I could feel her fighting off the shivers.

"This isn't just about looking for the Storymaker," she murmured. "That wraith won't stop. I could feel how much it despised me...that it *wanted* me to suffer."

All right, that monstrosity had just earned the top spot on my list of things to kill.

I just needed to figure out how to *do* it, since Storycraft was out.

"So you want to keep going?" I didn't really know what answer I was hoping for; I just knew whatever it was, I'd follow her to the edge of the world and then step off it. Like always...every version of our story.

"I want to go where you think it's safe."

I couldn't promise safe—not after what we'd tangled with today.

But at least I could promise better than a massacre.

CHAPTER 43
WHAT ONCE WAS EVERYTHING

A T DAWN, OVALIA SENT us off with our satchels restocked, with a warning to keep to the lower passes to avoid landslides and early snowstorms and the Misspoken manifestations which had sunk their roots into the higher peaks to avoid the Sha's coalitions. And to Jaik, she offered a scrap of power that left her breathless in her rocking seat on the porch: a Storycrafted lantern of vivid, blazing light—a fresh bloom of the same sort that had sent the wraith on the run. That had quite possibly saved my life.

A terror that had kept me awake much of the night.

"It won't last forever," she warned us. "No more than the barrier would. So ride quickly, and dally for nothing."

"You've got that right," Jaik muttered, clipping the lantern on his belt. "Appreciate it."

To me, Ovalia offered a parting embrace; swift, trembling with the strain of all we had both endured, but gentle and full of such unspoken feeling that my throat ached for it.

"I have always known you were gifted, Miss Addie," she murmured against the shell of my ear. "But to have faced what you have, and to still seek a redeeming of sorts for the woman you were, and are, and have yet to become...that is precious. It was truly an honor to be a part of your becoming."

The words lingered as we rode away, led by Jaik's map and his knowledge of this slice of the Vensair Mountains. As we went, it was him who told *me* stories...of times past in this span of Mithra-Sha, which had been a frequent haunt of ours.

Villages we traveled by, to whom we had long ago brought aid. Dams built and blockades gutted by the power of storytelling or the might of soldiering. Jaik pointed to places where the landscape itself had been altered by our work, and to homes and spaces where people lived and thrived because of us.

Because of *me*. Because of that power I had once possessed...the power Ovalia had demonstrated in saving Rivrand.

It was if our fingerprints were impressed on this swath of the country...a swath that, until months ago, had been a corner of a map even my eyes rarely visited when I found it on bulletin boards in Krylan. And that I had certainly neither memory nor ambition of ever setting foot across for myself.

But now, in so many ways...it was beginning to feel like a part of me.

It seemed only fair—only fitting—that rain returned with our ascent to the chillier, higher passes. As if the Vensair Mountains were determined to offer us the same welcome we'd been so glad to cast off after Belaris...to remind us what had befallen us there.

And with that memory, the rumors floated to us on the wind.

It came first from peddlers we shared the path with, wide-eyed and scurrying, glances cast back perpetually over their rounded shoulders; and then from soldiers whose presence began to thicken, surging from outposts along our shared border with Hadrass-Drui to patrol the forests with keen eyes and clenched hands wrapping their blades and rifles.

We traveled with pockets of them here and there, just long enough for Jaik to flash his title and take reports, and always it was the same tale: that Misspoken manifestations were being spotted nearer and nearer to the cities and civilizations that dotted the mountain range. They were behaving strangely, rallying and circling, then *waiting*—and then, all at once, attacking.

The same pattern as the skeletal crews that had sacked the two fleet ships before finding us aboard *The Cathan*.

Like nothing they had ever seen, the soldiers all claimed. And I wished *we* hadn't seen it before—because seeing made me feel no more prepared for the threat it posed, when Jaik and I peeled off from another contingent of soldiers beneath the dusky veil of falling rain...having heard the same story all over again.

"So, this thing is *smart*," Jaik growled, brushing damp hair from his brow and squinting down the trail. "It's choosing its targets, all right."

My knuckles popped with strain as I gathered the reins snug to my belly, glancing on either side of the path at the wavering shadows that changed shape beneath the racing storm. "Places we've been?"

"Got it one." Jaik shook his head. "Makes sense. Belaris first, then Rivrand, where Ovalia's living, now it's hitting all these places we helped in the past. Either that thing, or the Storycrafter who made it...they know what matters to us."

Perhaps the Audra I'd once been could have fathomed that...thought her way through it. Perhaps she'd known her craft with such intimate familiarity that she could surmise how someone forged this abomination that meticulously minced its way through the mountains, seeking us wherever we might be impressed upon to travel...where we had traveled *before*.

But I wasn't her. All I had was disbelief and fear rotting in my heart as we rode, tarring my insides with the same terror I'd faced when that creature had shackled me in Rivrand.

Just what precisely had I done to someone that they would craft a wraith so powerful and so cruel that it ransacked its way through the country, all in the interest of finding *me*? Who had dared to dream up such a ruthless creation that it made *other* Misspoken beasts tremble...that they would *heed* it, giving purpose to what was created without it?

And that purpose...

"Jaik, all these towns it's attacking..." I nearly choked on the words—on the implications of the terror and suffering that flared out from our very footsteps through these mountains. "You know it's trying to draw us out."

"Yeah. So we've gotta hole up." Determination etched every line of his face as he gathered the reins, urging Kova ahead. "I know a place we can wait it out for a couple days, give it a chance to get ahead of us...somewhere built to keep Misspoken manifestations out. It's about a day's ride...we can make it if we push."

That day of riding proved to be among the worst days of my life.

Tension strained in my temples and throbbed through the center of my head like a bar rag wrung out and yanked in opposite hands; I could barely bring myself to blink, watching every shadow for a hint of ember-hearted threat. And there were *plenty* to watch as we jogged through the might of the Maker's weather, navigating slick uphill lurches and slurry downhill slides, past perilous mountain crags and sopping fields and questionable caves. Several of those dangled a sinister promise of shelter in their shadowy depths...and the possibility that the wraith might come alive from within.

Was it *made* of shadows? Did it *come* from shadows—*any* shadows?

I didn't know. And I didn't dare risk it.

Just after dawn, Jaik finally slowed our footweary pace, and I dared to blink my itching, aching eyes; we'd reached a sharp vee in the path where it jutted into the midst of a pair of streams. An ancient landslide had scooped handfuls of stone and snapped trees over the water, forging something like a makeshift lean-to.

Fresh, flowing water, and shelter from the rain that didn't seem inhabited by animals. A dearth of darkness while the world lightened to a misty gray.

And Jaik, his silhouette carved of waxing light as he took in the forking streams, the clusters of stone and toppled pines. "I think I know where we are."

For another quarter-hour, we pushed on through the storm, twisting down a game trail until all at once, it wove out and broadened into a span of open rock. Grass furred the edges of the cropping, and to our right, a waterfall tumbled over stones to fill a pool just large enough for bathing.

And straight across from the game trail, the most glorious sight of all: another cabin.

My breath caught as I stared at it: rich red wood, a brickstone chimney, dark windows. A rick of wood covered against the side. A hitching rail and lean-to for the horses.

"What is this place?" It felt as if it had been plucked from one of those dreams I never could quite recall.

"Outpost. Sort of." Jaik's tone was as quiet as mine—nearly breathtaken. "There's little cabins like this all through the Vensair Mountains, like Ovalia's probably used to be, too...for soldiers and the Sha's people to use. But no one else knows about this one...Tobyrus Lothar thought it got swept off in a landslide."

"Why did he believe *that*?"

A flicker of a smile touched his mouth. "Because that's what we told him happened to it. So we'd have one place in Mithra-Sha where we could be our-selves...be together without worrying about someone finding us and reporting to him."

A blush dappled my cheeks, tingling with the cold that soaked through my skin. "*Oh.*"

Jaik nudged Kova forward, taking in the cabin from front and side. "This one's built special...*you* rebuilt it with your Storycraft. Made it impervious to attacks...and it's got a warning system in place. Misspoken manifestations used to run these mountains a lot, so you set up bells and whistles to warn us if anything came close."

An ache settled in my chest, hard and gritty as a pebble biting in the sole of a shoe, at the admiration and affection with which he spoke of the woman I'd been before. A woman capable of such feats to defend us...when all *I* could offer was a dagger in my hand. And barely that.

Jaik didn't seem to notice that small resentment turning my exhausted yawns to a scowl. With a jerk of his head, he led the way to the cabin. "Let's get inside before anything catches us, huh?"

We untacked swiftly, rubbed the horses down, then carried the saddles and bags to the cabin; Jaik opened the door without a key, but with a swift pattern of twists to the doorknob that seemed like pure muscle memory. And then we were inside, dripping rainwater all over the floor of the loveliest log cabin I had ever seen.

Exposed beams hung low over the entrance and the broad doorway to the kitchen and dining area. Across from us, the ceiling vaulted upward to embrace the height of the smooth river-rock fireplace and to encompass the staircase winding up from our left to the open balcony stretching out over the room. I spotted two doors—one I suspected was a bedroom, the other a washroom.

Jaik strode to the fireplace, tossing his satchel and saddlebags on one of the sofas with a puff of dust and snatching up a log in each hand from the basket on the edge of the hearth. "You get the bedroom. I'll take the couch, keep an eye on things down here."

I fidgeted at the threshold, discomfort easing in for the first time since our departure from Vallanmyre; he moved with the ease of familiarity, of a routine...something I had once been part of and to which I was a stranger now.

"I can fix supper," I offered. Something to do...something to occupy my mind besides thoughts of ransacked cities and wraiths on the road.

"Sounds great." Jaik flashed a smile over his shoulder, then returned his focus to the flue.

I retreated up the stairs, not even one emitting so much as a creak beneath my sopping feet, and crossed the balcony to the second door.

The washroom beyond was simple, only a basin sink and a clawfooted tub. But the sight of it reminded me so sharply of a certain, much smaller washroom in Belaris that I hastily retreated and let myself in through the other door instead.

This bedchamber was modest: a single bed with a broad, short, and empty bookcase abutting the foot of it, slanting roofbeams, a wide window with a recessed sill ushering in a lovely view of the evergreens and the teeth of the mountains glinting dully through the storm.

I shouldered off my own burden onto the bed, reaching to stroke its thick duvet on my way to the window—

An echo of sensation whipped through me: the press of lips on mine. A hand hitching around my hip. Falling into a swirl of sheets, mouth-to-mouth, fingers tangled in hair—

Heat exploded through my chest, dizzying in its contrast to the chilly damp, and I gripped the bedpost for balance. With a few blinks, a few swift headshakes, the notions vanished; but the bruising sensation lingered on my mouth and tingled across my tongue.

Not merely a bruise...an impression like light trapped behind my eyes. A feeling like being loved and longed for. Like belonging so absolutely, it had redefined the very course of my life.

And when I blinked, it brought back the image of Jaik's face...dancing in the meadows and fields of Mithra-Sha. Our time in Fallshyre Bay. Our encounter in the washroom in Belaris and the way he'd stood his ground against that Misspoken abomination to free me. His face, sometimes the only light in the dark of the mountain tunnels. The way he'd found my gaze at my parents' table, in the halls of the Shastah. How he held my hand when I craved courage; how he let me be the tide that carried us, and him the wheel that steered our course.

The echo in my chest, and the sensations of those memories we'd gathered over the last handful of months...they were the same.

And, flipping *Luck*...that echo tantalized in its faded roar. It made me feel wild and free and craving and curious.

This place *I* had helped fashion...I had built it for us. Free of consequence and corruption. Untouched by the world beyond.

There was nowhere better to wonder. To hope. To *dream*.

Or...to do.

It was several minutes before I could catch my breath and scaffold my heart with that newfound courage; before I could bear to leave the room and pad downstairs, boots toed off, socks squelching a bit on the descent.

I found Jaik where I'd left him: at the fireplace, its contents crackling merrily now. His hands were spread on the mantel, his head bowed beneath his shoulders.

Trembling shoulders. A defeated stoop to his entire frame.

Hugging my elbows tightly to myself, I crossed the room to stand behind him, searching for words, for questions—for distractions.

None came.

I bit my lips together, a memory of beautiful bruising still pressed across them like a forgotten promise.

Tossing away caution with the same ferocity as my discarded saddlebags, I wrapped both arms around Jaik's waist, burying my face in the back of his shirt. His spine stiffened beneath my cheek, his muscles cording sharply...but he did not pull away.

"I hate that I can't remember what all of this means," I mumbled into his shirt. "What it means to you. What it meant to me."

"Yeah." A raspy reply, shuddering with bitten-away emotion. "It was sort of everything back then."

"I know it's not everything anymore." I tightened my grip around him. "But it's not *nothing* either, Jaik. Not for me."

An unsteady laugh. His fists tightened over the mantel's edge. "What's that supposed to mean?"

"It means..." I tugged my lower lip through my teeth, weighing the words—debating them how I thought a Storycrafter might. Knowing that what they conveyed would write a new ending.

"It means I want you to kiss me."

A violent shudder wracked through his body; then he shoved back from the mantel, twisting in my grip, staring down at me. "*What?*"

"I know you used to kiss me in this cabin, Jaik Grissom." I slid my hands up to his shoulders, inward to grip his collar in both hands. "Show me how you did it back—"

The last word lost itself in a gasp as his mouth crashed down over mine.

Beautiful. Bruising. Desperate. Desiring.

I lost myself in that kiss, my fingers raking up the sides of his neck to tangle in his hair; his one hand snared a fistful of shirt in the small of my back, hauling me curve-to-curve with him, and the other steadied the nape of my neck and guided my head so our lips could better meet. Again. And again. And again.

The fire roared and fanned out behind him, its inferno lighting up the embers beneath my skin. I couldn't be close enough to Jaik Grissom; I couldn't pull him near enough to satisfy.

Teeth nicked lips. Tongues danced together. It was my turn to guide *his* head, so that every inch of my lips could explore his, satisfying the question that had haunted me for weeks, now. And he took to my leading like a waltz, his grip gentling, his mouth following suite.

Passion mellowed into pleasure. Kissing simply for the sake of it. Until at last I pulled back, just enough that the tip of my nose and the edge of my brow brushed his; that I could meet his eyes in the narrow space between us.

"Flipping *Luck*." If his gaze was drunk with desire, his tone was absolutely gutted by it. "*Ayjay…*"

"Whatever happens," I panted, stroking my fingertips through the ends of his hair, "promise me you'll keep kissing me that way."

"Anytime you ask, tiger." His nose brushed mine, and he angled his head for another kiss—fleeting and far milder than the last. "What brought *that* on?"

"Upstairs, I just felt…I felt like we'd done that here before. And that I wanted to do it again."

"Yeah, we did." He brushed my hair behind my ear. "This was the first place you told me you loved me."

My teeth grazed the tip of my tongue.

I couldn't say it. Not now—not yet.

Reading my silence, Jaik added hastily, "Listen, I'm not asking you to try to be the Audra I remember, I just…I'm just asking for one last chance to love you the way I never got to before." A vulnerable, jagged laugh fell from his trembling lips. "That all right?"

I had never even imagined someone *asking* if they could fall in love with me. But it was somehow the safest I had felt in as long as I could remember.

"I think…all of my favorite memories are of you, whether they're the ones I remember or the new ones I'm making," I whispered. "Whatever my story is, it feels like you're always the best part of it. And I think I'd like another chance to fall in love with you, too, Jaik Grissom."

The relief shattering through his eyes was almost heartbreaking to behold; when he dipped his head, I stretched up for another kiss, but his face buried against my shoulder instead.

"Flipping Luck, I missed this." His warm breath ghosted against my skin; it made me acutely aware of how alone we were, and just how much mischief we could get into in this cabin, all alone like we were.

So I slipped backward, and he let me go; but I didn't retreat far.

"Help me make dinner?" I took his hand, tugging him after me, toward the kitchen.

There was no more I could bear to say tonight…nothing more I knew how to offer him yet. But with my lips pulsing from the heat of his kiss, I could admit this much: what I felt for Jaik Grissom was not mere friendship. Not mere trust.

It was deep. Visceral. It was written on my bones, scripted in the depths of my heart. It was something that not even twisted Storycraft had fully erased.

It was inked in my blood itself. And with every pulse of my heart, that blood flowed swifter and farther, saturating every inch of me with the certainty that wherever my story went from here, I wanted him to be a part of it.

Perhaps even the best part.

Whether we were making food together, or playing cards beside the fireplace, or kissing each other senseless...

I just wanted Jaik Grissom. Whatever way I could have him.

So, it was a day of chasing...not after my memories. But chasing after *him*. And realizing that, whatever came from the rest of it, whether we found the Storymaker or not...

Nothing would ever be the same again.

CHAPTER 44
SAFE IN THE DARKNESS

WE SHELTERED IN THAT cabin a full week—long enough to be certain that no Misspoken manifestations stalked its grounds. Long enough to recover a bit from our wounds in Rivrand. And long enough to enjoy what had never been ours before: the chance to simply be together, shutting duty and desperation away.

Though our journey after we departed those safe and sacred confines was gruelingly swift, I didn't mind; eager as I was to find the Storymaker, and wary as I was of encountering the wraith again, quicker was better. And the kiss Jaik and I had shared strayed a hand across the pages of our story, rewriting bits and pieces with a new sort of flourish.

Tales—from him and others—had told me that was not my first kiss with Jaik Grissom; but he behaved as if it was, treating the moment in the cabin and every one after with a cherishing reverence that was truly the stuff of romantic storybooks...and my heart stretched out for more. More kisses, passionate and fierce; more kisses, slow and savoring. Waking kisses, goodnight kisses, dismounting kisses...kisses stolen in the midst of training with the blades, kisses popped on cheeks and shoulders while we made camp.

Kissing Jaik was something my body knew how to do with the same skill as tending bar, and I craved it at the same rhythm. As if some part of me *did* remember what it was like not to have the choice...and coveted it ferociously.

Some of the terror soothed, tempered with the newfound warmth between us as we rode by mind and map, beholding breathtaking pockets of Mithra-Sha where summer clung in blistering, vibrant emerald hues and ascending into stretches where autumn flared in ember-bright spans, the treetops possessed in a riot of fire tones that burned up my breath just to look at them.

Of one thing I was absolutely certain: I had never witnessed a change in seasons so stunning in Krylan.

Yet it didn't feel as if the seasons were the only thing changing; *I* was changing. Some if it for the better—the joy in kissing Jaik. The warmth whenever I slept in the curve of his body. The homecoming that built itself like a shelter around my heart.

But those were not the only changes waiting on our horizon.

Shadows stalked my dreams; frequently, bouts of unease and anger, grief and disquiet joined the swirl of tempestuous uncertainty that had marked my emotions since we'd departed the Tailbone City.

More difficult than feeling it was that Jaik *knew* I felt it now. I could no longer spare him from it, not after how honest I'd been with him after the confrontation with the wraith in the village.

Oddest of all was that it wasn't entirely terrible to have those emotions be known. It wasn't as horrible as I had feared it might be, that Jaik Grissom was watching out for me.

"How you feeling, tiger?" he asked one night when we stopped to make camp; we'd chosen a pair of lateral groves, untacking and brushing down the horses in one, then building a fire and setting the lantern burning bright in the other.

That lantern was the only reason I had managed to sleep at all since Rivrand; only the darkness in my dreams found its way through that undying glow. Even in the cabin's confines, I hadn't been able to slumber without the lick of silver light against my eyelids.

I cleaned sweat-sticky horsehair from my palms on my riding trousers before I handed over more kindling for Jaik to build the fire. "Honestly...I'm feeling everything still."

"Heard that." He snapped the branches and stacked them neatly in a tower. "Anything I can do to help tonight?"

Some nights, there was. Sometimes we talked about what was frustrating me. Sometimes I confessed the things I was afraid of. Sometimes we sat, fingers entwined, and he reassured me he was there—that I wasn't alone.

Tonight didn't feel like the night for any of those things. All the emotions seemed more tangible, somehow, sharper—tangled up in my chest in corkscrew loops. And the tightness cast them into a more vivid relief of sorts, like thorns springing from a rosevine.

"No, I don't think so." Crouching on my heels beside him, I trapped my palms between my knees. My mind wandered of its own volition—as it had every sunset since Rivrand—to memories of blood-red pulsing in the heart of shadow. At the heart of everything.

"Jaik," I murmured, "may I ask you a question?"

He snorted lightly. "Audra Jashowin, asking before she talks? Only in this life."

I rolled my eyes, but that spurt of warm irritation did nothing to soothe the anxious thoughts clamoring in my head, the same barbed cacophony that had found a home under my skin with those vivid flashes when the wraith had grabbed hold of me.

Scooting nearer to the fire, I took up the flintrock and struck a few sparks onto the kindling. "When we faced the wraith, did it feel...familiar to you in any way?"

"What—you mean the abomination like no one's ever heard of, not even the former Headmistress of Fablehaven Academy?" Jaik scoffed. "Nah, can't say that it did, tiger." A beat, while my neck warmed and his posture shifted—a slight rocking from one haunch to the other. "Wait, why? Does it feel like that to *you*?"

I scratched at the itching warmth that tipped my ear. "No."

"Ayjay, come on."

"It's probably nothing. Just my imagination running away with me."

"I mean, yours was always better than most." The kindling caught alight with the next shower of sparks. Jaik cupped a hand around the fire and blew, like an actor in a performing troupe breathing fire for the awe of the crowd.

Except that I was his only audience, this forest the sole witness to this conversation—to the tremble in my hands and the deep thoughts turning his tilled-soil eyes nearly night-dark.

"Why don't you tell me what you're really thinking?"

I dropped my gaze to my trapped hands, rubbing my thumbs together. "It started back in Belaris. When it touched me, I had a sense of...I don't know. *Familiarity* is the only word I had for it. And in Rivrand, it was worse. It came with...not just emotions. Flashes. Images."

Jaik blinked. "Memories?"

"They might be." I shuddered to believe they were, with all the pain that punched behind each one. "But I wondered if maybe you and I had faced this manifestation before. Possibly in the Illusionarium?"

Brows scrunching, Jaik shook his head. "Not a chance. I would've remembered it if we had. But let's go back...explain what *familiar* feels like."

"I don't know!" Huffing a breath that stirred my bangs, I flattened my hair back from my temples with my palms—then slid them down to cup my neck, that flash of irritation dimming again. "It doesn't make any sense. But whenever that wraith touches me, it feels like it...parallels me, somehow. My emotions, the ache in my chest. I don't know what to do with that. I don't know what it *means*."

"I'll tell you this much." Jaik tugged me nearer, and I fell against him, curling up into his side beneath the shelter of his arm. "It means we need to find out what's going on in this country, and we need to get you safe. Get your memories back. Ayjay, no matter what's happening, our goal doesn't change, right? We stick to the course, and one way or another, we'll find our answers. Whether we figure it out for ourselves, or the Storymaker tells us."

Inevitable answers. That thought sustained me through a quiet dinner, through the beginnings of a gentle, warm mountain rain, through finding a shelter beneath a few boughs we wove together and huddled beneath. Curling up on the mossy ground, my body nestled into the curve of his, I was quick to find peace when Jaik's arm slipped under my head so as to keep his sword in reach even while he held me close; I huddled with my face tucked into the dip of his throat, shielding my eyes from the lantern's light. In a few moments, I slipped away into dreams.

Perhaps if I hadn't fallen asleep so swiftly, things would have been different.

Perhaps if we had both kept watch, and not just Jaik, things would have gone differently.

But we didn't.

So neither did they.

CHAPTER 45
SHADOWS ALIVE

ONE MOMENT, I WAS lulled to slumber by the heat of Jaik's body, the quiet lullaby of his breaths. The next, my eyes popped open to a banked fire and ethereal lanternlight glow, my heart thundering against my ribs like it was seeking the best ones to escape between.

It was a moment before I realized what had woken me: the pleasant drumming of the chilly rain had changed. It hadn't stopped—not entirely. But it was muffled now, as if we'd moved deeper under shelter. Fewer drops pattered on the undergrowth around us.

It was eerie. Abrupt.

I rocked my hips, scooting backward, deeper into the warmth that sheltered my body. "Jaik?"

"Yeah. I hear it." His tone was sharp, watchful—alert. A soldier on guard.

Every hair on my nape rose at once, and I rolled in Jaik's embrace, blinking the canopy of the forest above into focus.

Nothing seemed aberrant, at first, besides the quiet. Moonstroked shadows, swaying boughs, leaves trembling in the wind—

And then a notion plucked my heartstrings out of tune. It played a screaming refrain of warning like a tavern musician missing a note.

Because those shadows...those weren't leaves. The branches didn't bow in the wind. And in the heart of the darkness—light ignited.

"*No!*" I howled, lurching to my knees. "Jaik, it's *here!*"

Cursing Fickle Luck, Jaik sprang to his feet, stepping over me as I scrambled backward on my hands and knees; his sword was already in his hand before I even reached my dagger, useless though it would be.

Useless against the wraith as it spooled down from the treetops—undeterred at all by the lantern in whose glow we faced it now.

CHAPTER 46
NEVER A CHANCE

SCREAMING EVERY PROFANITY I'D ever heard in the *Pourhouse* from swarthy sailors and smart-mouthed soldiers, I flung myself toward the lantern; but Jaik sidestepped into my path, hooking me around the waist and dragging me the opposite way.

"Leave it, Ayjay, it's not working anymore!"

And he was right; impervious now to the very iridescence that had sent it fleeing from Rivrand, the shadow wraith dropped its jaw in a warbling snarl and wove toward us, growing as it advanced.

Six feet. Seven. Eight. Ten. Towering as high as the *Spirited Sunrise* trees that decorated town squares at wintertime, this inversion of all things light and pure advanced on us—backing us out of the glade, into the deeper forest.

Jaik and I sidestepped, moving around its edge, forcing it to revolve on a column. But it twisted endlessly, never needing to sidestep itself, never once taking its burning, fiery pit of a stare from our faces.

There was an odd rebuke in that look. Predator abashing its prey for the audacity to flee.

"That thing," Jaik snarled, "that is *not* normal."

"So let's not be normal, either."

I gave him a shove—then dove past him, snatching up the lantern and swinging it in a wild arc. Whether it was my reckless audacity or a last bit of fear for the light that had spared Rivrand's survivors, the wraith snatched itself away from my strike.

Then Jaik caught my wrist, hauled me back to him...and we were running for our lives.

Leaving the horses. Leaving my dagger. Leaving *everything* behind, running with just the cloaks on our backs, a lantern, a sword.

A prayer to the Storymaker that this wasn't where ours ended, as we plunged into the undergrowth with the darkness peeling back from our boot tips, feeding the height and span of the wraith that pursued us.

Its advance was not shadow-softness; it was the terror of tree limbs cracking like bones. The crunch as soil churned under the yank of barbed darkness. It was a screaming, vicious dissonance that pursued us for nearly a mile, running with all we had...knowing that the forest was the worst place to make a stand against a creature like this.

We needed space to maneuver. Room to dance.

At last, panting, my side afire, we tumbled out of the treeline into another clearing and stumbled to a halt, arms tangled across each other's fronts, slowing the brief descent that lay ahead of us.

A shallow slope to nothing.

The wraith had backed us to the edge of a gorge. Far below, river water tumbled in a ceaseless churn.

"All right, back—back!" Jaik spun me with one hand across my front—then cursed and shoved me behind him as the wraith wavered up from the treeline, surging unimpeded into the open.

My heart faltered in my chest; my bowels clenched.

"When you see an opening, take it. Get back to the horses," Jaik rasped under his breath. Then, before I could answer—voice my protest or give into the terror weakening my knees—he feinted to the side, smashing his blade against a rock jutting from the soil. "Hey! *Hey, ugly*! Over here!"

The wraith's head whipped his way, fiery mouth grinning wide—sprouting a barrage of teeth like iron bars over a blazing furnace. It lunged for him...and I speared for the treeline with all the strength in my shaking legs.

I had half a moment to register Jaik's shout—not one of pain. One of shock morphing into horrified fury.

One moment to slam a heel in the rain-damp earth and start to pivot, instinct kicked awake by Jaik's cry racing ahead of what my mind struggled to fathom.

One moment to behold the shadow-carved figure descending on me...a feint of its own.

I swung the lantern high, warding the beast back for just a moment; but it was only a course-correction, a duck and swivel beneath the shaft of opalescence.

Then the wraith was upon me.

Its spidery hand slammed my chest with a world-throbbing *shove*, and as my feet kicked out from beneath me—as I hurtled backward through the air—time seemed to slow.

The true blow came not from its hand, but from the surge that snapped out behind it, like a parchment unfurled and tumbling down over my face. Suffocating me.

Hate. Grief. Shame. Terror. Rage.

Pain erupted through my back as it slammed against a tree; I buckled down among the roots, hips and knees and a host of other joints screaming and popping at the awkward bend they made in the descent. But I couldn't gather strength enough to unfold, to seek relief—to do anything but watch, gasping for the breath torn out of my lungs, as the wraith advanced.

Over my chest—over my heart, where its palm had contacted—my skin blistered. Throbbed. Broke out in fiery pinpoints of anguish.

Hate. Grief. Shame. Terror. Rage.

The wraith loomed across the span between us, shadows reaching and expanding, gathering up from the hem of its cloaked figure to elongate its head, its neck, its torso. So that its face came at level with mine; so that it heaved its fiery breath against my pain-squinted eyes, my throbbing face.

Let me tell you a story—

My eyes slammed shut at the gust of its breath burning up what little I had to offer.

A soldier's wicked, belligerent scowl.

A bloodied shipdeck.

A Sha's impassive face.

Heat soaking and staining my arms, my chest, an impossibly heavy weight dragging me down, down—

"You Storycrafters are all alike—crafty, covetous pieces of slag—"

"I had no choice. You couldn't leave, not like this. Not with him."

Pain erupted in my shoulder, in my side, arching my body in a mortal twist that struggled to escape the agony that climbed every crack of my flesh, meeting in a cruel twist just below my arm.

She was a bleeder.

I'll do what I can for her...

Don't...don't you say my name like that—

"—Get your mug off my wife!"

Not a memory. No, not that cracked, furious snarl.

And then Jaik was there, lunging between us, heedless of both shadow and flame. Unafraid of the thing's fuming breaths that sapped the strength from *my* limbs.

And for the first time, I watched the wraith change course.

Saw it turn its sights from me to someone else.

It recoiled, and redoubled, rising in its size, rearing back to strike like a coiled serpent, collar aflare.

"Jaik, go," I choked—not even enough breath to cry out in earnest. "Jaik—*please*—"

"Not a chance."

Sword braced with both hands, he launched himself at the wraith.

And all at once, it stopped retreating.

Shadow solidified into steel in the creature's right hand, a weapon forged in the span of a heartbeat; my mouth dried to the last drop when I beheld the sword it wielded.

A dark, mirrored echo of Jaik's; another fire-guarded blade, this one summoned from the inky tendrils of the creature itself. And it stroked with a form that was eerie, exact, *strikingly* known...something I saw, and felt, but couldn't bring into concretion in my clamoring thoughts.

It matched Jaik flawlessly, blow by blow, stride by stride. Shadow and flesh dueled through the trees, a ringing cacophony of steel on shadow as Jaik ducked and twisted like a dervish, fighting to slip past the wraith's guard.

Yet even its swings were more calculated than any Misspoken manifestation had a right to be. It was too precise, too vicious, far too aware. Whatever had forged this creature, shaped it, it *had* been made *other*. Different from its kin.

Jaik. I tried to wheeze his name, to cough it out, to call him back from the fight...but was there really any hope of that, when his blade alone might be the means of felling it?

Mortal weapons had failed. Storycraft had failed. What more did we have than this?

And Jaik fought just like that—like a man making his last stand. He fought even more ferociously than he had in Rivrand. He was a feral vision, hair slapped in slick strands across his eyes, mouth peeled open in a neverending snarl, face grooved with brutality that would have made me feel safe if he'd faced any other foe.

But not this one. Not this.

My hands scraped backward, gathering splinters like loveletters to the same fate Jaik and I always faced...moments like this. Fighting and falling and fearing for each other.

It's never going to stop.

Catching purchase on the slippery wood of the trunk behind me, I dragged myself swaying and bending to my feet. But something worse than a bruised back and creaking joints made my knees buckle as I watched him fight.

Despair deadened every limb. It weighed my head like an anvil, so much that I struggled even to fix my eyes on the duel of shadow-and-Storycraft blades in the night.

This world is never going to stop taking you away from me.

I trembled, panted, fighting to straighten my legs.

It will never end.

The wraith was shifting, thickening, strengthening with every swing.

No matter what, I always lose. I always lose you.

A triumphant shriek pierced the night, stopping my heart altogether.

The wraith broke Jaik's guard with a whip-quick swivel, faster than I had ever seen man or creature ever move; bracing Jaik's blade overhead, it whirled beneath, jamming an elbow into his ribs. And then a second blade—a dagger, an inky sketch of the one *I* carried—formed in its hand.

And struck.

Fabric gave first.

Then flesh.

Jaik plunged to the earth, the shadow blade buried to the hilt in his leg.

CHAPTER 47
RAGE INCANDESCENT

For a heartbeat, the world blurred away.

For two, there was nothing. Not even drumming rain. Not the river's rushing cry.

There was only Jaik, laid out in the soil, stricken, gasping with agony. There was the shadow-knife stuck in his flesh. And there was the wraith, sheathing its sword by a swipe of the blade down its flank that restored the shadows to intangibility.

The wraith, closing in on him. Crouching before him and slinking on all fours like a seductress, sniffing at the blood that pooled around his fingers.

The ill sensation that had sent me retreating aboard *The Cathan's* deck when Jaik had been set to duel Wilkes rose in me again...a nausea that sickened to the very marrow of my bones.

How could I move—how could I breathe for it? For all the emotions cresting in a drowning tide at the back of my throat?

Hate. Grief. Shame. Terror. Rage.

Rage.

RAGE.

Rage was not a wave.

Rage was an inferno, rage was iridescent, incandescent. Rage lit me up from the inside out, belting from me in a scream that ripped my throat in two as I shoved up from the tree. *"Get away from him!"*

And the wraith...hesitated.

Its fingers drew back from the handle of Jaik's blade. It cocked its head back, shadows rustling in an oddly captivating fold from the murky features of its wasted face as it looked up at me.

As it regarded me with a wary sort of curiosity.

And that was all the advantage Jaik needed—to lift his sword with a chest-wrenching cry and slash backhand with all his might.

Steel grazed smoke, riving a burning scarlet gash across the wraith's middle. It doubled back, screaming, gathering its shadowed fringe to itself in a spidery crawl, its form morphing and folding and burbling like hot molasses in a tavern cookpot. One moment its face formed here, the next there, and the shrieks the took on a form I couldn't begin to fathom.

They were almost like sobs.

Brutal, wrathful, *rageful* cries as it clawed away from us, to the treeline. To the fringe of shadows where, in response—

New voices raised the call.

Low snarls rumbled from the undergrowth; shadows shifted in slinking, slithering swaths. Though the night muted the definition of things, it couldn't erase the texture of them—of bristling hair and heaving hackles, of towering racks of antlers on heads mounted two to a single neck. Nor the glow of white, vacant eyes igniting in the dark...far too many, at far too great a height.

The wraith had gathered another army around it...Misspoken beasts, by the look of it. Perhaps game someone had been desperate enough to try to Storycraft during the lean years of drought when stories lost their endings.

Once more, they heeded the summons of a void master; once more, we were cornered by manifestations. And perhaps they could bleed, like the spiders in Rivrand; perhaps they could be felled.

But there was only one of me; and there was Jaik, bleeding before me.

There was no hope of fighting them, of defeating the wraith. Not when it was growing, shifting, *strengthening*.

So I did the only thing I could think of.

I grabbed Jaik under the arms, heaved us both backward in a kicking fit of legs stirring at the leaflitter, sword plunged into the sward, fighting desperately to stand—

Then I leaped with all my might into the gorge.

CHAPTER 48
COMING FOR BLOOD

T HE WATER SNATCHED US away the moment our legs touched its whitecap rapids.

Everything dissolved into a downhill tumble that matched the chaos thundering in my head. It was all I could do to keep one arm around Jaik and stroke wildly with the other, to keep our mouths above water. The rest, we gave over to the river...letting it bury us. Erase us.

Make us untraceable.

I lost count of the minutes we were at the current's mercy, or which direction its serpentine twists carried us. Between high, tree-studded canyon walls so narrow we barely squeezed through; down slick, smooth stepped waterfalls where the riverstones tugged up my tunic and scraped my bare back, setting new pain alight all along the bruised flesh.

It seemed miles of bone-aching cold and wet before the current finally showed mercy; before the sloped shore receded to chest-level, then to eye-level...then to muddy banks that could've been fished from.

I had no breath to spare for words; I simply tightened my grip around Jaik's chest and kicked out for shore.

We floundered into the shallows where I dropped back, shoving at Jaik's weight with my shoulder, pushing him up out of the water to the river's edge. He dragged himself through the mud until his torso was clear of the swirling shallows; then he collapsed to his chest and rolled onto his back.

Propped on his elbows, his shaking fingers seized sharply, violently around the shadow dagger still plunged deep in his calf.

"Stop!" I yelped, crashing to my knees next to him and swatting his hands away. "Jaik, stop, let me—!"

"It's burning, flipping *Luck! Agh*, it *burns!*" Jaik's heel raked in the mud, a wilder fear than any I had ever seen scouring his wide, wet eyes.

Bundling my hands in the folds of my cloak, I gripped the knife near his flesh, jolted again with the familiarity of its lay...the way the wraith had forged a dagger so alarmingly like mine.

I allowed myself only once to look, to soak in the grisliness where the hilt met weeping skin. It already gushed blood again, though it had been more than a quarter hour since the fight, and that spent in the water. Then I wrenched my gaze up to Jaik's grime-smudged face.

"Look at me, Jaik," I panted, and his eyes shot to mine. "Let me tell you a story."

A swift, sharp blink. "What—?"

With a twist and a yank, I wrenched the dagger free.

The moment it left his flesh, it burst into strands of smoke, carried away on the wind. A creaking, broken bark of a sound wrenched out of Jaik, and he tumbled to his side, burying his face in the filthy forest floor, slamming his hand again and again into the mud. I swiped my hand on my cloak and scrambled over Jaik's leg to grip his shoulder. "I'm so sorry, Jaik, I'm sorry, I had to—"

"I'm fine," he choked, fingers clawing into fists in the mire, "I'm all right—"

"No, you're not! *Jaik*!"

"Yeah...yeah, all right, I'm..." He crumbled, a crooked sound somewhere between a broken laugh and a sob punching from his chest. "*Ah*, this hurts! *Ah-ha...*"

Panic begged to break its fetters and fly free at that guttural gasp, but I noosed it with all my might. Tucking one hand behind Jaik's neck and seizing his collar with the other, I hauled him up to his seat, shoving him gently back against a stump hewn to the quick at the edge of the shallows.

"Stay with me, Jaik." Gripping the tattered halves of his trouser leg, I tore them wider; my stomach turned over itself at the brush of my fingers on the abused flesh around the wound, the mess of blood that oozed from the sundered skin. And in the veins around it...

Shadows. A slow-spreading stain.

The lump in my throat bobbed and blistered. *No, no, no...*

"Hey...does it look as bad as it feels?" Jaik panted.

"It..." I faltered, one finger following a spidering vein. "It needs a...a torniquet."

I gripped the hem of my Storycrafter's cloak in my teeth; and before Jaik's stutter of protest could fully form itself, I ripped the hem, stealing a strand of smoky fabric for my own.

"Why would you *do that*?" Jaik croaked. "That's your *cloak*!"

"I know precisely what it is, and I know precisely what I'm doing." Memory guided my flying fingers back to his leg, winding the fabric just beneath his knee, tying and cinching with all my strength. Words and notions floated through my reeling mind—instructions from Naomi's book that I'd read some evenings to quiet the well of emotions bubbling in my chest. Simple, basic wound care.

This was far from simple, far from basic. Who knew what that wraith had done to him?

But *I* could only do one thing at a time. One step at a time. Slowing the bleeding...that was where it started.

"Ayjay," Jaik rasped, the faintest argument seething under the damp roll of my name through his lips.

"What was it like, fighting that abomination?" I cut across him quickly, shrugging from my cloak and wrapping it fully around the weeping wound on his calf.

Trembling fingertips wound into my hair, tugging just enough to sketch discomfort in fiery traces through my skull—just enough to tell me how fiercely that touch was an anchor for him. "Seemed like it was going all right. Up until it stuck me."

I dared a glance up to catch his crooked, mirthless smile. "You saw how it hesitated, didn't you? When I screamed at it?"

"Yeah." His head knocked back against the tree, the arch of his throat lurching through several staggered swallows. "That was...different. Can't say I liked how it screamed when I cut it, either."

"Do you think that was a mortal blow?"

"We'd better hope so, the way it was yelling its head off...otherwise it's probably going after blood next time. I don't think it'll take its time again if it knows we can hurt it."

Panic zipped like lightning along the backs of my teeth; I swallowed it, let the tingling burn warm me as I pressed a hand to the tree above his head and hauled myself upright. "Then we need to go. It could track us at any time."

"Yeah. About that." A faint shudder rocked the line of his shoulders, stealing a bit of their strength; in its absence, he bowed a bit more, caving in on himself. "Ayjay, listen, I'm not...I don't think I can move."

Fear reared and roiled; I smothered it with a grit of aching teeth, with a shove of my cheek along the length of his. Stubble scraped my damp skin, the hot blood and leather scent of his clothing filled my nostrils and erasing the tang of my own panic as I brought my lips to rest against the shell of his ear.

"You listen to me, Jaik Grissom," I hissed, sliding my hand from his neck to lift his head a bit from the tree, winding my fingers into his soaked hair. "I may not know everything, but I know this: you and I have spent our lives doing one foolish and insane thing, over and over...staying together. Whatever's come for us, whatever way the coin flips, whichever face Luck turns our way." A violent shiver wracked through him, and I blinked away the filmy heat of tears again, pulling his head into the crook of my shoulder. "You have never given up. You have *never* stood down, not once, whenever I've needed you. And right now, I *need you* to get on your feet, so that we can get out of this forest and get you the help you need."

The hoarse, panting breath that wafted against the side of my neck might have been an attempt at laughter. "Flipping Luck...if I knew taking a...a knife to the leg was what I needed to get you to talk to me like that, I'd have gone tangling with that wraith a long time ago."

A hysterical smile scratched at the corners of my lips. "You still might get another chance. But first, I need you to *move*."

His arm slung around my back, hot and heavy—far too heavy, bearing almost none of its own weight. "Help me."

I swiveled to press a kiss to his temple. "Always, Jaik."

We found our feet together—an awkward, stumbling tangle of disarrayed limbs, him struggling to push all his weight into his unhurt leg while I tilted and tipped, balancing his injured side. It was a broken dance, but we found our rhythm even in that with his arm swooped around my back, and in a handful of moments we were stumbling through the undergrowth.

"Just hold on, Jaik," I muttered through gritted teeth. "I'm getting us out of this."

"I know. I'm not scared." His fingers latched around my hip, biting in almost to the point of pain. "Listen. Keep us going southeast, and we'll get to Galent eventually."

Galent...the place of refuge we'd sought all this time. The hope of a better place to make a stand.

He was entrusting our course to me. Trusting me with *everything*.

So I set my jaw, and my sights, and started us moving through the shadowed undergrowth. "Galent it is."

CHAPTER 49
TELL ME A STORY

T HE FOREST WAS NO longer a friend.

Whatever beauty it had once possessed was lost in a shroud of bloodstains and bandages hastily-tied from strips of our shirts and my cloak, washed again and again. Birdsong muffled under labored breaths. Wide-reaching horizons dimmed by a glaze of tears. The mottled undergrowth turned to a hedge of bitter greens, a maze that sprouted brambles while we traveled. Every passing inch of it loomed the same—a confusing blur that trailed southeast, flanking the higher peaks of the Vensair Mountains.

Or perhaps we weren't traveling that way at all. I only had the sun's rising and its trek along the arch of the sky to guide my sense of direction, and I wasn't proficient in these things...or if I was, I didn't remember it.

And Jaik...

Jaik was only barely helpful. Frequently slumped against me as we made agonizing progress at the pace his one leg could manage, he peeled his head up to croak vague directions whenever I brought myself to disturb him and ask. Beyond that, I had the brush of his fevered brow against my temple to taunt me—to remind me that despite my hectic force of will, we were horseless and moving on three legs between us.

The only running we were doing was running out of time.

The first day, we managed a short bout of camp—enough for me to unbind Jaik's leg and wash the wound, stomach churning at the reek of the swollen, turgid flesh. Already it was as solid as the binding of the healer's book left behind in our saddlebags, with horses likely torn to tatters by the Misspoken beasts the wraith had summoned to be our downfall.

For the scant hour I could bring myself to rest, I sat with Jaik's head in my lap, one hand carding his hair from his sweat-soaked brow while I tried frantically to recall everything Naomi's book had said about wound care. Herbs and poultices that could stave off infection and stop bleeding and treat envenomed limbs.

But even when I remembered this or that name or description, there remained a lack of the curatives themselves everywhere I searched for them, in all the places where Naomi's book suggested they ought to be. Beside the river we kept to our left as we traveled, in all the low-lying, boggy areas and at the bases of certain trees. Everywhere I searched, it was little less than a graveyard for growing things. As if someone had gone on ahead of us, picking over this portion of the forest. Trimming it clean of poultice ingredients...clean of hope.

The second hopeless day of alternating our staggered progress and foraging whenever Jaik needed to rest—which was more frequently now than yesterday—I returned with empty hands and a now-familiar rage storming in my chest to our small campsite where I'd left him as comfortably as I could. He was precisely where he'd been when I'd slipped away a half-hour ago: sprawled beneath the shade of an oak tree, draped in my drab gray cloak, head cast back and hand over his middle.

His leg reeked. Even from a distance when I approached, the pungent odor had my nose wrinkling of its own accord. And knowing that smell came from his *wound*, from a hurt I couldn't help, couldn't *heal*...

Grinding out a snarl, I ripped my hands back through my hair, stalking to his side.

One eye slid open; his free hand drifted up to shade his gaze against the sunlight glaring through the trees. "Got anything?"

"If I did, I would already be tending your leg." I hovered over him, considered peeling back the bandages and examining it, but...

What was the use? I knew what I would find.

"It's all right, Ayjay, don't worry." Jaik let his hand fall from over his eyes. "It's going to be—"

"Don't!" The word barked out more forcefully than I'd meant it to, with the weight of me falling into the leaflitter at his side. "Don't you say it's going to be *fine*, Jaik, I can't find anything to help you, I can't do *anything*, and I'm so afraid..."

I dropped my face into my knees, hiding away from the words that had nearly escaped. That hurled themselves relentlessly against the inside of my skull, the back of my tongue, the hard lump in my throat.

I'm so afraid you're going to die.

All of my fears from this entire, mad quest surged in my chest at once, strangling my rage—most powerful of them all the terror of losing him, after I'd dared to let him nearer. Dared to care for him...to begin to fall in love with him again.

His fingers worked their way heavily across the space between us, catching mine and prying them slowly from the soil where I'd buried them to brace on either side of my body. Exhaustion slowed even the brush of his thumb against my knuckles, but he persevered for the sake of that comforting touch.

Because that was what Jaik Grissom did—whatever it took to make his way back to me.

"Ayjay, hey, can you...can you tell me a story?" he croaked.

My face sprang up from my knees, my eyes finding his—dim, weighted slits, the brown depths nearly robbed of any light at all. "Jaik, I..."

I don't know how.

I don't know how to tell a story you're not part of anymore.

Silence and forest-song enclosed us for a long moment, his thumb still making its way back and forth across my knuckles...slow as the handwriting of an arthritic, half-blind scribe.

"It's all right," he said again, quieter this time. "I know you, Ayjay. You're going to tell them again...when it's time. I just wish..."

"That it was now?" I muttered, dropping my gaze to our hands—and turning my fingers to lace between his. "So do I. Then, maybe, I could get us out of this mess."

"*We're* the mess," he mumbled. "But I never wanted to get out of it."

Somehow *that* was what dragged the tears from along my lashes; I dashed them hastily away with my free hand. "You're so ridiculous, Jaik."

He said nothing to that.

For the first time, it struck me how limp his fingers were—making no effort at all to squeeze mine.

I jolted from my haunches up to my knees, looming above him, my gaze hunting his slack face. His shuttered eyes...no wink of brown left like a horizonline to draw me home.

"Jaik?" Panic pierced my voice up through three octaves. "Jaik, *answer me!*"

He didn't. Even when I screamed his name, gripped his shoulders, shook him with all my might...he didn't stir.

"No, no, no…" Caught between a broken chant and a desperate sob, I hooked my hair behind my ears and dipped, pressing my lips to his, cradling his feverish cheek in one hand. "Wake up, Jaik. Jaik? Jaik, *please…*"

He didn't peek open an eye. Didn't tease me. He hardly breathed except in shallow, aching pulls.

Salt skimmed my lips as I fumbled frantically for the pulse at the side of his neck—still strong, but far too quick. Cursing Luck, I tugged his head into my lap, wrapped my arms around his shoulders, shook him and shook him—

I was shaking, fear twisting my bones almost entirely out of joint, making a ruin of my composure. My strength. Everything I had left to give.

"I'll try!" I wept against his filthy hair, squeezing my eyes shut and pressing him as tightly to myself as I could. "Jaik, I swear on Luck, I'll try again…I'll tell any story you want me to, just please, *please*, open your eyes—"

But he didn't.

Not all that day and into the night. Not when I held him, not when I rocked him against my chest, not when I sobbed his name. Not when I fumbled for words to keep my vow…a promise kept too late. Stories told to no one who could hear anymore.

He never woke, never reached for me, never comforted me…not while I wrestled all alone with the terror that I might have heard his last words—his final plea—and been too terrified to answer.

CHAPTER 50
CALLED BLUFFS

F OR TWO DAYS, JAIK fevered and worsened, unconscious. The shadows took strange, spiraling turns through his veins, along and under his skin, like tattoos branded below the flesh.

I did everything I knew to do—tying tourniquets, straying as far as I dared from the campsite to search fruitlessly for herbs. But still the patches where they ought to have grown were picked dry, stalks utterly bereft of flowerheads and seedpods, and I couldn't risk searching for the next stream, the next pond or pool. Not when Jaik shuddered and groaned more with every passing hour. And not when the curlicues of that venom closed my throat with an unspoken, paralyzing fear.

This sickening was purposeful. The wraith hadn't meant to kill him.

It was hunting us. Waiting until we were at our weakest to land the final blow.

That notion haunted me for those two days, firming into a nib-sharp certainty piercing me through the belly...a constant stomachache that erased what little appetite I had. I hunkered low in the underbrush every day, afraid to light a fire—afraid to even keep the lantern alight.

And so that was where I was when the sound roused me from sleep on the third day of Jaik's unconsciousness: my arm draped over him, my face pressed into the back of his shoulder, holding him as the shivers ripped along his frame again and again.

The brush of a frame parting undergrowth. The sway of foliage beneath the pass of a hand.

I pushed myself upright, one palm still splayed on Jaik's chest—frozen. Holding my breath. Waiting.

Another whisper of sound, across from the first.

Enclosing us.

Terror spiked, slamming like a blade through my skull—and then it bled away, ink running down a page, and all at once in its wake, something new wrote itself on the parchment of my heart.

A frigid, furious calm.

This had not just happened to Jaik...it had been *done* to him. And now the Misspoken manifestations had come to finish their work.

Not while there is still one single breath in my body.

Jaik's slumped form barely shifted as I wrenched the sword from the sheath on his hip and spun up off my knees. Stabbing the fire-guarded blade into the soil, I planted my feet and stood over Jaik. Stood between him and whoever was coming—and raised the blade at shoulder-height, braced outward, the same way I'd seen him do.

"There's no sense sneaking," I snarled with all the bravado I hadn't lost watching Jaik slip away from me, one second of suffering at a time. "I know you're there. So step out into the open so we can *end* this!"

It was the most courageous bluff I had ever made.

And they called it.

CHAPTER 51
STORY-MADE

MY ONLY SMALL CONSOLATION was that the figure who emerged from behind the trunk of the nearest, broadest tree was not a writhing wraith forged of shadow. But what he *was* should have frightened me just as much: a man garbed in fighting leathers beneath a cloak painted the colors of the forest to blend in—core greens, deep sables, moody browns and grays. Not even the knives and axes bound across his body made a whisper when he moved, stalking with catlike grace toward us.

No sound echoed from beneath the tread of his boots; nothing like I'd sensed before, that'd woken me from the restless edge of slumber.

I'd only heard him because he'd wanted me to. And I didn't know if that boded well or very, very badly for us.

Who was he, and why had he come upon us *now*?

I searched his cloak's dappled shades and my memory for a lick of familiarity...for the chance to determine if he was a Storycrafter.

If, possibly, he was *the* Storycrafter...the one who'd formed the wraith and unleashed it against us.

But even if he was...he had not come for this reckoning alone.

Other figures slipped out of the shadows on his heels, and my stomach plunged lower with every hooded newcomer's arrival. But I didn't give ground, even when the first man approached, hood still cast up, posture casual, leonine, frighteningly graceful; and he didn't show a flicker of fear, as if he knew that he'd caught me off guard. Knew that I was struggling wildly to get the measure of this threat, a surrounding in our sleep like I'd expected, but not from the foes I'd been braced to fight.

He halted just shy of the blade's tip; his eyes flashed in the sunken-sun shadows, glittering like the stirred depths of an inkpot, shimmering at the touch of light.

A tremor wrapped through my arms, jamming my shoulders tightly together. I couldn't bear to look backward for an ambush; I didn't dare take my gaze off this broad-shouldered threat who moved through forest and shadow like he was born of them.

"I know that blade." His voice rumbled, deep as a tremor moving through the mountains beneath our feet. "Story-made. Fire-handled. I'd know it *anywhere.*"

Before I could muster a breath—to warn him off or threaten him, though there was little doubt he and his band could rip me in pieces if they chose—he spoke again. Words that sheared through my defenses like they were ancient parchment, crumbling at a touch.

"That's Jaik Grissom's sword."

One hand flashed up, dashing the hood from his head—revealing thick auburn hair twisted into a knot at the nape of his neck, unmasking those rich brown eyes from the shadows. Concern streaked the lines beside them...laugh-lines. Sun-squinting lines.

"Addie, is that you?"

The next breath stumbled its way through my lungs—because only the friends I'd forgotten ever called me *Addie.* And the way this man spoke the name, with a cave-in of his courage, a disbelief and concern so intimate my heart echoed it even without an ounce of recognition...

The sword dipped, suddenly heavier than the weight of carrying Jaik all this way.

"It's me," I gasped. "I—we need help."

The man's gaze leaped past me, finding the tattered, unmoving heap of cloak behind me...and his eyes blew wide. "Oh, Luck, *no.*"

He brushed past me, and I let the blade fall, turning with the knock of his shoulder against mine; watching as he knelt and drew aside the sodden cloak from Jaik's leg to examine it, his touch so infinitely gentle it sprang tears to my eyes.

"Ah, *Jaik,*" he rumbled, deep in his chest. "Brother, this is *bad.*"

Two wobbling steps nearer, and I broke down beside them, stubbing the hilt into the soil. "I did my best, but I'm not a healer, and this isn't—"

"I know you're not." The man squeezed my shoulder, his gaze darting past me to his companions. "Lidya, head back. Tell them to expect us—and have the infirmary ready."

An infirmary.

Help, at last.

The man turned to me, took my shoulders in his gloved hands, and peered deeply into my face. "Look at me, Addie."

I did, though I had to blink twice to clear the heat from my gaze enough to focus on him; a frown slit between his brows, and he studied me longer than I could bear. Seconds I wished he'd have his eyes on Jaik instead.

"You don't know me, do you?" he murmured at last.

My next blink freed a tear, heat slithering down my cheek. "I'm so sorry. But you have to help us."

"It's all right." His fingers squeezed tight over my shoulders. "You don't have to know me...I know you, and that's what matters. The name's Gillian Cross. You've got friends here...*Jaik's* got friends. And we're going to help you. Just got to follow me."

CHAPTER 52
TO GALENT

IT TOOK GIL AND one of his men, Tayler—who paused to wrap me in a sideways embrace beneath the brawn of his sable arm—to mount Jaik on a horse. Another member of their group reintroduced herself to me with a nod and a brisk, "I'm Kassa, the regiment healer. I'll stabilize him before we ride."

And that was how we found our way to Galent: Kassa riding with Jaik after packing some sweet-smelling poultice against his leg, me astride a mount with Gil, the rest of them thundering ahead on their own horses to prepare the way.

It was half a day of travel that felt like a hundred by the time we galloped off the barely-perceptible game trails and broke suddenly through a wall of trees, into the town of Galent itself—a sight that filled every spare inch of me with muted, tattered wonder.

These people had built their home on the trappings of a storybook. Woven among the soaring columns of ancient trees, the stone, wood, and wattle-and-daub homes and shops sprouted like mushrooms on tiers of rock climbing up along the hillsides. Stone bridges crisscrossed over tumbles of water that fell through the rock, joining tier to tier, home to home—places where neighbors could cross spans of arched rock and enter each other's upper rooms. Voices drifted on the wind, echoing like music off the crops of stone, blending into the birdsong floating down from the vaulted treetops.

Home—a life—built into the foundations of Mithra-Sha itself. A story written into rock and root.

I had no memory of it. But the sense of safety...the *relief* of arriving...poured through me stronger than the terror and fury and every other emotion I'd wrestled for so many days.

Before Gil urged his mount across the first bridge that crossed this side of the roaring river, I was already weeping.

We loped along the footpaths and stone bridges, winding toward the upper tiers—passing through a plaza of circled homes, where wide eyes watched the regiment stream past, bound for the town's uppermost level.

"That's the infirmary." Gil gestured toward a looming edifice with thick eaves and wood-paneled sides, perched above the rest of Galent by a small span. "Best air, best access to water. Hold tight, Addie. Almost there."

I was already clinging to the saddlehorn for my life. And already praying that Jaik was holding on even tighter than me.

CHAPTER 53
TALES OF US

THE TAPESTRIED AND HIDE-STRUNG walls of Galent's infirmary were beautiful at first sight...and rapidly became almost painfully familiar with the toll of passing time.

I refused to leave after our arrival while the healers swarmed the bed in the small, single-windowed room, assessing and then acting, applying salves and tinctures and pulling oils that were meant to counteract the infection spidering through Jaik's veins. And when they had done all their work—assuring me that, strange as it was and as quickly as it had come, infection was infection and could still be treated—I couldn't bear to draw myself away until I knew for certain that was true.

So I stayed, even when my back and shoulders ached from the firm chair at the bedside. I stayed, sustained on the sights of the golden-red trees swaying through the open shutters. I read the few books on the lampstand table, over and over, to myself at first and then aloud to him, my fingers woven into his so that I would feel if he so much as stirred.

Nothing.

When those books ran their course, their words still resonating in my head, the ink emblazoned behind every blink of my eyes...I kept my promise. I tried something I had not dared to do ever since he'd first told me who I was. Who I *had* been.

I told Jaik Grissom stories.

They were nothing of note...short, stumbling vignettes built from gossip threads woven throughout Krylan. But there was something in them that made my heart race, no matter how mundane the tale; it felt almost rebellious, forbidden, and that made it all the more alluring.

Stories held no power for me anymore...but that did not mean I couldn't tell them. And, after all, *no* stories had brought power to bear in Mithra-Sha for some years; but that had not stopped people from weaving a different sort of beauty with them.

Just like Reiko had told me, back in the Shastah.

So, for Jaik, I told him every tale I could think of, until a cadence emerged from the telling. Until I began to fathom intrinsically how stories began and middled and ended. In quiet, with confidence growing, I spun narratives about the world. About the places we had been.

About *us*.

I whispered fantastic imaginings of where we were going and what we would find along the way. Stories of mythical places and treasure troves and wonders yet undiscovered, waiting for *us* to find them.

And when my mind ached, when my imagination shriveled like waterlogged pages soaked with anxious thoughts as days passed and he still slept on...I went to his satchel, rooted through it, and found the journal he had first showed me on the bartop in the *Pourhouse.*

I read him its stories, written by two different hands...stories of seamstresses in cellars and soldiers on battlefields. Of lost souls and found hearts. Of those who wandered in the dark and those who shed light for them to stumble home by.

These tales I had started; these stories Jaik had finished. I wept over them, stroking tears away before they could plop on the pages and mar the ink, and broken laughter bubbled from my throat each time I reached the place where the careful, elegant script shifted to a sharper, sloppier scratch. Where the somber tales turned all of a sudden, each and every time, and faith began to bleed into the narrative. Where the story pivoted from hopeless to hopeful.

How fitting, that every story in my life became a happier one when Jaik Grissom helped me tell it.

I couldn't go on reading once that thought struck and settled; it pierced like a thorn beneath my flesh, and the tears turned from joy to grief and anger again.

Tucking the journal beneath his pillow, I slumped against the edge of the bed, draping one arm across Jaik's hipbones. And I cried myself into the murky depths of slumber.

CHAPTER 54
ALWAYS HAD SOMEONE

MORNING STRUCK OFF WITH the loud, violent clap of hands startling me to the fringes of a shadow-soaked dream; then the backhanded pop of knuckles on my thigh jolted me fully awake an instant before a strident feminine voice barked, "All right, enough of the breakdown at the bedside...it's honestly a bit too saccharine for my tastes."

Blinking sleep from my sticky eyes, I squinted at the figure who slipped past me to dump herself unceremoniously on the edge of Jaik's bed—so near our knees knocked together. Tall, fair-haired, with well-muscled arms, she shoved Jaik's legs to make more room for herself.

"Flipping Luck, what do they *feed* him?" she complained. "I swear on every coin toss I've ever made, he's taller than when I saw him last."

I scrubbed the haze from my eyes with the back of my knuckles. "I don't—"

"Remember me, I know. Gil and the regiment filled me in." She jutted out a hand, fingers half-gloved by a leather gauntlet. "Elyssabet Stanos. Glad to meet you *again*, Addie." A smirk tilted up one side of her mouth. "We were close the last time you visited."

A new corner of the pit in my stomach chipped away, yawning wider than ever. "I'm so sorry, I—"

"Feel horrible, wish you remembered me, so on and so forth." A breezy roll of her hand softened my shame. "Truth is, so much has changed since you were here last, we might as well start over with a blank page." Clapping her hands on her knees, she shoved to her feet. "Gil sent me to pry you out of that chair and get you down to the town hall for the afternoon meal. Said I have full permission from him *and* from the elders to use any force necessary. So, what'll it be? Are you coming on your own two feet, or do I throw you over my shoulder?"

For the first time in days, the urge to laugh manifested in a ticklish sensation at the back of my throat. Though I remembered nothing about this woman, I needed none to be certain of two things: the first, that we had absolutely been friends, and dear ones at that; and second, she would make good on her threat in a heartbeat.

Still, my gaze strayed back to Jaik, inert as he had been ever since the forest. But with the way Luck always seemed to flip the coin these days, he would stir as soon as my feet crossed the threshold. "Will...will someone stay with him, in case he wakes?"

Elyssabet nodded. "Gil's on his way."

Relief unspooled the breath I held deep in my lungs. Slowly, I pushed myself up from the chair, wavering a bit on aching, unsteady legs. Elyssabet caught my elbow, a flash of true concern spearing through her eyes...then softening when I gently tugged myself free.

"My own two feet," I said with as much of a smile as I could manage. "Now, let's go, shall we? If Jaik's going to be his usual ornery self and wake up the moment I leave, it's better we just get it over with."

Though my heart—and my thoughts—lingered in the infirmary, it was still wonderful to be out in the sunshine.

I had seen Galent painted in depthless shadows and sharp silhouettes by the first light of sunrise; in midday, it was something else entirely. Touched by the fiery hues of early autumn, the town braided itself among the trees like lovers' fingers linked together. Some of the homes were even perched among the lofty branches themselves, accessed by steps carved out of the bodies of the tree trunks. Others peppered the twisting avenues built of river-smoothed paverstones, lining the way to a broad plaza framed with shops and buttressed by a lofty, wood-and-stone communal hall.

That was where Elyssabet led me, her chatter a welcome balm after so many days filled with the sound of my own voice, and occasional conversations with the healers who came to assess Jaik. She pointed out things that had changed since my last visit—new homes in the treetops, fresh riverrock walls built along the bridges, and more—though I wouldn't know the difference; then we ducked into the warm, smoky interior of the communal hall, and I decided it was my new favorite place in all of Mithra-Sha.

At the far wall, a fireplace boomed and crackled; children roasted sausages and marshmallows over the flames, their laughter lightening the dark atmosphere of thick, sable roofbeams and hide-pelted floors. Tables framed in benches stretched the entire length of the hall. My attention hopscotched over them to the banquet counter against the far wall, where baskets of bread and a vat of stew were placed out for the lines of townspeople to enjoy—where Tayler, Lidya, and a handful of other faces swarmed, shoving each other out of the way for a meal, throwing nods our way.

Elyssabet nudged me, and we ducked into line, snatching up trays and bowls from the racks on the wall. "There's nowhere better in all of Galent than this place right here."

"I feel as if that's true of everywhere I look in this town," I admitted. "It's just so...welcoming. Cozy."

Like coming home.

"Well, that's nice to hear *you* say, of all people."

"What do you mean?"

Her gaze raked me up and down, and she snorted lightly. "You sure you want to know?"

Gratitude almost crowded out the hunger beginning to bubble in my stomach. "I appreciate you asking, but I really think I do."

"You've got it. Well, a long time ago, there was this soldiering outpost, like a lot of the ones out here in the mountains," she explained as we edged nearer to the banquet; the aroma of chicken and spices saturated my senses with my next inhale, and water flooded my mouth. "They've been around for...Luck only knows how long. Mostly keeping watch on Hadrass-Drui at the border, because they had some sort of upheaval with their elites centuries ago. The kind of thing that made past Shas nervous, you know?"

We reached the table at last; Elyssabet ladled generous portions of the creamy white stew into both of our bowls, then snatched three rolls apiece and plopped them onto our trays.

"Off we trot." She led the way to an empty pair of seats at the end of one of the long tables; situated across from one another, we tucked into the first truly warm meal I'd had in days...a blessing I hadn't had time to miss since we'd escaped the wraith.

I buried a shiver at the thought of that monstrosity beneath a spoonful of stew that warmed me from the inside out.

"Anyway," Elyssabet went on—a merciful and much-needed distraction, "soldiering outpost, long and storied history as such. Well, the Lothar lineage sort of forgot about it with power trading hands from fathers to sons, so the soldiers stopped waiting for orders from Vallanmyre. They learned woodcrafting and homesteading and turned the outpost into a town."

I swirled my spoon toward her. "Which became Galent."

"That'd be us." A flash of a sharp smile that gleamed all the brighter as she knocked her spoon against mine. "And an old town built by old soldiers raised on old ideals...they were really challenged to give up the old ways. Like letting girls learn swordplay and marksmanship."

A snort scraped the back of my throat. "Are you serious?"

"Let's just say that sitting out here waiting for trouble from Hadrass-Drui that's never coming, this town was well behind the good sense that spread across the rest of Mithra-Sha." Elyssabet blew off her next spoonful of soup. "But I grew up following Gil and Rowdi, my brother, everywhere. We trained and played together our whole lives, and both of them thought I deserved a chance to be part of a regiment. The town elders just wouldn't give me the chance."

I eyed the sword lashed to her hip, the rifle leaning against the table's edge. "What changed their minds?"

She shot me a grin. "*You* did."

I nearly choked on my next slurp of soup, coughing wildly at the searing heat that made my eyes water and nose run. "I...what?"

"You were the first Storycrafter to visit Galent in generations." Elyssabet leaned across the table to pound me on the shoulder. "*Master* Storycrafter, no less. You and Jaik had put your heads together to pull in all the old soldiering outposts and their commands, to strengthen the borders once trouble started brewing with Amere-Del. Jaik found us in some ancient army records, and one day you two came strolling into Galent and shook up everything like a fermented jar of onions."

Disbelief bolted through my chest like a blow. "You're serious."

"Oh, absolutely. And so were you." Elyssabet toppled back in her seat and helped herself to another bite before she added, "*Seriously* enraged the town elders wouldn't let me or any of the other girls try out for the regiments. You gave some grand Storycrafter's speech about how people should be judged on their merit alone, and Jaik pointed out how you were one of the youngest Master Storycrafters ever to wear the mantel. Then he offered to fight me, to make it a fair show of my talents...he said the army wouldn't give Galent back its station unless they caught up with the times." Smugness wreathed her tone, hinting at that particular story's ending before she added, "It was a tie—knocked each other out after a half-hour duel. But a tie was good enough…after that, the elders couldn't have saved face if they didn't put me in the ranks."

"That…does sound like Jaik." My chest squeezed with a yearning for that cocksure confidence, the swaggering grin that must have accompanied his challenge even back then.

"It should sound like *you*, too, because you told them you'd be checking in on the regular to make sure *everyone* was given an opportunity to train as a soldier who wanted to." She shook her head. "In the space of two weeks, I went from having nothing to everything. Just because you two sniffed us out of the woods."

"And…how are you now?" I ventured, swirling my soup and gathering a spoonful of meat and beans while I studied her face.

Elyssabet's answer came with a catlike grin. "Just earned my full rank as a soldier a few years ago, and now Gil and I lead our regiment together." Her eyes sparkled with a mischievous, infectious joy. "They keep us on our boot-tips, but you know…I wouldn't have it any other way."

"I think I know what you mean." And, truly, I was beginning to.

Life could be dangerous, and frustrating, and an absolute whirlwind of an adventure tale…and still be joyful. A journey could be long and difficult and still make way for quiet cabin kisses and breathtaking views of the best a country had to offer.

Struggle did not demand we give up. Sometimes, it demanded we persevere.

"What about you?" Elyssabet forewent the spoon to slurp her last bite of stew straight from the bowl. "What's life like for you now? Where did you land?"

"Krylan," I admitted.

"*Krylan*!" Barking a laugh, she banged down her bowl and wiped her mouth on the back of her wrist. "That's the last place I expected *you* to land, being so close to the Ameresh border. So, how was it?"

"It's…" I blew out a breath, stirring the forelock that had strayed too far into my eyes this last handful of days. My brow was beginning to itch from the oils. "Do you want the truth?"

"Oh, Luck, Audra Jashowin *asking* if someone wants the truth? Not telling you she's going to give it to you, whether you want to hear it or not—because hearing it is best for you?" I pinned her with a halfhearted scowl, and she tossed her hair back. "*Fine*, fine. Yes, I want your truths, Addie. All of them."

I bit my lips together, trapping the retort that she surely didn't want *that* much. Instead, I gave her the one promised: "Compared to all of this, life in Krylan seems incredibly…"

"Boring?"

"Lonely."

Elyssabet eased back in her chair, folding her arms slowly over her narrow waist. A dark sort of sorrow settled in her eyes, like midday shadows dappling a forest floor. "You know…you were a lot of things when I last knew you. Ambitious, bold, loud-mouthed, brilliant, feisty. But one thing you never were was lonely. You always had your friends back in Vallanmyre, a family you wouldn't shut up about. And you always had Jaik."

"I know." Tightness balled in the base of my throat. "From the sound of things, I always had *someone*." A smile etched up the corners of my lips. "And so many of them I've forgotten."

"You really didn't have anyone like us in Krylan?"

I shook my head, scraping the bottom of my soup bowl. "I had my cat, Sheeba. But this has been so different. This whole journey, it's been horrific at times…so often I've wanted to give up. To go back. But…" My fingers tightened around the spoon until bone strained under skin, begging for release as much as the words building up on my tongue. "But it's also been so *wonderful* to not be alone. And to know that my life amounted to something more than I ever believed it could. Not just filling tankards and helping erase a day's sorrows, but…"

"Actually doing something that would matter after you were gone." A pure and priceless understanding shaped Elyssabet's grin.

"*Yes.*" The word rushed from me on a sharp breath—and more tumbled after it. "Other than Leatrix possibly being frustrated to death with my replacement…I don't think anyone at the *Pourhouse* or anywhere else in Krylan truly cares that I disappeared. But when I'm out here…I feel my own fingerprints everywhere. On people I've touched, with stories I've told. My craft. My *life* meant something out in this world…even if I don't remember it, people remember *me*."

"I know *I* certainly do." Her eyes shimmered as she leaned her folded arms on the tabletop now, bending earnestly toward me. "You changed everything for me, Addie. For this whole town."

And nothing could have warmed me more.

CHAPTER 55
COME BACK TO ME

IT ALMOST ESCAPED MY notice just how long Elyssabet managed to keep me out of the infirmary. What began as a simple meal elongated to a tour of Galent, with more twists and turns tacked on at every corner of the town I confessed I had no memory of.

So our return was by the longest route, winding on foot through the streets I'd glimpsed by horseback, admiring pumpkin patches and apple tree groves and a more radiant array of fall hues than I had ever seen. Elyssabet first cajoled, than adamantly insisted I try a cup of golden turmeric milk from a vendor stall; while I sipped its delicious, nutty foam, she walked me through her family's orchard and down a steep slope behind it to the communal training grounds.

There I was reintroduced properly to the rest of the regiment—to Tayler and Lydia, laboring and graoning through their paces after the meal in the hall; to Kassa, the healer who'd stabilized Jaik, who bandaged a sprained thumb on Evani, the youngest and brightest-eyed girl among them; to Rowdi, Elyssabet's brother, who slapped me on the back in hearty greeting so hard I coughed up all my air, and Ronna, who slapped him upside the head for it before planting a kiss on his cheek; and to Andray and Quinn, a pair of archers who glanced away from their targets to greet me and *still* managed to strike the bull's-eye.

My head was awhirl with good food and too many greetings, sights seen and faces met all over again, and my feet and calves thumped from the uphill climbs and downhill descents by the time we finally returned to the infirmary. It was only by the swathing of dimming daylight along the now-familiar walls that I realized with a jolt Elyssabet and I had been gone most of the day.

Despite footweariness, my strides lengthened at the thought, an eager sort of desperation carrying me down the last wood-walled corridor to Jaik's room—where we found Gil with his feet up on Jaik's bed, ankles crossed, playing a hand of cards, and checking Jaik's for him.

Jaik, still unconscious, cards on his chest and head turned away from his friend.

"Ah, another bad hand." Gil shook his head. "Luck really doesn't love you, Jaik."

"Please tell me he's not betting his belongings." Elyssabet dropped herself on the arm of Gil's chair.

"As Luck would have it, I actually already won his boots, his rifle, and his sword."

"The sword is not up for bets," I warned, propping myself against the doorframe and breathing through the drop of despair that came from seeing Jaik as inert as ever.

Gil grinned. "No memories and she's still fighting for what he loves. Now, that's a story if I've ever heard one."

It was good to have their company as I wrestled the steeping grief in my core, and I gladly accepted the round of cards they invited me to play; their banter was a soothing cadence that softened the sting of Jaik's ongoing slumber. It helped pass the next handful of hours until I could think of sleeping again...and Elyssabet, keen as ever, seemed to catch the moment my distraction overwhelmed the fun of the game.

"I think it's time we let her get back to her morbid bedside vigil." Slipping the cards from my hand, Elyssabet bumped them into a neat, expert stack. "Besides, the only thing she's got left to bet is her underwear."

"Not true. I have my cloak," I protested.

"Which you'd never bet." Gil winked, shoving to his feet.

I caught his wrist. "Thank you for staying with him today, Gil."

"It's the least I could do." A bit of his booming liveliness slackened as he glanced at Jaik; uncertainty wrote the furrow between his brows. "Healers say he should wake any time now."

Elyssabet pocketed the cards and slipped from the armrest, settling both hands on Gil's shoulders and squeezing. "Actually, what they said was whenever his body is healed enough to handle the pain awake, he'll come around. And that it *could* be any day."

Gil bobbed his head faintly, one hand crawling up to clasp hers more tightly over his shoulder.

A pang of painful yearning bloomed in my chest at that casual contact. I had wished with all my might that even once this last week, Jaik would have returned the sharp squeezes I gave his fingers.

And...nothing.

"Come on, Gillian. Patrol." Elyssabet's voice jerked me from my thoughts, and I blinked, raising my eyes to hers; knowingness shimmered in her stare, and the dip of her chin she paid me was a silent commiseration.

Pressing my lips thin, I nodded back. "Thank *you*, for today. For the meal and the tour."

"Oh, trust me, Addie, it's not just today. You and me, at the dining hall, tomorrow." Elyssabet aimed her fingers at me over Gil's shoulders. "I won't take no for an answer."

I flashed her a smile. "Who am I to argue with a soldier?"

"Ha!" Gil scoffed. "*Arguing* was more your calling than being a Storycrafter, Jashowin."

"Oh, get out and let her mope." Elyssabet shoved him toward the door, casting me a parting wink before she and Gil disappeared into the outer hall, their good-natured arguments peppering the air.

The woosh of my sigh filled the echoing silence in their absence.

Alone again. I had never despised it more.

Rising from my place against the wall, I edged to Jaik's bedside, halting with a hand braced on the footboard to rub a cramp from my calf. I truly was not looking forward to another night sleeping in that chair...particularly after a full day of touring the village.

A notion occurred to me then—a bit reckless, a bit improper. It had me peering through the arched doorway across the room, neck itching as if I'd be caught just for having it.

But no sign of the day's healer in the hall beyond.

Well...and if they found me and yelled at me for a lack of propriety, then so be it. From what Elyssabet had told me, I'd never been bothered by challenging the rules of this town. Why start now?

Sliding onto the bed, I wedged myself in the narrow gap of the mattress at Jaik's side; lifting his limp arm, I pulled it around myself like a blanket, wriggling as close to him as I could. Then, with my head tucked over his thudding heart, I laced my fingers with his and hugged his arm around me.

"Jaik, I need you to wake up." I pressed a kiss to the line of his jaw. "I need you to come back to me."

CHAPTER 56
MAKING A STAND

I N THE SLIM SPACE between waking and sleeping, where dreams tangled with the threads of truth and the world was fantastical and flighty and full of possibilities, both good and ill...everything was scarlet.

Deep scarlet. Blood-red.

A forest floor drizzled in crimson. A golden chamber paved in sanguine shades.

My hands coated in blood.

A future of this...

A world torn by this...

Hate. Grief.

I have lost you so much. *I don't think I want to remember what it feels like to lose you all over again.*

A sob lodged in my throat, a silent wail tearing at the boundaries of the half-awake, desperate to claw free from dreams and make itself manifest in the world.

A scream for love stolen away. For all that had slipped to the tips of my fingers—and might still be torn from my grasp.

Ayjay...

A bloodied leg. A chest rived open by a betrayer's blade.

Shame. Terror. Rage.

I'm right here, hey...

Painful, stammering breaths, the world splitting apart at the seams, flesh rending, bone snapping, minds and memories undone—

I'm dying to see how this one ends.

"Ayjay, hey! Hey, stop—*look at me!*"

I gasped awake—screamed myself awake—slapping and slashing with both arms, swimming in a sea of fabric. Antiseptic and blood stung my nostrils, and my mind ravaged itself on confusion, on dreams, on things that felt too clear, too close, too *cutting* to just be a vision—

A hand wrapped the back of my neck, anchoring me a heartbeat before my palms slipped from the bed; my heart jolted at the nearness of falling, a surge of terrifying clarity that emptied my thundering ears to hear a strained, panting rasp as that broad hand steadied me on the bed's edge. "Whoa, whoa. Take it easy, tiger. You really that eager to get away from me?"

Another blink. My vision swam, hazy with sleep, with tears—hardly daring to believe that what I heard was not part of those terrifying scarlet dreams on the verge of waking. "*Jaik?*"

"Yeah?" A hoarse, throaty chuckle, edged with nervousness. "Who else are you thinking you'd wake up in bed next to? Something I need to know—?"

The last words slammed out of him in a rough gust as I shoved away from the edge of the mattress, yanking my knees beneath my body and thrusting myself across the bed to wrap my arms around him.

His bare shoulders, perfectly fitted beneath the grip of my hands, rising and falling with measured, even breaths. His skin, no longer fever-burned like in the forest when he'd slipped away. When I'd thought I'd heard his voice for the last time.

"Flipping *Luck*." I buried my face—hid my tears—in the fluttering pulse on the side of his neck. "I thought I was going to lose you, Jaik."

Again.

And maybe this was everything I had feared since I'd begun to know him again—everything that had tried to convince me to flee from him. From this. From *us.*

But holding him now, I found that mattered so much less than the joy—the relief—of holding his living warmth against me, trailing my fingertips up and down the arch of his spine, tracing his scars and his muscles and knowing he was *here*. Awake. Alive.

Jaik.

My Jaik.

"Aw, Addie...hey." His hand tangled in my hair, his cheek shifting, days of stubble scratching against my temple as he dropped his face to my shoulder in turn. "Sorry, I didn't mean to scare you like that. I know you're—"

"*Stop* right there, Jaik Grissom." Planting my hands against his chest, I pushed back to meet his exhausted, sheepish stare. "Tell me you are not about to apologize for being stabbed by—"

The wraith. My tongue almost formed those words, but a shudder bit them short.

Until now—until I had seen his waking eyes, felt his fever broken with my own hands on his body—that suffering had been the greatest horror I'd carried away from the forest. But now it was cringing back, making way for other things.

Sundered shrieks. Steel and shadow ringing together. Jaik's anguished cry as the wraith's shadow-dagger plunged through his skin.

Bile sweated in my mouth.

Jaik grimaced as if his thoughts followed the same paths back to the forest glade. "I didn't mean for it to happen like that."

"Neither did I. But we don't need to have that conversation yet." Gripping his cheeks, I searched those earthen eyes, touched with amber light spilling through the window behind me. The fever glaze had chipped away, revealing that cocksure, taunting brightness I'd come to search for in every part of this country we'd traipsed through. "How do you feel?"

"Leg's sore. Stiff." He bent the knee halfway, then grimaced, letting it slide flat again. "How long was I out?"

"Days." Among the worst of the life that I *could* remember, true or fabricated—but I wasn't going to tell him that. Not when guilt already lurked in the corners of his stare. "We made it to Galent. Gil found us."

Jaik blew out a long breath. "Figured he would, if we got close enough. His regiment likes to patrol up north, bring herbs back for healers like Kassa."

Well. That explained the dearth of flowers and seedpods along our route.

Jaik's hand encircled my upper arm, and with a gentle push, he laid us both back on the bed, facing one another; he tugged the blanket up around my shoulder, then trapped it beneath his elbow. "You want to tell me what that screaming was about?"

Wincing, I tugged my lip between my teeth; now that I was awake, and the dreams blurring to a dagger-edged, crimson haze, those screams—and the tears—needled with a touch of the melodramatic. "Just...nightmares."

"Mmhmm." His hand slid down the length of my blanket-shrouded arm, then back up to my shoulder; his eyes followed the motion, then flicked to mine. "That happening a lot since I've been out?"

"What do you think, Jaik?"

A sigh blustered from his flaring nostrils; he shifted nearer, pressing a kiss above my left eye. "Sorry."

This time, I knew well enough it wasn't shame undergirding that heavy word; it was grief.

Grief that I had traveled that brambled forest alone. That I had faced the possibility of his death alone. That I had confronted one of the deepest fears scripted on every page of my life's story now...and that it had written itself into my dreams.

"I'm just glad you were here to wake me from it this time," I murmured.

We lay with those thoughts for a long while in silence—thoughts of the things we endured, and what we could and couldn't save each other from. I lost all sense of time, wrapped in Jaik's arms, tangled in the starched sheets; it was the nearest to home I'd felt in days.

There was no more space between us, only words and sweet, slow kisses, and stirring occasionally simply to graze our hands over one another. It might have been hours later or the following dawn when we both stirred to the echo of taxed hinges, the door sailing open—a familiar, booming voice filling the space that had shrunk considerably now that I'd moved into the bed.

"There he is! Jaik, my brother, how in fickle, flipping Luck are you *doing*?"

"Gil," Jaik groaned, hefting up on one hand and snaking the other arm from behind my neck to thrust it Gil's way. I lay on my back as Gil's long legs gobbled the distance in two strides; he seized Jaik's hand, tugged him fully upright, and gripped the back of his neck, kissing his brow.

"Healers sent for us, said there was a change but wouldn't tell us what!" Gil chortled, freeing Jaik and flopping back into the chair. Spanning his hands on his thighs, he swept his gaze between us—brows jumping and waggling. "No need for worry, by the look of things."

"Nothing happened," Jaik grumbled. "Not with this leg, anyway."

Slowly, Gil shook his head. "I tell you, Jaik, you've got a nose for trouble like no one else I've ever met."

"Except for Audra." That sweet, needling remark heralded Elyssabet's arrival, twin platters of steaming sweet yeast buns in her hands. I nearly wept as the intoxicating aroma brushed my nostrils, and launched myself upright to catch the dishes when she thrust them my way.

"Right, but I sort of think of them as..." Gil wound his first and middle fingers around each other, "same soul, two bodies."

"Luck sure loves us, eh, tiger?" Jaik smirked, lifting one of the buns off the platter; I guarded the other against my chest, sticking out my tongue at him. The smirk transformed to a cackle, and he tore into the sticky bun with a savory moan, leaning back on the bed's iron headboard while he regarded Gil side-long. "So...what'd I miss?"

"Few days of town gossip." Gil shrugged. "The whole regiment threw down a betting pool on whether you'd wake up or not."

"Flipping opportunists," Jaik muttered. "Tell the winners they owe me a cut, since I did all the work pulling through."

"Same old Jaik." Elyssabet alit one haunch on the arm of Gil's chair—the same position they'd taken up last night, yet today it all felt brighter. Easier. "And still dodging the same old questions. You heard Gil—how are you doing? Feeling all right?"

"Feeling more like I got impaled through the leg by a Misspoken knife." Jaik tossed back the rest of the sticky bun, then rubbed his bandaged calf; that half-idle motion sparked in my mind with the memory of his agonized fingers strangling the bloodsoaked hem of his trousers. The wetness of his wound beneath *my* fingers.

I swallowed, slowly tugging my bun into much more manageable bites.

Elyssabet shook her head, brows knitting together. "We've gotten piece-meal scraps from Addie about that...sounds like this wraith that's hunting you is real trouble."

"Trouble like nothing *we've* ever heard of," Gil grumbled. "And you know we've seen our share of those beasties out here."

"Pretty sure no one's faced anything like this." Jaik shot me a sidelong glance..

Gil shifted in the chair, tucking one hand behind his head and sliding into a tension-freeing stretch. "Looking at that wound and how many things the healers had to throw at it to get the swelling down and stop the infection spreading—that's one nasty bastard."

"You got that right."

"And it's not just hunting," I added glumly. "It's bringing other mani-festations to its cause."

Elyssabet's frown deepened so sharply, it cast her eyes in shadow. Jaik's hand drifted to the small of my back, then wound its way up to the nape of my neck. And for the first time, absolute seriousness stamped Gil's features; he leaned toward me, shoulders bowed, hands pressed together...paying me the full weight of a Galent regiment leader's attention.

"Come again?" he said gruffly.

"Couple times now, we've seen it leading a pack," Jaik explained, while I fought back a shiver at the memory of gaping, humanoid mouths and glittering white eyes sparking in the undergrowth alongside the gorge. "In Rivrand, and out in the forest. We heard it stirred things up outside Belaris, too."

"Before that, it seemed like it rallied Misspoken manifestations to sack ships," I added. "One of which we were sailing on."

Elyssabet cursed Luck this time. "What kind of story could have made *that* possible?"

"That's the thing. Most of the manifestations it's bringing around are your run-of-the-mill kind, probably left over from the lean years." Jaik's thumb brushed along my nape in a slow, steady pressure. "But the wraith itself?"

"Neither of us can think of what sort of story could've made it," I confessed. "Or who would have been powerful enough to do it."

Silence dusted the room like ashes for a moment; then Gil shifted in his seat. "Might never figure that part out. But what about dealing with it, brother?"

"We've tried rifles, that didn't work. Storycraft either," Jaik replied.

Elyssabet straightened in her seat. "Are you *serious*?"

"Unfortunately, yes." I scrunched the heels of my hands against my aching eyes. "It *was* frightened off by a certain kind of Storycraft, but even that wasn't enough to destroy it completely. And now it's not even scared of that anymore."

"Only thing it's really seemed hurt by is this." Jaik tapped a finger on the hilt of his sword, propped against his bedside.

"So what you need is to get close enough to run it through." Gil cocked a thoughtful brow. "We can make it happen. Fortify and dig in. Get ready for what Misspoken nonsense comes our way, give you your best chance to finish the job."

Jaik shifted nearer to me. "What do you think, tiger?"

Pressing my lips against a terrified breath that ached to wobble free, I forced a nod. "That's why we came to Galent. Let's make our stand."

CHAPTER 57
A THOUSAND THREADS IN A TAPESTRY

SOLDIERING WAS BUILT IN the very bones of Galent—in the structure of its edifices, in the carving of its footpaths, in its defensible tree towers and fortified stone walls. Even without the history Elyssabet and Gil had morseled out to me, my time in the army-rich Tailbone City brought those qualities to light. In the weeks that ensued, as we fortified homesteads and town avenues, it became clearer every day how the anticipation of siege and strife were a way of life for these people. A generational consideration.

And yet...

There was not the fear in them that had choked Belaris. There was no bent toward suspicion or hands raised in cruelty. The same discipline that had set these people's ancestors at their posts in the Vensair Mountains and held them unwavering long after even the Sha had forgotten them...it carried on to these current generations as a way of living. Not a weapon wielded, but a fortification of the heart and soul that stoked the embers of my courage into flame.

There was truly nowhere better to make our stand. Nowhere assured to have such inherent soldiering strength, something to combat whatever Misspoken manifestations struck next.

We might not have story at our disposal here, but we had the sword in plenty.

Swords, and strong backs, and shoulders—all put to the paper of life, rewriting the angles and avenues of Galent, etching themselves down and out through the winding side streets and broad thoroughfares in layers of defense. New watches were raised, new avenues of escape laid and then concealed.

Storycraft was a barreling force against which sword and shield could often do little. But these manifestations could only strike what lay before them; so we peered deeper, thought around the edges. Jotted notes in the margins where they could not be easily read.

For nearly a fortnight, that was our life—two weeks of strengthening and steadying, while reports from the regiments told of Misspoken manifestations circling distant pockets of the mountains like carrion birds, slowly closing in on the lower portion of the Vensair range.

Two weeks with neither note nor notion of the Storymaker, ahead of or behind us. As if He, too, had taken pause. As if He watched, and waited to see what would become of us.

Anxious energy rattled in my hands and bloomed in my chest, tempered with counts of fives and fours and threes and twos and ones. My dreams festered, quieted only when I curled into the warmth at Jaik's side each night—first in the infirmary bed and then, once the healers declared him fit enough, in a small inn that refused to accept payment for our board.

Even though he was still recovering, Jaik was often awake before me, first hobbling, then hurrying with Gil through the streets, possessed by fervor of a different sort altogether.

We both felt it, though we only dared whisper it in the quiet of our small room, long after dark had fallen and the shadows beckoned secrets to be spoken in the safety of the deepening night: we could go no further than this with the shadowed haze of the wraith's violent intentions streaming behind us like an ashen cloak, blanketing our comings and goings in a pall.

Either this ended, or it ended us. But we would not bring the havoc of Misspoken manifestations and desperate vengeance to one more town. Particularly not towns so full of life, so full of *joy*—just like Galent.

It was almost infectious, that joy. It reeled me out of despair time and again when poor sleep and pits in my stomach threatened to overshadow everything else.

And then that joy somehow found me at a tavern one evening, sitting across from Gillian, a day's worth of sweat and grime from hard labor seeping out of our pores. We leaned against opposite sides of a crooked tabletop, elbows propped, hands locked—struggling with all our might to win an arm-wrestling match and a free ale.

Sweet beaded down my temples despite the ferocious tail I'd tied my hair back into; shoving against Gil's hand was like a Misspoken manifestation trying to bowl over the wooden pikes we'd drummed into the soil between the buildings at Galent's outer edge—or so I hoped. If our fortifications on walls, doors, and windows held as fast as the bulging muscles in Gil's upper arm, there was hope for us yet.

"Come on, Ayjay!" Jaik roared, clapping both hands on my shoulders from behind.

"Cheating!" Gil runted—a satisfactory amount of strain in that single word, considering I was fighting for my life against the thrust of his arm.

"What, by touching her *shoulders*? It's not like I'm packing my grip around that ham loaf you call a fist!"

A roar of laughter went up from the tables and chairs circled around ours; Rowdi whined audibly as we passed another five-second interval, and he lost another coin for the time.

"You've got this, tiger," Jaik murmured against the shell of my ear.

My arm wobbled as a shiver spidered down my nape; Gil's grin broadened, eyes crinkling, a genial sort of savagery stroking the lines around his eyes.

Elyssabet hooted, swirling one finger through a strand of hair at the base of Gil's sweaty mop of curls. "For honor, Gilly! For glory!"

"For Galent!" the regiment cheered as one, Andray and Quinn knocking their own frothing tankards together.

"On second thought, brother, keep it right up," Gil gloated.

Oh, no way in flipping *Luck* I was letting *that one* slide.

"So tell me, Gil," I panted, "how long *have* you have and Elyssabet been in love?"

Crunch. His elbow slipped on the wood, and swifter than I could blink, I had his knuckles trapped against the tabletop.

A beat of silence. Elyssabet froze, staring at me.

Then Rowdi lunged to his feet, kicking back his chair, fists thrown skyward. "I—flipping—*knew it!* You all owe *me*, pay up, pay up *right this instant*—Kassa, don't you even think about slinking out that door—"

Gil grimaced good-naturedly when I squeezed his hand, then let it go. "Wondered if you were ever going to remember that."

"I don't remember—it's just obvious, how you two are with each other." I tossed Elyssabet an apologetic smile.

Folding her arms on Gillian's shoulders, she rolled her eyes. "As if you're one to talk."

Heat freckled my cheeks and dipped the tips of my ears; I pushed back my seat—carefully, mindful of Jaik balancing on the back of it—and hurried to the counter, clapping a hand on the smooth wood. "Excuse me—barkeep!" When the salt-and-pepper-haired woman swiveled my way, I laid a hand over my heart. "I'll have that tankard Gil promised."

"Good for you, love," she chuckled. "Let me pull that for you."

I could hardly believe this was my first time in Galent's most popular watering hole. The two-story edifice was open-sided even in autumn—Elyssabet claimed they only shuttered the four walls in the dead of winter. Tonight, that meant easy access to the wraparound porch that laced the lower half, and a clear view of the mist-shrouded pond around which the tavern perched. Three bridges connected to the porch itself, each one capped in Storycrafted amber bulbs that retained and burned off sunlight throughout the night; gleaming light from windows on the upper level fell past the tavern's gables, adding their glow to a sweet, sleepy evening atmosphere.

The second level was accessible only by a grand, spiral iron staircase; according to Tayler, that was rented out for private assemblies. Their regiment liked to use it when they needed to strategize for full days.

Tonight, someone was being wed there—and enjoying an endless stream of celebratory drinks. The faint strains of lute and fiddle floated down the steps as barmistresses and masters came and went, keeping the wedding party in bubbly bliss.

They weren't the only ones.

I couldn't remember the last time I'd felt so light—so *safe*. We were fortified, we were surrounded by soldiers, and we hadn't seen a trace of an aberrant shadow in weeks.

So, for now, I wanted to believe that the wraith *had* fallen at Jaik's hand. That the Misspoken manifestations out in the hills were just that...wandering manifestations waiting to be culled by soldiers and Storycrafters.

That we could have this happiness and not have to pay for it...something as free as the ale the barkeeper shoved my way, with a smile and a flourish.

I took the tankard tentatively, eyeing the thin top on the brew.

Well, it is an unpaid drink. Nothing to do but sip.

A poor choice, indeed.

"Oh, this..." I sucked in my lips and squinted my eyes, my whole face retreating from the unpalatable thinness of the flavor. "Oof."

"Pulling ales it not my specialty," the barkeeper admitted with a sheepish smile. "Keeping things up and running is. Unfortunately, we're a bit understaffed tonight, what with the wedding and half of my best tenders on the fortification efforts."

Gratitude cooled the faint bite of nausea in my belly. "Well, I was a barmistress for years in Krylan. Would you like an extra pair of hands?"

The older woman straightened, slinging the bar rag over her shoulder. "Can't pay you, Miss."

"I don't need pay!" I vaulted the counter with a thrust of hands, landing beside her in the familiar span behind. "I'd just like to help."

A dimple carved into her cheek, mischief sparkling in her eyes as she slid the rag off again and draped it around my neck. "Show me what you can do, then."

There was something wonderful about being behind the bar again; repetitive, familiar motion soothed the edge of blistering emotions that burgeoned with the swift autumn onset of night. Tending bar belonged to a different time for me, before shadow wraiths and missing memories; it helped, somehow, to stand tonight with a foot in each world.

Anvera, the barkeeper, hovered over me like a raven over a shimmering stash for the first hour; then she retreated to manage the orders arriving further down the counter, convinced I wouldn't drive her reputation into a pit in one night. I served faces both familiar and forgotten—some of the regiment placing orders for more complicated mixed spirits just to test me.

It was even a little enjoyable to show off what I had learned in Krylan...to earn their praise for a well-made drink. To cheer on the arm-wrestling tournament that continued at one table while the others took up dice and cards—and to call out the cheaters while I studied their hands in the lulls between customers.

One of those lulls after a lurch of new orders from the wedding feast above found me swabbing out glasses and lining them below the counter, just soaking in the sights and sounds of Galent. The chirring insects around the pond's edge; the misty glow cut by the tawny globes. The faces smoothed by candlelight in this place.

Faces I had come to care for in our weeks here.

Faces I'd once loved.

Leaning my hands on the bar's edge, I soaked them all in through a haze of tears cresting in my eyes.

I'd thought I'd had everything I needed back in Krylan—or maybe I'd just told myself I wanted for nothing to make what I had seem like enough.

But this feeling, this...this *warmth* bubbling up from my core, this smile that made my cheeks ache, this *joy*...

I had never felt anything like it before. Not one moment from the time I'd woken beneath that bridge in Vallanmyre had ever compared to *this*.

Perhaps that was why I had enjoyed the crew of *The Cathan* so much, and our friends in Vallanmyre, in Fallshyre Bay, and these soldiers in Galent. Maybe that was why, in all these places, I'd felt a yearning for stories again. Not because they were like a barscape, these people like customers, but...

Like *characters*.

They popped and blistered as if they were embers cast up to mingle with the stars. Each one vibrant, each one beautiful, each one branded across my eyes with every blink.

Elyssabet, built with the swaggering pride of a woman who'd proven her station, time and again...and relished it.

Gil, his strut and charisma strung like battle charms across his smile, a man born to defend this beloved place.

Tayler, Kassa, Lidya, Ronna, Andray, Quinn, Rowdi, and Evani—Gil and Ely's entire regiment, soldiers I had labored beside all these weeks, names and faces I had known once and who were imprinted on my heart again. All of them dancing, drinking, reveling together as if no danger awaited...and each carrying the fear of it differently, behind glittering smiles, in the slam of goblets together and mead and cider tossed back.

Each of them leading their own stories. And all of those stories entwined, like threads of smoke and scarlet, plot after plot intermingling into a tale that forged the world.

For the first time, I saw it all through the Storymaker's eyes—thousands of threads spun from His tapestry. Thousands of stories branching away from the first Wellspoken one that had shaped all the known world.

We were all characters. All of us stories. All of us epics waiting to be etched into the fabric of the world.

And mine...mine was just beginning to take shape. The past unraveled from its knot. The future becoming so achingly, beautifully clear.

The best part of it was making its way to meet me now: Jaik, limping toward the counter even as I filled a last stein and slid back across to meet him...one character finding another in every iteration of their tale. Unwilling to be parted, whatever happenstance or tragedy penned their story.

"Nice work, tiger," he greeted me with a wolfish grin.

"Nice work, *you*," I tossed back, pushing the stein his way. "I saw that last arm-wrestling match...that makes you the champion, I take it?"

"That's me." He winked. "Good thing I didn't take that knife to the bicep, right?"

"Your liver might disagree on the luck of it."

"Eh." With a shrug, Jaik gulped his drink, leaning against the edge of the counter beside me. "Haven't seen you smile like this in a long time."

"I think I love it here," I admitted. "It's a good town. And these are good people."

"Some of the best I know."

We stood in companionable agreement of that, pitched back against the barcounter, listening to laughter and heckling and conversation all raised against the sweet refrain of strings and flutes and drums.

It sounded like love's first dance—the last of the night, when a wedding party made way for the bride and groom to pen the end of their ceremony with a private turn on the dance floor. Marli and I had always loved those moments best; when our parents' friends had wed, we'd always watched in rapt attention, chins on fists, daydreaming of when it would be our turn. What song we would choose, whether we would practice the dances beforehand or not.

Marli had always been a firm advocate for learning to dance *with* your partner. I'd always felt differently—that it was better if you knew the steps first, so you wouldn't stumble through life.

Perhaps if I'd been more willing to risk, to let go of everything and just *fall,* then my story would've gone a bit differently.

"Do you think," I murmured, tipping my head against Jaik's shoulder, "that if we'd had the chance to be married properly, it would've been like this?"

"Oh, yeah." Jaik slipped an arm around my waist. "Matter of fact...this was where we were planning to run to, when we tried to get out of the Shastah."

Shock tilted my chin up with its sharp fingers, my wide eyes finding the grief that half-masted his. "You're joking."

"Nah." He slid his free hand into his pocket, nodding across the tavern to where Gil and Elyssabet played a game of one-card-up. "They knew about us. Sort of figured each other's big secret out in the same fight. Gil and Elly mostly kept it to themselves just to make things simpler as soldiers, but by then they knew us well enough to guess it wouldn't work out if we stayed in the Shastah."

"They were going to let us live here?"

Jaik shrugged. "We planned to make our way through the Vensair Moun-tains on our own time. Stay at the cabin for a while, pick our way southeast, make it to Galent eventually. No one really cared about this outpost as much as we did, even the Sha, so we figured once he blew through every place he thought he could find us, we could probably settle out here. Live a normal life." He scoffed quietly, then buried the sound in another sip of ale. "Yeah. I had it all laid out in my head...I'd ask you to marry me in the cabin, first place we were ever honest about what we meant to each other. Then we'd get married right here in this flipping tavern."

Warmth bubbled and simmered and spilled over in my middle at the notion; and perhaps it was the hum of the ale in my veins, or the safety of this place, or simply that we had waited too flipping long being anything but reckless in search of reward. But when he banged the stein down, I twisted into Jaik's grip, wrapping my arms around his neck, breathing him into the depths of my lungs. I backed him against the counter's edge so there was no space between our bodies.

"Marry me, Jaik Grissom," I whispered against the side of his neck.

He slammed one hand back to cushion against the counter's stern edge. The other explored my hip, the dip of my spine, then rose to fist in my hair—tugging my head back until our eyes met, the desire in his reflecting the heat that burned in mine.

"Yeah. Right now?"

I framed his bearded cheeks with both hands. "*Right now.* You are my favorite part of this story. And I don't want to wait one more second before we write one worth remembering."

Because I was certain of one thing, without any doubt whatsoever: memo-ries or none, I was Jaik Grissom's, and he was mine.

And tonight...

That was precisely who I wanted to be.

CHAPTER 58
OUR HOPE AND HAPPINESS

I F I COULD HAVE written my own story however I liked, it would have begun with every day this way:

Waking up tucked in the curve of Jaik's body, his arm strung around my waist. Mellow golden sunlight streaking in through the windows of our room at the inn, freckling the bedsheets that swaddled us and gilding the hairs on Jaik's other arm, tucked under the crook of my neck and around my clavicles, his hand cradling my opposite shoulder.

The brush of his breaths on the back of my neck. The way I could bury my nose in his wrist and breathe in the tinge of campsmoke and pine and leather that hovered perpetually over his skin. The shivering sensation when I pressed a kiss to the pulse at the heel of his palm and felt every steady beat rising to greet my lips.

Last night's memory of stumbling, laughter-and-drink-soaked, up to Gil's regiment and telling them to follow us. Pulling aside the town officiant when the wedding party streamed from the tavern, and Jaik, Gil, Elyssabet, and I bantering and harassing him good-naturedly until he was finally convinced Jaik and I were more than just a sloppy pair of lovesick strangers who'd found each other at the bar counter.

Which was, amusingly, somehow less ridiculous than the truth of who we were and how we'd met. And how we'd fallen in love, once, twice, *three times* over.

Lucky threes, Elyssabet had teased as she and Kassa, Evani, and Lidya crowded around me on one side of the arm-wrestling table.

A gray thread unraveled from the hem of my cloak, twined around my finger. Jaik's mouth on mine, sealing a vow etched on our bones long before we'd ever spoken it, in a life I didn't even remember...but that I knew with every fiber of me was true.

I'd meant it back then. I meant it now.

And in a cacophony of cheers from the regiment, after we'd slammed our tankards together in a toast and thrown back deep droughts of the tavern's finest ale, Jaik had snagged me back the back of my head and kissed me breathless as if he couldn't wait a second longer to do it.

And then he'd lifted me up to wrap my legs around his waist, still kissing me—and carried me out of the tavern all the way to this bed.

I wished to Luck for a thousand nights like that. Surrounded by friends, spurred by spontaneity, making the same choice over and over again—choosing Jaik Grissom. Choosing the things I truly wanted, shaping the life I'd almost never dared to dream of.

Thousands of mornings just like this, and I would have been happy.

But I couldn't even have this one…not really.

It was a moment before I realized what had woken me, and only when it sounded again: a series of sharp, rapid knocks on the door.

Jaik groaned, a sound that teased my nape and vibrated against my back and puddled heat in my core; then he slowly unwound his arms from around and beneath me, scraping himself up off the mattress, pinching the bridge of his nose as he rolled over. "Ah, flipping *Luck*."

"What is it?" I demanded, twisting to face him; well-worn fabric slipped down off my shoulder as I moved—*his* shirt, one I barely remembered slipping into the night before.

"That's a…soldiering pattern," he grunted, tossing off the blanket and reaching for his trousers. "Must be Gil."

"Then it must be *trouble*." I gripped the hem of his shirt, raking it over my head.

His hand, large and warm, pressed over my hair—stilling me in motion. "Keep it on." He tugged down the collar to meet my eyes. "Wish I could wake up to you wearing my shirt *every* day."

The way he said it stopped me to the uttermost, not even a breath lifting my chest as Jaik surged up to sling on his shirt and coat, his sword and rifle.

Why can't you? I wanted to shout at his back. *What does that mean?*

But before I could ask, the door sailed open, framing Gil in the opening—broad hands braced to the wood, his tall frame swooping in. I cursed, whooping air back into my lungs as I towed the blanket up as high as my chest. "Gil! *Knocking*!"

"Been doing that," he shot back. "Don't get your undershorts in a knot, I didn't even see them. Jaik?"

"Let me guess," Jaik dropped back onto the bed to tug on his boots, "Misspoken manifestations?"

Gil's grim nod unleashed a deluge of shivers that wracked through my whole body. This was far too much like Rivrand—far too much like a pattern of its own. "Bands are closing in—scouts saw them crossing the village hunting grounds this morning. Direwolves, two-headed elk that eat flesh, snakes bigger than a house...that's just the start of it. All headed this way."

Jaik's eyes latched onto mine, sharing memory in the space between us—the creatures that had assembled with the wraith, rising up at its tortured beckoning.

And that was the death of my last, fragile hope that Jaik had felled the wraith for good.

The death of our fleeting peace.

"Sounds about right," he grunted after a moment.

Gil swayed deeper into the room. "You ready for this?"

Jaik tied one boot and spoke without glancing up: "You and your regiment go after them. I've got my work cut out for me." He tossed a mirthless smile my way; it did absolutely nothing to thaw the terror that iced my body to the bed. "Same as Rivrand, right? One group pulls the manifestations in, one goes after the wraith."

Gil grimaced. "You really think that sword of yours will be enough?"

"Didn't exactly get a chance to prove it last time." Jaik knotted his other boot and straightened, favoring that leg far, *far* more than I was comfortable with, given what we were about to face. "Let's give it another shot."

Gil squeezed Jaik's shoulder, then nodded to me and slipped from the room; I hurled off the blanket and yanked on my own trousers, stuffing my feet into my boots just as Jaik rose and went to the door.

All at once, every shred of safety burned away. All that remained was the tumult, the chaos that had rocked through my core ever since Rivrand—embers ignited at the inevitability of what we faced today.

We had prepared. We had expected it.

And I *still* wasn't ready. Not after last night. Not after a glimpse of what the future could be—what this wraith, like so many other things before it, sought to steal.

Our hope. Our happiness.

"Jaik, *wait*—" My protest was almost lost under the grind of the door sweeping open.

"Not really time for that."

"Yes, there is!" I hurtled after him, falling into step as he took the stairs two-at-a-time down to the inn's vacant parlor. Gil must've warned the keeper already to join the preparations put in place for this cruel inevitability. "It's too soon, your leg isn't healed. You're no match for it!"

"Yeah, well...better me than you."

Stung, I nearly missed the last step; my boots clomped heavily on the polished wooden floor. "You're being ridiculous."

"Maybe. But that's what being in love does to people." Jaik tore the inn's door open and stepped out onto the stoop; I kept pace with him, drumming down the steps to the dusty path that wound through the heart of Galent. It surged with activity, more than I had ever seen—mothers and fathers hastening children indoors, husbands and wives and lovers kissing one another goodbye as Gil rounded up his people. Elyssabet caught my gaze from Gil's side, tossing me a reassuring smile that was anything but.

I didn't want any of them to go. But Jaik most of all.

"Jaik, stop...don't do this. Don't go, don't face it. You don't stand a *chance*." Heat blazed in my eyes as he twisted to glance at me over his shoulder, never breaking stride on his way toward Gil's group. "We both saw how it grew, what it did last time. And after you wounded it, that wraith is going to see *you* as the only real threat."

"Sure is." A rueful smile cocked up one corner of his mouth. "That's *why* I have to go."

"No! You can't do this." I wound my fingers in the crease of his elbow, tugging him back—as if that would keep him with me.

As if it ever had.

"That's where you're wrong, Ayjay. *No one else* can." His arm flexed against my grip, hand falling to the hilt of his Storycrafted sword. "You made this sword for me, all right? We've tried *everything* else, even Storycraft itself, and this blade's the only thing that scared it. Really made a difference. So, the way I figure it, either this works...or nothing will."

"You can't take the risk that it *won't!*" Desperation sharpened my tone to a quill's tip. "You, of *all* people. You're the Sha's *bodyguard—*"

He swung back to face me at that, catching my jaw in the cradle of his grip and halting us both in our tracks; his thumb brushed the divot of my chin, his eyes searching mine.

"Yeah." His voice was husky. "But before I was his, I was *yours*."

My breath slammed to a halt in my throat.

A crooked smirk scripted itself against the lines of Jaik's lips as they hovered above mine—a story I knew all too well.

"Still am," he breathed.

Then his mouth crashed over mine—a kiss that pulsed with promise. A kiss that swore to be the first of hundreds. Of thousands.

A vow he couldn't be sure to keep this time.

He was the first to break free, to slip into the ranks with Gil and the others and start barking orders—orders I couldn't discern over the roaring of the pulse in my ears. I jerked backward when Elyssabet laid a hand on my arm, her grim countenance swimming in my vision.

"We'll guard his flanks," she murmured. "And we'll *all* be back soon."

I wanted so desperately to believe her. To believe in *them*.

But all I could think—as the regiment pulled together and moved off, carrying Jaik in their midst and Elyssabet on their fringes like stones and leaves borne in a drowning current—was that all of this was happening because of me.

And how wrong it was...how *unfair* it was...that I was the only one who could do *nothing* about it. Who couldn't fight—who had no power against this enemy.

The one being left behind.

CHAPTER 59
FAR FROM ENOUGH

GALENT RAPIDLY DESCENDED INTO a muted sort of chaos.

The remaining regiments ushered us left-behinds into shelters—children and pregnant or nursing mothers to the most fortified locations, stone hollows chiseled deep into the hillsides. Others went to their homes, trusting in the shoring up of rock and wood that sealed their windows and doors, that we had helped put into place over the last fortnight.

Hastening through the streets, I locked eyes briefly on a familiar face in the vaguest of terms...the bride from the tavern last night. The woman whose soldiering husband had carried her down the spiral staircase without a hitch in his stride, their smiling faces like twin lanterns lighting up the dark.

She didn't smile now. Anguish scripted her features in the most vicious strokes as an older woman—almost her twin in appearance—ushered her toward one of the staircases up to the lofty edifices strung among the treetops.

Her husband was nowhere in sight.

A pit gaped in my stomach, my hands flexing at my sides with the absurd urge to reach for hers—to hold on and squeeze and reassure her that her husband would be all right.

That...both of our husbands would be.

But that promise was not mine to keep. Not when the distant, harrowing screeches of Misspoken manifestations floated from the autumnal valleys, chasing us all indoors at a run.

So I returned to the inn. Alone.

Foolish, perhaps, given I was the one in whom the wraith showed the most interest. The one it had dragged away and tortured in solitude, stirring up those dark emotions that pierced like knives in my chest even now, with every breath.

But that also meant whoever I might shelter with would be in equal danger; and after Rivrand, after seeing its people slaughtered by those ravenous, Misspoken spiders—

I would not see anyone in Galent suffer that same fate.

Besides, we had fortified the inn well...windows boarded with stone beams too dense for even a shadow to slip through. Two regiments guarded it—one on the ground floor, one on the roof. I had a dagger, a rifle, and plenty of soldiers within screaming distance.

It was as safe as I could be, with that wraith still haunting these hills.

Yet the confined space might as well have been a cage, not a fortress of safety. Awash in the dimming sparkle of the lantern Ovalia had gifted to us, I wore the floorboards white with pacing, naming and numbering things I saw and heard and tasted and felt and smelled...none of which did a single thing to calm my nerves.

They were out there. Jaik, Gil, Elyssabet, and the regiment.

The wraith and its driven servants.

Clashing. Confronting. Waging battle on *my* behalf, while I was trapped here, only a dagger and a rifle to defend myself. Only a hope and prayer that they would return.

No. No. I couldn't think like that—I couldn't let myself travel down roads to bloodstained forest floors, to towering city walls, to muddy streets and seasprayed ship decks.

I couldn't let the hate, the fear, the grief consume me now.

Jaik *would* come back. They all would. And this would be just another story we told around a fire, like the kind we'd told around bar tables last night.

Not good enough!

The wishful wail of my heart dragged my feet to a halt at the bedside, a chill ripping its way down my spine with no concern for the pain it unleashed in its wake.

If this was all that came from the life I lived now—if this was all I could be—

Not good enough.

I wanted *more.* More than being a sideline spectator, more than being the one who heard the tales after others lived them. That *had* been enough, perhaps, in Krylan...to experience vicariously through gossip chains strung across the breadth of the country. To sail on the words of seamen, to witness through the words of others. To keep my adventures in the mind, in books, and never at my fingertips.

That *had* been enough...before I had tasted the sea breeze for myself, tangled with skeleton sailors, witnessed healing with my own eyes, climbed the backs of the mountains, fought with enemies of my own forging. Before I'd been loved and kissed and held and cherished by people to whom I was a friend, a sister and daughter, a wife—a legend.

Unforgettable. Irreplaceable.

The Audra that I was, that I had been for as long as *I* could remember...I did not want to be stuck like her. Lonely. Hiding discontentment beneath resignation, beneath cheery smiles and the motions of life. Settling for half of everything she knew she was capable of. Even the hatred, the fury, the grief and despair, the shame and conflict inside myself were better than being numb. Fading to only an echo of who I was made to be.

I did not want to lose Jaik Grissom again. I did not want to lose *myself* again.

Both hands pressed over my mouth, I choked on a surge of longing and terror that tore the breath out of me.

This is not enough!

I did not want to hear stories anymore. About myself. About the world. About the past, the present, the future, and realms that did not exist yet and might never be truly given shape.

I did not want to tell them, either.

I wanted to *live* them.

To wind myself up in their threads until it was all that kept me standing. To dance across every word like stepping stones to the next tale, and the next one, and the next one. To build a bridge between the life I'd left behind and the one I'd been sculpting dreams of since we'd set foot aboard *The Cathan*.

I wanted to *breathe* stories again...to devour them, to drink them down into the very core of me and give life to new ones from all that I had consumed. I wanted them to pour out of every inch of me...out of hands that shaped their edges and a tongue that stumbled with the sheer joy of telling them, out of feet that couldn't stand still when every step brought me deeper into whatever tale I was telling, out of smiles and embraces and tears that flowed endlessly, cathartic, healing.

Like the tears that scoured down my cheeks now, braided into the wild, gasping sobs sneaking between my fingers.

I wanted stories that swept my listeners away, and me with them, until all we could do was hold hands and hold tight and try not to lose ourselves in the beauty of them—and then to be lost anyway, in that glorious and brilliant way that made us all feel seen and known and loved by something larger and more beautiful than we could fathom. Like skies and stars and wild and wonderful places all living inside of a person, begging to be set free.

I wanted my *own* story, written by my own hand, guided by the One Who had penned so many new chances into it that they were notched into my bones. I wanted to step forward and shake hands with my Maker in the place where my memories fell to shreds, where the well in my middle had gone dry.

I laid my hand over that churning chasm at my core. Squeezed my eyes shut tight.

If you would still seek Me, you will find Me—when you seek with all your heart.

"I'm ready." Those two words sent fresh tears jumping to my eyes. "Storymaker, come close. I need this, I need You now...with *all* my heart."

Those words zipped under my skin like a stroke of lightning. My heart thundered in resonance.

"*I'm ready.*"

A whisper. A plea. A prayer.

And, then from the corner confines of my lonely cage—

"Hello, Audra."

CHAPTER 60
THE WANT OF LETTING GO

IT DIDN'T MATTER THAT I'd forgotten. That I'd lost everything.

The moment I heard that voice, I knew—and was known.

Because the Maker of all stories, the Maker of the Wellspoken World, leaned against the closed door of our room, arms folded behind his back. And when His eyes met mine, my knees met the floor—a clap of bone and cartilage on wood that hardly resonated past the roaring churn of shock that thundered in my ears.

He looked just how I'd seen Him last—but not in the story Jaik had told me about Erasure.

The white hair and brows. The dark, lively eyes and attire the color of parchment. Everything *exactly* the same as when I'd seen Him last...

When I'd spoken to Him in the bookbinder's shop in Vallanmyre.

"You...that was *You*?" I choked. "You were—You were right *there*..."

"Yes. But you were not yet prepared to stand before Me." He slid a hand into the pocket of His robes—and withdrew a stunning leather book, its tooled surface as soft as his smile. "You rejected the opportunity...your journey was not yet complete. You were not ready to make the choices that lie before you now."

"But people were hurt—Jaik almost *died*—!"

Again. The word stuck in my throat.

He might be dying right *now*, and here I was, frozen on my knees, hands pressed into the floor, trembling like storybook pages blown in a storm as the Storymaker Himself straightened from the doorframe and stepped toward me.

"People would have been hurt regardless." He knelt, prying my hands from the floor, holding them firmly in His. "And you would not have been able to help them. Not as you can now."

I'm ready. My veins singing with determination; my heart ironclad with resolve. My very being aching for stories—for Jaik. For salvation.

"Now," the Storymaker repeated, drawing me up to my feet, "what do you wish to ask of Me?"

I thought I knew precisely what I would answer; but the words rewrote themselves in scratches and scrawls somewhere between my head and mouth. "I have so many questions. Can...can You tell me what happened to me? The day I undid the Tearing?"

The Storymaker drew in a deep breath, and blew it out just as slow and steadily. Then He said, with the same careful precision I had to imagine had shaped the world, "When you faced the opportunity to rewrite that particular narrative, you had a choice to make. You could have kept your power, every drop of scarlet in your cloak. However, in order to do that..."

His dark, grave gaze lifted to mine.

"I would have had to write Jaik back out of the narrative."

A slow nod. "But you chose a different path. Instead of unraveling the power from *him*, you gave it from within *yourself*. You wrote your own power into the tales of others, to give Storycrafters back their endings."

I slipped one hand from His, fisting my trembling fingers in my ash-gray cloak. "Does that mean Jaik is still an amplifier?"

"Only to some. Certainly to you."

That quieted me for a moment. "Is...is that why I've felt so drawn to tell stories again since he came back into my life?"

"No." A smile curved one side of the Storymaker's mouth. "That is because stories are a part of how *you* are written, Audra Jashowin...how I formed you. That is your truth, regardless of whether those stories hold power beyond the joy they bring you."

The way He said that word—*joy*—swelled between us. It rose in my throat like a lump, a knot of tears tangling behind my eyes. "What about my memories? Why does everyone else remember everything, but not me? Did You take those to punish me?"

He held my gaze this time, even as He slowly shook His head. "Your memories would have returned with all the others...if they had found a place to rest."

My fingers flexed, caging tightly around His. "I don't...I don't understand—"

"Audra."

The softest, simplest way anyone—even Jaik—had ever spoken my name.

And now the tears *did* slip free.

How many times on this mad quest had I told Jaik I wasn't certain I wanted what waited at its end? How much had I feared losing him again...so much so that I wasn't certain I'd wanted to remember it happening before?

Hadn't I spoken with the Storymaker Himself about how badly I wanted to step off my own path?

Maybe I hadn't just been running from my past since Jaik had found me. Maybe I'd been trying to escape the grief, the guilt, the *shame* of the first Tearing since before I'd even known the truth about what it was and why it had happened.

"I wanted to forget," I whispered. "I wanted to let go."

"Yes. I knew that you would, when we spoke in Erasure."

"But letting go—"

A simple, solemn nod.

And it struck me all at once—a scream deafened in forest rain. A familiarity in the touch of the dark. Falling through inky shadows that were so *kindred*...that knew me. Sought me out. Changed me in ways they hadn't done to anyone else.

Every encounter with the wraith that had left me drowning in those feelings of hopelessness, of fury, of hate, of despair. They were still here now...blunted, somewhat, in the presence of the Maker of all stories, but they passed through me like a wind stirred up in the wake of His walking.

Oh, Luck.

I knew. I knew *exactly* who had made it—*how* it had been made.

How it always found me. And why it always came when my struggles peaked—my hate before we'd ever entered Belaris, my grief and shame in Vallan-myre, my rage in Rivrand...my terror after, when I'd told Jaik about the wraith's familiarity. The terror that had carried me through to Galent. That lingered in me now.

Each and every time, it had come as if I'd called it. As if it sensed me in those moments, found me in the swells...sought me out in the depths of my struggles.

And each time, it was larger, and fiercer, and mightier...impervious to our defenses. Even to Storycraft, and Storycrafted *things*.

Which meant, if it had grown again...changed *again* since we'd wounded it with Jaik's blade in the forest...

My hand freed my cloak, flying to my mouth instead. "Maker's *tales*—"

The Storymaker took my wrist gently, tugging my fingers down and capturing them again in His. "I have kept that manifestation contained for two long years on Erasure—but when you chose this journey with Jaik, to pursue Me, it sensed the change. It was time for you to face it, Audra. As you are facing all of this now." His gaze locked on mine—there was nowhere to avert, to hide from the intensity of that stare. "Yet even as you've come along the path, you have fled from your sense of purpose. Trying to give it up at every turn. Why is that?"

And now I knew—I knew it like the resonance of screams that broke with betrayal. Like the pulse of a beating scarlet heart.

"Because it has cost me *so much*," I choked. "It has caused me so much grief...fighting for it. Using it. Sharing it. I don't even have to *remember* it to see how much pain it's caused, to me and to others. And if that's all it's ever going to be, pain after pain, then why would I want it back?"

"Have you not also seen the *joy* it has brought?"

My next blink freed no tears—not when memory gusted through me, a warm wind chasing away the dark of night.

A snowstorm at the end of spring. A boy's future redeemed. Villages spared in the mountains. A sword that saved so many lives—ours included. Lio, lost and found again with her crew. Galent and Belaris, forever changed. A thousand stories told for the betterment of Mithra-Sha.

A world broken and reshaped and made right again.

"Somehow, that makes it seem worse," I admitted softly. "To know I could climb so high, but even so, it's going to hurt again."

"Oh, yes." The Storymaker brushed a thumb along my cheekbone, catching the next tear that found its way free. "The power of creation is never without cost. Your creation can always rebel, always twist and turn in its freedom of will. But creation also holds a great capacity to change things for the *better*...a story told at just the right time, in fact, can change *everything*."

From the folds of His drab robe, He withdrew a parcel wrapped in brown butcher's paper—and handed it to me.

"Go on," He urged when I hesitated...because how could I begin to fathom a gift from Him? "I've kept this for you."

Fingers trembling, I tore away the paper—igniting a fresh shock of familiarity at what greeted me within.

The same book He had offered me in Vallanmyre—familiar in its pristine condition. As heart-achingly beautiful as I remembered.

"What *is* this book?" I breathed, sketching my fingertips over its hand-hewn edges. Every stitch, every imprint of mountains and meadows and the engraved oval frame spoke of care, attention, and love...of a vessel created with purpose for a special story.

"Nothing. Yet." The Storymaker dipped His head a bit, peering at me with that piercing intensity that beckoned me to the earnest truth of what we discussed—far beyond logic. To something known by the depths of the heart. "It is where you will choose to rewrite your story...or not."

"Rewrite...?" My hands snared tight around the deckled pages, and I found myself recoiling a bit from Him—from the impossibility of what He suggested. "With Storycraft?"

His brows arched—inviting more of the questions simmering on the back of my tongue.

"Even if I wanted it, how could I have it back?" I burst out. "I tore the power out of myself to give it to the rest of the Storycrafters...I kept nothing for myself."

"That is true, and it was a selfless choice. But tell me what you have learned of your memories, from this journey with Jaik?"

It was incredible how swiftly tears burned the backs of my eyes at the murmur of Jaik's name.

"That the people who love us hold onto the parts of us we forget," I whispered. "They keep them alive for us when we'd rather let them die."

"So it is with the One Who loved you first...Who formed you, and the power within you."

He stretched out His hand; and there in the center bobbed a single beadlet like blood, welling in the center of His palm.

The breath caught in my throat, the way it had when Jaik and I had crested the mountain behind Belaris. It was just how the body seized and quieted to the very farthest reaches when facing something powerful and beautiful beyond belief. Something majestic and terrifying.

The very definition of creation.

"You have asked to be rid of this power, over and over," the Storymaker murmured. "To be free of its harms and its joys. You cast it out of yourself and fled from the memory of it, all this time. But still you have sought Me, even when the seeking terrified you. And now, face-to-face, I will give you one last chance to choose what it is you desire, Audra. I will honor the choice, whatever you make...but know that this opportunity will not be offered again."

I couldn't breathe. I couldn't stop *weeping*.

"After all you have learned, and endured, and what you know now," the Storymaker added gravely, "which life will you choose?"

Wind whispered against my nape like the stirring of a closing book—deckled edges settling together, pressing *the end* between the pages. Sealing it with finality.

It could be the ending for me, too. A chance to relieve my suffering...to ensure I never encountered the trenched depths of power misused. Of stories unfinished. Of the anguish that came with lost endings and beginnings too hopeful to bear.

But it would also be the end of something so precious. So glorious, even. Something that had brought me so much joy, I'd gone to the ends of the world to try and redeem it. Something that had given my feet the path to walk, a sense of purpose since I was a child.

Something that, if I sacrificed it in the depths of despair, I would never reclaim in times of joy.

"Am I strong enough?" I whispered—half to myself, half to Him. "To do right by it, in the good and the bad?"

"I would not have offered it to you otherwise." The Storymaker shifted nearer, that scarlet drop shimmering above his palm. "You relied long enough on your own strength, Audra. Lean into Mine now. It is there you will find your weakness made perfect."

I could no longer make out the shape of His face through the cast of my tears—so I could almost believe it was blurring. Annealing into a younger countenance, hair darker, clothing the color of well-loved parchment.

Still so familiar. Still a piece of home.

"And...will You stay with me? While I face this?"

"And beyond. To the end of all time. You are never forsaken or forgotten, Audra Jashowin."

He was right. The time for forgetting was over.

"I'm ready."

Over and over today, I had said those words—but for the first time, I truly knew what they meant.

And I truly meant them.

The Storymaker's smile was soft as sunshine, bright enough to erase every shadow that had dwelled in my heart since Belaris. He wrapped His hand around mine, and heat tore through my body—etching like the glow of His grin on every strand of my being.

Crimson-red. Fire-bright.

"And this, Addie," He murmured, "is my new favorite part of your story."

CHAPTER 61
SWORD AND STORY

JAIK

I T'S FUNNY HOW PAIN is sometimes the part that makes everyone's stories the same.

I'd known pain as a kid who was always felt second-best to his Storycrafter brother and sister. Pain as a new soldier recruit without a lot of friends. Pain trying to sneak into Ayjay's trust…some of the worst flipping pain of my life when I'd realized I was betraying someone I actually cared about.

Pain not knowing if I'd ever have a chance with her as more than just as her bodyguard. Pain when we realized what we'd be risking if we let ourselves love each other like we wanted to. Pain, just a constant ache, watching the Sha wear her down until she was a shadow of who she used to be.

Pain when a blade went into my chest. Pain waking up in an infirmary, alone, thinking the scar over my heart had come from a plow blade. Pain for years after that, like something had been ripped out of my life. Pain that came with finding Ayjay and losing her again, and again, and again—

Pain when she rewrote the whole world, right in front of me.

Pain when she looked at me like a stranger in a tavern in Krylan.

And now I had this new pain I should've been used to:

The pain that came from knowing I'd let her down.

The wraith painted the whole sky shadow, it turned day to night—covered up the sun that would've been pouring into this clearing otherwise. And it wouldn't stop screaming, like its voice was a weapon—a whole new blade jammed into my ears while its tendrils pinned my legs and arms, wrestling me onto my back on the leaf mold.

Gil, Elyssabet, the rest—they were still fighting for their lives somewhere over the next ridge. In between the wraith's shrieks, the snarls from the rest of those Misspoken abominations punched through. The regiments were keeping them at bay, so only the wraith had managed to slip through…just like we'd known it would.

I'd just hoped for more of a flipping *fight*.

But the thing was smart, smarter than any Misspoken manifestation had a right to be. It remembered exactly which leg it'd stuck its knife in...and this time, it wasn't keen on dueling. Just dodging and feinting, keeping me on the defensive, which had worked for about as long as my leg held up.

Not long enough.

Tearing on manacles of shadow rope so thick and sharp, they bit in like wire, I tried to haul myself out of the thing's reach—back to the sword it'd ripped out of my hands. At least it had cowered away from it once or twice while we'd squared up, but that seemed like it had just been learning. Because, first chance it got to go on the offensive, it'd focused on getting that blade out of my reach.

And after a lot of dodges and some solid swings from both of us, it finally had.

"Flipping *Luck*!" My palms ripped on the shadows, opening up new welts where the skin was already rubbed raw from losing my grip on my sword. Pretty sure my thumb was halfway out of joint, too, but that didn't matter much when that thing was clawing after me, looking like it was about to pop all the rest of my joints out of alignment, too.

It had gotten...bigger. A *lot* bigger. A lot nastier looking, too...every tooth turned to a fang in that burning forge of a mouth. Eyes burning up like fire. And the red pulsing in the center of its heart was brighter, almost hurt to look at...the same way trying to blink its edges into focus had my head pounding.

The flipping thing wouldn't stop *moving*...swaying left, dodging right, rippling up and back, then throwing itself toward me. Like it was expecting me to throw a punch—and you know, maybe I *would*, but the edges of its body had me trussed up like cattle waiting for the brand.

And I had a feeling that brand was coming right from its mouth.

Staring down its fiery gullet, *my* throat dried out.

So, this was going to hurt. But I'd made up my mind when I'd decided to come out here...I wasn't going to make a sound. I wasn't going to draw any attention.

Still. When it flipped back the shadow-sleeve from its shriveled-up arm and brought that dagger in concretion—looked like the same one it stabbed me with before—my leg bucked up under me like it was trying to get away.

Fingers dug into the soil, pinned down with that thing towering above me, I had time for one thought. One prayer.

Keep her safe if I'm not there to do it anymore.

Luck. Same thought I'd had in the golden Shastah halls, last time a knife had gone into my heart.

It pulled back, then *flew* down—

"*Stop.*"

Not a scream. Not even hardly a shout. But enough power in that one word that me and the wraith, we both froze.

Its knife half a foot from my sternum. My chest not even rising to meet the tip of the blade.

With that *thing* leaning over me, shadows smothering my whole body like a wet blanket, we looked at the same time.

To the edge of the clearing, some of the trees ransacked from our fight. And to the woman walking out of that carnage with her head up high, shoulders back.

No armor. Just a tattered-up gray cloak and a look in her eyes like she could bring the world to its knees.

"*No!*" The word ripped out of me like it had the power to push her away—get her out of here, send her back to Galent where this thing couldn't hurt her. Where it could just get it over with, take me instead...leave her *alone.*

But it was too flipping late.

The wraith snaked back, gathering most of its shadows into itself...letting in more daylight, but keeping the locks around my arms and legs. Keeping me pinned down so I couldn't close the gap to my sword and just *end this.*

Didn't stop me from trying...yanking, struggling, swearing, pulling the thing's fiery attention back to me.

Good! Keep it over here—

"Stop," Ayjay said again—this time, I didn't know exactly which of us she was talking to, because she usually aimed that annoyed tone at me. "Don't look at him, I'm not here for him. I'm here for *you.*"

She said it—but the way her eyes jumped to me for a split second, brows scrunched up, lips pinching tight like there was a sob stuck behind them...

It gutted me.

She hadn't looked at me that way since I'd walked into the Shastah's Convening Chamber for the second Tearing. Like she was seeing all of us—who we'd been, who we were, what we could've become—all at once. Like reading your favorite story over and over, even when you knew it couldn't have a happy ending.

Then she blinked, and it disappeared. She swiveled back on the wraith, and kept walking toward it.

"I know what you are," she breathed, stepping toward that incarnation of ugly writhing in shadows at the edge of the clearing. "And I know what made you."

It cowered away from her, teeth bared, snarling.

"You're *me*."

That choked whisper about stopped my lucking *heart*.

That twisted, corrupt *thing* that had been chasing us ever since we'd made landfall, that'd led a bunch of other Misspoken manifestations straight to us, made this journey a living nightmare—she couldn't *seriously* think that was—?

"You're the unfinished thread of the last story I told...from the Tearing." Audra kept sliding closer and closer to the wraith. "You're every unfinished tale I never got to tell, every doubt and fear that my stories would never be enough, every piece of me that raged about how *unfair* it was...that this was done to me, to *us*, and that we were the ones who had to pay the final cost." She stretched her hand out like she was talking down a spooked horse...not offering her empty palm to a piece of amplified Storycraft that could tear it off in a blink. "It wasn't one thing that happened at the Tearing, it was three. My power divided among Storycrafters...Jaik's life written back into the world...and you. All my hate, all my rage made manifest. So I could forget everything that hurt me...so I could hide from my shame. My grief. My hate and despair...my *rage*."

Shadowed tendrils rose, grazing her fingertips. And right then, staring at the two of them facing each other down—not trying to get between them, for once, even though every inch of me hollered that that's where I needed to be—

Flipping *Luck*.

Those shadows, the way they formed up, even the way they *moved*...

It was like a cloak. A shadow-cloak, hood pulled up over its head, streaming off its shoulders. A cloak that broke up, spidered out, and yanked back, shifting it closer to her with every breath.

No black and white cloaks for Storycrafters, Ayjay had told me once or twice. But this was different.

It was the dark side of *Audra's* cloak.

"You're every terrible thing I've been running from." Her gaze shot my way, then leaped back to the thing. "And you set the world out of balance, just like the Tearing did. An equal price."

"*Ayjay...*" Warning bristled up my hackles and escaped out my throat; that thing was winding itself higher up her arm, wrapping its glossy threads around her.

"It's all right, Jaik." Her voice wobbled, but her face was set. Surer than maybe I'd ever seen it. "This is why we haven't been able to stop it, not with rifles, not with blades, not with anything. Because it belongs to me...it's *my* manifestation. All of the things I was ever afraid of, amplified into one terrible piece of a story."

The shadows spun as high as her shoulder, and the thing *still* had enough to spare to keep me pinned down.

"Ayjay, forget it! Just run—just *get out of here*!"

"She's a piece of me, Jaik," Audra's second hand joined the first, stretched out...and this time the thing shot those tendrils around her without hesitating. In a second, it had her shackled up to the neck. "I can't leave her any more than I could leave you."

The shadows were up to her chin, now, sliding over her *mouth*—

"I'm ready."

She leaned her head back. Shut her eyes.

"Audra, *no—*!"

The wraith shifted in a blink—forged itself into chains, whipped Audra's arms out to the sides, ripped a yelp from her that had me writhing like I could get free. Like I could do anything more useful than belt out her name against the noose this thing had on me.

Then its center rippled, and it reforged that shadow-dagger, the same one it had dueled me with—and launched it.

Straight into Audra's chest.

"*Ayjay!*" Her name fired out of me like a rifleshot, like it was Storycraft, too—right when that weapon *slammed* into her.

Blood red exploded across her cloak, spilled down her back, and if the impact made a sound, I didn't hear it. I couldn't hear *anything* except the empty hole where my heartbeat should have been and the way I was *screaming,* "No—no, no, *no!* Audra! *AYJAY!*"

And then that stopped, too.

Because that scarlet didn't just pour down her cloak.

It poured *up* it.

Climbed straight up over her shoulders like fingers fastening the clasp shut at her throat. Drenched the hood over her hair. Leaked down to every inch, from the backs of her legs to the top of her head.

And Audra—my tiger, my flipping *Ayjay*—

She ripped her arms down to her sides, tearing that thing off its feet, crashing it down on its chest in front of her; then she wrapped both hands around the dagger and yanked it away from where it had stuck, barely ripping the front of her top, dripping a little blood from right above her heart.

"But here's the plot twist," she seethed. "If you're a piece of me, then I'm every part of you, too. Which means Jaik can't hurt you, Ovalia couldn't end you...but *I* can."

The dagger hung in front of her, caught in a whisper of scarlet threads twisted between her fingers like heartstrings. Then she flicked her wrist, and it dropped into her hand.

"This is *my* story now," Audra snarled. "And it's time to close your chapter."

CHAPTER 62
NOTHING LEFT TO FEAR

T HE ENTIRE WORLD BURNED in shades of *red*.

Power coursed through me, over me, *in* me. It lit me up like firelight, burning off the fear that had hitched my steps almost every stride through Galent—until the Storymaker had left me at its edge, with a squeeze of broad hands to my shoulders and a murmur in my ear of, "I will be with you. Even when you cannot see Me."

Now...now I *felt* Him.

That kernel of power He'd placed in my hand burst in bolts of crimson power, surging through every weave of fiber in my Storycrafter's cloak as I lunged at the wraith, swiping for her chest—sending her reeling off-balance.

For the first time that I'd ever faced her, *I* had the advantage.

So I seized it with all my might, blocking the tines of shadow she thrust at me, cleaving them off like scorched cloth and overgrown vines. Unburying a grave full of power that had slumbered for too long in the center of me.

I went to war for the people of Galent. For Jaik Grissom, trapped in shadow shackles, bellowing my name.

For *myself.*

The wraith and I battled through the clearing, to the forest's deeper edge—then plunged into it, the creature on the run. Me, chasing my fears for once, instead of fleeing from them.

The darkness of the undergrowth tangled with the shadows ahead, whipping them skyward like the hem of a windborne cloak. But now that I focused—now that I'd faced the truth of *what* I was facing, what I'd been avoiding in some fashion or another ever since we'd set off on this quest—she couldn't escape me. The wraith burned before my eyes, and every twist she took to evade my pursuit, that crimson core flared in a pulse guiding me onward.

I couldn't falter or fail. I had made this creature, created it in a horrible and wonderous moment when I'd had the choice to face what I'd lost...or run away. And it had hurt people...hurt Jaik, hurt *me*.

No more. This story ends today.

The thought drove me ahead in a few flying steps, gaining momentum with a well-placed lunge over a log and landing just shy of the wraith's heels. I didn't pause to think—I swung with all my might, slashing the hem of her cloak before it could wrench ahead again and pull her out of my reach.

She went down in a tumble of shadows and screams, every angle of her contorting with faceless bulges as she fought to morph back to her feet. But I couldn't give her that chance.

She'd only just begun to unfold—to stretch into that grisly height I could only imagine she'd gained as my fears had grown and my doubts flourished—when I reached her. And though the instinct repulsed me, I did as I had seen soldiers do.

I gripped her by the hinge of the shoulder, finding mealy, decay-pocked flesh and knobby bone somewhere below the writhing shadows. And I drove the blade with all my might into the scarlet center of her...the unbeating heart where all my torn-out terrors resided.

"This is the end," I seethed. "It's time to come back where you belong."

The wraith doubled over, emaciated hands clutching the blade, hunting with almost wondering slowness over the shadow-forged steel—

Then seizing. Tightening.

Sliding the dagger *deeper* into herself.

Shock almost separated my fingers from the grip; I clung on by the very clawed edge of reason, even when sense screamed at me to let go...to *run*. The wraith yanked me toward her, driving the dagger almost to the crossguard in her chest; I stumbled, skidding on the damp leaf litter—then followed my own momentum, bashing my shoulder into her half-tangible form and thrusting her backward. At the same moment, I heaved, whipping the blade free.

Shadow tines slapped my cheek, raising bloody welts that pushed tears from my eyes as I whirled and fled—no thought in my clamoring mind except feral instinct to put distance between us for a heartbeat.

Between me and this *thing* I had been so sure I had just destroyed.

Plunging deeper into the grove, I set my teeth against the pain spearing into my temples as the wraith shrieked and wailed behind me. *Maker, don't let Jaik hear that and come running*! The last thing I needed was to defend us both when I didn't even know how to do it.

Smashing my back against one of a pair of trees growing from the same root cluster, I bent double, clutching a stitch in my side and fighting to quiet my snarling breaths.

That should have worked! My thoughts pounded nearly as harshly as my pulse in the back of my jaw. *I stabbed her right through the heart—a scarlet heart! What else is supposed to end her?*

I held the dagger aloft before me, clinging so tightly to the grip that my knuckles pierced whitely against my flesh.

Why wasn't it working? I was armed, I had my power, I had a blade—

My gaze latched onto it. And my gut clenched.

I had a blade.

But I was not the sword in this story.

Terror crunched my fingertips, winding them tighter than ever around the dagger's grip. *I can't do this. I don't remember* how *to do this.*

Storytelling was no longer my strength. But...

Lean on Mine now.

"Please, don't ask me to do it this way," I choked.

The only answer came with the splintering of branches punched aside by withered, wraithlike hands, reaching, searching, finding their way toward me—and by a faint bead of warmth building in my chest. Peace like none I had ever known before, spreading out to saturate my trembling limbs.

If I was meant to do this with a dagger, He would have given me one.

I released the blade. The moment it tumbled from my hand, it pulverized into shadow and rapidly withdrew...seeking the likeness of its master.

I was unarmed. All except for the might given back to me...the shard of power that turned my cloak bloodred.

Squeezing my eyes shut, I whispered the words I'd heard at the advent of fantasy and fables unleashed around Krylan for nearly two years.

Let me tell you a story.

The wraith's next screech tore through the forest as it sighted me—whether by my voice or my terror or its own hunting, I couldn't be certain. My gaze ripped open again, and I lunged just shy of its swiping hand as it tore between the trees, jaws lengthening and shadowed fangs snapping for flesh.

I couldn't stop moving—I had to think *and* move—but I'd done that before. It was like tending bar and talking to customers…pirouettes and pivots. Like a meadow. Like a dance.

In a time and place unknown to our kind, in a land both exactly and nothing at all like ours, there once was a girl who lost the power to tell stories.

One day they were there, and the next, they were gone. Her mind turned to a void as bleak as the world she faced…a world that made her stories seem a commodity, meant for simpler times. In hardship, they had such little use. Her voice seemed so shriveled and small, lost inside herself…and all the joy she had once felt in escaping to faraway and fantastical places faded away.

The wraith clawed through the grove, its next blow slashing a hairsbreadth from my face. The last two words burst out in a yelp as I dodged barely out of reach, tripping and catching myself on a cluster of thorny brambles.

But not even the scrape and jab of sharp tines could pierce the swelling *excitement* within me. Words dredged from my depths with every gasping inhale and exhale…words like I'd learned in books that lulled me to sleep for so long in Krylan. Like the adventure I'd lived since departing port with Jaik. Like the stories we'd formed *together* in the journal he carried with him.

Pieces of me, spun in scarlet, coming alive with every breath from my lungs.

Had it been a slow whittling away of her power? A sudden severing as if by a sword? Looking backward, she couldn't be certain…all she knew was that it seemed the power was gone forever. That there was no longer a place for stories in her life, in the lives she touched with every turn of her feet.

Because what worth could stories have in the face of travesty, in a world full of so much suffering and injustice? How could she go on telling them when she had been so badly hurt so many times, when her body failed her, when her mind became her own enemy, when those she loved were dying?

Every word fell like a lodestone from my mouth as I darted away from the wraith; and it pursued, shadows clawing relentlessly, hewing clots of dirt from the forest floor as it scrabbled through the tightly woven undergrowth to reach me.

To silence me.

A giddy sort of desperation spiked in my chest at its feral screams. Because...why would it be shrieking, trying to drown out my voice, unless my voice was *exactly* what was needed now?

Striking a hand out backward, I caught hold of the next nearest tree at my back and heaved myself to my feet. Keeping my eyes on the wraith, I retreated as swiftly as my feet would allow, my mind racing miles ahead of every step.

In time, she grew to resent the impression that stories had left on her life. What was the purpose of holding on to such a memory when it only caused pain?

Every word seemed a struggle now, every thread of storytelling tangled up inside of her. She craved an escape. She craved a life without the shackles of forgotten talent climbing up into a noose around her throat.

Heat stamped my palms as I gripped a pair of trees and thrust backward, dodging the wraith's next scrambling strike. A swift glance at my fingertips sent my pulse stuttering.

The faintest tendrils of amber dust sifted against my palm...cords of storytelling trying to shift into something tangible. Something *real*.

The power of creation made manifest in my tale.

A wild whoop of shock and joy burned in my throat—then cut short at the wraith's next powerful slash, slapping a handful of trees loose from the soil and catching me across the chest with a limb. All the breath whooshed from me at once, and I skidded backward across the soil, rock and root catching at my back, slamming down the notches of my spine...stealing any air I tried to gasp in for myself.

I fetched up hard against a tree, squeezing the last breath from the depths of my lungs. Head rocking, eyes dancing with tinges of gray and distant blurs of red, I choked and clawed for life; dimly, mutedly, the sounds of struggle reached out to me.

The wraith, still shredding through the forest...hindered by its size.

Fear grown so large, it could no longer quite reach me. It couldn't yet touch me where I lay.

Fear.

This was what I had feared...a destiny of only this. A life defined by moments of joy and brushes with death an instant later.

But now was not the time to fear—not the next brush with death. Not even this one.

This was the moment to fight for the joy on the other side of it.

Digging my fingers into the earthy loam, I heaved and staggered back to my feet; cuffing blood from the corner of my mouth, my tongue sweating with it where teeth had pierced flesh at my impact with the tree, I measured my breathing. Steadied it. Made it obey *me.*

And then I swiveled to face the wraith, her hands gripping the tree, wrenching them apart in a vast grip, her seven foot height still rising higher beyond.

My stomach dropped into my toes...but I didn't let it pull me back to my knees.

Not this time.

I had done my kneeling today—at the feet of my Maker.

I had nothing left to fear.

She came to a crossroads, this storyteller. To pursue a world beyond stories...to let her own ending be written for her by the choices of her forsaken land, by the struggle, by the pain of it all. Or to hold on, with all of her might...to fight for the tales she told, and the reason she told them.

For only she could decide whether her gift perished. Whether she ended another tale at all. Or whether she pursued her craft, to the ends of a suffering world...to give what light she could. To write it back into herself when hers faltered.

With a roar, the wraith lunged—and by the guide of sheer instinct, I flung up my hand.

Her shadow shackles slammed against a rippling wall of iridescence.

Of *light*—the very same light Ovalia had unleashed in Rivrand, to save her people. But now it glowed in *my* palm, shimmered between *my* fingers...and with half a thought, it *shoved,* forcing the wraith back several stumbling strides.

Triumph burned in my throat as *I* pursued again.
No longer chased. No longer hunted...nor hunting.
Choosing *my* crossroads. My own path.

*And, no, she decided...she would not falter. And she would not fear. Her Maker
had given her everything she needed to fulfill her purpose.*

*The power of story was not some fleeting convenience meant for times of prosper-
ity, for happy days alone. It was not something to be discarded when life became
difficult, something she would let go of and fall away from because anyone else
told her she should. Or that she must.*

*No...she would fight for it. For her own story. For the stories that others dreamed
to tell. It would start with her, but it would not end with her. Not if she blazed
a trail. Not if she proved to herself and others that it could be done!*

The wraith fell back again and again as my voice lashed out—as conviction steeled every word. As determination blazed hot in my chest and forged
itself into fresh shields of light. And though the wraith's blackened edges
struck at mine again and again, it did not pierce. It found no way through.

This was *my* story. And I had decided I would finish it...whatever the
cost.

*She was worthy. Her tales were worthy. And no matter how bleak the turns in
the path, no matter how dark the days ahead, she was determined they would
not be made shadow, but light. A light for her footsteps, and for all those who
would walk the perilous journey of creation after her.*

*And she set out into the broken world, with her bruised body and battered soul,
to do just that. To etch her own epic into the face of history.*

And just like that—with my next step, with a drift of crimson on the
corners of my vision—I knew what I had to do.

Why the Storymaker had done this exactly the way He had. And how it must be finished.

In a broken and sundered world, stories are a power that will not be silenced. The stories we tell ourselves, that we tell each other, that we write by our very living, and the story that made us all, can echo beyond the ages...and redefine them.

Stories have the power to shape us. To change us.

Words are a weapon. We raise them as a battle cry.

And I raised it high.

Not a sword.

A *book*.

Plunging a hand into my pocket and yanking the deckled-edge tome free, I cracked the spine, spread its blank pages wide, and faced them out toward my enemy—my own darkness, the most rotten and outcast parts of me.

And the Misspoken manifestation *fractured*.

Not shadows -not shards—but *letters*. Inky words splintering into a thousand fractals. She exploded outward, the spirals of her twisting around themselves on the air—smaller words forging larger etchings against the brilliant sunlight.

Fear. Fury. Disbelief. Grief. Hatred.

An endless, repeating banner heaving and slithering through the sky...trying to soak in. Trying to taint everything.

Tears seeped down my cheeks as I stepped nearer to her shattered form.

"I'm done running," I panted, "and I'm done trying to write the hardest parts out of my story. There *is* no story without them. The good and the bad I've faced, they're the two halves of who I am...and that's shaped me into the person the Storymaker made me to be."

Rage scalded the air in the form of a scream—but it had lost its resonance. Turned tinny with its own sort of fear.

"*I'm* not afraid." A smile cut through the wash of tearstains on my cheeks. "Not of you. Not of your shadows, not anymore. Not when I know Whose light I'm standing in. It's time for you to give up your power and go *back* where you belong...to be a part of my story. And not the part that decides where everything ends."

Before my eyes, the winding ropes of words began to crumble. Falling apart into chains of letters...and then to only the letters themselves, floating apart on the breeze like embers and ashes.

And all of those letters drifted precisely where I'd told them to go.

To the book the Storymaker had given me.

The first stroke of fragmented letters against the pages struck like an anvil, wrenching my shoulders backward in their sockets; but I dug in my heels, I stood fast—not in my own strength, but in *His*. In the knowledge of this second chance He had gifted me, and how it was changing everything.

So I braced, and gritted my teeth, and held on...as more and more letters hurtled through the air, as they stabbed through the pages like knives, as the pain spiraled through my arms and crashed into my head. As I began to shake, from my ankles to my fingertips, feet curled in my boots, the whole world swallowed in the thundering of Misspoken power going to the only place it had left—

And then...strength of a different kind.

Familiar hands climbing from my hips, to my shoulders. Bracing me. Holding on when I quaked on the edge of breaking.

"I've got you, Ayjay!" Jaik rasped in my ear. "Don't let go, tiger—*don't let go!*"

A new warmth...sacred. Kindred. Igniting in my muscles, pushing back against the pain. Reaching into every inch of me that wanted to buckle, to fall and never rise again.

To the end of all time.

A joyful sob cracked from my chest, and I squeezed my eyes shut, leaning back into the steadiness of Jaik's chest, into the tangible presence of the Storymaker. The three of us, together, absorbing this might beyond reckoning.

A threefold cord that nothing had broken yet. That nothing ever could.

And at last, with a mighty thunderclap, with a piercing shriek morphing into a hiccupping breath—almost like a gasp of relief—the last of the letters jammed into the book. The pages ruffled with a roar so violent it jerked me clean off my feet and out of Jaik's hands; I slammed down in the soil, pain jolting through my kneecaps, hands splayed on either side of the book as it tumbled from my grasp, skidding in the mud.

It came to rest like the brush of a palm over weathered writings, the front cover falling gently open, baring a floating inscription that inked itself on the very first page:

Let me tell you a story.

And in a moment—in the turn of a page—I was utterly undone.
And made utterly new.

LET ME TELL YOU A STORY

THERE ONCE WAS A woman who had everything.

A family she adored, who adored her in kind—even if they were sometimes too proud to admit it. Friends she trusted with every piece of herself. A man who began as a rival, who turned to a friend...who became something so much more.

She held power in her hands, gathered in the folds of her scarlet cloak. She brought stadiums to their feet and villains to their knees. She lived and loved fiercely, until she burned her life out to embers. To ashes. To mere echoes.

Until the thing she loved most, of everything she had, was ripped away.

There once was a woman who lost everything.

She spent years running in the only direction that seemed right...away from everyone and everything she had ever known. Toward the vaguest impression of where she might find a fresh start. Where she might come home to.

And, Maker, was she *right*.

She'd had no ending in sight...but she'd found hers again. In the hands and heart of love lost and reclaimed. In a shift of her own story she'd never foreseen. Through a wild and wicked adventure that had unveiled the truth of what she was made of, what *all* stories were made of...and the part she played in telling them.

And then she had a choice to make. And she made the only one she could think of, to write an ending that mattered.

There once was a woman who gave up everything.

Who settled for less. Who contented herself with the quiet life. Who let no one truly come near. Her companions were cats and books and the people she allowed to approach only to arm's length...until the doors of her life blew wide, ushering in strangers who knew her far better than she'd ever known herself.

Strangers who remembered power and passion and purpose and *love*. Strangers who ushered her on a new adventure, a grand one that brought her face to face with just how beautiful and broken life could be. So that she could choose for herself...the quiet, the content, or something far more.

Far, far more than she had ever dreamed.

There once was a woman who had, and lost, and gave. And then she reached out with all her heart, and was given back her measure.

Let me tell you *her* story.

CHAPTER ONE

T**HE TANG OF INK** and parchment kissed my nose. Feather-soft pages pressed against my cheek like flower petals. The wind smelled of damp, torn earth and autumn decay, somehow both sweet and musty, and someone was saying my name.

If I cracked my eyes open, I'd be slumped over my textbook in one of Fablehaven Academy's rotunda rooms, most likely dampening the page beneath my cheek with an excessive amount of drool. That would account for the scents swirling like delicate script in my nostrils, the strain in my back and hips, the tightness in my shoulders that pinched like a quill nib against tender flesh—and that voice repeating my name, somewhere between furious and frantic, because once again I was disturbing a lesson...but it was hard to keep up with it all.

Sneaking out to meet with Naomi and do our classwork together, practicing Storycraft in the smallest tales whispered between the cracked courtyard stones, darting home to do my laundry and steal some of Mama's scones to share with my classmates...it was a full life.

"Audra—hey, fun's over! You're scaring me, tiger—"

Tiger.

None of my professors ever called me that.

Only *one person* had *ever* called me that ridiculous name.

My next breath, deeper, allowed an invasion of other smells—blood. Body odor. Animal musk. And a warm undercurrent of leather and woodsmoke.

I crinkled my nose, but there was no fighting the sudden, violent urge to sneeze. It erupted out of me, sending a zinging sharpness into the corners of my eyes.

"*Jaik,*" I wheezed.

"Open your eyes for me, Ayjay."

"Bossy boots." But I obeyed.

And there he was, crouched before me, a bruised, bent version of the man I loved, sunk on his knees in the mud. Powerful hands encircled my upper arm, and he peered at me with those soil-rich eyes, chestnut hair falling across one of them in a messy toss, worry and disbelief scripting the lines around his eyes.

"*Bossy boots?*" he echoed sharply.

"That's what you are," I mumbled, pushing a hand into the soil and levering myself up. The ache persisted—most likely from fighting for my flipping *life* against the wraith—but the softness on my cheek lingered, too, like a brush of fingers.

Like the touch of the Storymaker's hand.

My gaze leaped back to the book, fallen open before me, faintly impressed where my head had dropped against it. And winking up from those pages in glossy ink freckled in gold—like letters read in a ship's creaking belly, beside hearths, in homesteads near and far—were six simple words. The beginning and end of everything I had ever known.

Let me tell you a story.

And it struck me, all at once, blowing the breath out of my chest, sitting me back hard on my haunches and knocking me clean out of Jaik's grip.

I remembered.

I.

Remembered.

Everything.

And then the sobs came, a fast, furious torrent bordering on hacks and screams, and barely before the first one was out, Jaik lunged for me; he wrapped one hand around my neck and the other arm twined against my waist, and he pulled me into his chest as I wept.

Stunned. Relieved. With a soul-shuddering pain and wonder that took the breath completely out of me.

I remembered every bit of it—Fablehaven, and the Master Storycrafter trials. Our journeys after, and how they'd come to a violent end. I remembered Vallanmyre, and Dalfi—the doors slammed in my face, the tavern that opened itself to me. The Undying Tale, and the way it ended.

Jaik, the stranger who'd once meant *everything*, coming to hear my story. *Our* story.

Galan. Hectra. The Misspoken manifestations in the forest, the colors coming alive in Dalfi again. A snowy alleyway in Fallshyre Bay. A ship like home.

The crew. *Julas.* Our return to Vallanmyre in chains, and then—

The Tearing. And my swift escape to Krylan, where I'd sold my ring, and made myself disappear.

Until my friends came back for me. Until *Jaik* kept his promise—like he always did—and found me again.

And somehow the *first* thing that I managed past the hacking sobs—the first words that escaped the jumble of prayers and apologies and the love lodged like a stone in my throat—absurdly, it was, "I'm—going—to—*kill*—Lionyra Vara."

Or Kassian. Or whatever my friend was calling herself now.

"Wait, what—*what?*" Stricken laughter jolted from Jaik, and his hand slid from my nape to my shoulder, pushing me out a bit from him—farther than I wanted to be right now. And possibly ever again. "Where did *that* come from?"

"You know flipping good and *well* where it came from," I blubbered with a devastating lack of dignity. "She didn't tell me who she was—*none of them* did."

Jaik's fingers stiffened. Tightened into a fist over the folds of my cloak.

"What."

No inflection to that word. No grace to the heave of his throat, to the sudden sheen that coated his eyes.

As if it wasn't me he was asking. Not really.

And all at once my brain caught up with my thundering, battered heart, and I realized he didn't know what had sent me bowling over into tears. Why I was crying so hard I could barely catch my breath.

This man who had spent so long and given so much of himself loving every version of me in this messy tale my life had always been...he didn't even realize what I knew.

"Oh, *Jaik*." I shifted nearer to him, gripping the collar of his shirt, searching his eyes...finding the first tear that slipped over the lid and disappeared into the scruff and stubble darkening his cheeks.

"Ayjay." There was a warning in his tone—a plea against hope. Begging not to be given that joy, and then have it taken away.

But I wasn't going anywhere. Not now, not ever again.

Nowhere that took me away from him . Or away from the truth of who I was.

"I know you," I wept, framing his face with my palms. "I know every piece of you, Jaik Grissom. I know exactly who you are. My pain-in-the-rear bodyguard. My favorite farmhand. My flipping *husband*."

Profaning Luck, Jaik seized my temples in both hands, fingers tangled in my hair, and *crushed* his mouth over mine.

I now knew enough—knew *everything*—to be absolutely certain he'd never kissed me this way before. Not even in the cabin. It was like someone breathing life back into me...like a homecoming after a war. Like love pulled back from the very edge of death.

Like he would never let me go again.

And that was good; because I wasn't ever letting go of *him* again, either.

Not my memories of him. Not the man himself. *Anything.*

We were both weeping, panting, laughing when we finally broke apart; I pressed my kiss-bruised lips to the muscles that joined his shoulder and neck, a place that turned him wild. And my laughter doubled when he groaned, dropping his face into my hair.

"Hey, there, soldier," I teased; he fisted his hand in in my hair, bringing my head to rest above his heart. "I'm back."

"You're *home.*" A half-growl, half-sob ransacked his lurching throat; then he pulled me up to kiss him again.

And if this was all the joy we ever had—kisses on battlefields and bones aching and blood staining our hands, and breathtaking kisses with a home in each other's arms, and every single memory we shared of every time we'd done this before, with a lifetime of chances ahead to do it again, and again, and again...

It was enough.

It was *more* than enough to make all the hate and grief, the shame and terror, all the rage and every other awful thing endurable.

"I'm home," I gasped with laughter when we finally broke apart. "And now...I want to see the regiment. I want to go visit my family and tell them *everything.* And Noni, and Reiko, and Mahalia, and Raz...poor Raz."

That man, laboring under his father's title, with no Master Storycrafter at his side, and his bodyguard and best friend snatched away on this mad quest with me...

I owed him a drink. Possibly *several.*

"And after that," I rambled, straightening Jaik's collar, my fingers flying as swift as my tumbling thoughts, "once we're all sick of each other again, we have to go sailing. The crew, I have to see them...I need to apologize, and thank them, and hug *each and every one of them...*"

Syd, Lanah, Reinera—my forgotten friends who had shared my sorrows and my stories. Who had sailed me into danger and back again, over and over, with such unwavering faith. And Lio—*my* Lio—the former Delina of Amere-Del. The one who had been precisely what I needed, twice over...a friend who had chosen to become a friend again, without a hint that she'd ever known me before. Because that was what I'd needed.

Emotion gathered thick in my throat. Jaik's lips brushed the top of my head, his snort of laughter stirring my hair. "Already got it all figured out, huh? Got the whole story plotted?"

"Today, I do. And maybe tomorrow, I won't." I nuzzled my head under his chin, breathing in his woodsy scent and the warmth of this racing heart. "Stories can be like that sometimes...they'll take you by surprise. But I know what I *will* want today, and tomorrow, and every day after that, until the end of my tale...and it's you, Jaik. It's *our* story."

His throat bobbed, and he cradled my face against him. "Nowhere else I'd rather be, Ayjay."

That made two of us.

Thank you. I set the silent prayer free as I wound my fingers around the nape of Jaik's neck. *Thank you for everything.*

A breeze tugged at my hair—both warm and cool, smelling of ink and growing things and *living.* A breeze that had long ago chased me down the Spine, to Krylan. And to the seaside, to begin this quest with Jaik, when I'd almost turned away instead.

This time, it ushered the bellows of familiar voices, soaked with exhaustion but heavy with triumph.

Gil. Elly. The regiment, victorious, and searching, coming our way.

"Addie? Jaik? Where in flipping Luck are you at—what just happened?" Gil hollered. "All those manifestations just took off like bats out of a cave...what'd you two do?"

"*This time!*" Elly yelled.

"You want to break the news?" Jaik laughed as he planted his good foot and staggered up, hauling me to my feet with him. "Or should I?"

"Maker, where do we even begin?" I scoffed into the tattered folds of his shirt.

But I would find a way. With my memories settling over me in the warmest weight I'd ever known. With Jaik turning us to face the sound of footsteps tromping through the sullied undergrowth.

With a cloak of deep red, not quite scarlet, drifting over me.

A mantle. A calling I had once and for all, and truly, made my own.

This is your story, Audra, that familiar wind whispered in my ear.

All of it...the tales yet to be crafted, the people I would tell them to, the future I would build and who would be in it. The woman I had been, and lost, and was becoming now.

I was shades of all of them...scarlet red and blush rose and dapple gray. I was pieces of every Audra I had ever been...and I loved every one of them fiercely, flaws and beauties and all, through the Storymaker's eyes.

And I loved Jaik Grissom, my favorite part of my own story, who pulled me under his arm and walked with me side by side to greet our friends—all of them bruised and battered but alive, pushing into the open, a circle of backslaps and hugs and joyous cries already rising higher than the waning sun.

Just one piece of the family I had finally, *finally* come home to.

Tell it well.

EPILOGUE

T HE SHASTAH HALLS WERE no longer a gilded tomb.

For days after we'd returned to Galent—while Jaik had sent word for an airship, and we'd awaited its arrival, soaking up every moment with Gil and Lyssa and their regiment—I'd struggled to fit my hands around the shape of this next chapter in my life. What it would look like...who and *what* I could be.

Master Storycrafter, a professor at Fablehaven Academy, a part of Arias's council, a member of the combined sword-and-story that thrust into the hearts of Misspoken manifestations across Mithra-Sha, making our country safe again...so many things I could be. That I *wanted* to be, moment by moment.

It was Jaik who had reminded me, the same day as the airship's arrival in Galent, that we didn't have to sort out everything yet. Just the next page...and I already knew what that entailed.

So here we were...striding hand-in-hand through golden walls that had once marked death and despair for us. But not now...now, I knew it for all it was, and had been. And I saw it for what it was about to be: a space held for a reunion my heart had been *aching* for since the day I'd read the pages of my own story and remembered who I was.

There was a version of Audra who would have gone to her family first. And there was a version who would have spent her time tangled up in the sheets with her husband, admiring the iron band around her finger—a simple piece soldered by an ironsmith in Galent, inlaid with veins of red and gold. Still another who would have hurried straight to the nearest fight, to put to use the stories that bubbled effervescent on her tongue.

But the Audra who was all three of them...she approached the door of the Sha's Convening Chamber, where the walls whispered of such bitter loss, and of so much weight and grief...and she knew.

She knew precisely where she was needed first. Where her stories could be of the greatest help.

And what it meant, to carry that weight...and wear it well.

But even that Audra slowed, her hand slipping from her husband's, when she caught the sound of upraised voices within.

The last voices she had ever expected to hear in this place, raised in deft and foul argument—voices of seaspray and skeletal forms. Voices of shadowed wrath and fury. And also a voice of powdered-sugar sweetness and rainstorms and fireworks.

"Is that...?" I half-turned toward Jaik; his hand had already encircled the back of my neck, his thumb rubbing the top of my shoulder.

"Yeah." He frowned. "Yeah, I hear it, too."

It would've been wonderful to sink into his casual touch...the sort that had signatured every day we'd spent together since my memories had been restored. The kind that welcomed every sunrise and sent off every sunset.

But a new fire lit in my chest at the sound of an argument ahead—a scarlet ember stoked to brilliant, fiery life.

A part that was so flipping *familiar* with being at the center of every argument that happened behind those walls. And a part that couldn't wait to meet the voices raised in impassioned argument between them.

Satchel bumping against my hip, heavy with the weight of a journal and a cloak wadded within, I surged out of Jaik's grip and shot for the Convening Chamber's only set of double-doors.

"Ayjay—hey—wait!" Jaik barked behind me. "Count to five, tiger!"

Absolutely flipping not.

Slamming both hands into doors that had shut me in and kept me out more times than I cared to recall, I stormed straight inside like I belonged there.

Because now, I remembered—I *did*.

"*Lionyra Vara*!" I roared—then drew up short, puffing out a breath, embarrassment scribbling all over my chest. "Oh."

The Convening Chamber was by no means sparsely occupied; not only was Arias present, one of the three shouting voices, along with Reiko, Mahalia, Naomi, and Wyat—but there was Lio, whose unusually strident tone had summoned me like a call to battle.

And she had a cluster of sailors at her side.

Captain Kassian, naturally—the absolute ass. And Hasser, Syd, and Lanah, who were slack-jawed at my arrival.

For a moment, no one said anything—except for Syd, who flicked a hand halfway up and croaked, "Lionyra Kassian, actually—" before Lio swatted his hand down, staring at me wide-eyed.

Eyes that were already gathering a slim film of tears—of dawning comprehension at a name that had belonged to us when we'd first met. Not how she'd introduced herself aboard *The Cathan*.

The tension broke when Jaik stepped to my side, his hand grazing the small of my back...a silent question that went unanswered as Arias slumped forward, elbows propped on the table, rubbing his temples.

"Ah, look who arrived just when I need him most," he huffed. "Jaik, do your duty, will you, and throw the Captain out on his leather-clad backside?"

"Touch me, Fishbait, and I'll give you a hand to match mine." Ryker flashed his four-fingered hand our way; the other fell on the sword at his side.

"Y'know, actually, I'm curious how this one plays out." Jaik folded his arms, slumping back against the doorframe. "Love to hear what they're doing in the Shastah, too. Didn't think Kassian could go on land without growing a tail."

"After all the times you told me merfolk can't be real," Naomi folded her arms, stabbing Jaik with a glare like a quill tip punching through parchment, "*now* it suits you? As an *insult*?"

"Actually," I piped in, "he never said they *couldn't* be real...just that it was even less likely than you ever finding a man who could meet your standards."

Naomi scoffed. "Well, he's still right about—"

She broke off. Blinked. Met my sheepish smile with a mouth slowly falling open—and damp eyes to match Lio's glistening stare.

"Addie?" she breathed.

The whole room caught its breath as Naomi Weathers and I met each other eye-to-eye, face-to-face, for the first time in too many complicated, Luck-loved years.

"Oh, bloody depths," Ryker grumbled. "Here it comes."

"Flipping *Luck*!" Naomi launched from her seat and scaled clean over the table in a smooth bound of flying skirts; her tackling embrace knocked me reeling straight back into Lio's arms encircling my collarbones from behind.

And then I was crying again—we were *all* crying—as they held me, pressed between them like a flower in parchment pages...something beautiful and beloved, perfectly preserved all this time. Two of my best friends in the whole of the Wellspoken World holding onto me with all of their might, and I finally, *finally* knew every single reason why.

"I'm so sorry," I rambled, working an awkward arm around each of them. "I'm *so sorry* I gave you up—I swear on the Maker's tales, I won't let *either* of you go for the rest of my life—"

"Just shut your ramble hole for *once*, Addie," Naomi's tears stained my sleeve, "and then promise me you'll *never* shut it again."

"Never, ever." A vow I hadn't made to her since we'd been little girls—which made it all the more precious now. "I love you so much, Noni."

"I love *you*, Addie, you impossible, wonderful, amazing person."

We held and swayed each other for more minutes than I cared to count; it was Naomi who drew away first—only to cradle my face for a moment, then to flick rivers of disturbed kohl from below her own eyes as she stepped back—and into that gap, the others slipped, one by one. Syd and Lanah first, speaking over each other in half-shouts, telling me all about *The Cathan* and its surviving crew, about Wilkes and Reinera and how *thrilled* they were going to be to know our quest had succeeded—*well, not Wilkes, he sort of tried to capture you when you were Master Storycrafter, do you remember that? But he liked you well enough this time, so go easy on him*—until Reiko elbowed them aside.

"Thank *Luck* you're back," she swore, knocking her fist against mine when I raised my knuckles for the familiar ritual. "You told me *last* time you weren't going to leave me to handle this alone, and what'd you do?"

"You would *never* believe what I did," I admitted.

"Show-off."

"That's me."

Before I could turn to the table—to Arias and Mahalia, who'd held back with a Sha and Shadress's perfect poise, but their damp eyes fixed on me—Lio turned me at last to face her, gathering my face in her hands.

"Hello, Addie-cat," she murmured. "You look *whole*."

Fresh tears spilled down my cheeks. "I have you to thank for so much of it."

"Whatever part I played in your happiness, it was my honor."

"And *mine* in yours." I wrapped my arms around her and hugged her to me with all my might. "Flipping Luck, I missed you. I can't believe you married a pirate who *captured* you."

"You fell in love with a man who once betrayed you, as well." She pushed me back a bit, meeting my playful scowl with a mischievous wink. "Perhaps we are alike in every way."

"You take that back." I nearly popped her on the shoulder—then hesitated. "How...how are you? Really?"

"Quite possibly the best I have ever been." Her eyes gleamed with emotion—with earnest truth.

Still, I found my gaze darting to Ryker...because, as messy and complicated as *he* was, as their past was, there was no denying the fierce love that had guided his defense of her aboard *The Cathan*.

And there was no lack of that love now as he watched us reunite—the same sort of love that had readied me to face my own past. The shadowy echo of my own *self*.

Our gazes met, that kindred, world-tearing emotion sharing space in the air between us...but before I could say any of a hundred things that swirled to life at its rising, Jaik cleared his throat and snapped his fingers, drawing Ryker's attention away.

"So? How'd you get here? Didn't think that watertight coffin of yours could row across the ground."

"Aye, you really thought you got funny on your little adventure, did you?" Ryker cocked a brow. "We walked, mate. Left Gyddy and Siu in charge, Cam and Wilkes and Reinera with them. That suit you?"

Jaik blinked. He dipped his chin, just a bit; the intensity that flickered in his eyes was a story unto itself—one he hadn't shared with me yet, that must have nothing to do with sundered memories—and he didn't speak it now as he shrugged, tearing his gaze from Ryker. "Eh. Sort of wish they'd left *you* behind."

"Never. Where I go, he goes...always," Lio said, and with a last squeeze, she let me go.

I brushed past her, stalking up to Ryker and shoving him with all my might. He took it like he'd been *expecting* it—and, good. He *should* have, after he'd captured my friend and then *married* her.

Still, it would've been nice if he'd done more than rock back on his heels and shoot me a slag-eating grin. "Oddball."

"Captain *kidnapped-Lionyra-Vara-and-convinced-her-to-marry-me!*" I shook him by the ridiculously soft folds of his well-worn leather coat. "Maker's tales, I don't know if I should hit you so hard you beg me to kick you in the groin, or kick you so hard you beg me to punch your pretty face!"

"Wait, *pretty?*" Jaik protested. "*That's* pretty, Ayjay? *Seriously?*"

"Don't whine at me, I'm wearing *your* ring!"

"*Ring?*" Mahalia shot up from her chair at last, thrusting it back with a shriek so piercing we *all* flinched as she darted around the table to grab my hand...turning it this way and that, examining my iron ring. After a moment, she groaned, dropping my fingers like they'd scalded her. "No—*Addie!* You promised I could design your wedding gown!"

"I didn't remember!" I protested—though guilt wrote its sharp curlicues on the corners of my heart. "There's still time for a ceremony—"

"Oh, bloody *joy*," Ryker muttered. "Just what I need...one more wedding. Gyddy's nearly sank me in the depths. Don't even remember the better part of Syd and Lanah's, and *Wilkes'*—"

"Still have the scars from that one." Syd shuddered. "Inside and out."

"Excuse me!" It just figured they were pirating the list to my own wedding, after they'd pirated *Lio* as well. "I didn't invite you, *Captain Kassian—you* are *not* invited!"

A gentle but firm hand seized my wrist—and at the slightest bit of pressure in fingers I knew best suited for kneading dough, but that I was now aware from a story of her own could wield a blade with killing precision—I let go of Lio's husband, pivoting to face her instead.

"While I would have, at one time or another and in one fashion or another, immensely have enjoyed the spectacle of watching the Master Storycrafter and Captain Blackhand come to blows," she smiled gently, squeezing both of my hands in hers, "it would, perhaps, be in poorer taste than moldy loaves to wish a beating on the father of my child. However well-deserved it may be."

I rolled my eyes. "You're just afraid I would—"

All the breath rushed from me at once.

I blinked. Lio blinked back, arching a brow, one side of her mouth tilting up.

Had it ever taken me *so long* to comprehend a story—one written in golden-glowing skin, in sparkling eyes, in a particular bunching of dimpled cheeks, in thicker-than-usual waves of dark hair and a belly that rounded just a bit differently from how I recalled even from aboard *The Cathan*, a few months ago?

"The father of your...*wait*," I choked. "*Wait.* He got you *pregnant*?"

"I bloody hope it was me," Ryker muttered under his breath.

Lio tossed an eyeroll past me at the sulking pirate captain—not just her *husband*, but the father of her *child*. "You know I have eyes only for you, Bash."

"Aye, but it's not *eyes* you need for—"

"Stop, stop!" Wyat yelped. "I don't want to hear what you need for what!"

Ryker's grin, if possible, widened. "Lad, you just fully gave yourself away."

"Stop! *No!*" Mahalia wailed, covering her ears and squeezing her eyes shut. "Not in front of my *brother!*"

"What? We're all adults!" Arias argued. "We know how babies are made!"

Red-faced, Wyat shot a look at Mahalia. "It's not that—I don't—"

"Flipping Luck, do we need this lesson?" Naomi groaned. "Here? Now?"

"Lio!" I rattled her hands furiously between us, dragging her attention back to me—earning moans of relief from every other person in the room, though I paid them barely any mind as I searched my friend's grinning face. "You're pregnant!"

"*Yes.*" Wonder—joy—and perhaps a tinge of fear—colored Lio's tone; her hand parted from mine, hovering over the folds of her stomach as if she ached to cradle the life growing within. "That's the reason for this entire, ill-fated, utterly *disastrous* meeting. Gyddy discovered, when we came ashore at Fallshyre Bay...it's taken us that long to make the crossing to Vallanmyre, to request an extended leave of absence from the fleet."

"That long because you were emptying your guts in every ditch between there and Vallanmyre." Only the scrape of the Captain's hand around the back of his neck betrayed any concern he'd had for her condition. "Thought Hasser would have to string a bucket under your chin if we were going to make it more than a mile at a time."

"I would've welcomed either of you to try," Lio shot back crossly.

"Possibly you should *lead* with that exposition next time, Kassian." Arias sank back in his seat, rubbing both hands down his face. "I would have agreed without the verbal sparring match if I'd known there was a child's life involved! Why must it always be a fight with you?"

"Because I don't take orders from your scrawny arse."

"Actually, you do. You're a part of my fleet, I pay your crew—otherwise, would you have bothered to come to me to make the request?"

"Just didn't want you sending your goons to..." Ryker trailed off when Lio cleared her throat; then, cursing under his breath, he spread his hands on the edge of Arias's table, bending nearer. "Shore leave. We could use it."

"Naturally, it's yours." Arias's tired gaze traveled between Ryker's scowl and Lio's beaming smile...and softened with an emotion that knocked the breath from my chest.

Regret. Melancholy. Sorrow. All of it scripted around the warmth at the middle of his grin, that beat like a scarlet heart in a shadowy chest.

"That sort of joy should be defended at all costs," he murmured. "I'm happy for you both. And there will always be a place for *The Cathan* among the fleet, when the time is right for you to return."

"If that time ever comes," Ryker muttered; but he leaned away with a curt nod, which—I knew from experience—was as good as a hug and a handshake from the surly Captain.

"And there goes the best ship in our fleet," Reiko scowled. "Just *wonderful*."

Ryker flipped her a two-fingered salute. "Appreciate the flattery, lass."

"I'm not flattering you, I'm flipping *furious*. Way to strand us, Kassian."

"'Ey, you'll manage." He hiked a thumb my way. "The way I hear it, this one's good for ten of us."

"Twenty, if we're just talking you against her," Jaik ribbed, shrugging up from the wall and clapping a hand on Ryker's shoulder.

The Captain shrugged him off. "Don't get bloody *cozy* with me."

But Jaik only braced a hand on his shoulder, shaking him fiercely. "Congratulations, Kassian. I mean it."

Scoffing, Ryker rolled his eyes—but he clapped Jaik on the wrist after a moment, giving him a rough squeeze before he plucked his hand away and tossed it back down at his side. "Right. Time to set sail, Raiders."

"Oh, no, you don't." I wrapped an arm around Lio's waist, tugging her against me. "Not back onto that ship to cloister yourself on some gold hoard a hundred miles away from here—"

"Aw, that's cute!" Syd leaned his shoulder into Lanah's. "She thinks we're *real* pirates."

"—and come sailing back with a baby in a few months!" I shot him a glower, and he rubbed the back of his neck. "No, my *friend* is going to be properly celebrated."

Mahalia reared her head up, hopeful eyes pinned on me. "Does that mean what I *hope* it does?"

"Dinner. At my parents' house. Cake, flowers, *gifts...no*!" I barked when half the crew—and Arias—groaned. "I don't want to hear it, not *one word*. I just got all of you back, do you really think I'll let half of the people in this room sail off into the sunset right now? Not a chance!"

"Or you'll—what?" Kassian challenged. "Tell a story, turn us all into toads?"

"It wouldn't take much to change *you* into a slippery, bug-eyed nuisance, so don't tempt me, Captain." I hugged Lio tighter against me—and she hugged me back, meeting her husband's scowl with a demure grin.

"I did miss her, Bash," she murmured. "Very much. A week here, two at the most...it's hardly too much to ask, after all we've endured to find our way back to one another.

It might've seemed a saccharine jab, and nothing more—if not for how she rested her head against mine.

Grimacing, the Captain fell back on his heels. "Bloody depths. How do you handle it, Fishbait?"

"Both hands," Jaik shot back without missing a beat. "And never letting go."

I should have kicked him for that remark; instead, I found myself blinking away tears.

Emotions were certainly going to be the most difficult thing to navigate in settling into the Audra I was, and had been...and was still becoming.

"So, we're going?" Wyat asked hopefully.

"You heard her." Jaik clapped Wyat by the arm and hauled him to his feet. "Hope Mama Jay's ready for guests."

"She's always ready," I reminded him—because I remembered it now, too. How often she'd had the hearth roaring, a cup of tea or coffee and usually a few loaves of sourdough with butter, honey, and salt flakes warming on the stone windowsill for when I brought Naomi, or Jaik, or Reiko, or even Arias and Mahalia to visit.

So many parts of the world that so often were just open doors, in my past, my present, and my future—waiting for me to come home.

My throat thick, I opened my other arm to Naomi; she leaned into my side, enveloping me in the scent of cotton and freesia...another piece of home I'd forgotten. That I would never let go of ever again.

"*Come on*, big guy." Jaik dragged Arias up next, slinging an arm around his neck. "As your bodyguard, I'm telling you...safest place for your sorry-looking hide right now is Mama Jay's kitchen. I'll even let you win at another arm-wrestling match."

"*Let me*, ha." Arias pinned Ryker with a glare. "There are still logistics to be sorted out, about your leave of absence. This discussion isn't over."

"Seems to be," he drawled, hooking his thumbs in his belt and aiming a kick at Syd's haunch to usher him and Lanah out the door. "Unless you want to arm-wrestle for that, too, mate."

"Just banish them all," Reiko murmured in Arias's ear as she slipped past him. "I can Storycraft a little box—"

"Don't you *dare*," I warned.

She rolled her eyes. "Here we go...back for two minutes and already tossing around her clout."

But there was no venom to battle the relief in her gaze or the ease of her stride when she fell into step with the crew of *The Cathan*; and as I walked arm-in-arm with Lio and Naomi through the golden halls, it felt as if the ribs of the Shastah breathed. As if its very walls expanded to make space for me again.

To welcome me home—to a better future. A far brighter one than I'd ever dreamed.

Just like that, I watched it change...the way the burden eased when I was here. The way I slotted so perfectly back into this life I had left behind.

Purpose. A new story to help write...and to hear, and make better. As a Storycrafter, and as a woman who had lived so long in this place, with these people. As a friend and a daughter, a sister, a wife, who knew all of the characters in my own tale by heart.

As Audra Jashowin. All that had ever meant, and ever would.

Perhaps this was a piece of why the Storymaker had offered me back that kernel of power. Not only for myself...but for what stories meant to others.

To my friends. My family. My country. To a world who needed tales like mine...that only I could tell.

The narrative had already been changed for me. *By* me. And now, for others who craved it as I had—the beauty, the wonder, the change, the best of all the world could be—for people who had lost so much hope, and had so many questions, and so much uncertain wonder on the horizon—

It was time to tell them a new tale.

When we emerged from the Shastah into a brilliant golden-pink sunset, crossing the glass bridges that hemmed together my birth-city, Naomi and Lio pulled away from me; Naomi to fall in beside Hasser, discussing all manner of healing things, and Lio to speak with Mahalia and Reiko about their storybook.

All of these half-finished tales in my life, all blending together so beautifully. All written by the same hand, guiding them together in a story that made up the truth of who we were.

I couldn't bite back a grin—it grew and grew, almost pushing tears from my eyes when Jaik fell into step with me, winding our fingers together.

"What are you thinking, tiger?" He nuzzled a kiss against my temple.

"Just...about how much I love this place, and these people," I admitted. "And how happy I am to be with them again. With *you*."

"Yeah." His voice husky, he rested his cheek on my hair. "I feel that, too."

Ryker dropped back beside us, slipping his hands into his pockets, eyeing us from beneath knitted brows. "So. Looks like you found your compass and stars."

The words made no sense to me, but Jaik chuckled under his breath. "Yeah. Didn't even have to die for them this time."

"Not funny." I dug my elbow into his ribs; he snorted, pinching a giggle out of me.

"Funny enough," Ryker offered. "Still sporting gray, Oddball?"

"Red, actually," I grinned. "From the Storymaker Himself."

Ryker whistled, low and fluting. "You walk off my ship a bundle of nerves with a foot halfway back to Krylan...and you come back full of sass, wearing stars in your eyes and Fishbait's ring on your finger. Now, that's a story I want to hear."

"Good," I laughed as the crew all dropped back to circle around us—a captive audience, waiting for a Storycrafter's next tale. "Because it's one I've been dying to tell."

ABOUT THE AUTHOR

Renee Dugan is an Indiana-based author who grew up reading fantasy books, chasing stray cats, and writing stories full of dashing heroes and evil masterminds. Now with over a decade of professional editing, administrative work, and writing every spare second under her belt, she has authored dozens of books. Living with her husband, son, and not-so-stray cats in the magical Midwest, she continues to explore new worlds and spends her time in this one encouraging and helping other writers on their journey to fulfilling their dreams.

ALSO BY R. DUGAN

You can find other R. Dugan books, including...

The Chaos Circus (Young Adult Portal Fantasy)
The Curse of the Blessed (Adult Fantasy Trilogy)
Tales Of Wonder And Woe (New Adult Epic Fantasy Series)

at online retailers Amazon, Barnes & Noble, and more,
and at reneeduganwriting.com/shop

Find Renee Dugan online at: Reneeduganwriting.com
And on social media: @reneeduganwriting